Prologue

Captain Second Rank Sergei Andropoyov pulled the heavy sealskin coat even more tightly around his body and stepped out of the Naval Command Building into the bitter Arctic wind. He hated winters in this gray god-forsaken land. The sun never dared rise above the horizon and the icy wind, its fangs bare, howled in off the Barents Sea, just a few miles to the north.

At times Sergei wondered why anyone would ever build a submarine base in a desolate place such as this, but he knew the answer: water. When she was a mighty sea power, Mother Russia needed access to the world's oceans, and this was the best she had. The warm southern ports were all bottled up on inland seas, but here, ports on the bleak, bitter-cold Kola Peninsula offered a gateway to the West. Submarines could depart into a narrow ribbon of open water in the Barents Sea before disappearing under thousands of square miles of Arctic ice. Driving submarines out of this extreme environment demanded hard men and strong ships, but those sailors and boats had done their jobs for the motherland, and had done them well.

Captain Andropoyov pulled the fox fur hat even farther down over his ears and yanked the heavy fur-lined mittens onto his stiffening hands. He glanced around before stepping off the little stoop into the horizontally blowing snow. The dull gray buildings that made up the Polyarnyy Northern Fleet Submarine Base added no color at all, nothing that might alleviate the drabness of the landscape. They only served to funnel the icy winds into an even more concentrated blast of knife-sharp cold.

Andropoyov walked quickly to the slushy street that ran in front of the building and jumped into the backseat of the old black Zil waiting at the curb. He didn't utter a word to the tall, thin man who held the car's door open for him. Michman Tschierschkey slammed the door shut and scurried around to climb into the driver's side.

"Back to the ship, Captain?" he asked, rubbing his nose with both hands to get the circulation going again.

"Oh, *da*, Tschierschkovich," Andropoyov said without even looking up. "It is time for us to be sailors again."

The two men had sailed together for as long as Andropoyov could remember. Tschierschkey had been a draftee on board the old submarine *Kommosellet* when Andropoyov first reported aboard, fresh out of the Soviet Naval School at Stalingrad. Much had changed in the years since. The city was called St. Petersburg once again, the Soviet Union no longer existed, and the mighty Northern Fleet of the U.S.S.R. was nothing more than a rusting shell.

That is, except for Sergei Andropoyov's new submarine. The K-475, *Gepard*, waited in the covered sub pen at Shkval on Olenya Bay, newly completed and hungry for her first taste of the sea.

"We have orders, Captain?" Tschierschkey asked, his eyes wide as he turned to look back at his commander.

DANGER UNDER THE SEA

"Torpedoes passed astern!" Tommy Zillich yelled as he listened to the headset, his hands pressing the earpieces closer to his ears so he could hear everything going on out there. "We may be clear!"

Toledo was still angling sharply downward, toward the bottom, racing to get clear of the Russian weapons. They had all heard the deep rumble of the other submarine as it exploded. Now the control room was silent, everyone listening for the high-pitched scream of the incoming weapons.

That sound, as all the men aboard knew, would signal their immediate death.

A few of them breathed sighs of relief when they heard Zillich's report. Glass knew better. They weren't free yet. Those two torpedoes were still out there, still searching doggedly for them.

The sonar man confirmed his worst fears.

"Torpedoes! Both coming out of the baffles!" Zillich yelled over the 7MC. Now he had lost his calm demeanor. His voice was high and strained. "They're closing!"

The Russian weapons had crossed astern of them and then turned back, looking once again for *Toledo*. They were both still relentlessly coming after them.

FIRING POINT

GEORGE WALLACE
AND DON KEITH

A SIGNET BOOK

SIGNET

Published by New American Library, a division of
Penguin Group (USA) Inc., 375 Hudson Street,
New York, New York 10014, USA
Penguin Group (Canada), 90 Eglinton Avenue East, Suite 700, Toronto,
Ontario M4P 2Y3, Canada (a division of Pearson Penguin Canada Inc.)
Penguin Books Ltd., 80 Strand, London WC2R 0RL, England
Penguin Ireland, 25 St. Stephen's Green, Dublin 2,
Ireland (a division of Penguin Books Ltd.)
Penguin Group (Australia), 250 Camberwell Road, Camberwell, Victoria 3124,
Australia (a division of Pearson Australia Group Pty. Ltd.)
Penguin Books India Pvt. Ltd., 11 Community Centre, Panchsheel Park,
New Delhi - 110 017, India
Penguin Group (NZ), 67 Apollo Drive, Rosedale, Auckland 0632,
New Zealand (a division of Pearson New Zealand Ltd.)
Penguin Books (South Africa) (Pty.) Ltd., 24 Sturdee Avenue,
Rosebank, Johannesburg 2196, South Africa
Penguin Books Ltd., Registered Offices:
80 Strand, London WC2R 0RL, England

First published by Signet, an imprint of New American Library,
a division of Penguin Group (USA) Inc.

First Printing, July 2012
10 9 8 7 6 5 4 3 2

ALWAYS LEARNING   **PEARSON**

How little do the landsmen know of what we sailors feel,
When the waves do mount and the winds do blow!
But we have hearts of steel.

—"The Sailor's Resolution" (eighteenth century)

"We sail with the tide." Andropoyov met the gaze of the thin man, his eyes squinting in mock anger. "Admiral Durov will not be sympathetic if we are late because my insolent driver wanted to sit here in front of his head-quarters and chat."

Tschierschkey wore a broad grin as he turned and ground the car's starter. He already had the inside of the old Zil warm, just the way he knew Andropoyov liked it. The captain slipped off the heavy mittens and pulled the fur cap from his head, revealing a disheveled shock of white-blond hair. He sat back in the seat and sighed as the old *michman* pulled away from the curb, skewing a bit on the patchy ice in the roadway.

The ride over the steep, potholed streets back to where his boat awaited him would give Andropoyov time to reflect on the meeting he had just completed. Admiral of the Northern Fleet Durov had been his usual imperi-ous self, but as well as he knew him, Sergei had never seen him act quite the way he had this morning.

Over his career, Durov had single-handedly built the Soviet Northern Fleet into the largest, most potent sub-marine force in the world. Then, as he was not shy about telling anyone who would listen, he had watched it all be discarded by the spineless politicians in Moscow. On sev-eral occasions Sergei Andropoyov had seen him foam at the mouth as he ranted on and on about the castration of his beloved submarine service, all to appease the Ameri-cans and the clear-eyed capitalists in his own nation who would rather be rich than omnipotent, comfortable in-stead of supreme.

The old admiral had been much more subdued than

normal this morning. Oddly subdued, Sergei thought. Still, Durov had been in no mood for pleasantries. He acknowledged Andropoyov's greeting with little more than a grunt and a broad wave to take a seat. The glasses of tea were not even cool enough to drink without scalding their lips before the old man had rushed into the briefing, as if the information might grow cold and useless if it was not consumed at once.

"Sergeiovich, you have done well. I am told the K-475 is ready ahead of schedule for her first sea trials. She will do the *Rodina* proud. Our first new submarine in ten years! As much as I would love to show her off to them, even the Americans with their damnable spy satellites have no idea she exists. Nor do most of the bureaucrats back in Moscow. We must keep it so as long as we are able." The admiral sipped his tea and eased back in the plush padded leather chair, crossing his legs, a near smile on his lips. Andropoyov tried not to stare. He had never seen the old man so relaxed. Andropoyov had to listen hard to hear his words when he spoke again. "You will get under way with the evening tide, Captain. The K-461 will escort you to your operating area. You have not been certified to carry weapons yet, so K-461 will be your guard."

"I understand," Andropoyov said. He sipped his tea, not sure what else to say. He could hear the ticking of the admiral's desk clock, the shriek of the wind as it gusted around the corner of the building.

Durov stared into his glass for a long moment, as if he was studying the liquid for something that might be hidden there. He set the glass down and opened a drawer on the ornately carved antique wooden desk. He withdrew a large buff-colored envelope sealed with red wax and imprinted with the emblem of the Russian Navy.

"Here are your orders, Captain. Open them after you submerge, which you will do as soon as possible, before you reach the mouth of the Murmansk Fjord." He slid the fat envelope across the desk. "There are no American satellite overflights tonight, but we expect an American submarine is out in the Barents Sea doing what they so arrogantly call a 'gatekeeper mission.' You will slip past him without being detected. Is everything understood?"

It was obvious the briefing was over. Andropoyov stood, saluted, and answered crisply, "Yes, sir! *Gepard* will not fail you, nor the *Rodina*."

"Yes, I know. You will give your all."

Even the man's words seemed cold, detached, as unfeeling and aloof as the wind off the Barents Sea.

Andropoyov lifted the envelope, surprised by its heftiness, turned on his heel, and marched out of the office. He was happy to have a mission for his new boat, but still thrown a bit off balance by the odd demeanor of his admiral.

Now, as they pulled away, he looked out the Zil's side window, back toward the headquarters building, toward Admiral Durov's window. His breath fogged the glass and the squatty gray building was lost in the blowing snow before he could get it wiped clear.

Admiral of the Northern Fleet Alexander Durov watched the old Zil pull away from the curb. He turned abruptly from the window and stared hard at the other man who now sat in his office.

"There he goes, the impertinent little ass. Are you ready for your mission?" Durov asked.

Captain Second Rank Igor Serebnitskiv set the crystal glass of vodka down hard onto the priceless Louis XIV table. Trickles of condensation ran down onto the ancient shellac, ruining the surface, but Serebnitskiv paid no attention. He took his feet down from where they were resting on the polished wood of the admiral's desk and rose to stand at the window, beside the older man.

"*Da*, I am ready. *Volk* will sail as soon as I am back on board. I think I will take special pleasure in ridding the world of Sergei Andropoyov. I have suffered enough of his arrogance. Ever since Stalingrad, I have been forced to absorb—"

Durov held up a hand to cut him off and cracked a rare smile. "Just don't be too eager, nephew. Much more is at stake here than your own personal vendetta against our Captain Andropoyov. You must be patient, make sure the American is in place first. Andropoyov is a sacrificial lamb. His loss will be the impetus we need to overcome those weak-kneed old men in the *Dumas*." The admiral flushed red, his eyes narrowing. "Their cowardice is robbing the *Rodina* of our rightful place as the world's leader. Their stupidity will send our beloved motherland right back to medieval times. You will be the catalyst that drives them from the Kremlin."

Serebnitskiv stiffened. "I will not fail you, Uncle. Now I must go to my ship."

Durov gave an offhand wave of dismissal, but then grabbed his nephew's shoulder in what had to be a painful pinch. The younger man refused to flinch.

"Remember the old Roman warriors' saying: 'Return either *with* your shield or *on* it.' If you fail me . . . if you fail our union . . . it would be far better that you not return at all."

Serebnitskiv summoned all the confidence he could muster, nodded, and strode from the room, closing the heavy wooden double doors behind him.

Durov listened as his nephew's steps echoed down the hallway and through the door to the outside. He opened the bottom drawer of his desk and removed the telephone stored there. He dialed a number and waited for the clicks that signaled the encryption device was engaged. He began talking as soon as he was sure of the voice on the other end of the line.

"They sail this evening. All is going well. Our part of the plan is in motion. There is no turning back now. We must meet to discuss your progress. The *dacha* at Sochi the day after tomorrow. We will expect a full report of your progress on the New York front."

He returned the phone to the drawer and leaned back in his chair. By the time Serebnitskiv did his work, Durov would be on the warm beaches of the Black Sea. If anything went wrong, deniability would be more plausible if he was far away.

He could feel the excitement pulse in his veins. All the gears of this complicated machine were in motion. It was something he desperately needed. A military man required action in order to maintain life. Years of careful planning, of clandestine meetings, of nurturing the relationships with the Organizatsiya, the Russian Mafia, were culminating in a glorious series of events.

He returned to the window, sipping the cold black tea without tasting it, gazing off into the distance where the wind whipped white tops on the fjord's surface.

Soon he would no longer need to swallow his pride like bitter bile. Soon he and his nation would achieve the glory they had so long been denied.

How fitting that it would all be set in motion out there, beneath the surface of that dark, icy sea.

Chapter 1

The vicious storm raged out of the north, hundred-knot winds lashing the sea, churning waves to the height of a ten-story building before crashing back down with the awesome force of tons of seawater. Wind-driven spray froze into hard bullets that whipped across the maelstrom. Deep gray sky and gunmetal-colored sea blurred into one, the horizon obliterated by the dense fog of driving ice and snow.

Deep beneath the surface of the punishing Barents, the American submarine rocked as gently as a porch swing on a calm summer night. The easy motion was a quiet reminder of the terrible winter storm that raged three hundred feet above. The officers of the USS *Miami*, SSN 755, were seated around the wardroom table, taking their time finishing their dessert and coffee. The remains of dinner had been cleared. The men still present discussed the day's events and plans for the next. The sub's navigator and engineer half listened as they played cribbage at the far end of the table.

Commander Brad Crawford pushed away an empty ice-cream bowl and leaned back in his chair, stretching mightily.

"So, how is the whale watching going, Doctor? Figured out what they're saying to each other yet?"

Dr. David Croley, lost in his thoughts, looked confused when he glanced up from his own dessert dish. He pushed his reading glasses back up on the bridge of his nose, smoothed down a few wild strands of what was left of his hair, and gave a carefully considered answer to the captain's offhand question.

"The taping is going very well, Commander. Of course, in the strictest sense of the word, we are not trying to determine the content of their communications, only the modality of the interchange."

The tall, balding scientist was the lone non-Navy person at the table. Dr. Croley headed a small team of oceanographers from the Woods Hole Oceanographic Institution, on board *Miami* to study the migration patterns of narwhals. While the animals' summer travels were well documented, little was known about the winter activities of the Arctic-dwelling whales. Few people could see these vocal, sociable, tusked whales during the colder months, the horrible weather up on the surface a prime reason why. The Navy and the *Miami* were assisting Dr. Croley, allowing him to track the mammals across an entire Arctic winter.

Commander Crawford held up his hands in mock surrender and laughed. "Doc, I just wanted to know how it was going. Are the narwhals cooperating?"

"Of course, of course. I understand," Croley responded. "We are getting some excellent tapes. I think we have found at least six new pods. It is very exciting, doing research out here, being in the same waters with the *Monodon monoceros*. We could never do this type of research without your submarine. Why, just this afternoon we taped and identified several new types of communications sounds, an especially curious manifestation of harmonic—"

Andy Gerson, *Miami*'s executive officer, jumped to his commander's rescue. "Skipper, it's time for the nineteen-fifteen satellite downlink. Remember? You were going to observe Lieutenant Wittstrom going to periscope depth."

Crawford smiled. The doctor was a nice guy and could even be quite interesting to talk with once you got past all the gobbledygook. When he got wound up on the subject of his favorite whales, the conversations could be interminable. Crawford figured it was much like a submariner talking to civilians. They, too, tended to get verbose, speaking a language not understood by normal folk.

"Yeah, sorry, Doc. I better get up there. Mr. Wittstrom is coming along nicely. He'll make a good officer of the deck when he qualifies. Tonight will be a special challenge for him, though. You better make sure everything is stowed for sea, XO. We're going to get knocked around a lot while we're up there."

Crawford pointed to the overhead as he rose. He stepped out of the wardroom and into the centerline passageway. Barely shoulder-width wide and running from the chief's quarters in the bow to the crew's mess, this hallway was the major artery for the ship. On the port side were the corpsman's diminutive office and the crew's berthing spaces. To the starboard were the wardroom and officers' staterooms. Ladders led from the passageway down to the torpedo room and up to the control room.

Commander Crawford bounded up a ladder and entered the control room. He stepped to the forward starboard corner and watched the sonar repeater for several minutes. The furious storm above them created a din that drowned out most noises a surface ship might make. *Miami*'s sophisticated BQQ-10 sonar system computer enhanced the signals to counteract some of the storm's racket, but it couldn't be one hundred percent effective. Crawford saw no trace of another ship anywhere nearby, nor did he expect one in this lonely stretch of ocean on such a blustery night.

"Okay, Mr. Wittstrom, you ready to go to periscope depth?"

The young junior officer gulped, but his voice seemed assured when he replied, "Yes, sir. I think so. I'm coming up to one-five-zero feet to clear baffles."

Crawford nodded. "All right. Let's go."

As *Miami* rose from the calm depths, the churning of the sea became more obvious, and the submarine's pitching and rolling increased. By the time she leveled off at one hundred fifty feet below the roiling surface, the sub was rolling more than twenty degrees to either side. The bow rose and fell at least fifteen degrees. By then, everyone had to hold on to something solid just to keep from being thrown off balance onto the deck or down a ladder.

Wittstrom turned the sub to make sure that no ship was approaching them from astern. The sonar was blanked in that direction by the sub's bulk. Its screen still showed only the noise of the storm.

"Captain, no sonar contacts," the junior officer reported. "Request permission to come to periscope depth to copy the broadcast."

Crawford looked hard at the sonar repeater. "Mr. Wittstrom, what is the sea state?"

"Captain, sonar reports a sea state 'eight,' maybe 'nine.'"

Crawford looked up at Wittstrom. "That's what I figure, too. That means wave heights somewhere between thirty and sixty feet. I'd suggest we come around to course 'north' to face into the seas. That will limit the rolls a little."

As *Miami* swung around to her new course, the rolls calmed a little, but the pitching worsened.

Wittstrom braced himself and shouted, "Number-two scope coming up!"

He reached above his head and rotated the large red ring there. The periscope slid smoothly out of its well. As the eyepiece cleared the well, he snapped down the two black handles and stuck one eye to the eyepiece. He started to walk a slow circle, rotating the scope and looking out at the empty blackness.

That's all there was. Ominous, complete darkness. Not even a hint of light.

Without removing his eye from the scope, he shouted, "Dive, make your depth six-two feet."

Wittstrom continued the slow rotation. Submariners had long since dubbed the waltz he was doing "dancing with the fat lady." He was looking to see if there was any obstacle, like a ship's bottom or an unexpected ice keel, that he could see in time to avoid it when they surfaced. There was not much chance of that in this pitch-black, storm-tossed sea, but it was still necessary to make certain. Rescue was a long, cold ride away.

With Wittstrom satisfied the way was clear, *Miami* slid up toward the surface. The pitching and rolling worsened until she was bucking like a frenzied bronco, rearing wildly in some very cold, wet rodeo. The diving officer and his two planesmen were working with every bit of skill and strength they had to keep *Miami* on depth, but they were no match for the sea. She was quickly broached, bobbing like a cork on the surface of the seething ocean.

A horrendous crash came from the galley, below the control room. Dish stowage was not equal to the sea's might. Clipboards, books, coffee cups, anything not tied down, fell to the deck and slid noisily fore and aft, port and starboard, as the sub heaved and pitched. Crawford grabbed the stainless steel railing surrounding the periscope stand and held on with both hands.

They couldn't waste much time up here. Someone could get hurt. Mercifully, the radioman soon announced over the 21MC circuit, "All traffic aboard and accounted for."

Crawford was just opening his mouth to order the boat back down when Wittstrom beat him to the punch, shouting, "Diving Officer, make your depth three hundred feet. Lowering number-two scope."

He reached up and snapped the red ring clockwise. The scope slid back into the well as *Miami* once more headed to the peaceful calm of the depths.

There, it promised to be much safer on this particular night.

*   *   *

"Dmitri, how is the testing going?"

Alan Smythe stepped into the elevator just ahead of the man who ran his company's testing department. He pushed the button for the twenty-seventh floor while the door hissed shut, and then he leaned back against the rail as the car whooshed upward.

Dmitri Ustinov glanced over at the slightly built Englishman as if he might not have heard the question. Although a mere twenty-two years old, Ustinov possessed a keenly trained intellect hidden in a bear's body. Despite his heavy, continuous brow, droopy eyelids, and a stooped stature that made him appear on first glance a bit dense, the man possessed a unique skill set well suited for his present project. His knowledge of complicated computer systems along with his familiarity with the inane, convoluted rules for trading stocks and other securities was already well celebrated. Even at his young age, he was the chief engineer for testing the revolutionary new Opti-Marx equities trading system.

"Problems with the integration to the National Market System," he answered as they glided past the fifteenth floor. His accent still carried a hint of his native Russian though he had been in the United States for a decade. "The Securities and Exchange Commission is looking at how we are doing that. It will be several weeks until we get a ruling out of them."

Smythe grunted acknowledgment. Damn government bureaus worked on their own timetables. He was accustomed to such roadblocks, but they were still hard to stomach. "What does Chuck Gruver over at the NYSE say?"

"Not a lot of help. He is so damned head up and ass down in the changes to the Intermarket Trading System that he does not have time to help us on this side."

"Not surprised. About time they fixed ITS. That ticker tape should have been donated to the Smithsonian a long time ago." The elevator door parted and they walked out into the large open office space of OptiMarx, Inc. The big room was divided into a myriad of cubicles. Alan stepped to the left, toward the hallway that led to his office, while Dmitri headed to the right. Smythe stepped into his corner office. Opposite the door, the room's glass wall looked out from the New Jersey shore, across New York Harbor, past the Statue of Liberty toward Lower Manhattan. Ferries scurried across the Hudson River to the north as helicopters buzzed back and forth between the heliports on either shore. Smythe slid into the modern black leather chair behind the smoked-glass desk, the panoramic view now at his back. He had hardly begun riffling through his morning e-mail before the intercom on his desk buzzed its annoying interruption.

Without even a "good morning," his omnipresent executive assistant, Cheryl Mitchell, announced that Mark Stern wanted to speak with him. He sounded, she noted, "Pissed, as usual."

Mark Stern was the leading investment partner for the West Coast venture capital firm Private Pacific Partners. It was Stern and PPP who were providing the stacks of cash that kept Alan Smythe and OptiMarx afloat.

Smythe grimaced. He took a deep breath before he picked up the telephone and spoke. "Morning, Mark.

You're up early. It's . . . what . . . six o'clock out there on the coast?"

"Alan, I know damn good and well what time it is," Stern growled. "My question is, do you? We've shoveled over fifty million into that company of yours to date. So far, all we've gotten for our money are more and more delays. That excuse you have for a chief technology officer is giving us some cockamamie story about 'ITS' and 'SIAC' and 'POPs' and half a dozen other acronyms that make no sense to us at all. We don't want alphabet soup, Alan, unless it's 'ROI.' We want return on investment. Is that so hard to understand?"

Cheryl had stepped into the office to deposit a stack of folders on his desk. Smythe hit the MUTE button on the phone and muttered under his breath.

"Damn VCs. They have egos the size they *think* their dicks are and brains the size they *really* are."

Cheryl waggled her finger and looked at him over the tops of her half-glasses. "Play nice," she mouthed, then turned and left. Smythe unmuted the phone.

"Mark, calm down. We've just had a little delay while the SEC reviews our plan. Couple of days. No big deal. We're still on schedule. Testing the algorithm is going well and that's the tough part. Ustinov is doing a great job."

"Well, maybe you oughta make Ustinov your CTO instead of that idiot Andretti," Stern shouted into the phone.

Smythe held the phone away from his ear while the venture capitalist vented some more. He put the receiver back in place and spoke again, calling on his most soothing voice. "Mark, ease off a bit, old chap. Remember, what we are doing is revolutionary. There are going to be unexpected glitches. Carl Andretti is performing miracles every day. We need him. Now, I'll give you a call this evening, just before I leave for the coast for the board meeting. I'll have the latest numbers for you and an update on the progress. It'll be good news, I promise."

Smythe hung up with a happy "Cheerio!" He massaged the bridge of his nose. God, he hated these calls! Venture capitalists were the worst scum of the world. They had to be endured. They were the ones with the money, after all, and it took money to build empires.

Now, next on the agenda, he would have to deal with that idiot Carl Andretti. He shouted at the door, "Cheryl, get Andretti and tell him I want to see him right away."

"Should he wear his asbestos drawers?" she shouted back.

"It wouldn't be a bad idea!"

Captain Second Rank Sergei Andropoyov climbed the long ladder from the control room to the bridge of the Russian submarine K-475. He loved this new boat, so much more modern than the old rust buckets he had served on so far in his Navy career. Most of those boats were now tied up over at the Polyarnyy main piers, moldering into oblivion.

Gepard was brand-new and equipped with enough technological advances to make her equal to any American submarine. She was an Akula II–class boat—*akula* being Russian for "shark," a name most appropriate.

Andropoyov climbed through the hatch, leaving the cozy warmth below, and stood in the cockpit at the top of the submarine's sail. The huge cement and steel structure of the submarine pen stretched above him and far to either side. The piers were all empty, except the one where K-475 was tied up, and another down the way where K-461, the *Volk*, an older Akula I sub, sat. She was ready to follow him out into the Barents and stand guard while he tested *Gepard*.

The commander remembered how it had been a few years ago, when this building was always buzzing with furious activity. Boats preparing to go out into the cold, dark waters of the Barents Sea to challenge the Americans and to protect the *Rodina*. Boats returning from arduous patrols, needing rest and repair. This eerie quiet was most unsettling after all that purposeful activity.

The giant doors at the end of the pier were open already, revealing Olenya Bay and Murmansk Fjord beyond. A biting cold wind howled out there, close and strong enough to find a way to reach in to chill them even inside the sub pen. A rusty old icebreaker stood by at the building's entrance, smoke whisping from its single large stack. It would break a path through whatever ice there might be in the bay and fjord and lead K-475 out to the open water of the sea.

Andropoyov glanced at his watch. He turned to Dimitriy Pishkovski, his first officer. "Dimitriy, I believe it is time. If you would be so kind as to get us under way?"

The short, swarthy white Russian smiled. "I will be happy to, Captain. It is good to be heading to sea once more."

Pishkovski said a few sentences into the phone at his ear. The knot of men standing on the pier broke up and scurried off to stand beside the bollards, ready to tend the lines that still held *Gepard* tied up in the pen.

He spoke again into the phone. The men standing on *Gepard*'s broad rounded main deck released the lines from her cleats and let them slide off into the water. The line handlers on the pier growled and cursed as they pulled the ice-cold, wet lines from the water.

Pishkovski ordered the two small reserve propeller systems to twist *Gepard*. Unlike American subs, she had a small electric-driven propeller a few feet to either side of her mammoth main screw. They were designed to bring her home if anything happened to the main propulsion system, but they were also very handy for maneuvering in close quarters. By having the starboard screw go astern while the port went ahead, Pishkovski was able to twist *Gepard*'s bow away from the pier while walking the stern out, too.

With two meters of black water between the sub and the pier, Pishkovski ordered the main propulsion system to drive K-475 out of the sub pen. The water at the stern churned white as the six-meter-diameter, seven-bladed screw started to turn. The black sub cut through the water smoothly now that she was back in her natural element.

The rusty old icebreaker churned ahead of her, crunching through the layer of ice covering the bay, leaving a broad trail of crushed and crumpled ice floating on the black water. The high, steep hills surrounding the bay hid the sky except for a small patch overhead. A thick, heavy layer of ominous clouds reflected the lights from the Polyarnyy Naval Base and the Severomorsk Shipyard farther down the fjord.

Andropoyov stamped his feet, attempting to keep them warm as he stood on the hard steel deck. The wind whipped across the sub's bridge as they moved into the bay, its force so brutal he had to shout to be heard.

"I feel a storm, Mr. Pishkovski. The Barents will not be a nice place to loiter on the surface. We will dive before the last turn of the fjord. Please make sure there are no delays."

"Yes, Captain. There will be no delays." The first officer clapped his mittened hands together hard. "Damn, it is cold!"

The icebreaker made the wide, sweeping turn from Olenya Bay out into the Murmansk Fjord. The fjord faced due north and the high rocky hills on either side channeled the Arctic wind into a bone-chilling blast down the narrow stretch of water. Anyone unlucky enough to be standing unprotected was dealt the full force of the cold. Exposed skin froze in moments. The two officers huddled for protection below the edge of the cockpit, drawing slight comfort from the meager trickle of warm air drifting up the hatch from below. They took turns rising to look out at the water ahead before ducking back down out of the blasting wind.

The two ships steamed north into the Kol'skiy Zaliv, the wide mouth of the fjord that opened into the Barents Sea. Farther north was nothing but the frozen wasteland islands of Spitsbergen, Franz Josef Land, and then the polar ice cap. The surging breakers of the open sea prevented ice from building out here. The sub began to pitch and roll in the growing swells.

Andropoyov smiled even though the wind made his teeth ache and his cheeks sting. "It is good to feel the sea again, aye, Dimitriy?"

Pishkovski shouted over the wind, "Yes, Captain. It is good. It will be better, though, when we have dived and are down in the warm control room with a cup of tea."

Andropoyov nodded and answered, "I agree. It is time. Signal the icebreaker that we are diving. Then we will lie below."

Pishkovski aimed the Aldis lantern at the icebreaker and flipped the shutter handle. The icebreaker returned the flashing light signal and swung around to return home. The two officers scurried down through the hatch, closing and dogging it behind them.

Their mission had begun.

Chapter 2

Igor Serebnitskiv stood in the open bridge cockpit of the K-461, watching with great interest as the *Gepard* sailed out of the submarine pen and disappeared into the blackness of the night. The lights of the icebreaker leading the submarine away were all that marked the new boat's progress.

He didn't try to hide the rueful grin on his face. *Gepard* was a beautiful boat, so much newer and more capable than Serebnitskiv's beaten and rusty old *Volk*. He couldn't help chafing at the thoughts of Sergei Andropoyov riding high up there on *Gepard*'s bridge, driving a boat that should have rightfully been his own to command. Years of careful manipulation to be first on the list of commander candidates had been wasted. Political leverage had been applied, bribes surrendered to all the right bureaucrats, all for naught. To make the sting of the slight even more unbearable, his uncle, Admiral Alexander Durov, commanded the submarine fleet. With all that capital, Serebnitskiv could never understand why he had been passed over for command of K-475.

After this morning's meeting, he understood one important thing: his uncle's scheme and the part he was to have in it. Durov was playing a much larger game of no-return chess, and it was one in which the admiral's nephew would have a most pivotal role. His success in this mission would propel him to heights within the Russian military he could never have anticipated. As he watched the running lights of the ice breaker being erased by the snow and spray, he could hardly wait to be in motion, to assume the rightful place of importance his skills and connections and political savvy deserved.

Still, his voice was low and unhurried when Serebnitskiv muttered the orders to get K-461 under way. K-475 had already disappeared around the point of land into the Murmansk Fjord when *Volk* slid out of the silent, darkened submarine pen. The ice was beginning to refreeze as the older sub crunched its way through on its own journey toward the deep death-cold waters of the Barents.

Dmitri Ustinov flopped down in his worn office chair. He stuffed a sugary cruller into his mouth as he waited for his computer to boot up. His bad luck to have to ride up the elevator with his sissy British boss.

When the icons on the desktop blinked into place, he looked around the office, then clicked the mouse button to check his e-mail. Sure enough, there was one there from Roman. The message was an innocuous recap of an uneventful weekend trip to the Hamptons. He clicked the button to send the message to the printer on his desk, then deleted it from his in-box and mail server and erased all traces of it from the hard drive on his computer.

Once again, he glanced around the office space to see

if anyone might be watching him. He grimaced and mentally kicked himself for being so skittish. The paranoia of his boyhood education in Moscow was imprinted on Dmitri Ustinov's psyche. He was still certain that shadowy forces monitored all e-mail, that some all-seeing someone was always watching him, spying on every move he made. The mere fact that he received an encrypted e-mail would alert whoever watched that he had something important to hide. It was much better to conceal everything by hiding nothing, by conducting his business in broad daylight where it would attract the least amount of unwanted attention.

With another series of mouse clicks and an eight-digit password, Ustinov brought to life the accounting program on his computer. He converted each letter of the e-mail to a number and then typed in the number sequence backward. A macro churned away for a second, and a ten-figure total appeared in the answer block. Ustinov memorized the number, shredded the e-mail, and closed the program without saving his work.

Yet again, he gave a fleeting look around the office, making sure no one had observed his actions, no matter how innocent they might have seemed. The telephone next to his elbow jangled, startling him. He snatched the offending device before it could shriek a second time and jammed it to his ear. "Ustinov."

"Dmitri, morning. This is Chuck Gruver over at the New York Stock Exchange. We've been working with your people to test some of those new modules for post-trade clearing."

Ustinov had been expecting this call. He leaned back

in his chair. "Yeah, Chuck. Is there some problem? Functionality not working out?"

He put his feet up on his desk and caught sight of the pretty young programmer in the cubicle across the hall from his office. Marina Nosovitskaya had first gained his attention the day before. She was quite a treat, too, with dark, slanted Asian eyes above high Slavic cheekbones, her long hair gold and flaxen. Her tight leather jeans and sweater did little to conceal a perfect body. He couldn't believe he had not noticed her before, but now there was enough interest that Ustinov had taken the time and trouble to pull and review her records. She was as smart as she was beautiful. She had graduated with the highest scores from the prestigious Department of Applied Mathematics and Information Technologies at the Vladivostok School of Mathematics and Computer Science. Definitely worth further interest when he had the time. Russian immigrants to the U.S.A. needed to stick together, after all.

Marina must have felt his gaze. She looked up at him from her computer screen and smiled shyly, the glow of the monitor shining in her eyes. Ustinov stared right back at her, flicking the cruller crumbs from his shirt and tie before returning the smile. All the while, Gruver prattled on and on about the testing difficulties they were having with the new software. Ustinov grunted occasionally to verify that he was listening, but he never took his eyes off the pretty young programmer.

She would soon be his. Of that he was certain.

Gruver said something then that broke through Ustinov's pleasant distraction.

"One other thing. I was doing a little white box testing on some of the modules. Maybe you can clear something up for me. There are some lines of code in there that I don't understand. They don't seem functional at all."

Ustinov paused for a second and phrased his reply very carefully. "Oh yeah. I know what you are seeing, Chuck. Do not worry about those. It is check and monitoring code the SEC insisted on us putting in there. Their people put it in so they can track things later if they ever need to. We debugged it on our end already. It is good, solid code, even if it did come from the government."

Ustinov held his breath and waited. Would Gruver buy the story or would he ask more embarrassing questions, questions that would be infinitely harder to answer?

Instead of asking for more information, Gruver snorted. "Yeah, damned government geeks! They gotta have their mitts in everything."

Ustinov allowed the breath to escape from his lungs. The NYSE techie had bought the cover story, just as the controllers had maintained he would. Just in case, Ustinov changed the subject as subtly as he could. "Hey, Chuck, we need to get together and have some fun for a change. I found a great new joint down in the Village, on Sullivan between Prince and Houston. It is the best jazz in the city, and you know how great jazz attracts great women. I even have an idea of somebody I might invite to go. How does tomorrow night sound?"

"You're on, my communist comrade. We been bustin' our hump on this project and we owe ourselves a night on the town."

Ustinov was smiling when he hung up. He dreaded having to spend a whole evening with that dweeb, Gruver. He had just sailed a high fastball right past the guy's bat for a strike and the guy didn't even know he was up to bat.

He congratulated himself on coming up with such a patently American metaphor as he stood, headed for another cup of tea and a better look at the lovely Marina, the princess of cubicle twenty-six.

Commander Sergei Andropoyov stood in the corner of the K-475 control room and watched as his crew operated. A few months before they were a motley gaggle of ill-trained novices. After untold hours in the trainers, they were now performing like a precisely matched set of complicated gears.

So, too, it appeared, was his brand-new submarine.

Dimitriy Pishkovski stood beside the periscopes, scrutinizing each panel and gauge spread in front of him. To his right, one *michman* was pumping water to the various trim tanks to compensate for stores and material they had loaded aboard for the long mission. Keeping the weight of the boat balanced, on an even keel, would be a vital and continuing task. It was even more important on this initial dive when they had no experience to draw on, just the designer's best theoretical calculations. One misplaced digit in some obscure computation somewhere and they could plunge to the bottom. Or, embarrassingly, not be able to dive at all.

At the forward end of the control room, a meter in front of Pishkovski, two other *michmen* tested the bow and stern planes. Working together, the two sets of planes, located far forward on the hull and just in front of the screw all the way aft, controlled both the up-and-down motion of the sub and the fore-and-aft angle.

All was in readiness. The pride was obvious in his voice when Pishkovski called out, "Captain, we are ready to submerge."

Andropoyov nodded and glanced around the control room one more time. He was satisfied with what he saw. A slight smile played at his lips. "Very well, First Officer Pishkovski. Submerge the ship."

Pishkovski ordered, "Michman Tetryasoi, open the ballast tank vents. Full dive on all planes. Make your depth thirty meters."

The vents opened on command, allowing air to escape from the huge ballast tanks that wrapped around *Gepard*'s thick pressure hull. As the air roared out of the top of the tanks, water flooded in the open grates in the bottom. *Gepard* sank lower and lower into the inky black water until there wasn't even a ripple on the surface of the ocean to betray her presence. At thirty meters, the sub leveled off and headed out into the Barents Sea.

Michman Tetryasoi pumped water to and from several of the trim tanks, compensating for minor inaccuracies in the engineers' calculations. An extra five thousand liters pumped to the forward trim tank, while another ten thousand liters pumped from the after trim tanks. Pump some; then watch the bubble in the glass tube of the inclinometer. Pump a little more; watch some more. After a few minutes, Tetryasoi nodded that he was satisfied. *Gepard* was ready.

Pishkovski stepped over to stand shoulder to shoulder beside Andropoyov. "Captain, the engineers at the Severomorsk Design Bureau did well."

Andropoyov nodded. "Yes, Dimitriy. It appears they did well." He glanced around the busy control room one more time. "Dimitriy, I will be down in my stateroom. It is time to open our orders and see what Admiral Durov's plans are for us and our shiny new toy. Please stay here and supervise. Call me when you detect the K-461 or if there's any sign of an American boat tailing us."

Commander Andropoyov accepted Pishkovski's nodded acknowledgment. He turned and disappeared down the ladder.

Igor Serebnitskiv descended the ladder from the bridge of the *Volk*, seeking the warmth of the control room. The sea spray coated his thick black beard with a matting of ice. More frozen spray clung to his heavy fur cap and bridge coat. Soon, though, the melting ice puddled at his feet on the immaculately clean deck.

Serebnitskiv accepted a glass of steaming hot tea someone offered him. He stood there, still dripping, and sipped the liquid as he watched the K-461. She, too, disappeared below the waves, an hour behind the K-475. He ordered a course out to the northeast, staying close to the coastline. They would pass within a kilometer of Zsapadnyy Kil'din, the island that guarded the eastern approach to Murmansk.

Despite his political connections and the rather corrupt way he had achieved his position in the Navy, Igor Serebnitskiv was an experienced and capable submarine captain. He knew the tricks and games of playing with the Americans out here in these forbidding waters. His equipment was no match for theirs, but he knew his cunning and intellect evened the playing field. Connections and politics served him well in the morass of the Russian military, but it took skill and guts to patrol beneath these frigid waters.

Serebnitskiv knew that the sea noise close to the shore would hide his older, noisier boat from the listening ears of the inevitable American submarine out there. He would hide here in this acoustic underbrush until he could dash across the shallow Pechorskoye More and keep cover again in the noise of Novaya Zemlya, the haunting, forbidding island that separated the Barents Sea from the Kara.

He was aware that Admiral Durov had ordered Andropoyov to take a direct route to the test area. The American submarine would certainly detect K-475. They would realize they had found something new, something unexpected swimming out to sea from Polyarnyy. In their excitement, they would miss the *Volk* as she steamed a circuitous route well to the east. The American would never suspect he was sailing into a trap, the wily wolf snared by his own hungry greed as he stalked the newborn lamb.

The trap was a well-planned one, but Serebnitskiv knew he would have to move quickly if he hoped to get into position. The problem with taking the long way around was that it took longer. There would be no time for niceties, like communicating with the Central Command. No matter. He relished the independence of being in command at sea.

A long period of enforced separation from the meddling of the land-hugging bureaucrats was an unheard-of luxury.

Igor Serebnitskiv measured the distance he had to travel, walking the brass dividers across the chart that plotted out the submerged route. He calculated the *Volk* would need to journey over sixteen hundred kilometers, while the *Gepard* would travel a thousand. Their rendezvous was a point over four hundred kilometers north of the winter ice line and two hundred kilometers west of the icebound coast of Novaya Zemlya. His uncle, Alexander Durov, would have had to think very hard to imagine a more isolated stretch of ocean.

Serebnitskiv punched the distance into his computer and added the time it would take to arrive at the rendezvous point. He needed to be in place at least eight hours before Andropoyov got there so he could search the area and find a good place to hide. The computer churned for a second or two before it spat out a speed of forty-five kilometers per hour. They would have to move fast in very shallow water.

Serebnitskiv turned from the chart table and shouted to his first officer, "Make your speed forty-five clicks."

Before the shocked officer could even reply, the commander turned and strode out of the control room. He could feel the sub accelerate as he walked down the passageway to his tiny stateroom and a swig of something stiffer than the hot tea.

Alan Smythe looked up as soon as he heard the tentative knock on his door. Carl Andretti stood there waiting for Smythe's nod to enter. The tall, overweight chief technical officer for OptiMarx walked in, closed the door behind him, and plopped down hard onto the black leather couch that ran under one of the long windows that looked out over the harbor. His tie was crooked, his jacket wrinkled, and a loose button showed a white chunk of his ample belly.

"You wanted to talk with me, Alan?"

Smythe pushed aside the report he was reviewing and laid the gold Mont Blanc back in its case. He deliberately removed his reading glasses and placed them next to the report, then shifted them around as if their exact position on his desk was of some importance. He looked over at Andretti. "Yes. I had a most disconcerting discussion a bit ago with Mark Stern. I understand you and he have had a conversation or two."

Andretti answered nonchalantly, but there was just a hint of alarm in his small, deep-set eyes. He licked his lips after every few words. "Yeah, he called me yesterday afternoon. He said he wanted to talk about schedules. I swear that guy thinks he has my job. I told him we were having some problems integrating the quote feed and setting up the communications protocols. Nothing earth-shattering and he seemed okay with it."

Smythe nodded, then spoke in a quiet, deliberate voice. Andretti had to lean forward on the couch to try to hear him. "Carl, I wish you would let me know when you take these calls. We've talked many times about how we want to answer their questions. The board members, and particularly Stern, are not as up to speed on technology as they think they are. Even those PhDs out in Chicago who came up with the OptiMarx idea in the first place are so far behind the technology curve they may as well be using slide rules."

Andretti seemed relieved as he nodded in agreement. They were on common ground, unified against a common enemy. "You can say that again, Alan. Those bastards in their ivory towers. They're always talking about market structures and all that other gobbledygook that has no real-world application in—"

Smythe held up his hand, stopping his chief technical officer in midsentence. His words were clipped, his precise British accent even more pronounced when he lectured. "Carl, just let me finish what I want to say. What I need for you to do is to understand that we . . . you and I . . . are sitting on a gold mine here. Neither the VCs nor the inventors have any idea what a mother lode we are about to dig into. They think we are going about building a better stock trading system." Smythe rocked back and forth in his chair. "If we play our cards right, we won't simply be able to retire to some South Sea island. Carl, we'll be able to buy the damned island with our pocket change. The beauty of it is that we can do it without anyone having any idea what's going on." Smythe turned his chair a bit so he was now facing Andretti. The bright morning sun reflecting off the water and through the wall of glass gave his face a harsh, brittle look. "The two of us have to work together here, Carl. If we are going to pull this off, I can't afford for you to go off on your own and plant little seeds of doubt. Do you understand, Carl?"

Andretti nodded but didn't say anything. Smythe continued, his voice even lower now.

"Good. Now I need you to have a project status report ready for Stern this afternoon. Good numbers, all perfectly on schedule and on budget. Understand, Carl?

Nothing for them to question at all. We'll discuss the rest on the flight out. I want to see that special trading module you're working on. Wheels up at six this evening. I'll meet you at the Executive Aviation Terminal at Teterboro."

Andretti nodded. "Got it. I'll have the full report ready in a couple of hours."

The big man stood, turned, gave Smythe a quick wink, and walked out of the office. He was all the way across the office suite, at his desk and behind closed doors before he allowed a slight smile to flit across his broad face.

He reached into his jacket pocket and turned off the tiny digital recorder. Another disk to lock away in his safe. Another bit of insurance just in case anything went wrong in this intricate, dangerous game in which he was involved.

He gritted his teeth. How dare that girlish Brit bastard talk to him like a truant schoolboy! If it weren't for the great harvest he was about to reap from this whole thing, he would punch the son of a bitch in the face. Let him know who was doing all the work here. Remind him who deserved the lion's share of what they were about to bring down.

He forced himself to breathe normally, sat at his desk, moved his mouse to awaken his sleeping computer, and went to work on the reports Smythe had demanded.

Chapter 3

The 21MC speaker broke the silence inside the American submarine's control room.

"Conn, sonar. New contact on the towed array. Best bearing either zero-three-five or one-two-five."

Commander Joe Glass leaned back and wiped the sweat out of his eyes. He pursed his lips as he glanced around the cramped space of the control room of the USS *Toledo*, SSN 769. This boat was different from the old *Spadefish* where Glass had most recently been the executive officer. The bright fluorescent lights of *Toledo*'s control room illuminated a scene that could have been lifted right out of a Hollywood science fiction movie.

The forward port corner looked more like the control station for a starship. The diving officer and two planesmen faced a wall of flashing red LED displays and liquid crystal screens that would have done Captain Kirk proud, but it gave them all the information they needed to drive the boat through the inky blackness of the North Atlantic.

To their left, the chief of the watch sat facing an imposing wall that held still more displays, gauges, and switches. A myriad of heavy steel pipes and thick wiring bundles ran from behind his desk to the farthermost ends of the boat. From here, he could operate the complex high-pressure air, hydraulic, and trim systems. Over his head were two large brass handles, the emergency-blow "chicken switches" that forced massive amounts of forty-five-hundred-psi air into the ballast tanks that would rocket them to the surface in an emergency.

The entire starboard side of the control room was dedicated to the computerized fire control system, the BYG-1. Here they analyzed and scrutinized every shred of data *Toledo*'s sensors could dredge up. The information was turned into "solutions," information to use to better aim the torpedoes and missiles the submarine could shoot.

The center of the room was dominated by the periscope stand with the two shiny steel barrels protruding from the wells in the deck and extending through the overhead, up into the sail above. From this central location, Commander Joe Glass could observe and direct the complex operation of the boat.

This was the first opportunity for Glass to watch his crew in action since taking command of the boat the previous month. The *Toledo* was one of the newest Los Angeles–class boats in the Atlantic and she was out now, running drills, breaking in a new captain. Glass couldn't keep the grin off his face. He felt like a teenager with a new sports car, and driving the shiny new boat was the most fun he had had since joining the Navy.

Now the fun was about to begin. The announcement on the 21MC confirmed that they had found their quarry. The TB-16 towed array, a two-hundred-foot-long line of sonar hydrophones on the end of a tow cable that stretched out far behind the *Toledo*, was designed to search the depths for the faintest trace of noise from another submarine. Its great sensitivity meant that the *Toledo* could search vast areas of the ocean and hear other submarines before they were even aware she was there. The problem was the array couldn't tell from which side the noise was coming. The contact they had just detected could be on either one of two possible bearings, one correct, the other one the ambiguous bearing.

From his position, Glass watched Brian Edwards, his executive officer, lead the fire control party as they tried to ferret out every bit of information they could. The tall, thin XO was good, and he knew it. He made a perfect counterpoint in many ways to Glass, his new commander, who was short and stocky, quiet and thoughtful. The young XO had already shown a bit of cockiness, a tendency to make decisions quickly and move on, as opposed to Glass's deliberate and studied manner. Edwards had two years' experience on board *Toledo* and knew everything there was to know about her. It showed in the self-assured way he went about his business. And sometimes in a flash in the young officer's eye when he disagreed with his new commander or thought Glass was taking a bit long to make a decision.

Glass smiled as he watched Edwards work. He decided that when the shit inevitably hit the fan, he would rather have someone at his side who was good and knew it than be saddled with a hesitant dolt. There would be ample opportunity to imbue the young man with some humility as time went on.

Now Glass, Edwards, and the rest of the twenty men seemed to already be working smoothly enough together, even as they were packed into a space the size of a cheap motel room. They were quietly and professionally doing their jobs. Edwards had trained them well.

The XO stepped over next to where Glass stood. "Captain, sonar reports a contact on the towed array. Designate sierra three-one, bearing zero-three-five, and sierra three-two, bearing one-two-five. Received frequency is five-zero point two. Very weak contact."

Glass nodded. "Very well, XO. Is this the guy we're looking for?"

Edwards shrugged. "No way of telling for sure yet. He's the only contact we have, though. He's coming from the right direction and the right frequency."

"Okay, it's the best we got. Let's track it and find out if this is our little playmate."

Edwards stepped over to look at the computer screen for the BYG-1 fire control system. Pat Durand, the lieutenant operating the system, looked up from the complex display of numbers, dots, and lines. He nodded at Edwards. "XO, we have a curve. Ready for a maneuver."

Glass watched the young lieutenant's fingers dance across the keyboard of the system. The kid was as much a magician as advertised. He played the computer keyboard as if it were a concert piano. He even had a pronounced bob of his head as he worked, like some musician playing with feeling.

Edwards was checking the paper geographic plot the team was using to record all of *Toledo*'s moves and to note any information they could scrape up on the new contact. It was laid out on a small glass-topped table at the rear of the control room, behind the periscope stand.

A small X-shaped light, the "bug," moved beneath the glass to show the sub's current position.

"Captain, recommend we come left to course one-eight-zero to resolve bearing ambiguity," Edwards said.

Glass smiled to himself as he turned to face the young officer. How many times had he been in the same situation the young XO was now in? How many times had he told his commander, Jon Ward, how he should steer the old *Spadefish*? Now here he was, listening to the recommendations from his XO on how to drive his own nuclear submarine. It was what he had been working for since he was a kid, growing up back in Iowa. He had a bedroom wall covered with pictures of submarines, bookshelves full of plastic models of subs and ships he had assembled. Sometimes it was still hard to believe he was here, commanding this sophisticated piece of equipment and her ready crew.

"Helm, left full rudder. Steady, course one-eight-zero," he ordered.

Glass could hear Edwards muttering into the headset he wore, warning the sonar operators that they were turning. The sonar array was on the end of a two-thousand-foot-long cable. As the sub turned, it played "crack the whip" with the flexible array. Any information gathered during the turn was useless and had to be discarded. When *Toledo* was steady on the new course, the array would take several minutes to stabilize and integrate so they could once again locate the contact.

During the entire time they would be deaf. Often when the array was once again stabilized, the contact would be gone. There would be no choice but to start the hunt all over again.

The compass swung around, the only indication to anyone on board the *Toledo* that the boat was turning. The indicator steadied up with the arrow pointing at "one-eight-zero," due south. Now they would have to hang on for the array to stabilize behind them, five minutes of anxious waiting. There was nothing to do but hope the target would still be discernible. It was a time that tried men's patience. It was a game that required slow, stealthy stalking of the prey. Nothing like high-speed, high-adrenaline air battles, with everything decided in a few terrifying seconds. This was more like the slow, deliberate tracking of a big-game hunter. Find the prey, sneak up on him, and shoot him before he even knew anyone was there. Otherwise, the hunter could become the hunted.

Edwards held his headphone close to his ear, concentrating on what he was hearing. He held his hand up, signaling silence. "Sonar reports regain of sierra three-one, bearing zero-three-two. Drop sierra three-two, track sierra three-one."

They were back in business. The other submarine had not gotten away. They had verified that the target to the northeast was the real one.

Edwards stood next to Glass once more. He slid the headphone back off his ear, easing the pressure a little.

"How do you think everyone is doing, Captain?" he asked.

The XO was aware that this was Glass's first time to evaluate the team under pressure. He was hoping to make a good impression. "Okay so far. We'll see how it goes."

Hunting a submarine with another submarine was a competition played out entirely in the dark. The hunter listened for the other guy and tried to determine where the quarry was located and where he was going. The only real information to work with was the bearing and the received frequency of the sound—range, speed, and course had to be inferred from those two snippets. The usual game plan was to be quiet and listen a little, try to determine how the bearing and frequency were changing, change course accordingly, and then do it all over again. After several iterations of checking all possible answers and discarding the wrong ones, the only answer left would be the correct one.

This all depended on the target cooperating by staying on the same course at the same speed. Otherwise, it meant starting all over again or losing the game.

"Master Chief Zillich reports he is starting to get hints of some other tonal lines showing up," Edwards said. "Nothing definite yet, but looks like it could be our guy, very distant."

Glass nodded. Ever since he first received his orders to command, he had heard stories of Tommy Zillich and his legendary exploits with a sonar system. The crew viewed his abilities as mystical. If Master Chief said there was a flying saucer out there full of little green men, you could break out the Martian dictionary.

"All right, XO. Let me know when we have a curve. I want to bracket the range estimate and spiral in on him. I want to shoot from a range of five thousand yards, broad on his quarter. Do what you have to do to get me there."

Edwards answered, "Yes, sir!" and stepped back over to look at the fire control computer screens.

Pat Durand looked up as Edwards leaned over his shoulder. The young lieutenant had stopped clicking away on his keyboard for a moment. He looked worried.

"XO, I heard Master Chief's report, but my stuff is telling me this guy is pretty close. The only solution I can fit is at five thousand yards." Durand pushed a button on his panel and tweaked a small knob on the keyboard. "Frequency's going up, so we know he's closing."

Edwards watched the computer screen for a moment. Durand was very good, but Zillich was the acknowledged master. It would be much simpler if they both heard the same things.

"Try a solution farther out," Edwards suggested, making another of his patented snap decisions. "I'm going with the master chief on this one."

Not convinced, Durand nodded anyway and tweaked the dials some more, making it look out through the black water at longer ranges. The display now showed the target out at over nine thousand yards, moving across the screen diagonally at twenty knots, just as Zillich had said. Durand shook his head, still unconvinced. This solution fit the data all right, but not as well as the close-range one. Durand looked up at the XO, who nodded, even more satisfied now that Zillich had the right answer. The distant target was the one they were looking for.

Edwards turned to Glass. "Skipper, we have a curve, contact sierra three-one, current bearing zero-two-one, estimated range nine-two-hundred yards. Recommend coming left to new course one-two-five."

Glass played the picture out in his mind. His executive officer's solution had the target heading from the northeast toward the southwest. He was setting up to sneak around behind him, all the while keeping him at a range where he would not detect *Toledo*. Once they were in place, they would shoot the target in the back. The first time the poor, helpless target would even suspect *Toledo* was in the area would be when he heard the ADCAP torpedo racing in for the kill. Assuming Master Chief Zillich was correct about where the prey was located, it was a good, smart tactic. Time would tell.

Glass turned to the helmsman and ordered, "Left full rudder, steady course one-two-five."

He watched as the rudder swung over to the left and the compass started to swing to port.

Suddenly the 21MC blared with Master Chief Zillich's excited voice.

"Torpedo in the water! Bearing three-five-five."

Glass didn't hesitate. He ordered, "All ahead flank! Right full rudder! Steady course two-four-five! Launch the evasion device!"

He watched as the broad white track of the torpedo appeared on the sonar repeater. It had come out of nowhere just as they started their turn. The hunter was now very much the hunted. Time to run!

Toledo jumped ahead as the throttle man, a hundred feet aft in the maneuvering room, whipped open the sub's throttles. Steam roared down the pipes to push the giant turbines faster. The steam sucked energy from the primary coolant, lowering its temperature, sending colder water racing back into the reactor core, causing the power to race higher and the core temperatures to soar. The reactor needed more cooling water to keep the temperature under control. The reactor operator stood and grabbed the large black reactor coolant pump switches. When he yanked them up, the giant pumps shifted to fast speed, sending torrents of coolant water into the core to remove the heat.

This entire, well-choreographed operation was completed in less than five seconds.

"Torpedo bearing three-five-five! Going active!"

Toledo raced desperately, trying to outrun the approaching torpedo. Twenty knots, twenty-five, thirty, and more.

"Torpedo still bears three-five-five! Classified as a British 'Spearfish.'"

Glass stood by the plot as he watched the picture of *Toledo*'s trail and the developing image of the closing torpedo. It was already past the evasion device, the noisy mass that had been released from one of *Toledo*'s signal ejectors to try to confuse the weapon's instrumentation. The Spearfish blew past the acoustic noisemaker without even a glance. Glass guessed that he now had a minute left to avoid this high-speed underwater bloodhound.

"Make your depth one hundred feet!" he shouted.

The deck angled upward as *Toledo* now stretched toward the surface of the sea.

"Skipper, we'll cavitate big-time that shallow!" Edwards yelled. "Everyone in the ocean will know where we are."

"XO, that Spearfish on our ass already has a pretty good idea where we are. I'm hoping to lose it in the surface noise. It's a long shot, but it might work."

They could already hear the machine-gun rattle of cavitation from the sail and the screw as bubbles formed in the very low-pressure areas behind the trailing edges of the sub and then collapsed, making a very noisy bang.

Zillich's voice broke through the din of the cavitation. "Torpedo bears three-five-six! It's range-gating now!"

"Launch another evasion device," Glass ordered. He knew it was a futile effort, but it just might be enough to deflect the incoming torpedo.

"Conn, sonar. Torpedo is in final attack. It has us for good!"

The plot confirmed the report. The incoming torpedo was now merging with *Toledo*. No one breathed for a moment.

"Conn, sonar. Torpedo in turn-away," Zillich reported, his voice heavy with frustration.

Joe Glass turned to Edwards and spoke. "XO, if that had been an actual war shot, we'd all be dead right now. You put your trust in an old salt's hunch rather than believing what the data told you. You had time to evaluate the data further before making your move. Sometimes it's better to be certain you're right before going ahead. I hope you learned a lesson today."

Edwards's answer was drowned out by a sudden blast of music over the sonar speakers. It was the song "Now Give Three Cheers" from *HMS Pinafore* and it had all the effect of a good, old-fashioned Bronx cheer.

I am the monarch of the sea,
The ruler of the Queen's Navee,
Whose praise Great Britain loudly chants. . . .

Glass couldn't help laughing. The look on Edwards's face was priceless. "There's your answer, XO. That damned *Turbulent* is having some fun at our expense. Looks like we buy the first round when we get into port. Now let's get back to work and make damn sure we aren't the only ones buying."

Many miles away to the north and east of where the *Toledo* drilled, *Miami* commander Brad Crawford had eased back down in front of his desk to review some of his never-ending paperwork. Just when he was making some headway, his phone buzzed. It was Bill Schutte, standing watch as the officer of the deck.

"Captain, request you come out to the conn. Sonar has picked up a contact on the thin-line towed array that I think you should see."

The TB-29A thin-line towed array was a thousand feet of ultrasensitive low-frequency hydrophones towed more than a mile behind the *Miami*. Its length allowed it to detect very low-frequency sounds such as those a whale makes. By being towed far behind the sub, it could hear sounds made in the water hundreds, and sometimes thousands, of miles away. The whole thing, array and tow cable, could be wrapped on a reel in one of *Miami*'s after-ballast tanks when not in use.

Crawford was already out of his seat and heading down the short passageway to the control room before Schutte had finished. He found the OOD standing in front of the BQQ-10 sonar repeater surveying a picture that looked like the profile of a growing mountain range.

Crawford stopped beside him. "What do you have, Nav? More whales mating?"

Schutte smiled. He pointed at the picture. "Skipper, we just started getting these tonals. Most of these look like our library for Akulas, but we're missing several in the fifteen- to forty-hertz range and this one at eleven hertz is brand-new. It's not in the library at all. We don't have any record of it that I can see."

Crawford looked at the display. Whatever they were picking up was a sub, but it was not fitting the pattern for known Russian boats. The building peaks showed a time history of sound energy at each frequency. It was shaping up to be a very interesting picture.

Schutte was right, it did look somewhat like the display from an Akula-class boat, the best sub the Russians had ever built and one equal to *Miami*. Those boats had all been tied up for several years now. Intelligence reports confirmed that none of them were even operational anymore. Now, if one of those "sharks" had come out to play, it would be interesting to see what she was up to.

The picture wasn't quite right. The major frequencies used to detect and track an Akula were gone, not showing up at all. There was the brand-new line, very low frequency and so quiet that even the TB-29's hypersensitive ears had almost missed hearing it.

Both men were thinking the same thing. This could be a new boat, and that was worth taking a closer look.

Crawford turned to Schutte and winked. "Nav, I think our whale watching is over with for a bit. Station the fire control tracking party. We're going shark hunting."

Chapter 4

Igor Serebnitskiv stared out the periscope of the *Volk*, but saw nothing. Even using the scope's low-light capability, he could make out little more than various shades of gray. He had raced his old sub to the rendezvous point as fast as she would go, driving his crew to arrive five hours earlier than planned. A very careful search of the area found exactly what he expected—no one else was anywhere around. Now he would have ample opportunity to find himself a cozy place to hide and wait for the parade to pass by.

The craggy, mountainous underside of the Arctic-winter pack ice would serve his purposes. All he had to do was find a notch where he could tuck *Volk* in and hole up. The upward-looking underice sonar helped to map out the upside-down landscape over his head, but it was no substitute for seeing what he was searching for. That would take the periscope, but he would have to be very careful. A low-lying ice keel could shear the scope right off if he wasn't watchful and careful.

Sergei Andropoyov and *Gepard* were due to arrive at their rendezvous point in little more than an hour, and Serebnitskiv wanted to find his hiding spot before they showed up and had a chance to detect his sub, which would be much easier with all of the K-475's fancy new equipment. Serebnitskiv wanted to be invisible before the inevitable trailing American submarine came by, too. If the Americans had an inkling that *Volk* was there, his long-evolving mission was lost. They would have to start all over. That was one message he did not want to relay back to his uncle.

Once hidden and unmoving amid the thick ice, *Volk* would disappear from the sonar screens of both Andropoyov's new boat and his American tail. The grinding and cracking noise of the frozen mass as it drifted southward would also conceal his presence.

Serebnitskiv stared through the eyepiece on the periscope, finally spying what he was looking for: an inverted valley that was wide and deep enough for *Volk* to fit her bulk into, but not so deep that it would mask her sonar hydrophones. The upside-down gorge's main axis pointed directly at the rendezvous point, a kilometer away.

Perfect!

The Russian crew maneuvered the sub so that it came to a stop, hovering just a few meters below the ice valley. They pumped a few thousand kilos of water from the trim tanks so *Volk* was positively buoyant, and the old boat eased up into the concavity.

All the while, Serebnitskiv watched through the scope as the boat rose. Satisfied that he had lined everything up correctly and there were no hidden ice keels to ram into, he lowered the scope. *Volk* nestled into the little valley with the top of her sail resting hard against the overhead ice. They were firmly in place, held there by the positive buoyancy of the trim tanks.

Serebnitskiv had learned this trick from the old submarine masters of the Soviet fleet. Called an "ice pick," the maneuver was used often when they ran up to these frozen wastelands to hide from the Americans during the Cold War.

It worked well then. It was working well today.

Now all Serebnitskiv and the *Volk* had to do was wait until that bastard, Andropoyov, and his shiny, new *Gepard* strolled by, with the Americans following behind, poking her in the ass.

The commander rubbed his hands together and ignored the odd stares of his crewmen. He had waited years for this, and he intended to enjoy every last second of it.

Aboard the *Miami*, Commander Brad Crawford watched the tactical picture develop on the screen in front of him. The new Akula sub they had just spotted was heading to the northeast, steadily steaming ahead, deep beneath the pack ice. The TB-29A array fed a continuous stream of information about the mystery sub into the BYG-1 fire control system. The fire control tracking party was extracting every bit of useful intelligence they could get and plotting it out on paper charts. This was sure a lot more interesting than trailing along behind a pod of whales.

Crawford steered the *Miami* back and forth across the Russian sub's track, solving for her course and speed. She seemed to be heading a little east of due north, straight and true with no variation at all. The solution showed her on a course of zero-three-five, traveling at a speed of eight knots. The Akula didn't seem to be in much of a hurry or to be the least bit suspicious that anyone might be trailing her. She hadn't changed course or cleared baffles since *Miami* had detected her twenty-four hours before. That was a very long time for any submariner to go without turning around to try to catch anyone who might be trailing him. It seemed as if the Russian skipper expected someone to be following him.

The pair of boats had left the open water over two hundred miles back. Now there was a thick layer of ice above them, stretching for many miles in every direction. If they needed to go to the surface for any reason, they would have to search for a polynya, a thin place in the ice to break through. In the winter up here, these holes were few and far between.

Crawford grimaced as he rubbed his aching neck. The excitement of the chase had begun to wane hours ago. His blue poopie suit was wilted and sweat-stained and his face felt like coarse sandpaper. He stared into the dregs of his coffee. It had long since gone cold.

Glancing around the control room, Crawford confirmed that everyone else looked as tired as he felt. Andy Gerson sat slouched on a stool in front of one of the fire control computer screens. He was hunched over, talking to Bill Wittstrom. Tired or not, they were trying to refine the solution some more, learning all they could about the unidentified sub.

Bill Schutte looked up from the navigation chart he was using. "Skipper, looks like he's heading for the north tip of Novaya Zemlya. You don't think he's making a transit around to the Pacific, do you?"

Crawford stood, stretched, and stepped over to stand beside the navigator. He looked at the positions of the two subs, *Miami* and the unknown Russian, on the chart of the Arctic Ocean. Their tracks were on a course to pass just clear of the northernmost tip of that piece of frozen real estate. From there, it was a straight shot past Franz Josef Land, a small archipelago of mostly uninhabited islands at the edge of the permanent pack ice, into the Arctic Ocean, and then to the Bering Straits and the Pacific Ocean.

Crawford scratched the day-old stubble on his chin for a minute, lost in thought.

"Possible, Nav," he answered. "It's been a while since they've done an interocean transfer, and I don't recall ever hearing about a winter one. If that's what this is, something's up and we're in for a long haul. We better find ourselves a polynya. It's time to tell the boss what we're doing."

Schutte pulled another chart out of the large roll he kept tucked under the table. He spread it out and put a coffee cup on each corner to hold it flat. The chart, the result of decades of polar research, showed the expected locations for polynyas in the wintertime Arctic. Still, it would be a real trick to find one so they could surface and get a quick message off to COMSUBLANT back in Norfolk. And do it while maintaining sonar contact on the Russian sub. They did not want to lose track of this intriguing boat right now.

Schutte shook his head as he perused the chart. "Not

much around here, Skipper. Looks like the best bet is over near Novaya Zemlya. Chart says there should be a few sensible heat polynyas over there."

"Okay, let's head over that way."

Gerson joined the two at the chart table.

"We still have good contact on this guy," he reported. "The twenty-nine is holding him fine out to twenty thousand yards. He's still steaming straight and normal, far as we can tell. Want to ease up a little closer and see if we can get any better info?"

Crawford shook his head. "No, XO. You weren't around when we used to play with these guys all the time. We're doing fine out here on the thin-line. If he is an Akula, we wouldn't be able to detect him on the hull-mounted arrays until we were inside four thousand yards. That's the same range he needs to be able to hear us. Getting counterdetected is bad."

Gerson nodded in agreement. "I see what you mean. Not a good trade."

"Besides, we don't know what he's up to," Crawford continued. "If he's not transiting to the Pacific after all, if he's out here getting ready for some exercise or something, we might get caught up in the middle of that nonsense. Nope, better to stay out here in loose trail until we can see what this guy is up to."

All three men stared hard at the mark on the chart that represented the Russian submarine, as if his identity and mission would magically come clear for them. There was nothing. The intrigue, the excitement of the hunt, had revived them.

Brad Crawford whistled tunelessly when he returned to his seat by the periscope.

Dimitriy Pishkovski pushed the buzzer button. He waited several seconds and pushed it again even harder, as if force might make the noise louder. He heard Sergei Andropoyov's groggy voice on the other end of the phone.

"Yes, Dimitriy, what do you want?"

The *Gepard*'s skipper had been catching a few minutes of rest in his stateroom.

"Captain, you asked to be awakened when we were an hour away from the rendezvous. We are ten kilometers from the point now."

"Thank you, First Officer. Any contact with the K-461?"

Pishkovski held the phone in one hand while he pressed the buttons on the sonar repeater with the other, looking at all the displays for the hundredth time in the last few hours. The captain had voiced the question that had been hounding him for the last little while. He looked up from the sonar scope and shook his head as he spoke into the phone's mouthpiece. "Captain, no sign of the K-461. I don't understand. We are at the right place and on schedule. I have checked the navigation. Where could he be?"

"I will be right there. Perhaps Igorovich Serebnitskiv has been delayed and will arrive later."

Or perhaps the bastard was playing games with them. Andropoyov didn't trust Serebnitskiv one iota. He had seen too many indications of the man's ruthless quest for promotion. He would stop at nothing to make Andropoyov look bad if it served his ambitions.

Pishkovski was unconvinced, too, and his voice showed it.

"Perhaps," he said. He put the phone down and resumed searching the sonar screen for some sign of their comrade.

Captain Second Rank Igor Serebnitskiv watched the sonar display with undisguised glee. The dim white line that was the *Gepard* built from the southwest.

Andropoyov, the haughty bastard, was walking into the trap, unaware of his fate.

Where was the American boat? There was still a single trace on the display. The rest of the screen was lightly dusted with the snow of background noise, not even the subtlest hint of another sub.

Serebnitskiv allowed the *Gepard* to sail right on past, a kilometer in front of his icy hiding place, unaware of his presence. Surely the American would be following, sniffing like a dog following a bitch in heat. He waited while the new Russian boat glided well past, beyond the range of his sonar, and disappeared from the screen.

He studied the display. Still no trailing American.

Serebnitskiv knew he was out there. He could feel it in his bones, smell the stink of the foreign boat fouling his home waters.

It was time to revise the plan. The American would have to be enticed into the trap more forcefully.

It wasn't the way Uncle Durov had ordered, but the

old man was back in the cozy warmth of his office, not out here beneath the pack ice.

Serebnitskiv made his decision. The success of the mission depended on his ability to improvise, and that's what he would do. Results were all that counted. His uncle would eventually acknowledge his brilliance.

The trace for the *Gepard* reappeared on the sonar screen, this time coming from the northeast.

She's looking for us, Serebnitskiv thought. How heartwarming!

When the *Gepard* was in front of the *Volk*, a kilometer away, Serebnitskiv keyed a button on the high-frequency underwater telephone, sending a special coded pulse into the water at a frequency well above human hearing. The pulse was received by two transponders hidden inside the ballast tanks on the *Gepard*. They had been secretly placed there three years before, when she was still being built, and they had sat there, undetected, waiting for just this signal.

One of the transponders was hidden in the after ballast tank, right beneath the massive main shaft, where it penetrated the pressure hull. On recognition of Serebnitskiv's signal, it shut a tiny microswitch, completing a circuit that energized a relay. The relay sent a small jolt of electricity into the primer circuit, firing a squib charge that ignited the main explosive charge waiting there.

Most of the explosive force vented downward and outward, instantly rupturing all the after ballast tanks. Sufficient energy jammed upward to bend the meter-thick shaft to a right angle and to punch a hole that was half a meter in diameter through ten-centimeter-thick high-strength steel and into the aft compartment of the new sub.

The other charge, sitting in the ballast tank beneath the torpedo room, also received and recognized the command signal. But a tiny leak had developed in the circuitry. The wiring to the microswitch had corroded through, so the circuit was not completed. The explosives sat there, inert, without the electric charge necessary to ignite them.

Serebnitskiv smiled as he both heard and felt the jolt of the explosion as it passed through the water and into the hull of his boat.

Now all he needed to do was wait while the wolf came charging to the squeals of the dying rabbit.

Michman Rudi Tschierschkey was lying in his bunk in the aftermost compartment on *Gepard*, trying to find a position to suit his aching muscles. Everyone else was forward, on the mess decks watching a movie, an old American Western that he normally would have wanted to see. Tonight he was too tired. Better to lie here in his bunk and try to get some sleep so he would be ready to go again in a few hours.

A long, hard day had been spent repairing the shoddy workmanship of the bastards at the Servomorsk Shipyard. Damn civilian workers didn't care, as long as they got their daily ration of vodka.

This afternoon's task had been to fix leaks in the still. Seawater kept seeping through bad solder joints into the distilled water, ruining it. He had to resolder most of them, and do it while bent double with his head and one arm inside the heat exchanger, a valve handle digging into his back.

He was getting too old for this. Submarining was a young man's game. Maybe after this exercise, it was time for him to retire and find that nice warm beach on the Black Sea he had been promising himself and his long-suffering wife for so many years.

The sudden blast ripped the covers off Tschierschkey and flung him violently upward, into the bottom of the bunk above him. For a few seconds he was knocked senseless. Then the unmistakable roar and rush of seawater under pressure revived him.

It was a submariner's worst nightmare: ice-cold seawater pouring in, the bilges already full, the boat sinking by the stern.

There was no time for panic. He pulled himself out of his bunk and fell hard against the after bulkhead.

Water was already waist deep, and bone-numbing cold.

Tschierschkey knew he had no hope of reaching the hatch and getting out of the compartment now. Even if he could, he wouldn't be able to lift its massive weight to shut it all by himself.

The sailor didn't have to ponder the situation. He was already a dead man. No retirement, no sitting on a beach on the Black Sea with his wife and children.

He would do what he had to do in order to save his boat.

Tschierschkey dove beneath the chilling water and fished around until he found the big red hydraulic handle that was mounted on the aft bulkhead. When his fingers located the handle, he yanked at it, but lost his grip as his cold, unfeeling fingers refused to obey the orders from his brain. He tried again, jerking it upward, forcing hydraulic oil into the piston for the emergency closure system.

The hatch slammed shut.

Rudi Tschierschkey floated there and waited as the compartment filled with water. Tears blended with the inrushing seawater as he thought of his wife, of his two boys, of the warm sand on the Black Sea beach that he would never feel beneath his feet.

The sudden explosion threw Sergei Andropoyov to the deck and slammed Pishkovski into the depth control station. The commander lay stunned and horrified for a moment as he felt the stern of his new sub begin to sink lower. He could see the depth gauge as his boat rapidly slid down into the depths.

Pishkovski was unconscious, slumped over, his body caught on some piping. Bright red blood streamed down from a gash on the first officer's head, dripping onto the slanting deck.

Andropoyov pushed himself erect and climbed over to the main propulsion control station. He did his best to cling to stanchions and pipes to keep from being slammed against the after bulkhead.

The *michman* who should have been sitting at the propulsion control panel was gone. Andropoyov spotted his limp form resting against the after bulkhead, where the blast had tossed him.

The captain yanked the controls to force the screw to answer an emergency "ahead" bell. He watched in disbelief as nothing happened. It didn't respond at all.

Gepard was no longer moving forward.

Instead, she was sliding backward into the cold black depths of the Barents Sea.

Every indication told Andropoyov that something was terribly wrong. The explosion, whatever had caused it, had resulted in flooding somewhere in the after part of his boat. If this happened in open water, the procedure would be obvious: He would blow the water out of the ballast tanks and bob to the surface as quickly as they could.

That wouldn't work beneath ten meters or more of granite-hard ice. The *Gepard* would be smashed like an egg against the ice pack if he tried to surface here, and that was if he could even get air into the tanks with this much angle on the boat.

Andropoyov was stymied. The depth gauge ticked away as the boat sank backward.

The depth gauge read three hundred and thirty meters when the stern of *Gepard* slammed into the muddy bottom of the sea. The tail of the sub plowed out a trench over fifteen meters long as she ground to an abrupt halt. The force of the bottoming tore Andropoyov loose from the grip he had on a pipe and flung him hard against the deck. He was fighting for breath once again, even as the desperation of their plight hit him full force.

The men trapped inside the *Gepard* were alone on the bottom of one of the most isolated and inhospitable seas in the world.

Chapter 5

"Damn! What the . . . ."

Aaron Miller tore his headphones off, shook his head hard and tossed his headphones on the deck, wiggling a finger in each ear. They rang from the blast, amplified by the BQQ-10 sonar receiver. The sonar screen blossomed into a white blob as the intense noise blotted out everything else in the sea.

Miller shook his head again. He reached above him to grab the microphone that was hanging there. Still deafened, he yelled when he spoke. "Conn, sonar! Loud transient on bearing three-four-seven. Sounded like an explosion."

Andy Gerson glanced at the fire control computer's solution for the mysterious Akula-class sub they had been shadowing for the last day. Sure enough, it was on bearing three-four-seven.

Bill Wittstrom was the first one to see the signal light blink out on the narrow-band tracker.

"Hey, we've lost the tracker on the Akula!" he yelled.

Commander Brad Crawford jumped up from the stool where he had been resting and stared wide-eyed at the sonar repeater. Sure enough, the noise signal from the mystery sub was abruptly gone. He punched the buttons, leafing through the displays in a vain attempt to find her again.

The clamor from the Russian sub had not faded away. It disappeared.

It didn't make sense. The explosion, loud as it was, would not blank out the narrow-band signal, only the broadband. Yet the sub appeared to be gone.

Crawford knew he needed answers, and he needed them now! He grabbed the 21MC microphone.

"Sonar, Captain. What happened to the Akula?" he demanded.

The sonar supervisor was just as mystified as his skipper. He was frantically punching buttons on the narrow-band stack.

"Captain, the signal's just gone," he answered. "It went away at the same time as the explosion. I checked the tapes. It just went away. Our equipment checks out fine. No problems at this end."

So that left one explanation. It was not a heartening one.

Whatever had caused the explosion somehow involved their mystery sub. That was not good. Not good at all. If the boat they had been trailing had some kind of accident on board, there could be fellow submariners out there battling for their lives at that very moment.

Crawford chewed his lower lip as he weighed in his mind the possibilities and potential courses of action. A sub in distress up here on top of the world, underneath all this ice, was pretty much on its own. There would be no way for it to signal that it needed help and no way for help to get to it in a hurry, even if someone knew a boat was in trouble.

He decided to go in closer and try to determine what might have happened. He would see if they might be of some assistance if anyone was left out there to help.

He glanced around the control room. All eyes were on him. Once again, the awesome pressures of leadership washed over Brad Crawford like a deluge of cold water. These men had no idea how to interpret what had just happened. Or any concept of what to do next. That was up to him, their skipper.

So now it was time to let them in on his plan. Trouble was, even as he opened his mouth, Crawford had no idea what that plan might be.

"Okay, so it looks like we lost contact with the Akula at the same time we heard that explosion. They were both on the same bearing. It is very possible the Akula suffered some kind of accident." He swallowed hard. "Here's what we're going to do. We're going to close the last position we had on her and see if we can find out anything. Everyone on your toes. We don't have any idea what we might be running into."

Sergei Andropoyov picked himself up off the deck and spat out what appeared to be tiny bits of tooth. He blinked twice and struggled to get his balance.

Gepard had stopped moving at last. The depth gauge read three hundred and thirty meters. The inclinometers showed a twenty-degree list to port and a ten-degree up angle.

No doubt about it. His beautiful new submarine was resting on the bottom of the sea.

The control room was deathly quiet. The humming noise of an underway sub was gone.

The lights were still on, though. They still had power.

Andropoyov looked around the control room. Dimitriy Pishkovski sat in the corner, holding a bloody cloth to his head wound and moaning. Some of the other watchstanders around the control room were picking themselves up, staring around in dazed disbelief, trying to assimilate what had happened.

Andropoyov walked around the control room, trying to assess what was working and what wasn't. Reports were starting to come in from the other compartments in the boat. He listened to them as he continued his visual check.

All over the sub, crewmen reported in. Except for the after compartment. There was nothing from there.

The captain checked the pressurization meters and was not surprised to find the after compartment was at sea pressure. After all, they had sunk backward to the bottom. There had to be a rupture to the outside sea somewhere in the after compartment.

Someone had managed to shut the hatch and seal off the inflow of water. Otherwise, the next compartment forward, the one that housed the steam-driven engines and turbines, would be flooded, too.

The reactor was shut down. That wasn't surprising, considering the shock of the explosion. The battery appeared to be working all right. Fully charged, too. That should last awhile. Several days if they were careful.

So there was hope. They should have enough time for

Igor Serebnitskiv and the K-461 to show up for the rendezvous, learn of their distress, and summon help.

The *Volk* might even be close enough by now to hear them. It would have heard the explosion, too. They needed to be signaling already so the old boat would know where they were and what had happened.

"First Officer, get up. I need you," Andropoyov barked at Pishkovski. "Station a watch at the underwater telephone. Signal *Volk* so she will know we are down here and so she can find us."

Pishkovski pulled himself erect. He still held the blood-soaked rag to the jagged gash on his forehead. He nodded and stepped unsteadily over to the underwater telephone. After flipping the toggle switch to turn it on, he picked up the microphone to talk. Before he could key the microphone, though, Andropoyov reached over and flipped another switch.

"Dimitriy, better use the topside hydrophone. The keel one is buried in the mud."

Pishkovski nodded and sat down hard, still holding the microphone. He began to speak weakly into its mouthpiece. "*Volk, Volk*, this is *Gepard*. Help us. We are sunk."

He repeated the plea over and over again.

The *michman* who had been taking the reports from the crew gave a wrap-up. "Captain, all compartments except the after compartment have reported. Fifteen dead, ten seriously injured, one missing. Compartment seven is reporting some leakage through the stuffing tubes from the aft compartment. They are attempting to tighten the tubes, but the bilges are full. No other flooding reported."

Andropoyov nodded. They were better off than he had any right to expect. Flooding controlled, damage apparently confined to the sub's rear end, resting reasonably upright and stable on the bottom. Deep, but not too deep for rescue. Thankfully, a comrade would be along shortly to get that process started.

At least they weren't out here all alone.

Meanwhile, there were fifteen killed and ten injured from his crew of sixty. That left thirty-five crewmen to work.

Trouble was, just now he had no idea what they should be working on.

Miami steamed toward the last known position for the mystery sub. Brad Crawford was torn between rushing in as quickly as possible to see how he could help and easing in cautiously until he could determine what in hell had happened.

He decided to err on the side of caution. *Miami* was coming in carefully and quietly.

Aaron Miller first heard the voice in his headphones. He couldn't understand what the man was saying. It was a foreign language, maybe Russian, but a weak, strained human voice saying the same thing over and over in a tired singsong. The frequency was the same 4.7 kilohertz as the newest Russian long-range underwater telephone.

Someone out there was alive and talking. Given the range of a typical underwater telephone, he was within a couple of miles.

"Conn, sonar. Hearing underwater telephone. Best bearing three-two-one. I think it's Russian, but I can't tell."

Crawford looked hard at the plot. The bearing pointed pretty close to where they believed the last position of the mystery sub had been. The Russian underwater telephone communications could be a plea for help. The problem was Crawford didn't know of anyone on board who spoke Russian.

A thought hit him. Maybe one of the Woods Hole scientists. Hell, they spoke "whale." Maybe they could manage a little Russian. Crawford sent for Dr. Croley.

The tall, gangly scientist arrived in the control room with a puzzled look on his face. Ever since the *Miami* had gone sub hunting, the crew seemed to lose all interest in narwhals and his research. He and his colleagues had busied themselves transcribing notes and listening to whale songs on tape.

Crawford looked up from the navigation charts. "Dr. Croley, thanks for joining us. We need some help. Does anyone on your team speak Russian?"

Croley smiled. "Captain, it's hard to do research on Arctic whales without speaking and reading some margin of conversational Russian. Most of us are fluent."

"Excellent! I need someone to translate for us." Crawford ushered the scientist into the sonar room and handed him a set of headphones. "What is this guy saying?"

Croley listened, pressing the earphones to his head and concentrating on the feeble, scratchy sound of the voice. He nodded as he listened. He snatched a pad of paper and began to write: "Wolf, Wolf, this is Leopard. Help us. We are sunk."

Croley looked up at Crawford, his eyes wide and his

face going ashen as he realized the implications of what he was hearing.

"These are the words," Croley said, pointing to the pad. "He is saying it over and over again."

Crawford nodded. It was what he had expected.

"Dr. Croley, would you please stay here and translate? Tell me if anything changes."

"Should we answer him?"

"Not just yet. Stand by."

The captain trotted out of the sonar room and headed back to control. There he gathered Gerson and Schutte around the navigation plot. This had now become a matter of life or death. They needed to figure out what to do. Crawford told them of the translation of the underwater telephone plea.

Schutte studied the chart. It was a little over three miles from their current position to the sunken sub. Water depth there was marked at just under two hundred fathoms. Deep, but still shallow enough that a sub could sink to the bottom without being crushed by the pressure. He looked up at Crawford.

"Skipper, if they are bottomed here we need to get help quick. There's nothing else we can do for them but say a prayer or two."

Gerson nodded his agreement, but Crawford noticed his executive officer's brow was creased with worry when he spoke. "Okay, XO, what's bothering you? Something's gnawing away in there. Spill it."

"The way I read what this guy is saying, he's calling out for someone named 'Wolf.' Or maybe a boat named 'Wolf.' Do you think there might be another sub that he's expecting to be up here, and close enough to hear his distress signal on the underwater phone?"

Crawford shook his head. "Not that we've seen. We're not detecting anyone else. Not even with the TB-29. Looks like we're up here all by ourselves, except for the poor bastard on the bottom. Let's go talk to him and let him know we've heard him, even if 'Wolf' hasn't."

Gerson nodded but he didn't lose his worried scowl.

Dimitriy Pishkovski was growing ever more tired and despondent. For hours, it seemed, he had been sitting here, repeating his plea over and over again, his pain-slurred words spilling out into the cold, empty Arctic water. Why bother? Would it not be better to fetch the bottle of vodka from his stateroom and enter the next life in a stupor?

He knew Andropoyov would never allow such an easy, cowardly way out. He had served too long with that old fighter. The captain would never allow anyone to quit. Not until the aloof, icy waters of the sea had overpowered them, strangling out the last breath from their lungs. The tough bastard would still be at the helm, trying to give marching orders to the sea.

When Dimitriy released the TALK button on the phone to listen yet again for a reply, there was a voice there. An odd voice.

"*Gepard. Gepard.* This is the American submarine *Miami.* We heard your underwater telephone. What is your status?"

Pishkovski shook himself. Had he imagined the voice? Who else would be up here in this place? Besides *Volk*, who, as far as he knew, had not yet arrived?

He raised his head. He winced as the pain shot through his temple and down the back of his neck.

"Captain, come quickly! Listen!" he shouted.

Andropoyov rose from the table where he was planning their survival. He listened to the words on the phone, spoken in Russian but with an unmistakable halting American accent.

"Dimitriy, we have been found by the Americans." He ran through his mind what the proper procedures would be. There had been a time when they would have refused any assistance from the Americans. When they would have taken their chances on the eventual arrival of *Volk*, wherever the tardy bastard might now be. When they would have accepted any fate besides surrendering themselves and their boat to the hated Americans. That was another day and time. "Tell them we need help, and we need it soon."

Pishkovski held the microphone to his lips. "*Miami*, this is *Gepard*. We are bottomed. An explosion . . . some kind of explosion . . . destroyed our propulsion and flooded the after compartment. We have injured on board. We need help."

The acknowledgment of receipt of the transmission from the American was the sweetest sound Dimitriy Pishkovski had ever heard.

Brad Crawford looked up at Gerson, a wry smile on his lips. "Well, XO, that tells the story. Only way to get them help is to get the DSRV here on a mother sub, and get it here quick." He turned to Schutte. "Nav, find me a polynya. We need to talk real bad."

They would have to surface to radio back word of the sunken Russian submarine and get a deep-sea rescue vehicle en route. No telling how long that might take or how much longer the *Gepard*'s crew could hold on.

Schutte checked the charts. "Skipper, I think our luck may have just changed. There should be one three miles east of here, toward Novaya Zemlya."

Crawford called over to Croley. "Doc, tell them we're going for help. We'll be back in a couple of hours."

Croley relayed the message while *Miami* ran for the hole in the ice as fast as she could go.

Then, unknowingly, they flew right past a shadowy shape, silently hovering nearby, its sail resting on the bottom of the ice pack, its bulk hidden by the sides of the narrow inverted ice valley where it lay coiled like a snake in its hole. *Miami* zipped past the hidden *Volk* much too fast for the Russian to react.

The polynya was right where the chart showed it might be. *Miami* eased to a stop beneath the thin ice. Crawford maneuvered around, much as Serebnitskiv had done earlier with *Volk*, making sure that *Miami* was lined up beneath the gauzy skin of ice so they could surface without hitting the thick pack ice surrounding it.

When he was satisfied, he ordered the ballast tanks blown dry. *Miami* shot straight upward. She crashed through the foot of ice that covered the polynya, sending shards of frozen ocean flying in all directions. Once she stopped, her sail stood high out of the water in the howling Arctic wind.

Crawford sent the carefully worded message to COM-SUBLANT, giving them the limited information that he had about the situation. He ended the message by telling them that he was going back to the helpless sub and that he would be out of radio contact for twelve hours. Crawford knew from experience it would take at least that long for the people back home to react to this shocking news and to figure out what to do next. He also assumed that *Miami* could be of better use back with the *Gepard*. From that position, they could offer moral support and guide the sub that was bringing the DSRV to the site.

With the message sent and receipted for, *Miami* dropped back down into the deep and turned to head back to where the *Gepard* rested on the bottom.

"No rush, XO. We got time to kill while we wait for help," Crawford announced. He ordered a safer twelve-knot pace. "I doubt those poor souls are going anywhere, either."

Now *Miami* steamed a little more than a kilometer in front of *Volk*, no longer racing at top speed to summon help. Igor Serebnitskiv had ample time to observe their approach and passing. He could line up his shot at his leisure.

Aaron Miller was the first to hear the unmistakable sound. His mouth dropped open in shock, but he was quick to shout the warning. "Conn, sonar! Torpedo in the water! Bearing zero-two-one!"

Years of intensive training kicked in by instinct. Crawford was stunned, but he went to work without hesitation.

"Ahead flank!" he shouted. "Left full rudder! Steady course one-four-zero!"

Miami leaped ahead in obedient response to his order. They were in a race against death itself.

"Torpedo bears zero-two-one!"

Miami flew through the water, her enormous screw pushing the seven-thousand-ton behemoth forward at better than thirty knots. Still, the torpedo was coming at seventy knots. It wasn't a fair race at all.

They had to stay outside the narrow sonar cone in front of the torpedo, the area where the weapon sensed its prey.

Miller couldn't believe his own words when he next yelped.

"Conn, sonar. Two torpedoes! Bearing zero-two-one and zero-one-eight! Signal strength is increasing!"

Crawford groaned. Two torpedoes—the son of a bitch was using standard Russian tactics. He had fallen into a trap. The bastard must have been "ice picked" out there somewhere, just waiting for him to amble by. Had it been the same sub that had made the distress call? Why would they be shooting at someone who was trying to help them?

"Torpedoes bear zero-two-one and zero-one-eight! Still closing. Both are active!"

How the hell could they manage to evade these two deadly weapons bearing down on them and then turn and shoot that bastard?

No way to outrun them.

Maybe they could lose them up there in the ice. That was their only hope.

"Dive, make your depth one-two-zero feet."

Gerson stared hard at Crawford. "Skipper, there are ice keels hanging down to at least one hundred and fifty feet!" he protested. "We hit one of those and we're dead!"

Crawford shouted right back, "We don't outsmart those torpedoes and we're just as dead. I'm hoping they lose us in the ice."

Miami angled upward and raced for the new depth. There was no time for anyone to spy the massive ice keel dead ahead. At thirty knots, they were outrunning the ability of the underice sonar to see what lay ahead of them. The keel only jutted downward to ninety feet, but that put it even with *Miami*'s main deck.

The jagged chunk of ice started to print out on the display. The sonar watchstander shouted a warning. It was too late.

When the sub slammed into the keel, the mass of granite-hard ice raked hard into *Miami*'s sail, shearing it off neatly. Tons of cold seawater flooded into the control room through the hatch, the chopped-off periscopes, and the dozens of other hull penetrations. The boat stopped dead. The men on board were slammed forward with the momentum, smashing into whatever unyielding piping or equipment protruded there.

She had just lurched to an abrupt stop, just begun to settle and sink away from the ice keel with the sudden weight of the inflowing water, when the two Russian torpedoes arrived simultaneously.

One passed under the engine room and exploded, ripping a massive gash through the thick steel of the sub's skin. Ice-cold water rushed in through the immense rupture. The force of the explosion lifted the massive main turbines off their bedplate and slammed them sideways into the hull. The huge steam pipes ripped free and poured live steam into the engine room, scalding everyone there.

The other torpedo exploded just outside the crew's mess room, the force blasting through the hull, sending red-hot shrapnel spraying around the crowded room, slicing through flesh, instantly killing the sailors there before they could even realize what was happening.

The doomed sub, defeated, sank slowly, inexorably into the deep, the sea continuing to rush in through rents and tears along her length.

By the time the *Miami* came to rest a thousand feet below, the sea had already jealously claimed as its own the once proud submarine and all the souls on board.

Igor Serebnitskiv laughed out loud and pounded the nearest bulkhead with glee. His crew stared at him, not fully understanding what had just happened. Some wondered if their captain had gone mad.

Serebnitskiv was oblivious of those looks.

It was done.

He listened to the sounds of ocean water as it rushed into the carcass of the dying ship. He could hear the sizzle of ice-cold water hitting steaming-hot pipes, and make out the crushing of bulkheads as they collapsed under the awesome pressure of the sea.

Then the final sound, the grinding and tearing as the sub's lifeless remains plowed into the stony bottom of the ocean.

He had been cursing himself for not pursuing the Americans when they went racing past him the first time. There had been no time to shoot and he dared not make noise that would alert them of his presence.

He knew they would not abandon another ship in distress, that they would be back. Americans were weak and predictable that way. He had been right.

Now there was nothing to do but wait a few dull, boring days until that annoying underwater telephone on *Gepard* went silent. Until there would be no chance of any witnesses remaining.

He could go home to tell his uncle what he had accomplished out here in this bitter sea.

Go home to toast the renewed glory of the *Rodina*.

Go home and help lead the new revolution.

Chapter 6

Admiral Alexander Durov sat on the porch of the seaside dacha, gazing out over the blue waters of the Black Sea. A warm breeze blew in, bringing with it the refreshing scent of salt air and the clamor of fishermen already heading out for their night's work. The sun burned a fiery orange as it sank into the sea. The lights of Nizhneye Dzhemete were already blinking on, adorning the hills along the shore to the north of the dacha with a necklace of white pearls.

Durov loved this place. It was so different from the frigid wasteland of the Kola Peninsula where he now spent so much of his time. His boyhood home was a few kilometers north of here. He had spent much of his early career at the vast naval bases at Novorossiysk, a mere thirty kilometers to the south.

Beautiful and comfortable as this place was, Alexander Durov knew the future of Russia lay much farther north, up there in the frozen Kola, with its open access to the world's oceans, not here on this warm, closed sea.

Boris Medikov sipped his vodka and watched the admiral, the red glow of the setting sun reflected in his still-clear eyes.

"Alexanderovich, you are a million kilometers away."

Durov turned to look at him and shook his head. "No, Boris, my friend, I am right here. I am enjoying allowing the healing warmth to soak into these old bones."

Medikov leaned back into the padded cushions of the overstuffed chair and sighed. He was a dark-haired, handsome man. He looked to be a full decade younger than his fifty years. It was his eyes, though, that most people noticed. They were dark, deep, and appeared to be hooded, even when they were wide-open.

"Ah yes. This is far better than the chill winds blowing through Moscow nowadays. I must confess, I find the nightlife around here a little slow for my tastes."

Durov grimaced and took a drink of his own vodka. "You Muscovites are all alike. You must have action and excitement in your lives all the time or you feel you are missing something vital to living. You never take the time to enjoy the quiet things in life." He waved his glass in a long, slow sweep around the horizon. "Just look out there. The serenity of this place is balm for the aching soul."

Medikov chuckled. "It may be enough to soothe an old man's soul, but as for me, I prefer a beautiful woman wrapped in furs to soothe mine."

"*Ne kulturny*, no culture," Durov mumbled, and shook his head as he rose from his chair. He ignored the slight sliver of pain behind his breastbone as he stood. "Come, Boris. I didn't pull you away from your women wrapped in furs to watch sunsets with an old man. We have important things to discuss."

He walked through the double doors and inside the dacha. Medikov had to hurry to follow in his wake.

The two men stepped into the admiral's bookcase-lined study. Well-thumbed naval history books shared shelf space with tomes covering grand military strategy. Interestingly, there were also texts there that discussed stock markets and international finance. Interspersed around the volumes were the trophies and mementos of a lifetime spent serving at sea. There were detailed ship models, well-used brass chronometers, and other nautical bric-a-brac. A huge Georgian mahogany desk filled much of the floor space. Off to one corner, facing a now-cold brick fireplace, were two red leather armchairs with a dainty tea table set between them. The table was burdened with a large bottle of white wine, chilling in a silver ice bucket, and two crystal wineglasses.

The two men took seats in the armchairs, each finding his own spot, as if they had often sat here and talked together. Medikov pulled the bottle from the ice and considered the label.

"Well, I see you've broken into that case of Chalk Hill Chardonnay we sent you, Admiral."

"In your honor, Boris," the old admiral replied. "I'm normally content with a simple Russian wine myself. Even your high-priced American contacts haven't spoiled me of that yet."

As he poured a glass for Durov, Medikov broached the subject that had been so far delayed by the spectacular disappearance of the sun into the Black Sea. "Speaking of America, I should update you on our progress there."

Durov tasted the wine. "Very oaky, not at all subtle like a good Russian."

Medikov chuckled. "Subtle? Americans seldom are. That is to our benefit. Our people are in place in the OptiMarx organization. They report the central algorithm has been modified for our purpose."

Durov nodded, then looked sideways at Medikov. "That is all well and good, but will the changes be detected?"

Medikov shook his head. "We control the internal OptiMarx testing. Even the Americans understand there is nothing like Russian training to make a good software tester. Besides, the changes are so well hidden and pervasive, without access to the entire code base no one could uncover it. Even then, someone would have to know what to look for and it would still take him a very, very long time to discover it."

Durov stood and paced over to stand in front of the large window looking out over the water. This time the darkening view was lost on him. Deep furrows of worry creased his brow.

"Still, there is always the possibility of its being uncovered," he commented drily. "This is not acceptable."

Medikov laughed humorlessly at the admiral's concern. "Alexanderovich, you would make a very poor criminal. You worry far too much. As I have told you, the changes are well hidden. Besides, even if they should be found and identified, everything there points at the greedy American stock traders."

Durov turned abruptly and faced the seated Medikov. When he spoke, his voice was forced and steely. "Boris, you are being unbelievably dense. Our operations are already under way. Regardless of who might get the blame, the code must not be detected. Anything that might upset the timing of our plan now would be disastrous."

Medikov set his wineglass down on the little table so he could use his hands to plead his case. "Alexanderovich, the profits are in the New York operation. It will make us all very rich. All this other is merely a sideshow."

Durov flushed crimson and slammed his fist onto the desktop. The formerly quiet eyes of the old admiral now blazed as intensely as the setting sun. "Do you not understand, you fool? The few baubles we might liberate from the American markets are meaningless. This is all for the *Rodina*."

A quick sip of the wine seemed to calm him, but Medikov noticed Durov's hands still shook with anger as he lifted the glass. The old admiral used his free hand to knead a spot in the middle of his chest. Medikov started to speak, but Durov stopped him.

"Now listen as I try to explain to you one more time what we are doing." Admiral Durov's voice took the tone of an exasperated schoolmaster tutoring a dull pupil. "For Russia to be a mighty and prosperous nation, the *Rodina* must be respected and feared throughout the world as it once was. Our people must be united, all with a common goal. Peter the Great understood that, and therein lay his power."

Durov removed a book from the shelf and thumbed through its pages. "He tried to build Russia into a Western country. The idiotic nobility tossed the idea as soon as they could for their own selfish purposes." He flipped a few more pages. "Lenin understood, too. So did Stalin. Then the political animals took over once again. Still, we almost made it. Do you understand that in a few more years we would have built an impregnable fortress for the *Rodina*?"

"Don't tell me you're an unrepentant communist," Medikov scoffed. "I know better."

"No, we are patriots, not ideologues. We were working on this plan when you were still rolling babushkas in Gorky Park for a few rubles." Durov took a sip of wine, allowing the insult to lie there in the room for a moment. Medikov seemed not to take notice. "Those fools in Moscow are bent on allowing our country to continue to disintegrate until we are no more than a mass of weak, feuding states, destined to suck and poke at each other until we are all bloodless. Those weak bastards must be removed. Now we have the tools to do it. The plan is under way. We should hear from Serebnitskiv soon. If he did his job correctly, we will be able to blame the unsuspecting Americans for the loss of our new submarine, K-475. We must be ready to move quickly in the ensuing international crisis. Now do you see why your timing is so important to the glorious future of the *Rodina*? To the restoration and eventual triumph of the most powerful union on the planet?"

Medikov nodded and sipped at his American wine.

The irritating jangling of the telephone at his elbow disturbed Captain Jon Ward's train of thought. He had the travel brochures fanned out on the desk before him. It would be the first vacation he and Ellen had taken alone since their honeymoon, twenty years before.

Two whole weeks! Where to? The Caribbean? Paris?

Rome? Ellen had been dropping strong hints about a cruise, maybe around the Greek islands. Ward wasn't sure. Just what a Navy man needed. Two weeks on a ship!

Ward listened to the phone shriek two more times, waiting for his yeoman to answer it and stop the noise. It was a lesson he had learned when he took command of his first nuclear submarine, *Spadefish*, years before. Captains shouldn't answer the phone themselves. They never knew when it might be Mike Wallace from *60 Minutes*. Now that Ward was in Norfolk, commanding a submarine squadron, it was an even more valuable lesson. The proximity of the media animals in D.C. was much too convenient.

Not this time. The yeoman stuck her head in the office door. This was a call he would take.

"Admiral Donnegan for you, sir."

Ward shoved the travel brochures aside and grabbed the phone. "Captain Ward."

"Jon, good to hear your voice. I haven't seen enough of you and Ellen since you took command of Squadron Six. Here we are, just down the road from each other. When are you coming up to see me in this five-sided puzzle palace?"

Tom Donnegan was an old and dear family friend. He had served as a surrogate father after Jon Ward's dad was killed when Jon was a young boy. The gruff, cigar-chewing admiral had been promoted to the job of Director of Naval Intelligence. That promotion forced him to leave his beloved Hawaii for the congestion and clamor of Washington and the Pentagon.

"We've been meaning to get up there, Admiral, but it's been so busy down here, as you can imagine. We're still getting settled in and learning the ropes. These LANTFLT sailors do things a lot different than we did out in the PAC."

"Ain't that the truth!" Donnegan said with a chuckle. There was a slight hesitation. Ward could picture the admiral shifting the cigar from one side of his mouth to the other, signifying an obvious change of subject. "Jon, I didn't call just for social niceties. I've got a job for you."

Ward knew it was time to get down to business. He grabbed a notepad and pen before he responded. "What you got for me, sir?"

"We received a message from the *Miami*. She was out on one of those scientific cruises, listening to whales up near the ice edge in the Barents. Brad Crawford . . . I think you know Brad. . . . He reported a Russian sub down, under the pack ice and with survivors."

Ward whistled. "Wow! We need to get the DSRV rolling pronto. I've got Joe Glass and *Toledo* exercising with the Brits over in the Irish Sea. That has to be the closest mother sub."

"That's what we figured, too. The DSRV will be airborne out of North Island within six hours. The C-5 should touch down in Prestwick, Scotland, ten hours later. Have *Toledo* alongside the pier in Faslane, ready to take it on board. I want her under way inside of twelve hours."

Ward glanced at the chart of the Atlantic and Europe hanging on the wall across from his desk. "Tom, it's over twelve hundred nautical miles from Faslane to the Barents. With the twenty-knot speed limit because of the DSRV, it'll take *Toledo* three days just to get there. Wouldn't the Russians be able to get there a hell of a lot quicker?"

Donnegan cleared his throat. "Jon, the Russians maintain that they don't have any boats missing. They are now, for some damn reason, resurrecting their old bullshit claim that the Barents is an inland sea—that it is their sovereignty and that we are to stay out."

"So, okay, they are embarrassed and don't want help. Same thing happened when the *Kursk* went down. We didn't butt in then. Why now on this one?"

Donnegan paused a beat. Ward felt a sudden chill crawl up his spine. On one of the brochures on his desk, a happy couple waved from the railing of a cruise ship.

"There's one more thing, Jon. *Miami* said she would be back in communications twelve hours after the original message. She is now twenty-four hours overdue. Tell Joe Glass he had best keep his eyes open up there."

The giant trailer eased out of the brightly lit hangar, making its way toward the waiting open cargo door on the C-5B Galaxy. This entire end of North Island Naval Air Station, near San Diego, hummed with sudden activity. Men raced about carrying boxes or directing forklifts loaded with pallets into the Galaxy aircraft's after cargo door.

The trailer's suspension groaned under the massive weight of the huge khaki-green-and-white cylinder that sat strapped to its bed as the tractor tugged it toward the waiting plane. Large black letters painted across the side proclaimed this to be DSRV-1, the *Mystic*.

A warm wind blew in off the dark Pacific, tousling Lieutenant Dan Perkins's blond hair as he watched his baby slide out of the hangar. Perkins never ceased to be amazed that he was now the officer in charge of *Mystic*. Amazed but proud. How had the Navy known to pick a mustang diver for the perfect job? Coming up through the ranks as a working diver, Perkins had always dreamed of this. Now it was true. He smiled every time he thought about it.

"Hey, Lieutenant," Chief Gary Nichols called out. "Better move or you'll get your toes run over."

Perkins jumped backward as the trailer rolled past. As usual, Nichols was doing his best to keep him out of trouble. Best damn chief he had ever worked with.

Perkins walked over to stand next to him and watch the process together. "Chief, you get any skinny on where we're headed?"

Perkins had learned a long time ago that the old Navy axiom was true: A chief always knew what was going down long before it came through official channels.

This time Nichols shook his head and frowned. "Not a word. Just the order for a full load-out. I suspect it's just another drill. You know. Fly us off to some godforsaken air base and back again, just to prove we can do it."

"Yep, I suspect you're right."

Perkins's reply didn't sound so certain. Something felt different about this one.

The DSRV with its trailer was moving up the ramp now and sliding into the gaping maw of the C-5 aircraft. It filled the giant bird's massive cargo hold with mere inches to spare all around.

The front cargo door hissed down and locked closed. The DSRV crew jumped into the aircraft through the diminutive crew hatch.

Minutes later, the four giant General Electric TF-39 turbofan engines dragged the bird upward and into the night sky. Within minutes the cheerful lights of San Diego disappeared behind them.

"Dimitriy, how is the crew holding up?" Captain Second Rank Sergei Andropoyov asked.

He had just looked up from the manual over which he had been poring for the past half hour.

"We've lost two more of the injured," Pishkovski answered sadly. "I expect we will lose Ludmila in the next few hours. He was burned badly by the steam pipes. There is nothing we can do but keep him drugged." He slammed his fist into a sheet-metal locker door in frustration. "Where is that damned American? What happened?" Tears spilled from his eyes and down his face. "Captain, why did he leave us down here to die?"

Andropoyov put a firm hand on his first officer's shoulder. "Easy, Dimitriy. I need you to be in control of yourself. The crew needs to see us both as strong and confident." He bent closer and, in a whisper, he added, "I suspect the explosions we heard may be why we haven't had more contact from the American. I'm beginning to suspect he may be suffering the same fate as we are."

Pishkovski looked at his captain, his eyes wide with fear. "That means what happened to us was not an accident!" Andropoyov nodded. "What of the *Volk*, Captain? He should have been here by now anyway."

"I don't know. I don't have all the pieces yet. Now we have more pressing concerns. Help me here. We need to get power back to the reactor before the battery is too depleted. If we can start it, we can last until we are rescued." He leaned over the reactor control panel and pulled the handle for a switch marked LATCH CONTROL RODS.

Nothing happened. Andropoyov tried again. Still nothing.

He looked at Pishkovski and said, "I don't understand it. Even when I've bypassed all the safety circuits, I can't get the control rods latched. I've checked every inch of the circuits. There must be a fault in the reactor compartment." He stared at the pages of the manual a moment, then shook his head. "I don't think we will have the reactor, Dimitriy. How much time do we have left on the battery?"

Pishkovski checked the meters on the electrical panel and did some rapid calculations. "Captain, if we turn off everything but the heaters and lights here in the control room, we have three more days." He checked his figures once again. He looked up at his captain with a desperate expression frozen on his face. "And then, it will get very dark and very, very cold."

Chapter 7

Joe Glass eased down into his chair at the head of the wardroom table. He would be able to devour a quick bite of lunch. The exercises they were conducting with HMS *Turbulent* were still going on, even as the *Toledo*'s captain paused for his first real meal in over eight hours. Glass was in much better spirits now than he was earlier, after the Brits had "sunk" his submarine in the drills.

They had just finished an approach on *Turbulent* and successfully "shot" her with an ADCAP torpedo. The retriever boat was up there now, picking up the exercise fish while the two subs repositioned for the next go-around. It was a good time to grab a hurried lunch with half his officers. They would wolf down their sandwiches and rush to relieve the other half so they could eat before the excitement started up all over again.

Brian Edwards was up in the control room, supervising the operation, so things aboard *Toledo* were in good hands while her captain took his dinner break.

Joe Glass was more than happy to be down here at six hundred feet and not up there on the surface. He could feel sympathy for the sailors working on the retriever boats, trying to wrestle four thousand pounds of wet, slippery torpedo onto a hundred-foot-long boat while being tossed around all the time by the angry wintertime North Atlantic Ocean.

Jerry Perez, the navigator, occupied Brian Edwards's customary chair to Glass's right. Short, with a dark complexion and jet-black hair, Perez was showing the signs of a developing paunch. He talked and moved the same way he mauled his hamburger and fries: slowly, deliberately. He worked hard to develop the image of a cool and collected Southern California surfer, but it was also obvious to anyone who watched him work that he had a razor-sharp and insightful mind.

Doug O'Malley, the boat's engineer, sat to Glass's left, across the table from Perez. O'Malley was the exact opposite of Perez. He was tall and red-haired, his body athletic and chiseled. Hailing from the upper Midwest, O'Malley spoke directly and with machine-gun speed.

Despite their physical differences, O'Malley and Perez were close friends.

"Skipper, how you think we're doing?" O'Malley asked as he gulped down the last quarter of his sandwich in one quick bite. "*Turbulent* is damn good and that Spearfish torpedo is one smart bitch."

Glass grunted as he bit into his own hamburger and held his answer a few seconds while he chewed. The burgers were dubbed "sliders" because they were so greasy they slid right down the gullet. This one still tasted delicious to a ravenous Joe Glass. "We got a ways to go. Your plotting team needs to work on the information flow. Too many details are getting lost in the shuffle."

Perez glanced over at O'Malley and shook his head. He pointed a French fry at his friend as he spoke. "Trouble is,

Eng, you spend too much time aft, speaking 'nuke.' You gotta learn to talk 'submarine' like the rest of us."

He gobbled up the fry. "Hell, Jerry, you know I can—"

Joe Glass held up both hands. "I've been your skipper long enough to have grown weary of you two bickering like an old married couple," he said, but with a smile. It was a sign that the rest of the crew was now comfortable enough with him and his command that they could banter like this in front of him. It had not been that way his first few weeks on board when everyone seemed to be walking on eggshells.

A buzzer interrupted their meal. Glass reached underneath the table, grabbed the JA phone handset, and pushed the TALK button. "Captain."

"Captain, XO. We just received underwater comms from *Turbulent*. She says we need to come up for an urgent message."

The other officers at the table could not help noticing the sudden frown that erased the smile on their skipper's face.

"All right, XO. Ask *Turbulent* to come to safety course north and to stay at periscope depth. Put us on course north and come up to one-five-zero feet. I'll be right up."

With both subs on the same course, the "safety course," they wouldn't collide with each other while they were at the same depth.

Glass replaced the handset, pushed himself back from what was left of his meal, grabbed a cup of coffee, and headed out of the wardroom. When he entered the back door of the control room, he found an orderly bustle of activity under way. Edwards was watching the fire control computers, checking the positions of all the surface contacts. Pat Durand was flipping through the displays on the BQQ-10 sonar repeater, looking for contacts and attempting to get clear in his mind the way they might be moving.

Sam Wallich, the chief of the boat, sat in the diving officer's chair, coaching the two most junior kids on board. The helmsman and the stern-planesman steered *Toledo* and kept her on the ordered depth. Their station looked like the cockpit of a large airliner, complete with control yokes and a wall of gauges and computer displays. The control yoke was turned to move the rudder, which in turn steered the sub. The other yoke was pushed and pulled to position the bow planes and stern planes to go up and down. There the similarity to an airplane ended. Unlike an airliner, there was no window to see where they were going or what might lie in their path.

Glass stopped beside Edwards. The two watched together for a moment as the computer screen displayed the best guess of where the ships on the surface were located.

"What's happening, XO?" Glass asked.

Edwards pointed to the speck of light nearest *Toledo*. "*Turbulent* is here, at PD on safety course. She reports no surface contacts. The only other contact we hold is sierra nine-two, bearing zero-seven-two, best range one-nine thousand yards, past CPA and opening. That's probably the retriever."

Glass nodded. No problems here. He turned to Pat Durand. "Mr. Durand, you ready to go to periscope depth?"

"Yes, sir. Ship is ready. Request permission to go to periscope depth."

"Proceed to periscope depth," Glass responded. He stepped up beside the sonar repeater to watch while the young lieutenant drove the sub up to the surface.

Durand reached above his head and rotated the red scope control ring and shouted out, "Number-two scope coming up!"

As the shining smooth metal of the scope barrel started to slide out of its well, Wallich called, "Speed seven knots!"

This safety check was to make sure the sub was traveling slow enough that the scope would not be damaged. Too many young officers over the years had raised periscopes while the sub was traveling fast enough that the force of the water bent it right over. Such a careless mistake would cost the taxpayers many thousands of dollars. More important, it could result in an aborted mission.

Durand slapped down the black handles, put his eye to the eyepiece, and started to walk a circle, looking upward to make sure they weren't surfacing under a quiet, unnoticed ship. He saw nothing but the gray-blue of the North Atlantic water.

"Diving Officer, make your depth six-two feet," he called out.

"Depth six-two feet, aye, sir," Wallich responded. He leaned forward, placing his head between his two young charges, and spoke. "Okay, you two, let's do this right. Don't embarrass me in front of the skipper. Rudder amidships. Full rise on the bow planes. Seven-degree up angle with the stern planes."

Toledo rose from the dark depths toward the light above. As Wallich called out the depth changes, there was no other sound in the control room. Every ear was strained to hear Durand's call if he should see an unexpected shape. To a man, the crew was thinking what he needed to do to get *Toledo* back down to the safety of the deep if an obstacle appeared.

The periscope broke through the surface. Durand swung the scope around through two complete circles, looking for ships close enough to hit *Toledo*. Glass had moved over to watch the TV monitor, showing him what Durand was seeing.

The young lieutenant called out, "No close contacts."

It was safe to breathe again.

Glass leaned over to Durand and said, "Raise the BRA-34 and download the broadcast. Let's find out why the boss wants to talk to us so bad."

The submarine had a pair of BRA-34 communications masts for both receiving and transmitting radio signals over a wide range of frequencies. They allowed the boat to stay safely hidden below the surface and yet still be in radio contact with ships and stations around the world.

Within minutes the radioman on watch was reporting over the 21MC circuit.

"All traffic on board and receipted for. Request captain come to radio."

Glass stopped next to Edwards as he headed aft to the radio room. "XO, keep an eye on things out here while I see what radio wants. Let's stay up at PD until we've taken a look at the traffic."

He stepped out the back door to the control room, ducked around the ESGN inertial navigation gyros hanging down from the overhead, and punched the combination into the cypher lock on the door to the radio room. The door opened to a cramped world of electronic panels, humming communications gear, and red-painted crypto equipment. This was the most secure room on the boat, and for good reason.

The radioman handed Glass an aluminum clipboard with the words TOP SECRET painted in two-inch high letters on its cover. Glass flipped it open, signed a disclosure sheet saying he had seen the message, and began to read:

TOP SECRET, SPECIAL HANDLING RE-
QUIRED

TO: COMMANDING OFFICER USS *TOLEDO*,
SSN 769

FROM: COMSUBLANT

BT

1. IMMEDIATELY PROCEED AT BEST SPEED TO RN SUBMARINE BASE FASLANE. MOOR PIER NOVEMBER TWO.

2. LOAD DSRV MYSTIC AND OTHER EQUIP-
MENT.

3. UNDER WAY IMMEDIATELY UPON COM-
PLETION ON-LOAD.

4. FOLLOW-UP ORDERS AND AMPLIFYING
INFORMATION TO BE DELIVERED BY SPE-
CIAL COURIER UPON ARRIVAL.

BT

Glass read the words again, trying to search for any
meaning hidden between the lines of the terse message.
Something was up, and whatever it was, it was important.
There hadn't been any mention of a submarine disaster
in the message traffic. That would be the most probable
need for the rescue vehicle. Glass closed the cover.

Well, he decided, there was no good to be served by
trying to guess the situation. Not until COMSUBLANT
decided to tell him more.

He hurried back to the control room. He almost
bumped into Edwards as he stepped through the door.
He handed the message board to the XO. Edwards read
it once, then read it again. He whistled as he looked up
at his skipper. "Wow! Wonder what's going down."

"No idea, but you better go grab the nav. Tell him to
put that second dessert aside and get his butt up here.
There's work to do."

Edwards chuckled as he slid down the ladder to the
middle level. It appeared Perez's fondness for sweets had
not escaped the skipper's attention.

Glass stepped up to the navigation chart that was
spread out on the port-side plotting table. Dennis Oshley, the leading quartermaster, was stooped over the table, plotting *Toledo*'s latest position fresh from the GPS

receiver above his head. He looked up when he realized Glass was standing there.

"Help you, Skipper?"

Oshley was always serious, rarely joining in the usual onboard camaraderie. Like everyone else on *Toledo*, he did his job well. Exceptionally well. Glass vowed once again to have a chat with him one day, see what made him tick. Maybe he could find out why the young man was so solemn all the time.

"Just seeing how long it would take us to get to Faslane," Glass said.

Oshley grabbed a pair of dividers and walked them across the chart from the position he had just plotted all the way to the Royal Navy Submarine Base on the west coast of Scotland. "I get a hundred and fifty-five miles, Skipper." He picked up a circular slide rule, a relic from an earlier time but sometimes still the fastest way to solve certain problems. "Let's see, at twelve knots, it would take thirteen hours."

"You hankering for a pint or two of stout, Skipper?" the quartermaster asked.

"That would taste good, but I don't think we'll have time to imbibe. Oshley, you better start plotting the most direct transit in. We can't wait around for the Brits to give us a submerged transit lane, so plan on a surface run all the way."

Oshley looked up at Glass. When he got no further amplification on the strange order, he shrugged and began maneuvering the parallel motion protractor to start drawing a course.

Glass had already stepped up to the periscope stand.

Durand was still looking through the scope, tracing a circle, watching for anything that might be approaching the sub. He leaned back from the scope for a second and rubbed his eye. "What now, Skipper? Go deep?"

"No, Mr. Durand. Surface the ship. We're heading for port."

Durand looked hard at Glass. "Did you say surface, sir?"

"That's what I said, Mr. Durand. Now get a move on it. We don't have time to lollygag around out here."

Ten minutes later the sub was surfaced, ready for the long, cold run on top of the ocean all the way into Faslane.

O'Malley stepped into the control room. He looked like a bright orange version of the Pillsbury Doughboy. The exposure suit he had donned was bulky and not very fashionable, but it was warm, waterproof, and floated should the wearer fall overboard, so no one complained.

"Request permission to open the upper hatch," he called across the room to Durand.

"Open the upper hatch, one inch pressure in the boat," Durand sang in response.

O'Malley bounded up the ladder. In a few seconds there was the unmistakable sound of air whistling past the partially opened hatch. Glass felt his ears pop from the pressure change just as he saw the HATCH SHUT light on the ballast control panel flash out. The wind rushed out of the boat as the air pressure inside equalized with that outside. In a few moments the whistling stopped. O'Malley swung the heavy hatch fully open and climbed up into the dripping-wet bridge cockpit.

Glass donned his own exposure suit and made the long climb to the bridge. The wan sun hung low on the horizon like a dim afterthought, a pale orange ball in the otherwise gray winter sky. This far north and this time of the year, it appeared above the horizon for a few hours each day, bringing scant warmth to a cold, dreary place. A bitter wind whipped the sea into whitecaps with the occasional gust sending bullets of spray against the Plexiglas windshield.

"Where to, Skipper?" O'Malley yelled over the wind as Glass emerged from the hatch to stand next to him in the cockpit.

"Steer zero-nine-zero until you get to the North Channel. We'll come to one-three-zero then until we're clear of the Mull of Kintyre. By then Nav will have charts plotted so you can see what's going on. Now kick her up to a full bell. We need to get moving."

Toledo picked up speed until the sea washed back across her bow, deep and clear until it crashed high up on the sail, then falling in frothing white chaos. A broad white churning wake stretched far behind as the sub plowed ahead through the winter sea.

Toledo slid on, steaming down the North Channel between Strathclyde, Scotland, and Northern Ireland, then turning east to enter the Firth of Clyde as they passed the lonely, barren rock of Ailsa Craig. Then they turned northeast to run between the Ayrshire coast and the Isle of Arran. The channel here was wide and deep with plenty of room for the ships traveling to and from the busy port of Glasgow at the head of the firth.

The firth narrowed to a couple of miles across as they passed between Garroch Head on the Isle of Butte to port and the Cumbrae Islands to starboard. Mercifully, the mountainous terrain shielded them from the cold wind blowing in off the North Atlantic. O'Malley and Glass were busy keeping track of all the shipping in these confined waters, making sure none of them got too close to *Toledo*. Boats of all types scurried about the busy waterway. Huge freighters, small coasters, and fishermen all steamed up and down the firth. Ferries made their scheduled runs back and forth across the stretch of water as well.

"Watch for those guys," Glass warned O'Malley as a large ferry weighted with cars and trucks and a railing lined with waving passengers steamed across *Toledo*'s bow. "They don't give way for anybody."

"So I see!"

As they made the long sweeping turn around Gourock, Glass pointed over to the opening of a loch on the port side.

"That's Holy Loch over there. Our FBM subs used to patrol out of there before the Tridents hit the water. I was there once as an ensign. The winds coming down the loch can hit a hundred knots. Real nasty." He chuckled as he reminisced. "So bad sometimes that the liberty boats couldn't make it out to the tender. There's a bar on Hunter's Quay that serves a selection of Scotch whiskeys you wouldn't believe."

O'Malley shivered from the cold. "I got to admit that sounds real good to me right about now."

"See that red flashing light up ahead, off the port

bow? That should be Roseneath Point Light." Glass pointed at a pinprick of light three miles ahead, barely visible against the brighter illumination of the towns that stretched on beyond the point. "The tugs should be waiting just around the turn."

They steamed past Strone Point and the broad entrance to Loch Long and started the long, hard turn to the northwest, skirting Roseneath Point to enter Gare Loch. Two Royal Navy tugs joined them there in Roseneath Bay with a friendly greeting. The little fleet steamed in formation as they squeezed through the Roseneath Narrows and transited the length of Gare Loch.

The bright lights of the Royal Navy Submarine Base at Faslane came into view.

As the two tugs pushed *Toledo* alongside the pier, Glass looked up and saw it for the first time. It was the shape of the *Mystic*, dangling like a gigantic hooked fish below a massive pier crane. That brought home once again why they were here.

That machine was designed to rescue submariners trapped deep below the surface of the sea. They had been summoned to deliver it to some place out there. It could be no more than a simple drill. It could also be that brother sailors were in deep distress and he and his crew and boat were their last hope.

Chapter 8

"I appreciate you and your people coming down for this meeting, Mr. Smythe." The tall, distinguished man had started the meeting at precisely nine a.m., at least three digital watches in the room all tweeting in harmony to confirm it. "It will be a quick one, but I felt it was important for us all to meet face-to-face one more time, considering how much more closely our staffs will be working together until the final implementation of your system."

Alstair McLain was the director of the Market Regulation Division for the Securities and Exchange Commission. With his full head of silver hair, strong, piercing eyes, and commanding presence, it was clear who was in charge here. The fact that he had the full regulatory force of the U.S. government behind him added to his considerable majesty.

Alan Smythe nodded in his direction and tried to sit up just a bit straighter in his chair. He knew his future, the future of OptiMarx, was as much in this man's hands as anyone's.

"Thank you," was all he said.

Smythe, Carl Andretti, and Dmitri Ustinov sat across the broad conference table from McLain and two of his people, a rather nondescript man in a bad suit and a pleasant-looking middle-aged woman. McLain waved his arm in their direction.

"I believe you know Stan Miller, my deputy. I wanted you to meet Catherine Goldman as well. Ms. Goldman is head of the Information Technology Branch and will be your key contact on the OptiMarx project from this point forward."

The three OptiMarx executives had been frequent visitors to the imposing SEC Headquarters Building, which stood just two blocks north of the Mall in the heart of downtown Washington. From this building, the powerful government agency watched over even the tiniest move of every player in the U.S. stock market. While the exterior and public spaces of the headquarters spoke of power and grandeur, the working areas were plain to the extreme. This conference room was one of the working spaces. Windowless pale green walls accented the utilitarian furniture. Each plastic chair bore its Government Services Administration serial number, proclaiming it to have been bought from the lowest bidder. The lone concession to human comfort was the coffee carafe and stack of china mugs in the center of the Formica-topped table.

The executives from OptiMarx introduced themselves to Goldman, exchanging pleasantries and trying not to neglect Stan Miller. It was clear that Ms. Goldman was the newest obstacle they would have to hurdle. She was a smallish woman, not unattractive at all, but with a strong air of all-business about her.

Dmitri Ustinov was thinking that if she would allow her hair to grow out, do something to hide the few gray strands, maybe pay a bit more attention to her makeup, she might be worth taking a run at. Alan Smythe was pondering if she was at all corruptible. Carl Andretti was wondering what his two partners were thinking about this new and unexpected development.

It was obvious that McLain was ready to begin again and the room fell quiet. He read from a prepared text he held on the table in front of him.

"We are meeting today under the provisions of SEC Policy Statement 34-27445, the 'Automation Review Policy.' The ARP inspection will be run by the New York Stock Exchange, but we will observe it. Catherine will head up our team that will be responsible for monitoring every step."

Goldman acknowledged the mention of her name with a quick nod of her head and smoothly picked up the very obvious baton that had just been handed to her.

"Gentlemen, we will be working very closely together over the next couple of months. We will be looking at all aspects of your OptiMarx system to make sure it is sized to handle the maximum expected volume. That is what ARP was chartered for." She stood and looked over at the three corporate executives. Even though she was only a little over five feet tall, she still radiated a force of presence that demanded respect. "We will also be testing all the trading and clearing rules, as well as compliance with SEC policy, as you would expect. When we're done, your system will be wrung out and ready for 'prime time.'"

As she talked, Ustinov leaned over and whispered to Andretti, "Damn, she sure sounds a lot tougher than she looks."

"I'll bet she's tough as she sounds and twice as smart," Andretti whispered back. "Watch out for that one."

Goldman stopped talking and cast a cold eye on the two men. "Questions, gentlemen?"

"Uh, no," Andretti stammered. "We're just discussing the schedule."

"I was just getting to the schedule, if you will allow me," Goldman said rather pointedly. "We will begin on Monday. Early Monday. The remainder of the schedule and the requirements documents are in these packages." She handed thick bound notebooks to each of the Opti-Marx executives. "Mr. Ustinov, I expect your team to be ready to go by eight o'clock Monday morning." She looked around the room. "Any questions?"

There were none. The meeting was over.

Andretti and Smythe walked out of the conference room together. Ustinov stayed behind to attempt to make small talk with Goldman. It never hurt to be nice to a bureaucrat, even if she happened to be a tough-as-nails woman. Both the other two men had seen the look in Ustinov's eyes. He was on the hunt.

Andretti waited for the elevator door to slide shut before he spoke.

"What did you make of that? They brought us all the way down here for a two-minute meeting and to hand us the paperwork they could have sent up to us by courier. Do you think we have a problem?"

Smythe half smiled when he answered, "I don't think so. This was all for show, to let us know how serious they are about keeping an eye on us. It gave McLain a chance to trot out his attack dog to scare us, to put us on our best behavior. Maybe to even throw us off our guard. She growled a bit, right on cue. Ustinov will use that Russian charm of his on her. He'll have her eating out of his hand. Besides, except for his tendency to chase everything in a skirt, he is so damned clean and innocent. He'll soon have her convinced that the only sinister plot at OptiMarx has to do with him getting into her pants."

Andretti was still chuckling at the idea of the young Russian programmer chasing the SEC inspector as they stepped out of the elevator into the marble-and-wood lobby. Smythe's limo was waiting at the curb to whisk them back over to Reagan Airport and the corporate jet.

Dmitri Ustinov was on his own.

Sergei Andropoyov shivered and pulled his coat even more tightly against his body as he made his way from one of the crippled submarine's compartments to another. It was cold in here already, even with a few of *Gepard*'s heaters still left on. They couldn't afford to use any more of them. They drained far too much from the limited battery supply.

Andropoyov could see his frosty breath in the eerie half-light as he fought to keep his true thoughts from showing on his face. He knew it was important that he make an appearance. The surviving crew needed to be reassured that everything was all right. Most of them were lying in their bunks, curled beneath their blankets, trying to stay warm while they heeded his admonition to avoid movement and conserve oxygen.

Oxygen wasn't the real problem. They had enough for a month or more, stored in the big flasks out in the ballast tanks, and there were enough sodium chlorate candles to give them breathable air for another week after that.

The problem was carbon dioxide. Each crew member breathed out one hundred and fifty grams of it every day, and without the air being cleansed, it would soon grow to toxic levels. If they had power, the scrubbers would remove it from the air. Without them, the alternative was to let the lithium hydroxide pellets absorb it. If they had power, the pellets would be held in canisters and fans would force the carbon dioxide–laden air through them. Without power, the fans and canisters were useless. The best way to get the lithium hydroxide in contact with the air was to lay a thin layer wherever they could. The pellets were already spread out on most of the horizontal surfaces in the submarine, on tables, empty bunks, even on the deck. The pellets disintegrated so that a cloud of obnoxious dust rose whenever they were disturbed.

Gepard carried enough lithium hydroxide to last for a complete patrol without the scrubbers, but the storage lockers where most of it was kept were all in the flooded after compartment. The ready stores were all they had now. Even if they were careful, there was only enough to keep the air breathable for a few more days.

"Otherwise" was a proposition Sergei Andropoyov did not want to ponder.

He paused in his tour at the reactor hatch. It seemed strange to see the doorway gaping open when they were at sea. Normally it would have been locked shut. If anyone were crazy enough to enter the hatch while the reactor was operating, the radiation would kill him in a few minutes.

Now the reactor was shut down. It presented no danger from radiation.

The captain ducked his head and stepped through. The place was huge, but crammed full with piping, valves, pumps, and wires. He noticed the temperature difference. After the cold in the rest of the sub, it was very warm in here. Even two days after the explosion that had sunk them, the reactor system was still quite hot. Andropoyov took advantage of the heat, removed his coat, and allowed the warmth to soak into his body. His hands tingled as the circulation returned.

Now, where was the first officer?

He found Dimitriy Pishkovski staring forlornly into an open electrical panel.

"Captain, I have found why the rods will not latch," he announced, the defeat heavy in his voice.

He pointed into the electrical panel. It was filled with charred insulation and melted wiring. All the interior surfaces were blackened with a heavy layer of sticky, oily soot.

"How did that happen?" Andropoyov asked.

"Damn shipyard! The lugs weren't tight. When the explosion happened, the wires must have gotten crossed. Burnt it all. Nothing we can do here."

Andropoyov looked over Pishkovski's shoulder at the confused, blackened mess. Even in a shipyard, it would take weeks to repair damage this extensive, and now there was no way to float this thing to a shipyard.

The captain shook his head in resignation. He squatted down and put an arm around Pishkovski.

"My friend, let us not share this news with the rest of the crew just yet," he said in a raspy whisper. They crouched there for another moment, the sweat soaking through their garments. It was so deathly quiet. There was no sound but their own breathing and the distant, ghostly *chink* of dripping water somewhere. Andropoyov stood and took a deep breath of the sultry air. "Come, Dimitriy, there is nothing more to do here. We will go see what we can do for the injured."

Joe Glass stood on the brow of his submarine and watched as the *Mystic* DSRV settled down onto the seating ring around *Toledo*'s after escape trunk. The workers rushed to check the latch mechanism and to hook up the power umbilicals.

Up forward, a strange-looking device slid down the torpedo-loading skid on its way to the torpedo room deep in the submarine. Glass still didn't quite know what to make of it. The bright yellow box had arms, propellers, and other spiky protrusions poking out at odd angles.

So that's what one of those robot subs looks like, he thought. Wonder why we're loading on one of those things.

There were four green-painted war-shot torpedoes resting on dollies, waiting their turn to be loaded. Why would he need war-shot torpedoes for a submarine rescue?

Crewmen brushed by him as box after box disappeared down *Toledo*'s forward escape trunk. The DSRV crew came with quite a load of extra stuff. Add to that the groceries they would need for wherever they were going and the result was a full-fledged stores load.

A couple of patrol boats cruised out on the loch, discouraging anyone foolish enough to be out on the water this late at night from coming any closer. Occasional headlights were visible up on the hill as cars drove by on the A-814 on their way to Dumbarton.

Glass was so intent on watching the flurry of activity around him that the voice of the topside watch startled him when he hollered for him.

"Skipper, XO on the phone for you!"

Glass grabbed the phone. "Captain."

"Skipper, you've got a phone call down here."

"Damn, XO! I'm busy up here. You handle it."

With all the activity on his boat, it would be a major chore for Glass just to get down to some place where he could answer the call.

Edwards hesitated for a polite second and then replied, "You'd better take this one, Skipper. It's Commodore Ward and he wants to talk to you on the secure line."

"Okay, XO. I'll fight my way down."

Glass dropped down through the forward escape trunk, squeezing past the mass of sailors who were standing there, passing boxes down. He nimbly stepped over the accumulated pile of stores that was building up on the mess decks. They would be walking on cans for a week, at least.

He scurried up the ladder to the control room. Perez and Oshley were bent over a pile of charts, planning their eventual track out of the confines of the base and back to open water. He squeezed past them and headed for his stateroom.

The deck of the passageway forward of the control room was missing, as was the deck for the middle-level passageway below. A long ramp angled up from the after end of the middle-level deck to the topside of the open weapons shipping hatch. The strange yellow box Glass had seen topside now dangled from the ramp and traveled down its length. It looked even stranger up close. The clear glass lens of an underwater video camera seemed like the eye of an intelligent alien being staring curiously at him. Was it malevolent or disinterested? He wasn't sure.

Glass stepped around the corner of the ramp and jumped into his stateroom. He could see all the way down to the torpedo room in the lowest level of the boat from here and he felt cold air spilling down from the open hatch above.

He plopped down in his chair and grabbed the outside phone. "Joe Glass here, Commodore."

"Well, Joe, it's good to hear your voice. How is it going out there?"

"Real good. This is a good boat and a good crew. They learn real fast. I gotta tell you one thing, though. When I climbed up on the bridge for that first under way out of Norfolk and the officer of the deck turned around and asked for permission to get under way, I looked behind me to see where you were standing. It took me a few seconds to realize he was talking to me."

Glass could hear Ward chuckling on the other end of the line.

"Joe, that happens to every new skipper on his first time out. I remember feeling the same thing myself the first time we got *Spadefish* under way." Ward paused for a moment for an obvious change of subject. "Joe, I've been looking at your exercise messages. It looks like you got your butt kicked on the first run."

Glass grimaced. He might have expected it. It was like a high school teacher inspecting a former student's first college grades.

"Yeah, *Turbulent* is real good and a lot quieter than we thought. We got in too close and she shot us before we were ready. We all learned a valuable lesson there."

Glass wasn't about to go into detail, to talk about Edwards's unjustified reliance on Zillich's "gut feel," or the slow response of the fire control party. He wouldn't share those things with anyone else, not even his old skipper. That kind of information was kept inside the lifelines. Outside the lifelines, any problem with *Toledo* was a problem with her skipper.

There was a serious tone in Ward's voice when he went on. "I'm glad you learned it when the lesson was cheap. Next time may not be. That's why we hold drills, Skipper. Let's go secure."

Glass felt a sudden shiver of cold go down his spine as he pushed the button on the secure phone. He listened to the electronics chirp and crackle for a few seconds, until the red light flickered to green. Ward's voice now sounded oddly distant and hollow.

"Hold you secure, Joe."

"Hold you the same," Glass answered. "Now, what's going on? This ain't some exercise."

Ward paused a moment before answering. "Day before yesterday, SUBLANT received a message from *Miami*. She was on one of those scientific exercises up in the Barents Sea at the ice edge. Had a load of eggheads from Woods Hole on board, listening to narwhals."

"That's Brad Crawford's boat, isn't it? He was in the same Prospective Commanding Officer class with me. A real good guy."

"Yeah, Crawford has *Miami*," Ward answered. "You're right. He's a good one. Real cool under pressure. Great service reputation. He seems to have all the right buttons punched. Anyway, back to the story. SUBLANT gets this message from Crawford. He says he picked up a new type of Akula coming out of Polyarnyy on his thin-line array. It was real quiet and not showing most of the Akula tonals."

Glass whistled and rubbed his chin. "A new boat out of Russia? They haven't even been getting the ones they have under way lately. I hear they have no money for upkeep and the boats that they have are rusting alongside the pier. How the hell are they going to build something new?"

"I have no idea, Joe," Ward replied. "An even bigger question is how they could keep something like that secret from us. Anyway, *Miami* reports trailing this new boat up under the ice. They get two hundred miles northwest of Novaya Zemlya when the Akula explodes and sinks. Crawford said he talked to survivors on the underwater telephone and they're in dire straits. They don't know what happened but they've lost their reactor power. They're on the bottom in a thousand feet of water and under a lot of pack ice."

"Jesus," Glass answered. "New boat. Not shaken down. Who knows what might have gone sour on the thing? Okay, so we tell the Russians what we know and they crank up an effort to go up there and get their guys. They're not that far from Polyarnyy. You still haven't explained why we're here in the middle of all this hurry-up and secrecy."

"You're getting ahead of the story, Joe. The Russians claim they don't have any boats at sea at all right now and that none have gone missing. Our last satellite pass did show all their boats accounted for, all cold iron sitting right there alongside their piers. To top that, they are bringing up that old claim again about the Barents being a territorial sea. They told us in no uncertain terms to stay out of there."

A clanging bell outside the door grabbed Glass's attention. He looked up to see one of the green war-shot torpedoes sliding ominously down the loading hoist. "Jon, you haven't told me why we're loading war-shot torpedoes if we're looking for a sunken Russian sub."

"Those aren't ordinary fish you're loading," Jon Ward said. "They are specially outfitted for underice operations. The sonar and the electronics are tuned for that environment. Those are the only four underice ADCAP torpedoes in our entire inventory."

Glass swallowed hard. "You still haven't answered my question. Why do I need them?"

There was a long pause on the other end of the line. Joe Glass could hear the faint hum of the secure phone line, the creaking of the hoist that was lowering the sophisticated ordnance into the bowels of his boat.

"Joe, *Miami* was supposed to communicate again twelve hours after her first message," Jon Ward answered. "We haven't heard a thing since. She has been overdue for more than a day now."

"What do you think, Jon?"

"I don't know. But, Joe, you better be damn careful up there."

Chapter 9

Joe Glass watched from high atop the sail as the big yellow-and-orange Royal Navy tugs churned up alongside his submarine, preparing to pull *Toledo* away from the pier. He took a deep breath. The chill wind blowing down from the north felt invigorating, even as the bits of sleet and snow it bore stung as they nipped at his face.

Dawn was still three hours away. It had been a long night, capping off a hard day. Glass knew he was about to embark with his boat and crew on a mission that had real purpose. There was also the uncertainty. He had no way to know if he and his men were ready for what they might find up there on top of the world, beneath the unforgiving ice.

His equipment was state-of-the-art, the best his government had, and he had worked with his men long enough to have confidence in their abilities. Uncertain missions were what he had trained for his entire Navy career.

He was as ready as he would ever be!

The *Mystic* was latched to the sub's back, rigged for the long transit to the polar ice. The special ADCAP torpedoes were stowed in the torpedo room, ready for tube loading later. Eric Hobson, the weapons officer, had put them to bed along with the unmanned submersible.

The crew, those not manning watches for the under way, were still stowing food for the run north. Dan Perkins and his DSRV team were finishing the final checks on their baby and stowing their gear for the long, rapid ride.

"We're ready to go, Skipper," Hobson yelled up to Glass. The weapons officer stood in the bridge cockpit just below him. "Tugs are tied and ready to take a strain."

The words were snatched away by the brisk wind. Glass had to lean in to hear him. "Very well. Cast off all lines."

Once under way, *Toledo* jumped ahead as if she, too, sensed the urgency of once again getting to sea, out of the loch, so she could head northward to whatever awaited them.

The crusty old submarine looked as if it had long since been abandoned to the Arctic weather. The signboard dangling from the sail was faded and barely readable. Vipr, it read, in dim yellowing Cyrillic letters. Broad bands of red rust streaked down the sides of the rounded sail. Great chunks of its anechoic rubber coating were missing, as if the sub suffered from the pocking of a severe case of acne. Her deck was covered with a thick coating of ice, blackened by dirt and grit blown across the fjord from the shipyard.

Two tugs that were laced to the decrepit hulk maneuvered it across the lead gray waters of Polyarnyy Harbor. Wind whipped the water into whitecaps, spraying everything with icy cold mist as the trio inched toward the lonely pier. There, four more dilapidated submarine hulks sat bobbing listlessly, apparently abandoned and wasting away.

A half dozen slovenly dressed sailors loitered there, ready to grab the lines as soon as the tug pushed the sub a little closer to the pier. They swung their arms across their chests and stamped their feet, all in a vain attempt to keep the blood flowing to their freezing extremities. Heavy clouds, laden with snow, hung overhead, their dark gray bunting hiding the stars in the night sky. The overcast also prevented any curious overhead eyes from looking down. Mercury vapor lights hanging on poles along the pier reflected off the low-hanging clouds, bathing the scene in a ghostly cold blue light.

The frail old sub kissed the camels floating alongside the pier. The men grabbed lines and tied the relic securely enough that even a howling winter storm wouldn't be able to break it loose. Their chore finished, the sailors walked briskly back across the narrow gangway and down the long pier, passing other similar boats along the way. Each one of them was every bit as forlorn and crumbling as the one they had just lashed to the dock.

Once they were gone, there wasn't another human being in sight, not even a guard standing topside to watch over the wraithlike assembly of dead subs.

The group rounded the corner at the end of the pier and headed off down the street toward the mammoth building that stood at its end. Once there, they entered the same covered piers from which *Gepard* and *Volk* had departed several days before. The bustling activity in here was in stark contrast to the deathly stillness at the open pier they had just left. Here, they walked down one long pier, past four other subs and workers who crawled all over them, before they climbed onto yet another smartly maintained submarine at the end of the line.

The clean, new signboard on that boat clearly read VIPR.

The group's leader saluted the officer who awaited them topside. "Captain, we are completed. The dummy sub is tied up in the same spot where we were."

The captain saluted back smartly. "Excellent! Once again the American spy satellites will tell lies. They will never suspect the switch."

He motioned them below. Their reward would be hot black tea and a chance to warm their numb hands and feet.

The pealing of the telephone woke Admiral Alexander Durov. He had not even realized that he had fallen asleep at his desk until the jangling startled him awake.

He shook his head to clear the fuzziness and cursed his own fatigue.

So much to do, so little time. Well, there would be ample time to rest when this was all done and the *Rodina* was once again secure in its destiny. For now, though, there was work to do, arrangements to be made, schemes to be put in motion, and no time for a nap. Not even for an old sailor.

His hand jabbed out and grabbed the phone. "*Da!* Durov here. What do you want?"

"Admiral, this is Captain First Rank Gregor Dobiesz."

Durov recognized the voice at once. Dobiesz was the commander of submarines for Polyarnyy and a key player in Durov's scheme. He was also one who loved the sound of his own name.

"The last switch has been made. *Vipr* is being refitted and loaded out with missiles in the sub pen. The mock-up is in her place at the pier. We will have all the boats ready for our mission in two weeks," the captain proudly announced.

"Dobiesz, you misbegotten Cossack idiot!" Durov growled back. "Was your mother a jackass? That is the only way to explain how any man could be so stupid as you! When I said five days, what part did you not under-stand? Can you not count to five?"

Dobiesz tried to break into the tirade before it got out of hand. His words now carried a distinct air of despera-tion. "Admiral, you must understand, the loading takes time. The missiles must be tested. The systems must be—"

Durov was in no mood to hear excuses. "I do not care about tests and checks. Those subs, all of them, will be ready to sail on command in five days. Do you hear me? Five days! If they are not, Siberia will be warm compared to where you will spend the rest of your days."

"Yes, Admiral," the shaken captain replied meekly. "It will be as you order."

Durov slammed down the phone. He breathed deeply, trying to calm himself. His old heart wasn't what it used to be. When he had been younger, an incompetent like Dobiesz would have evacuated himself at the mere sound of the admiral's voice raised in anger. Now the major ef-fect of his having to make a forceful point with an incom-petent underling was to leave his own heart racing and him gasping for breath.

Durov poured a healthy shot of vodka into the crystal goblet sitting on his desk. He reached into his jacket pocket and pulled out a small bottle of pills. Extracting one of the tiny blue capsules, he popped it into his mouth and took a heavy gulp of the fiery, clear liquid. His breath returned and his pulse settled back to its normal beat. He tugged a handkerchief from his breast pocket and wiped the sweat from his forehead, the phlegm from his lips.

Satisfied he was once again in control of his breathing, he grabbed the phone and dialed a well-remembered number.

"Yes, Admiral? What do you need?" Boris Medikov answered, his voice hollow on the phone line all the way from Moscow.

"Boris, we are on schedule here. Every boat will be ready to sail in five days. We still have not heard from *Volk*. We have to assume that the action with *Gepard* was successful since she has not reported in, either. Serebnitskiv may be delayed for any number of reasons, but we just do not know what is happening."

Durov swallowed hard when he finished his report. The lack of word from his nephew was troubling. The suspicion was strong that Andropoyov might have somehow been able to fire back, to take out his own stalker before going down. Both boats would be lost, but that was acceptable. Maybe it was even better in the grand scheme of things.

He could hear the silence on the other end of the line now, and Durov could picture the Mafia leader chewing on his lip for a moment as he pondered the report and its effect on the overall plan. Medikov's words were sharp, razorlike, when he spoke.

"For someone who was so critical of the most mundane and harmless holes in our plan in America, you seem to have your share of loose ends up there, Admiral. You do not even know if the ambush has taken place or if the plan has been set in motion yet."

Durov gritted his teeth. Who was this Organizatsiya henchman, this common hoodlum, to question the efficacy of his operations? He forced himself to swallow his pride for the moment. "Rest assured, we are successfully under way with the plan. Soon the world will know what has happened beneath the ice. Or at least our version of the tragic treachery that has occurred."

"So, let us assume you are correct. What do we do now?"

"The impending news will have its desired effect, you can be assured," the old admiral answered. He tried to ignore the shaking of his hands as he turned up the goblet and drained the last drops of the vodka. "As soon as you have everything in place in New York, we will make the claim that the Americans, once again aggressive and blatant under their new hawk of a president, are responsible for the loss of *Gepard*. If *Volk* should fail to return as well, we will blame them for her loss also. Once the media is on the trail, they will do the rest of our work for us. The world will be thinking of nothing else. The rest of the plan will proceed as we have laid it out."

There was a grunt all the way from Moscow, then a long sigh.

"Let us hope, for the sake of both our necks, that what you say is true, Admiral."

It was cold, so very cold.

Captain Sergei Andropoyov huddled in a bunk in the

dark berthing room. The numbing chill made even thinking difficult. Still, he had to continue to plan what to do in order for his crew to survive.

It was growing more and more difficult. All his thoughts were a slow jumble. He was fighting the palpable sense of shadowy dread that seemed to envelop him as surely as the black coldness.

All the crew, or at least the thirty-five who remained, were huddled together there in the berthing room, trying in vain to use their shared body heat to keep each other warm. The battery was now so depleted that Andropoyov had decided they could no longer afford to use the heaters. They would have to use the trickle of power left for the underwater telephone should rescuers approach again. Otherwise, no one would be able to find them.

He motioned for his first officer to join him beneath his blanket. He kept his voice low when he spoke. "Dimitriy, we must do something. We will all freeze here, even if the air lasts," he whispered. It wouldn't be good if any of the huddled, shivering crew members overheard their captain, even though they knew what was happening as well as he. Still, until their leader gave up, there was hope. "There must be something we can do. Do you have any ideas?"

Pishkovski shivered. He pulled the edges of the blanket closer around him and answered through chattering teeth, "Captain, it is still warm in the reactor compartment. A little radiation is better than freezing."

Andropoyov rose from the bunk. The air was fouled to the point that any quick movement left him breathless.

He wondered how much longer they could hold out in the forlorn hope that help would arrive. The calcium hydroxide would be depleted by now and there was little more to scatter about. He figured another day or two and the carbon dioxide would kill them if the cold hadn't done so.

He pondered his choices for a moment. A morbid thought tried to capture him.

Maybe it was better to wait here and freeze. Andropoyov had read somewhere . . . maybe in one of Pushkin's books . . . that freezing was a quiet, peaceful, painless way to die.

He shook himself and cleared the idea as best he could. He must keep fighting, use every trick he could think of to bring his crew through this if he had any chance of getting them home alive.

There was still the matter of what might have sunk them in the first place. If there were some fault in his boat that had caused this catastrophe, they would need to make certain it didn't happen again to some other crew. That was something they could never hope to do if they lay dead and silent at the bottom of the Barents.

"Come, Dimitriy," he growled as he turned. "Let's move everyone to the reactor compartment."

The remnants of the crew stumbled as best they could through the hatch and into the relative warmth.

Marina Nosovitskaya glanced up from her desk when the dark shadow fell across it. Sure enough, Dmitri Ustinov stood there above her, smiling wickedly as he stared down the opening at the front of her blouse. The lovely young programmer abruptly sat erect, pulling her blouse pointedly taut.

"What are you staring at?" she snarled in Russian.

Ustinov leered right back. "Now, is that any way to treat your boss? I was just admiring the lovely view and here you are, getting all indignant with me." His smirk grew even more pronounced. "You should be nicer to me. You never can tell what I might be able to do for a new immigrant to America like you. I have connections in this country, you know."

Nosovitskaya leaned back, drawing the gauzy pink material even more tightly across her breasts. An odd, seductive smile played on her full lips. Her nipples protruded invitingly.

Ustinov gulped. Beads of sweat broke out across his broad brow. The light in the office cubicle seemed to darken. Except for a ray of sunshine that played on those wondrous orbs. He could barely restrain himself. He fought the overpowering urge to reach out and grab them, right then and there, and show them some proper appreciation.

She leaned forward and leveled a commanding look at him, her eyes narrow and menacing. She spoke in a low, yet powerful, voice. "Uncle Boris warned me about you. He told me you were nothing more than a Georgian pig and that I should cut your balls off and jam them down your throat if you threatened me." She paused to savor the sudden look of terror that crossed his face. "You remember Uncle Boris Medikov, do you not?"

Ustinov's face went pale. He reached out to brace

himself on her desk to avoid keeling over as the blood left his head.

Boris Medikov, Ustinov's boss several times removed, was her uncle? Medikov would kill him for doing no more than he had done already, let alone the scenario he had been playing over and over in his mind since the first day he had laid eyes on the man's lovely niece. The truth was that Medikov could reach from Moscow to New York in the blink of an eye if he had reason to do so.

Nosovitskaya smiled a little easier now. She threw back her head, shaking out her mane of long blond hair. She seductively licked her lips with the tip of her tongue before she spoke again.

"I see you remember my beloved uncle Boris. He has a message for you. You are to make certain that the OptiMarx system is in full operation, with our modifications in place, within one month from today."

Ustinov looked around the office. Fortunately the room was still empty. Everyone else was out for lunch.

"One month?" he whined in protest. "That is impossible. It cannot be done. The ARP takes two months to complete. The system cannot be used until that test is done and the SEC gives its approval to go online."

It appeared that she wasn't any more interested in his frantic pleas than she had been his clumsy advances. She was idly staring down the aisle between the rows of cubicles, out the window at the far end of the office suite that opened onto the Manhattan skyline. He sputtered on for a few seconds. He stopped when it dawned on him that protesting was futile.

Nosovitskaya smiled. "Uncle Boris said one month. One month or you will find the bottom of the Hudson to be a very cold and dark place. I am here to make certain you are not distracted."

She stood and brushed past him, her breasts pressing against his arm. She stopped for a moment to look up at him through her thick lashes. Then she walked away, her hips swaying hypnotically.

Still, it was neither Marina Nosovitskaya's beauty nor the strong, lingering aroma of her perfume that had Dmitri Ustinov struggling to find enough air to breathe.

Chapter 10

Mark Stern eased his bright red Porsche Boxster into the parking space that was marked PRIVATE—PARTNERS ONLY! He hopped out of the little sports car, and, despite his age, showed no stiffness at all from the morning tennis game at the club. Ignoring the KEEP OFF THE GRASS signs, he strode across the immaculate green lawn, the straightest line toward the stone and glass two-story building that was set back in a grove of large old California black oaks. From the outside, the structure resembled one of the red-roofed classroom buildings down at Stanford, but those were on the other end of Sand Hill Road. The only external difference was the discreet polished black marble slab that stood near the stone walk. The gold letters on its front read PRIVATE PACIFIC PARTNERS.

That was the only indication that this was the Palo Alto home of one of the country's most powerful but secretive venture capital investment companies. It was no indication of the heady financial dealings that went on inside its walls.

Stern half nodded to the receptionist, ignored the open elevator doors behind her, and rushed up the stairs, taking two at a time as he headed straight to his private corner office on the second floor. He was a man on a mission this morning. The phone call he had received while en route to the office confirmed an earlier suspicion, and now it was time to do something about it.

Like the building itself, the interior of the big office was designed to impress, even awe, those who might have reason to be there. But this wasn't the subtle understatement of power of the public spaces; this was more blatant. The huge, ornately carved mahogany desk was centered in front of a picture window that framed a sweeping view of the Silicon Valley below. A matching conference table rested in front of the other glass exterior wall, looking out on an equally stunning view, but this time of the Santa Cruz Mountains. The black calf-leather and chrome chairs gave those fortunate enough to be granted an audience here a comfortably stylish seat while they listened to the great financier pontificate from behind his desk. The two interior walls were tastefully decorated with various pieces of modern art, all originals. The dark maroon deep-pile carpet and textured wall covering added to the rich elegance of the big room. One could smell money and feel its power here.

Stern sat for a moment, twisting his lip as he pondered his next move. He tapped the desktop with his fingertips and fought to remain calm, to keep his temper under control.

OptiMarx had promised to be a veritable gold mine from the beginning. That's why he had enthusiastically committed vast quantities of the fund's capital to the effort. Why he had just as willingly tossed in a large part of his own personal fortune after it. His due diligence had been as comprehensive as ever. Everything had turned up positive. The venture had appeared golden.

OptiMarx was a reputable company with a solid contract to modernize the nation's primary stock exchange. How could it miss?

Now, there was considerable risk. That limey idiot, Alan Smythe, was on the verge of ruining everything. At this point, Stern wasn't sure if the guy was incompetent or criminally stupid.

Did the son of a bitch think he could hide his silly little scheme from Mark Stern? After all, Stern had not managed to work his way to the top of one of the most powerful VC firms in the world by allowing small-time grifters and con artists like Smythe to pull their amateurish stunts on him. That wasn't the complication. If the SEC got suspicious, if they caught even the slightest whiff of anything amiss, they would ensnare OptiMarx and, with it, PPP's and Mark Stern's money in a morass so deep and sucking none of them would ever escape. The company would be so tangled up in endless testing, complicated reviews, eternal litigation, and constant inspections that the money would run out long before the system was close to launch. All that would happen even if they never uncovered Smythe's clumsy little scam.

Then there was the other matter, a slight snag that hit Stern even closer to home. It had seemed so easy at first, and had been necessary at the time. Stern needed to lay his hands on ten million dollars to cover a margin call when some of his personal high-tech investments went sour on him. His broker had not been very understanding. The boys at Bund Systems were much more helpful and had proposed a rather simple solution. They would be most happy to slip him the money he needed under the table. All he would need to do in return was arrange for OptiMarx to contract for Bund's hardware when they built the new trading system, even if it was little more than overpriced junk.

Now Alan Smythe was shying away from his end of the bargain, claiming the equipment was not compatible, that it would not meet the specs the Exchange was demanding.

It was time to rein this flunky in! Stern unlocked the bottom drawer of his desk and pulled from it a videotape. For the first time this day he allowed a small smile to play at his lips. This should do it. The private investigator who had secured the images on the tape had earned his fee well. Maybe he worked hard and made certain he was in the right place at the right time. Or maybe he had set the whole thing up. Stern neither knew nor cared how he did it. The slight grin widened to a full smile as he imagined the wheedling and whining he would soon hear from that pompous Brit ass. It was something he wanted to see in person.

He punched the button on his speakerphone and yelled to his assistant when she answered.

"Get Alan Smythe at OptiMarx on the phone. Tell him to get his ass on a plane out here immediately. Tell him I expect him to be here this evening. That I want no excuses from him or the checks will stop . . . as of close of business today."

Joe Glass sat on the bench locker in front of the torpedo tube control console. Despite the mess of new electronics and cabling that had been brought aboard back in Scotland, the torpedo room looked curiously empty considering that they were outbound on a mission. Six orange exercise ADCAP torpedoes filled a half dozen of the twenty-six stowage positions. One green war-shot was lined up behind tube two. The other three tubes were locked shut, with brass signs hanging from the heavy bronze doors. The signs read CAUTION, WAR-SHOT LOADED.

Tube two's door hung open, though. It was possible to see all the way down the twenty-one-inch-diameter cylinder to the muzzle door twenty-three feet away. The only thing in the tube was the little yellow robot sub. Its strange, misshapen, dwarfed form seemed out of place in there. This space was meant for sleek, deadly weapons of destruction, not the little toy of some eccentric oceanographer.

"Here's the difficulty, Skipper," Bill Schwartz was saying as he pointed to a hockey-puck-shaped blob of plastic. A thick cable protruded out of one side, while the other side contained an orderly mass of short pins. Schwartz was a civilian scientist and a temporary member of Dan Perkins's DSRV team. The middle-aged scientist pushed back his bifocals and shook his head. The mane of brown hair, streaked with gray, flew wildly, adding to his mad-scientist persona. "Damn quality control! Takes three of these one-forty-eight-pin connectors to get one that works."

Schwartz tossed the offending connector onto the deck next to the electronic test set he had been using. He grabbed another one out of the green sea bag that lay on the deck behind him and hooked one end of it to the set. He stood and leaned over to push the puck into the mating connector on the tube door.

He sat down again in front of the set. It was a box with several switches and a laptop computer attached to it. After a few strokes on the keyboard, Schwartz leaned back and pointed to the screen. "You see, Skipper? That's what it should look like. This is a good one."

Glass looked at the computer-generated graphic. It was indecipherable to him, but if it placated the scientist, all was well.

"So, where are we?" Glass asked.

Schwartz sighed and sat back, leaning against one of the heavy stanchions supporting the upper level of torpedo stows. He took a healthy swig from his coffee cup and sighed. "Well, the ticklish part is over. It's all grunt work from here on out. This is the first time we've tried to use one of these from a torpedo tube, you know. We couldn't have done it at all with the old-generation underwater vehicles."

Glass frowned. He couldn't believe that this Rube Goldberg–looking lash-up had not even been tested before. Or that the potential rescue of stranded submariners depended on it functioning properly.

"Why not, Dr. Schwartz? It seems like that gizmo would be the perfect tool for a lot of uses."

"Problem was the power supply. The old ones were electric driven, powered through the tether cable from the surface. There was no way to launch from the torpedo tubes without major modifications to the tube door, and even then, it would have limited the range so much it would not have been practical. You don't have room for several thousand feet of tether cable on board your boat, Skipper. Or a way to retrieve it once we've spooled it out. These new ones are powered with fuel cells. They use this little fiber-optic cable." He picked up a reel and showed him the end of a hair-thin piece of wire. "It gives us over ten thousand yards of range. When we're finished, we just cut what we've unrolled and throw it away once the robot sub is back in the tube. No retrieval needed."

Glass shook his head. "Slick, real slick. How good is this thing?"

Schwartz was in his element now. Someone was interested in his little ugly yellow baby, and he could talk forever on that subject. "The *Sea Scan* is several orders of magnitude more capable than any previous unmanned submersible. We attached a high-resolution side-scan sonar that allows us to do very rapid bottom searches over rather large areas." He pulled out a spiral notebook and flipped it open to a drawing of the robot sub. He pointed to a box attached underneath the device's belly. "This magnetometer will help us when we're looking for a downed sub, too. It detects masses of metal quite well. Once we've found something, these video cameras are linked to that monitor over there." He pointed to a screen among the mass of electronics and jumble of cables sitting on the torpedo stow above him. "Then we can see what *Sea Scan* has found and drive in for a close-up look. The real problem is knowing where she is in relation to both the *Toledo* and the sunken sub. We put in a very accurate miniature inertial navigation system and tied it to your sub's system through the fiber."

Glass looked at the jumble of wires and the stack of boxes and shook his head. The normally neat and orderly torpedo room looked like a junkyard with all this foreign stuff. He wasn't sure anything could work in this confusion of electronics, monitors and cabling.

He asked the question he had been thinking about ever since he saw the chaotic mess in the midst of his torpedo room. "How long until you have it all ready to go?"

Schwartz looked up from the monitor, its blue-white glow reflecting in his thick spectacles. "I'll finish the hookup this evening. Tomorrow we can flood down the tube and give her a test run in the tube. That soon enough?"

"Good. We go under the ice tomorrow evening. I want everything ready once we get in the area. Lives may depend on it, Dr. Schwartz."

The oceanographer Schwartz showed him a shy little grin. "Don't worry, Skipper. *Sea Scan*'ll be ready to go."

Catherine Goldman had a perplexed look on her face when she looked up from the screen she was reviewing. Something was fishy here. She still wasn't quite sure what it was, but something just didn't feel right.

She flashed on to another screen and read down the neat, orderly lines of source code that were displayed there. A little voice in the back of her head was telling her there was a problem here. It was a voice that rarely lied to her. So far, she just couldn't quite put it together.

Still, Goldman knew from years of listening to her own instincts that whatever was out of whack with this project would be made clear to her. She needed to sink her teeth into it more deeply and shake it out.

She leaned back and reached for the thick systems manual on the bookcase behind her and flipped through the pages. It wasn't any help at all.

She got up from the desk and stretched, trying to un-kink the knots in her cramped, aching back. Hunching over a computer all day just wasn't as easy as it used to be. She could remember days, not that long ago, when she would do this for eighteen hours a day for weeks on end, without giving it a second thought. She was an ea-ger young kid then. The world was exciting and fresh; the technology had so much potential for good. She rel-ished every challenge.

She was older now, more mature and realistic. Even a bit cynical, she admitted to herself. Things were much more complicated. A whole generation of hackers had grown up out there, and their break-ins and viruses were much more sophisticated than the crude efforts in the early days. The nation's stock and bond trading forums were always alluring targets, whether it was some kid in a basement somewhere trying to impress his friends or a well-planned plot by clever criminals or terrorists.

She grabbed up the manual and stepped out of the cramped little cubicle and walked down the hall to Carl Andretti's office. She ignored all the OptiMarx develop-ers in the cubicles along the way, their noses almost touching the monitors as their fingers danced on their ergonomic keyboards. The clatter of their fingertips on the keys rattled drily like the singing of cicadas.

She doubted that the fat chief technology officer

would be of any help. Goldman had concluded earlier that he was clueless when it came to the technical details of the system.

Still, he was the one to start with, much as she loathed any contact with him. Maybe he would say something that might give her some inkling, something to go on. It was surprising sometimes where elucidation originated.

She knocked at the door of the large corner office and then cracked it open when there was no response. Andretti looked up quickly from the phone call he was involved in. There was a startled, guilty look on his face. He held up a hand, mumbled something into the receiver she couldn't quite hear, and hung up.

Only then did Andretti stand, offer her a forced smile, and wave her on into his office. She couldn't help noticing the jelly stain on the front of his white shirt and the crumbs that clung to his patchy mustache.

"Good morning, Ms. Goldman. I didn't know you were in the building yet this morning. How is the government coming along in its never-ending task of protecting the poor American investor?"

Goldman brushed aside his feeble attempt at small talk. "Mr. Andretti, I've been in since seven. I have a question about the source code for the short-sale module. There are lines of code in there that I don't understand." She opened the manual and laid it on the desk in front of him. He stared at it as if it might burst into flames. "I can't find any mention of it in the documentation, either."

Andretti swallowed hard. He bent over the book and read for a few minutes, his lips moving as he did so. He looked up and shrugged his shoulders. "Look, I imagine it's just a little meaningless, extraneous code that got left in there somehow. Something legacy that didn't get purged. I'm sure it's nothing to worry about."

Goldman nodded, picked up the thick binder, turned on a heel, and walked back to her cubicle. He might be right. It could be nothing more than sloppy coding. Developers often inserted lines of computer code in a program for their own benefit and didn't bother to document it for anyone else who might stumble upon it. The pesky voice was still there, still singing loudly in the back of her head.

Something didn't ring true. She had no clear idea what it might be. She'd be damned if she let it rest before she found out for sure, before she hushed the nagging.

She shut the door behind her, sat back down at the desk, dumped out a couple of aspirin tablets, and swallowed them with a swig of cold coffee. She moved the mouse to wake up her computer, paged up on the monitor to the top of the section of code she had been analyzing, and once again squinted hard at the first instance of the troublesome commands she had found.

The little voice inside her head was screaming louder than ever.

The crew of the *Gepard* huddled together in the warmth of the reactor compartment. The space was designed for equipment, not people, so there was no place to comfortably sit or lie down. There was only a hard steel grating for a deck. The men didn't seem to care about that right now. They luxuriated in the warmth. The pitch-black space was silent, the stillness broken by the occasional low moan or grating gasp as someone tried to suck in a deep breath of the foul air or awoke from a fitful sleep struggling to breathe.

Sergei Andropoyov coughed and wheezed in the thick, tepid air. Breathing was becoming painful. Even the slightest movement left them gasping, so they all lay on the hard deck as still as they could manage. The captain had drifted off for a while, dreaming that it was the black, fragrant loam surrounding his boyhood farm home that now held them entombed, not the several hundred feet of icy water.

"Dimitriy, will we make it?" he whispered to his first officer. "Is there any hope left?"

Dimitriy Pishkovski remained silent for a very long time. Andropoyov had concluded that his friend and second in command might have given up and passed on. Then he heard a barely audible reply, a soft scratch of a whisper.

"Sergeiovich, it is in God's hands now. He will decide."

Andropoyov laid his head back on the rolled-up rag that was serving as his pillow. He had never known Pishkovski to be a religious man. In fact, in all the years they had sailed together, the subject had never come up. Now here they were, very near death, and his friend had found peace there.

Maybe it was best to accept the inevitable, to find tranquility wherever he could. He remembered the day before, when they were freezing and so near to surrendering to death. There had been an answer then. They had moved to the reactor compartment and prolonged their existence for another day.

There had to be another solution now, some way to allow them to hang on until Serebnitskiv and the *Volk* showed up and rescued them. Surely they would find them soon. Surely Pishkovski's God was not malicious enough to make them suffer so much, only to crush them when help was so near.

A sudden thought entered his head, a thought so obvious that his eyes opened wide and he gasped out loud.

"Dimitriy," he whispered.

"Yes, Captain?"

"The air masks! We can breathe the air from the flasks. It should last us for another day or so. They'll be here by then. I know it."

He could hear Pishkovski's slight laugh in the close darkness.

"See? I told you God would decide."

Admiral Alexander Durov paced back and forth in front of what was left of the fire in the fireplace, lost in thought. He was so preoccupied that he hardly noticed that the flames had waned, almost gone out. He stopped, snorted, and spat into the fireplace, but there were hardly enough embers left there to sizzle.

President Gregor Smitrov and his weak-kneed government were at it again. The Chechens were demanding concessions before they would participate in peace talks and that coward, Smitrov, was on the verge of giving in to the traitorous bastards. It seemed all they had to say was, "No more air strikes," and the Russian Air Force was grounded. They said, "Free our prisoners," and the criminals were back on the streets at once.

That was no way to crush a revolt!

The Chechen situation was bad enough, but the president couldn't even handle his own people. The oil fields in Siberia were shut down, the workers out on strike, demanding they have a voice in the industry. The food stores in Moscow, St. Petersburg, Kaliningrad and a dozen other cities were empty while the people went hungry. Troops were openly selling their weapons and missiles to the Syrians or to the Iranians, all so they could heat their meager hovels and keep their children from freezing during the long winter.

The country was disintegrating around the pie-eyed reformers and their frail-hearted lackeys. Their beloved country had become the biggest joke of the world. Two decades before, the entire planet quaked before their military might. Even the self-obsessed United States almost spent itself into bankruptcy to defend its shores, its corrupt government trembling from the perceived threat of the Soviet Union. All the while, the people's factories belched wholesome flame and their collectives brought forth abundant food for the tables of all its citizens, from Murmansk to Vladivostok, from the Laptev Sea to the Caspian. The map of the former empire straddled two continents, dwarfing all other countries on the globe with its magnitude.

Now they all laughed. The awesome industrial strength and once fearsome military was now rusting in the weeds while the greedy thieves in Moscow selfishly grabbed every morsel they could. In their haste to appease all the former empire's factions, they had allowed the union to splinter, fracture, break apart into a pitiful mass of impotent rubble.

Even now the newscaster on the television in the far corner of the room was reporting that Smitrov was off in Brussels, begging NATO for another handout. Already the lily white pansy had traipsed off, hat in hand, to plead for donations from every international organization, country, or charity who would give him audience. He seemed to believe that the world was there, waiting to give them assistance out of pure human kindness, that there would be no eventual payback necessary. There would be a payback, all right. One that would bear an awful usurious interest.

Durov knew it was true. History gave too many examples: Attila, Genghis Khan, Napoleon, Hitler. All had tried to crush the *Rodina* in her moments of weakness. Why would that fool Smitrov believe the modern world would be any different?

There was no doubt about it. The man and his peace-loving cronies would have to go. It was a time that called for strength, not contemptible beseeching. A time for true patriots to show the backbone necessary to save their beloved homeland from those who would give it away, piece by piece.

He bent, grabbed a poker, and stirred at the few remaining coals in the fireplace. A bright, angry flurry of sparks fled up the chimney and soon the blaze danced anew. In no time, it was roaring and crackling once more as it began devouring what was left of the logs on the grate. Its warmth soon filled the room.

There was a loud knock from the other side of the massive oak double doors at the far wall of the study. At Durov's word, they eased open and his aide, Lieutenant Vasiliy Zhurkov, stuck his blond head inside.

"They are all gathered in the conference room, Admiral. It is time."

Durov nodded. He remained there in front of the big fire a moment longer, warming his face and his wrinkled, drawn old hands at the flames. Then he strode to the great doors and swung them wide.

"Come, Vasiliy. You are about to witness history."

The old gray admiral and the strapping young lieutenant stepped into the large conference room. Zhurkov shut the doors and took a seat, while Durov walked to the head of the large table. He stood there for a moment, gazing down at the scene before him. He could still feel the invigorating heat of the fire on his face, on his hands. He narrowed his eyes as he looked at each man seated along either side of the broad expanse of the teak conference table.

There were six of the mightiest flag officers in the Russian military, all old comrades-in-arms and men he trusted. They represented the Army, Air Force, Navy, and Strategic Rocket Force.

Beyond these six were seated three men who wore rather nondescript business suits. They might as well have been salesmen or low-level bureaucrats from Moscow. Boris Medikov was seated at the foot of the table, idly studying the closed velvet curtains that hid the full-length windows, sealing this conference room off from the rest of the world.

Durov drew in a long, slow, deep breath. This was the

group of men who would lead the coup. Together, they would soon put the motherland back on the road to greatness.

Alexander Durov was their leader.

"Gentlemen, the hour is at hand," he began. Around the table, all eyes connected with his. Even those of Boris Medikov. "You will each now begin to put your portion of the plan into action. In three days from now, we will announce the unthinkable, treacherous sinking of our glorious new submarine, *Gepard*, by the deceitful Americans, and the loss of all her brave crew. If Serebnitskiv has not returned by then, we will announce that *Volk* was lost trying to defend her. We will express our dismay, our disbelief that the Americans would do such an unfathomable thing, despite their paranoia over the introduction of the first new Russian submarine in a decade. We can remain quiet. The media will do our jobs for us, enflaming the people of the world against the newly aggressive Americans. We will have unwitting allies within the bloodthirsty American press. Their own people will soon be marching in the streets. Our people will hear the nuances of the story, all placed in the proper light."

He nodded toward one of the civilians, the CEO of the nation's largest news organization.

"When the public outcry is at its peak, Mr. Medikov's New York operation will swing into full production. It will throw the American stock market into utter disarray and panic. Economic turmoil and protests by their own people will absorb the American attention so much, and with it the entire world, that they won't even notice our maneuverings here. Our plan will be assured of success."

Durov reached down and picked up a carafe of port and poured a glassful. He circled the table, pouring a glassful for everyone there.

Once back at the head of the table, he raised his own glass high. "To the *Rodina*!"

Everyone scrambled to stand and all drank deeply. They cheered.

All, that is, except Boris Medikov. He remained seated and sipped from his glass as he peered over the rim at the grinning, red-flushed face of Admiral Alexander Durov.

Chapter 11

"Captain, we're in the area," Jerry Perez reported as he glanced up from the navigation chart. "This is the position *Miami* reported."

Joe Glass nodded. "Very well, Nav. Let's start an expanding circle around this location at four knots." He paused for a moment, his face grim. "I want you to be very careful. We don't know what happened to either one of them, the Russian boat or the *Miami*."

Glass turned back to the discussion he was having with Brian Edwards and Dan Perkins. The *Toledo* was operating over two hundred miles from the edge of the thick, forbidding winter pack ice. The three specially designed underice ADCAP torpedoes were loaded in their torpedo tubes, flooded down and ready to go. The outer door for tube one was already opened. Only a few seconds would be needed to send that deadly fish on its way to a target. The sub was rigged for ultraquiet; every unnecessary piece of equipment was secured so *Toledo* was running even more silently than the surrounding water. At the same time, Master Chief Zillich sat in the sonar room, listening intently, using every bit of his experience along with the capability of the BQQ-10 sonar system to search out the ocean for any threat.

They had approached this location carefully, circling for a maddening ten hours, all to make sure they were alone. They had heard nothing, not a hint of a man-made sound amid the popping and groaning of the ice.

Glass stared at the traces as they developed on the sonar display repeater. He gritted his teeth and rubbed his chin.

"I don't like this," he growled. "Nothing here. No *Miami*. No Russian boat. Nada. What do you make of it, XO?"

"Damned if I know, Skipper," Edwards responded. "We drove up here to find a downed boat. Suggest we get looking."

Glass nodded and looked at Perkins. "Mr. Perkins, looks like it's time to unleash your mad scientist and his little toy. You ready to deploy the robot sub?"

"Yes, sir. Just give the order and Dr. Schwartz will start searching."

Glass turned back to look at the sonar screen for a moment. If there was danger out there, they had done all they could to detect it. Now they would have to stay alert and carry on. From what little he knew of the downed Russian sub, there was little hope of finding anyone alive by now. If the *Miami* had somehow run into the same trouble, there was no call for help from her, either. There was only the incessant gnashing of the ice and nothing more.

None of that bode well. Still, they had a job to do.

"Very well. Commence robot sub operations."

Bill Schwartz sat on the deck in the torpedo room, his legs crossed beneath him and a couple of pillows under his butt. As soon as he got the word, he flipped a toggle switch, watched a set of indicators for a moment, and then started nudging a joystick with his right hand. All the while, he watched a small video screen propped up in front of him on top of a stack of manuals.

To an outsider, he looked as if he was playing a video game. In truth, he was maneuvering a multimillion-dollar state-of-the-art robot sub, directing it down the length of *Toledo*'s number-two torpedo tube and out into the icy darkness of the Barents Sea.

The tiny robot responded to Schwartz's commands as he guided it downward, diving toward the seafloor. When it was a hundred feet above the soft, silty bottom, *Sea Scan* leveled off and began to move horizontally, starting a planned grid search of the area. Tiny electric motors drove the robot sub forward. Its magnetometers probed the bottom for any hint of metal that might be disturbing the earth's magnetic field while the side-scan sonar looked for any signs of debris. All of this information was fed back to Schwartz through the hair-thin fiber-optic line that stretched from the back of *Sea Scan* to where it penetrated the torpedo tube door on *Toledo*.

It was torturously slow and exacting work. The robot sub could only search a thousand-yard swath at a time and its forward speed was three knots. They were searching for a very small needle in a very large haystack. Schwartz settled back and sipped at his coffee as the *Sea Scan* did its work. When he thought he saw something, he would replay a piece of data on the video screen for either the magnetometer or the sonar. Every time it proved to be a false alarm, either a lone rock jutting up from the seafloor that attracted the attention of the sonar or a piece of junk metal, likely dumped there from some passing freighter. These waters served as a main supply route to Siberia during the few months when the ice receded, and the sea bottom was well littered.

Hour melded into hour as they searched fruitlessly. Schwartz stood to change the CDs that were recording all the data for later analysis. He stretched his aching muscles and attempted to find a comfortable position on the hard deck. Nothing out there but mud, rock, and junk. The novelty of watching the monitor had long since passed and the curious crew members had wandered off to other duties.

Dan Perkins and Joe Glass had come down to the torpedo room to look over his shoulder, too. They stared at the screen for a bit, feigning interest as they watched the screens display nothing at all. After a couple of hours, Glass, too, wandered off, heading back up to the control room, while Perkins stayed on.

Just when he was on the verge of dozing, Schwartz saw something. His eyes grew wide behind his thick spectacles. It was a blip, starting to develop on the magnetometer. It got stronger as the *Sea Scan* approached whatever it was. It became steadily more pronounced until the signal was jumping off the screen.

This was no stray refrigerator washed off some Russian icebreaker! This was something big!

Schwartz maneuvered the *Sea Scan* so the side-scan sonar could take a better look. Gradually, a long broken cylinder developed on the screen with one end bent ninety degrees to the main axis.

Schwartz whistled. This could be it. It had the characteristics of a submarine debris field.

Perkins awoke from his catnap and sat up when he heard Schwartz whistle, then grunt. He saw the sonar display and knew at once what it was. Schwartz nodded, confirming that their thoughts matched. Perkins grabbed an MJ phone, selected the periscope stand on the station selector, and spun the dial. He heard Glass's growling voice answer on the other end.

"Skipper, we've found what we think is a debris field. We're bringing the *Sea Scan* in for a visual look right now. The picture is patched to the periscope video display, so you should see the same thing that we're seeing down here."

Glass snapped on the video monitor and moved closer. Edwards squeezed in next to him, and both men watched intently. So far, there was nothing to see but an occasional pale, curious fish flitting through the patch of dim light that stretched out ahead of the robot.

Perez left his navigation plot to stand beside them. The control room was quiet as they waited, watching, not sure what they might see in the next few moments. The sense of dread hung thick in the cramped room.

The bottom came into sharper focus. There it was— the unmistakable shape of a submarine. One that had been tortured. One that had died a horrible death.

Those watching in the control room breathed once again, but several men groaned. Joe Glass felt a wave of nausea well up in his gut.

Sea Scan eased closer, approaching what looked like it might be the bow of the boat. The impact with the bottom had bent it over, cocking it off at an odd angle. As the robot continued its exploration, it played its camera on a section of the hull where they could make out a huge hole, opening into the innards of the dead boat. The signs were obvious, even through the murky water. A large explosion of some kind had torn a hole in the boat's skin, ripping inward from the outside and caving it in.

Sea Scan moved farther along the hull. They could see the wreckage of what once must have been the sail. Some gigantic force had ripped it almost off.

There was another hole, very similar to the first one, but lower down. An explosion had smashed into what once had been the engine room. Again, the damage was devastating.

Joe Glass swallowed hard and turned away from the screen, the horror of what they were seeing washing over his pale face. There was no chance of any survivors here, no one for them to rescue from this boat.

Something else was clear. This was no Russian submarine. They were looking at the final resting place for the *Miami* and her crew. There was no mistaking the source of the damage that had sent her to the bottom, either.

This was no accident. This sinking had been caused by hostile torpedoes. Someone had attacked them, sunk them, murdered them all.

"Nav, mark this location." His voice was dry and weak when he spoke. He cleared his throat and wiped the sweat from his brow with the sleeve on the back of his arm. "XO, we know what happened to Bill Crawford, but why? Any ideas?"

Edwards shook his head. He felt dizzy, stunned.

Andy Gerson, *Miami*'s XO, had been a friend and

classmate. Edwards had even been best man at Andy's wedding a couple of years before. Now he was gone. Someone would have to tell Trisha Gerson, would have to try to explain what had happened.

The XO couldn't help it. Tears streamed down his face and he made no attempt to hide them.

Glass gave him a subtle nudge and spoke quietly to him.

"XO, snap out of it. I know how you feel. Right now we've got to report this and make damn sure the same thing doesn't happen to us. The son of a bitch who did this may still be lurking around out there somewhere."

Edwards nodded and wiped his eyes with his sleeve. "Yes, sir. I'm all right. We'd better stow the *Sea Scan* and report this to SUBLANT."

Glass turned to Perez. "Nav, have Dr. Schwartz stow *Sea Scan* as quickly as he can. Find us a polynya as near as possible and have radio draft an OPREP-Three 'sub sunk' message." He paused for a moment before uttering the words he had hoped he would never speak. "Sunk due to enemy action."

"Yes, sir!"

Perez jumped into action, issuing a flurry of orders.

Edwards turned to Glass and spoke in a low, forceful voice, his words spat out through clenched teeth. "Skipper, I recommend that we treat all submerged contacts as hostile until we are out from under the ice."

Glass shook his head and answered quietly, "Much as I would like to, we can't do that, Brian. We have no idea who did that." He nodded back over his shoulder at the monitor, now gone dim as the robot sub was retrieved.

"Or who else might be out here. We don't want to start a war by accidentally shooting some innocent boat that's out here on a rescue mission just like we are."

Edwards, his face red, started to argue. "But, Skipper—"

"No 'buts' about it, XO. We'll be careful. We'll be ready for anything. But we shoot in self-defense only."

"Yes, sir."

"Captain, *Sea Scan* is stowed," Perez called out. "Request permission to cut and jettison the fiber and shut the outer door."

Glass nodded. He could not imagine what in hell they had stumbled into the middle of up here.

If everyone in the control room had not been busy, redirecting the sub and getting under way to the thin spot in the ice floe, they might have noticed the hard, firm set to their commander's jaw. The steely look of determination in his ice blue eyes.

Without even knowing it, the navigator headed *Toledo* for the same polynya that *Miami* had used to report *Gepard*'s sinking. Along the route there, she passed silently a thousand yards from where *Volk* sat in wait. The sonar man standing watch on the Russian sub had the fleetest instant to see the ultraquiet *Toledo* before she disappeared from his screen. He had already suffered several days of endless boredom since all the excitement had taken place. Now all they were doing was sitting here, ice-picked under the Barents, and with nothing to listen for but the continual groaning of the ice and the irritating snores of his fellow crew members. On watch or not, he was half dozing himself, his head resting in his hands above the console, a thin rope of spit stretching down from his lips.

Toledo passed by undetected.

Even Igor Serebnitskiv stifled a persistent yawn as he stepped into the control room of the *Volk* at the very moment *Toledo* passed. He idly flipped through the screens on the sonar display. *Gepard* had ceased her underwater telephone pleas earlier in the morning. That was a good sign. His own people were certain the air aboard the vessel would be too foul to sustain life by now, even if the cold had not finished them. He was still mystified why the double blasts from the planted charges had not destroyed the *Gepard*, how at least some of the crew had survived so long, but that would be a moot point by now. The mission had been accomplished. They were all dead by this time, including Andropoyov.

Still, he decided it would be prudent to wait another day, just to make sure, before surfacing, delivering the news to his uncle, and heading back to Polyarnyy in triumph.

He did see the blip caused by *Toledo*'s passage, but he disregarded it. It was so quick, so fleeting, it was surely some extraneous sea noise. The sonar man was one of the best in the Russian Navy. If it were something worthy of easing out from their hiding spot, he would have sung loudly and clearly.

Five minutes later, the noise the tired sonar man heard was unmistakable, and certain enough that his eyes popped wide-open. He was quick to wake his commander from the fitful nap he had begun in the seat behind him.

"Captain! I hear the sounds of a sub breaking through the ice!" he reported, then checked the readings. "Bearing zero-eight-three. That is the bearing to the polynya where the American surfaced before."

Serebnitskiv cursed. Something had told him to stay on station a bit longer, and now it appeared that had been good intuition. The damned Americans had another boat up here!

There was no option. He would have to destroy it, too. No one could be allowed to return with the correct story, or a lucky guess, about what had happened here. Besides, a vicious attack on the two "innocent" Russian boats by a ruthless pair of American submarines made an even better story.

The Russian commander grinned. Oh well, just another fool to fall before his smart torpedoes. He would ambush this one just as he had done the last one, shooting him in the back as he passed by, oblivious of the well-laid snare he had slipped into.

Now he and the entire crew of *Volk* were awake. Awake and ready to pounce.

With the OPREP-Three message sent and acknowledged, Joe Glass ordered Perez to take *Toledo* back down to six hundred feet and to return to the search area. They weren't finished there. They still had a downed Russian sub to find.

Another thought had occurred to Glass. What if the distressed Russian boat was a decoy? What if they were being set up for the same ambush that had cost them the *Miami* already?

"Nav, come to course two-six-zero and let's head back to the search area. Ahead, two-thirds. And, everybody, on your toes!"

This time by, the *Toledo* passed directly underneath the *Volk*. This time, Igor Serebnitskiv heard them just fine. He made no attempt to hide his hungry grin. He waited a deliberate three minutes while the *Toledo* opened out to a range of a thousand meters. Satisfied the American sub was where he wanted her, he calmly gave the command to fire two torpedoes.

The ET-80As roared out of the *Volk*'s torpedo tubes, already at seventy knots. It would take them forty-five seconds to cover the short distance to their target. The Americans would not have a chance. Even if they somehow managed to get off a shot, there was no way their torpedo could find *Volk*, hiding amid all the ice like a wolf in its lair.

It was a sure thing, a point-blank pair of bullets in the back.

Master Chief Tommy Zillich was listening to the towed array sonar hydrophones, well aware that there could be a stalker out there somewhere in those dark, icy waters. His mouth still dropped open when he heard the launch transients from *Volk*.

There was no mistaking the sound. Torpedoes inbound!

He grabbed the 7MC microphone and yelled the words all submariners fear.

"Launch transients! Torpedoes in the water! In the baffles. Best bearing zero-nine-zero and they're close!"

Without hesitation, Perez yelled, "Ahead flank! Launch the evasion devices! Right full rudder! Steady course south."

Toledo leaped ahead as the throttle man poured steam into the boat's big turbines. Fifteen knots. Twenty. Twenty-five. The sub's speed climbed. But it was no race because of the velocity of the Russian torpedoes. There was one hope, to get outside the acquisition cone on the two incoming fish so they would lose the scent.

The deck rolled violently as the sub banked through the high-speed turn. Maybe, just maybe, the evasion devices would confuse the torpedoes long enough to allow them to escape.

Glass ran out of his stateroom into the control room. He took in what was happening and realized at once how close they were to death. "Make your depth a thousand feet, forty-down angle! Keep me just off the bottom! Snapshot tube one on the bearing of the incoming weapon!"

He grabbed the metal stanchion by the periscope stand and held on. This was going to be close.

Or maybe not. Maybe they were dead already.

They had to get out of the acquisition cones somehow. Or else they would be little more than another skeleton on the floor, lying dead right next to *Miami*.

The deck slanted down steeply as *Toledo* clawed for the safety of the depths.

"Torpedoes bear zero-nine-zero," Zillich reported, his voice calm and workmanlike. "I have them on the sphere now. They're active."

"Weapon ready!" Weps yelled.

"Shoot tube one," Glass ordered, doing his best to match Zillich's all-business tone.

Thank God they had the torpedo loaded, the door already open.

He watched the weapons officer throw the brass handle to "Standby" and then to the "Fire" position. At least they would get a chance to shoot back. Glass knew that it would do little more than scare the bastard who had ambushed them. He was probably hiding in the noisy ice near the surface and it would be next to impossible for a normal weapon to ferret him out.

Toledo lurched as the torpedo ejection pump forced three-thousand-psi water up around the back end of the ADCAP torpedo and flushed it out of the tube. Sensors in the torpedo detected motion down the tube so that the Otto-fuel engine started as soon as the weapon cleared the enclosure and was outside. Its steering vanes pushed the four-thousand-pound weapon around until it pointed at a course of zero-nine-zero. All the while, the engine accelerated until the torpedo was traveling at better than sixty knots. It was already busy, searching for its target.

This was no ordinary torpedo. The special underice algorithms built into its software easily picked out the *Volk* from the surrounding ice. Still, just as it was programmed to do, the weapon looked away and then back, verifying that what it had found was a real submarine target. Its logic now satisfied, the ADCAP drove at maximum speed toward the target, its arming mechanism activated to sense any large metal object nearby, both by sonar and with an interferometer.

The weapon passed underneath the Russian submarine once, without the arming mechanism being triggered.

Serebnitskiv could hear the pinging of the onrushing ADCAP through the hull, even without the aid of sonar. There was nothing to worry about. It couldn't find them up here in the midst of all this ice. It would soon fly harmlessly by and eventually explode into the bottom when it ran out of fuel.

The ADCAP circled around and came back again, but shallower this time. The arming mechanism still saw the *Volk* plainly.

It sent an electric pulse to the firing mechanism, which detonated the firing squib.

The firing squib set off the six-hundred-fifty-pound PBNX warhead just as the ADCAP was beneath the sub's operations compartment.

The vicious shock wave tore through the double hull as if it were little more than tissue paper. Most of the superheated gas bubble vented through the rent in the sub's bottom, incinerating most anything it touched as it ripped and tore through bulkheads.

The crew members on the *Volk* had less than a millisecond to realize what had happened. Igor Serebnitskiv was thrown violently upward and across the control room. He had no chance to grab anything. He was brutally impaled on a protruding valve stem, high up on the outboard bulkhead.

Admiral Alexander Durov's nephew died instantly.

Even if the catastrophic explosion had not been enough, the expanding gas bubble it set off lifted the

Volk upward like some child's toy and crushed it against the ice pack above.

Smashed and mortally violated, the mangled, lifeless hulk sank to the bottom of the cold, cruel sea.

"Torpedoes passed astern!" Tommy Zillich yelled as he listened to the headset, his hands pressing the earpieces closer to his ears so he could hear everything going on out there. "We may be clear!"

Toledo was still angling sharply downward, toward the bottom, racing to get clear of the Russian weapons. They had all heard the deep rumble of the other submarine as it exploded. Now the control room was silent, everyone listening for the high-pitched scream of the incoming weapons.

That sound, as all the men aboard knew, would signal their immediate death.

A few of them breathed a sigh of relief when they heard Zillich's report. Glass knew better. They weren't free yet. Those two torpedoes were still out there, still searching doggedly for them.

The sonar man confirmed his worst fears.

"Torpedoes! Both coming out of the baffles!" Zillich yelled over the 7MC. Now he had lost his calm demeanor. His voice was high and strained. "They're closing!"

The Russian weapons had crossed astern of them and then turned back, looking once again for *Toledo*. They were both still relentlessly coming after them.

"COB, get me thirty feet off the bottom!" Glass ordered Sam Wallich. "Do it now!"

Wallich nodded and turned to his helmsman and his planesman. "Okay, guys. It's up to us. Keep the forty-down angle until I tell you. Then pull out with everything you got."

Wallich stared hard at the depth meter as it reeled off the numbers. It was too late to pray that the gauge was calibrated, that the chart was accurate, but he did anyway.

Hitting the bottom at this speed would be like driving a 747 into a granite mountain. There wouldn't be much left of a fine American submarine and its crew.

It seemed they had been diving forever before Wallich screamed, "Pull up now!"

Somehow, the *Toledo* managed to stop her sharp descent and pull out of the dive a few precious feet before her nose would have burrowed into the muddy bottom of the Barents Sea. With her momentum still at a maximum, she raced blindly across the seafloor, the screw kicking up a thick cloud of mud in its wake. No one wanted to ponder the possibility of a rocky crag or sudden undersea hillock popping up in their path.

Edwards could hold it no longer. "Skipper, suggest we come up to—"

"Hold her where she is! Stay on the bottom!" Glass ordered.

The two torpedoes that were chasing them dove down to follow the *Toledo*. It appeared that not even *Toledo*'s mad dive to the seafloor had been enough to shake the damned things.

The torpedos' sonars became confused, dizzied by the returns from the bottom of the ocean and the mud cloud spouting up from the sub's screws.

All at once, as if a string had jerked their noses downward, they dove and were gobbled up by the mud.

Their explosions erupted a hundred yards astern of where the *Toledo* raced away from them. That was more than close enough to shake the sub violently.

Edwards held on and waited for the boat to stabilize, for Glass to give the command to stop their hazardous, mad flight along the sea bottom. He looked over at his commander.

Glass stood there, calmly leaning against a stanchion, as if they had just scored particularly well on some contrived test.

"Damn, Skipper!" the executive officer said breathlessly. "That was a little too close for comfort."

Glass nodded. He hoped his men couldn't hear the pounding of his heart as it tried its best to escape from his chest.

Chapter 12

The awesome series of explosions rocked *Gepard* where she sat wounded in the sand and silt on the seafloor less than a mile away. Sergei Andropoyov came awake from his latest ragged dream with the first round.

Someone was out there! Someone might be looking for them after all. What were the explosions? Why would they use them? Maybe they were blasting through the ice. Or maybe there was some kind of fighting going on out there.

Whatever was causing all the ruckus, it was their last hope. At least someone was nearby.

"Sergeiovich, did you hear that? Someone is out there!" Pishkovski whispered, his voice muffled by the air-fed mask. "They have come at last! We will be home soon!"

"Perhaps, Dimitriy, perhaps," Andropoyov said, his words full of doubt and dry as the winter wind across the steppes. "We shall see. Start someone using the signal hammer. If we have a rescuer, they will need to find us. If they mean to blow us out of the water, it will end our suffering more quickly if we guide them to us."

He knew that the sound of the hammer pounding on the hull would not carry as far as the underwater telephone, but now there was no longer any power for it. The hammer would have to do.

One of the seamen, so tired and breathless he could hardly lift the hammer, began banging as hard as he could manage on the interior hull of the sub, a rhythmic bell-ringing that could have passed for some underwater death knell. The clang of it reverberated painfully through the tight confines of the reactor chamber, but it still brought hope to the men assembled there. At least it was something they could do to help ensure their rescue.

Andropoyov hoped whoever it was out there making all that noise would stick around long enough, would ride close enough to hear them. That they would be equipped to rescue them.

Otherwise, he knew, their time on earth was short, measured in mere hours.

He tapped his foot in time to the constant, eerie ringing of the hammer.

"Skipper, I heard breaking-up noises," Master Chief Zillich declared. Even in the intensity and terror of evading the Russian torpedoes, the old sonar man had listened to everything happening around *Toledo*. Nothing had escaped his notice.

"I believe you, Tommy," Joe Glass said with a grin. He would bet anyone that if he asked Zillich how many cod they had passed, he would be able to tell him, and probably the sex of each. The two stood there in *Toledo*'s sonar room, still analyzing what had just happened to them.

She was safely back up at six hundred feet now, but

the crew was still working on slowing their pulses, still giving thanks that they remained among the living after the harrowing near miss. Brian Edwards was already busy, getting everything back in fighting order, loading another ADCAP, and finding out what damage might have been done. Other than plenty of jangled nerves and a few bruises from being thrown about during the turn and dive, it appeared they were unscathed.

"I heard the explosion behind us while we were running from those fish," Zillich said, talking fast. He was still excited by what he had heard and the wild ride they had just taken. "Then it sounded like flooding to me. I heard what I think was something big hitting the bottom a minute or so after that. Hard to say about the time. I'm afraid I was a little preoccupied with the torpedoes. I got it all on tape, though."

Glass stroked the stubble on his chin. "So you think we got the slimy bastard, huh?"

"I'd bet so, Skipper. I'll look at the tapes to make sure, though."

"Okay, Master Chief. Let's get your people back to searching just the same. If he's still out there, I don't want him to go shooting at us again. I don't want any more nasty surprises. I still want to find that downed Russian boat if it's out there."

Glass turned on a heel and walked out of the sonar room into control. Doug O'Malley stepped over from the periscope stand to meet him.

"Skipper, Dan Perkins is asking to launch the robot sub again. He says they're all ready to go down there in the torpedo room."

"Let's hold off a bit, Eng. I want to make sure we're alone out here before we go outside and play again," Glass replied. He reached up to the controls for the sonar repeater and flicked through the screens, checking what Zillich and his team were seeing in the sonar room. "Tommy's pretty sure we got the bastard that was shooting at us . . . and likely the one that sank *Miami*, too . . . but I want to be positive. I want to make sure he doesn't have a running mate out there somewhere, ready to come after us, too. Tell Perkins that we'll do a careful passive search of the area first. Then we'll see."

O'Malley was about to relay the message to the scientists down in the torpedo room when a sudden bright spike appeared on the sonar screen. They both stared at it for a few seconds, saw nothing for a second or two, but then another one split the screen. O'Malley grabbed the 7MC microphone.

"Sonar, conn. What is the transient, bearing two-one-two?"

"Conn, sonar. We see it. We're analyzing now," Zillich replied.

As Glass and O'Malley watched, another spike appeared, then another. It was odd. The pattern looked to be rhythmic.

"Conn, sonar," Zillich chimed in. "Sounds like somebody hammering on metal. I think we've found the sunken sub. Best bearing, two-zero-nine. Best range estimate is two-one-hundred yards."

Glass stared hard at the screen. So Brad Crawford had been right. There was a sunken sub up here, and with survivors on board. Brad had given his life trying to rescue a fellow submariner in distress. *Toledo* and its crew had almost paid the same price. Now it was up to Glass and *Toledo* to make certain the sacrifice had not been for naught.

If there were survivors down here, and everything pointed to that conclusion, the Russians would have to be in a bad way by now. Glass shook his head as he added up the days. They had been on the bottom for two weeks! They had to be out of power and air. He could imagine how cold and dark and foul it must be inside the submarine by now.

There wasn't time to fool around.

On the other hand, if they had not sunk the aggressor that had fired on them, or if there was another boat still around, waiting to ambush them, *Toledo* could join *Miami* and this Russian boat on the bottom. He could take the cautious approach and search the area before proceeding. Or he could rush in and start the rescue right away, knowing the stranded men were likely near death.

Glass stood by himself in the corner of the control room. He appeared to be watching his crew as they performed their tasks. He was paying them little mind. He was spinning out each of the options in his head. This wasn't a decision he could share with Edwards or with anyone else on board. This was one of those knotty judgments that only a skipper could make. He knew that men could live or die based on what he decided in the next few minutes. It would be a decision he would have to make on his own and then stand by, no matter what.

When he ran the possibilities through his mind one

*   *   *

Sergei Andropoyov listened, still in disbelief. After all the pain, cold and suffering, it appeared that someone was here at last! They might all be rescued! It was a miracle!

He realized then that he had already conceded defeat in his own mind. He had kept up the front for the men. He must never allow them to see that he had surrendered.

He crawled through the inky darkness and grabbed the hammer from the seaman in midswing. The exhausted sailor collapsed to the deck, his breath rasping in his chest. Andropoyov tapped out his message in English, just in case it was the Americans who had come to help.

"Thirty-five alive . . . out of air . . . no power . . . hurry."

He listened with rapt attention as the taps were answered by something pounding back on the hull of his submarine.

"Understand thirty-five alive. Have DSRV. Can take seventeen each trip. Which hatch?"

Andropoyov paused for a second, having trouble thinking clearly now. The engine room hatch was closer, but no one had been back there since they had sunk. He didn't know what they might face there. He chose the forward hatch. That meant the crew would have to make their way through the operations compartment to the number-three compartment to get to it. It would be very difficult in the dark, particularly for the injured. What little instincts he had still intact told him it would offer their best hope.

more time, there was one correct decision. They hadn't steamed all this way to sit around while men died down here. It was time for action.

"Eng, tell Lieutenant Perkins to get the robot sub launched and out there over that noise. I want to see what that sub looks like," Glass ordered. He walked to the back of the control room and studied the navigation charts. O'Malley followed, a small grin on his face, and waited for the skipper's next order. Meanwhile, he looked over his commander's shoulder at the charts.

Over fifty years of U.S. submarine operations up here in these frigid waters had resulted in bottom topography charts of very high accuracy. They showed a flat, featureless seafloor in this area.

Glass looked up. "Oh, and, Eng, tell Perkins to get the DSRV ready to go. I think we may be needing it shortly."

Sea Scan arced down into the blackness of the deep. The robot sub's probing sonar looked out over the barren sea floor, but so far it was finding nothing of interest. The magnetometer was quiet.

Bill Schwartz had his tongue protruding from the corner of his mouth as he wiggled the joystick. He stared at the empty video screens and steered the little sub closer to the metallic pounding noise.

Suddenly the magnetometer spiked high. A very large metal object was in its field of sensitivity. Schwartz made a minor correction to *Sea Scan*'s course, aiming for the object. The sonar started to map out the long cylinder. It might just as well have been an instant replay of what they saw when they had found *Miami* a few hours before.

The difference this time was the hammering. There was someone alive down here, someone alone in the cold and dark who needed help.

Schwartz maneuvered *Sea Scan* until it was a mere ten feet above the object, hovering a few feet to the side. He flipped on the lights and the video camera and twisted a control on one of the boxes arrayed before him. The screen came into focus.

There was the unmistakable form of a submarine hull. The smoothly rounded sail was just at the edge of the light and, unlike *Miami*'s, seemed to be intact.

Dan Perkins moved close to the screen, his nose almost touching it, trying to get a better look as Schwartz steered. He watched for several minutes as the *Sea Scan* moved along the hull.

"Looks like an Akula class. That sail is unmistakable. She's bigger than any Akula I've ever seen, though," Perkins whispered, more to himself than to anyone else.

Schwartz stopped the robot's progress for a moment and fiddled with the zoom for a bit, tilting the camera up and down and panning slightly. "Yep. Damage in the bow. Looks like it happened when it hit the bottom."

Next, the robot sub moved over the stern and there they could see the gaping hole left by the explosion, the jagged metal pointing outward in long, treacherous spears.

Perkins gasped. "My God! Look at that! She has a hole blown in her stern you could drive a truck through.

I believe . . . yes . . . it's an explosion from inside. What in hell could cause something like that?"

Gary Nichols looked over Perkins's shoulder at the devastating sight. He shook his head in disbelief. "It's a wonder there's anyone left alive inside a mess like that. They were probably saved by all the compartmentalization the Russians use. What about the hatches? Can you tell if we'll be able to set *Mystic* down on one of them?"

Perkins cocked his head. "Good question. Bill, can you steer over so we can take a look?"

Schwartz played with the joystick for a few seconds and *Sea Scan* moved back up the length of the hull. The large round engine room hatch came into view. It looked to be normal. He steered the sub a little more until the forward hatch was visible.

Nichols nodded. He was satisfied. "Thank God they both look all right. The boat is lying over a little to port. It looks to be a thirty-degree list, but that shouldn't be any problem for *Mystic*. Hatch size looks like it's compatible with our mating skirt, too."

"Let's make contact now. Let them know we are out here," Perkins said. "Bill, put *Sea Scan* down on the deck aft of the sail and we'll tell them 'hello.'"

With Schwartz using a steady hand on the controls, the spidery little robot sub settled onto the rounded steel deck of the Russian boat, a few feet aft of the curved sail. They had no idea how many men might have survived such a catastrophic sinking, but they were about to give them some very good news.

He tapped out, "Forward hatch . . . air poisoned . . . using breathing masks . . . need more air."

The answering message penetrated the steel hull.

"On our way. Have seventeen ready under hatch. Will signal when seated and ready. Need you to open hatch."

Andropoyov summoned all the strength he could muster and hammered out the acknowledgment. He turned to Pishkovski to tell him to get the first seventeen men ready. He heard the faithful first officer already at work.

Dan Perkins climbed up through *Toledo*'s engine room hatch into the belly of *Mystic*. Gary Nichols followed him up the ladder and shut the hatch behind him. The two men climbed up and forward into the command sphere and sat in the pilot and copilot seats. *Mystic* came to life as Perkins shifted from the umbilical connecting them to *Toledo* onto internal systems.

He put on a set of headphones and talked to Glass through the underwater telephone. "*Toledo*, this is *Mystic*. Mating latch released. Flooding and equalizing skirt for undocking."

Nichols flipped a couple of switches that allowed seawater to fill the skirt connecting the DSRV to the mother sub. With the skirt filled and the pressure equalized with the outside sea, *Mystic* lifted off *Toledo*'s back. Next, Perkins pushed forward on the throttle so that the large screw began to turn. The rescue sub turned and headed for the bottom.

At three knots, the trip would take half an hour, but

they dared not pull *Toledo* any closer. They needed the standoff room just in case it was a trap. This would give Glass the distance to defend *Toledo* if he needed to.

The stricken sub came into sight through the DSRV's viewing window. Although Perkins had seen the damage on the video monitor, viewing it this close made it look much worse. No weapon could have caused this type of mayhem. The explosion had plainly come from inside the sub, but there shouldn't be anything back here that could accidentally explode. Just the barest tendrils of suspicion began to creep around the edges of his consciousness.

Perkins steered the DSRV until they hovered over the hatch; then he allowed it to settle down until it rested over it. Nichols started the pump that began to remove water from inside the skirt. That caused sea pressure to push down with ever-increasing force until the skirt was dry and the weight of the sea married them to the Russian sub.

Once satisfied they had a good seal, the two men pulled masks out from under their seats and put them on. If the air inside the sub was poisoned, they couldn't risk breathing it. Nichols stepped out of the copilot's seat and eased back into the rescue chamber. He checked one more time that the air masks were ready for his passengers and then looked through the tiny viewing port into the skirt. He wanted to make doubly sure that it was dry and seated properly.

He opened the rescue vehicle's hatch and grabbed the hammer that was clipped to the bulkhead. He stepped down onto the deck of the Russian sub and banged hard on the cold, wet hull. After the third strike, he saw the hatch almost imperceptibly crack open. He felt the freezing-cold air blast up around his feet. It filled the DSRV with a dreadful, chilling presence, like the breath of the Grim Reaper himself. It would take a while for *Mystic*'s air systems to expel the noxious cold gas and replace it with breathable air.

The hatch was swung open and that allowed Nichols to stare down into a darkness that was as deep as that of hell. In that instant, he knew why he had dedicated his life to the DSRV. The faces squinting up into his light were visible, even through their fogged masks. The expressions confirmed the unspoken horror and fear these men had lived under for the past fourteen days.

He grabbed the hand of the man at the top of the ladder. Though the man's grip was weak, the everlasting gratitude was effectively conveyed.

Gary Nichols passed several flashlights and Arctic clothing down through the hatch. He picked up one of *Mystic*'s masks, on a long hose, and dropped it down through the hatch. He signed for one of the crew to take off his mask and put on the one from the DSRV. A seaman, either much braver or much more anxious than the rest, grabbed the mask. He ripped his off, put the new one on, and scurried up the ladder. One after another, seventeen of the crew climbed up and sat quietly in the rescue chamber where Nichols directed them. Some of them seemed too exhausted to move. Others awkwardly hugged their shipmates.

They now knew for certain that their long night of terror was over.

When all seventeen survivors were on board, Nichols passed a note down to one of the crew waiting for his turn. Someone on board knew enough English to do the tapping when they first found the beleaguered sub. Now he was telling them he would be back in an hour, to just keep praying and be patient for a little bit longer.

Still, shutting the hatch on the remaining men, even with the knowledge that he would be back soon to get them, too, was the hardest thing Gary Nichols had ever experienced.

When Nichols gave the sign, Perkins flooded and equalized the skirt so the DSRV could lift back off the stricken Russian boat. It turned and headed toward *Toledo*, which was still hovering a thousand yards away and four hundred feet higher in the water.

The survivors huddled together in the rescue chamber, wrapped in the thick, coarse Navy blankets Nichols passed around. Most still had their eyes closed, protecting them from the bright lights after the darkness of their watery crypt. They breathed deeply from the abundant, clear, clean air.

Nichols gave Perkins a broad wink and a spirited high five as they eased closer to the mother ship.

Sergei Andropoyov sat at the reactor compartment door waiting for the Americans' return. Pishkovski lay on the deck beside him, illuminated by the yellow glow of the American lanterns. They had already determined that they would be the last to go, after all the others had been safely delivered to the rescue submarine. Now they lay there and listened to each other breathe.

They had come through so much together. It was only a matter of waiting a couple of hours until they would be safe on the other sub.

It seemed strange to Andropoyov now that it was over. He would be able to bring some of his crew home to their loved ones after all. He wasn't sure at that moment where he would find the courage to face the families of the other ones, those who would rest forever here in the cold Arctic waters.

Both men were silent. There was no need for talking now. Each was alone with his thoughts.

Both men realized that they each knew what the other was thinking. Pishkovski broke the quiet.

"Sergeiovich, I don't understand. Why did they do this to us?"

Andropoyov pondered the question for a long time before he formed an answer. As they had lain here all these days, fighting for every breath, not sure if they would ever feel the embrace of their wives or hear the laughter of their children again, one fact had become clear. Both men had independently come to the same conclusion.

"Dimitriy, I don't know, but of one thing I am deadly certain. Igor Serebnitskiv did not do this awful thing on his own. He is a proficient sailor, an accomplished submarine commander, but he has no imagination or initiative of his own. No, Admiral Durov is the one behind this. How or why, I do not pretend to know, but he is there."

"I agree, Sergeiovich. With God's help, I will one day make him pay. I am not a vengeful man, but when I looked into the faces of these brave men over these last horrible days, when I consider the bodies of those who float still in the wreckage of this fine boat, I have vowed that I will one day make Durov pay for what he has done."

Pishkovski could see the grim smile on his commander's face. "As will I, Dimitriy. As will I."

Chapter 13

Carl Andretti slammed his fist down onto the desk. That government hack bitch!

She had no idea how close she was to stumbling onto the scheme. She had the audacity to stand there in his office and ask him about it! They would have to take care of this problem before she had all the rest of those SEC bastards pissing on their carefully planned parade.

He grabbed the phone and punched in Alan Smythe's number. The ringing on the other side of the office suite went unanswered. That self-important Brit son of a bitch was never around when he was needed.

Andretti shook his head as he tried to will his furious pulse to slow. There wasn't time to hunt down Smythe. Besides, Andretti doubted the man had the stomach for what needed to be done. He would puff his European cigarette, wave his hands about in that maddening, feminine way he had, and prevaricate until it was too late to do anything about it. Until after Catherine Goldman had shoved a giant wrench into the smooth-running gears of their perfectly meshing scheme.

The CTO felt the gorge rise in his stomach, the acid welling up into his throat. He opened the bottom left-hand drawer of his desk and took a big swig from the

Maalox bottle he kept there. The stomach problems were getting worse, harder to control. He didn't know if his nerves would hold out until they saw the plan to its finish.

The chalky taste of the stomach medicine gagged him now. He reached behind him and yanked open the little refrigerator, pulled out the bottle of Dewar's, and filled the water glass on his desk. He took a healthy swallow of the amber liquid, felt its deep coldness on his tongue, then its warm, slow burn as it passed down his throat.

Funny. It did more to calm his churning gut than the Maalox had. It gave him a shot of courage, too.

It was time to make the call.

He punched in the phone number from memory. It was the kind of number one did not keep handy in one's BlackBerry or address book. No, this was one number best not written down anywhere.

The phone rang twice, an oddly hollow and distant sound, and then clicked mysteriously several times. The call was being forwarded through a labyrinth of systems, bouncing around the world several times until it was untraceable.

It was a thick, growling voice that answered.

"Yeah. Who is it and what do you want?"

"It's CA. I have a job for you. A certain difficulty requires your attention."

Joe Glass stood on the platform at the bottom of the ladder that led up to the after escape trunk. The noise of the whirling turbines, just a few feet aft, drowned out most other sounds. He could hear the metallic clank as the *Mystic* landed for the third time on the back of *Toledo*. The smell of hot oil permeated everything back here in the engine room. Those who might assume that nuke boats were antiseptically clean had never been on one for any length of time.

The skipper looked around him as he waited for the *Mystic* to settle in and the hatch to open. The room was filled with the Russian survivors. They were a haggard bunch, but many of them smiled thankfully as they sucked in deep breaths of clean air.

Doug O'Malley leaned against the bulkhead just outside the maneuvering room door, ten feet forward of where Glass stood. The guy was keeping a close watch on his little kingdom. If he was the "master of all he beheld," he was a cautious master indeed. Glass had never met an engineer who was more dedicated to his equipment than O'Malley was. That included Joe Glass, back when he was the engineer on the old *Hammerhead*. O'Malley knew every nuance of this complex power plant and was dedicated to making it perform.

The hatch clanged open above Glass and a pair of legs appeared at the top of the ladder. A short, paunchy man descended the ladder, gripping the rungs as if he was on the verge of losing his hold and falling. His slow, halting movements were those of an exhausted man. Glass watched the painful descent, wondering if he should step over and assist the man. There was something in the Russian's bearing that held Glass back. He was proud, determined to make the descent on his own. Glass stood where he was, waiting at the bottom of the ladder.

The man stepped onto the deck and found the

strength to pull to attention. He lifted his arm and executed a reasonably snappy salute. "Captain Second Rank Sergei Andropoyov. Request permission to come aboard."

Glass looked at the battered man. Even after all the hardships he had been through, he could still find great dignity. Glass smiled and returned the salute. "Welcome aboard the *Toledo*, Captain. Please accept my condolences for the loss of your crew members. We'll try to make you and the rest of your crew as comfortable as possible."

"Thank you, Captain. For my crew's sake, I thank you." He turned and introduced the haggard, worn man who had come down the ladder after him. The man was now attempting to stand at attention beside his commander. "This is Captain Third Rank Dimitriy Pishkovski. He is my first officer."

Glass returned Pishkovski's weak but sincere salute and shook hands with the two Russians.

The other survivors were already arrayed around the room, forming a ragtag, exhausted group. Sam Wallich had been busy passing out warm, dry blankets and steaming mugs of hot coffee. Others were leading the survivors off in groups of three or four, headed forward to a hot meal and a warm bunk.

Glass invited the two officers to accompany him to his stateroom. He walked with Andropoyov as they made their way forward. When they were out of earshot of the other survivors, Andropoyov made a quiet inquiry.

"Captain, the other American submarine, the first one, what happened to it?"

Glass stopped and looked into Andropoyov's clear gray eyes. He answered without hesitation. "That was the *Miami*. She managed to report your condition and was on the way back to you to assist when she was attacked and sunk." He swallowed hard and shoved his words through clenched teeth. "I had friends on that boat. The son of a bitch shot her while she was trying to help rescue you. The wreckage is a mile from your boat."

Glass couldn't be sure, but he thought he saw a flicker of sad resignation pass through those deep, sad eyes. It was as if some suspicion had just been confirmed. Sergei Andropoyov nodded solemnly.

"That's what I thought. We talked with them on the underwater telephone. Then we heard explosions. And then, nothing. No one came. No one until you."

Glass could not keep the anger and sorrow from his voice. "Why? Why would someone do that? The *Miami* was trying to help. Whoever sank them . . . and took the shots at us . . . what did they accomplish?"

Andropoyov looked around them. Another group of rescued Russians was coming up behind them.

"Captain, can we continue this conversation somewhere more private?" he asked.

Glass nodded and steered them on in the direction of his stateroom. As they walked, Pishkovski muttered to Andropoyov in Russian, "Captain, are you going to tell the American of our suspicions? You are guessing. It could be very dangerous."

"Dimitriy, where we came from was as dangerous as it gets," Andropoyov answered, also in Russian. "We must find the truth and seek justice, not only for ourselves but for our friends here and on the other boat, those who have both risked and lost their lives attempting to help us. The man who caused all this must be made to pay."

Pishkovski nodded. "*Da,* I agree."

Joe Glass piped up in his best schoolboy Russian. "Captain, I appreciate your sentiment. We must talk." A wry smile lifted the corners of his mouth as he noted the two Russians' surprise. "Three years of Russian at the United States Naval Academy. Pardon my accent."

For the first time in days, the two weary submariners smiled.

Catherine Goldman hesitated for a moment before stepping through the front door to Harry's Bar. The pseudo–English pub on the corner at Hanover Square was the historic after-market-close meeting place for Wall Street players. The atmosphere enveloped her while the clamor roared in her ears. Endless rumors and innuendo passed from lip to ear here at Harry's. Fortunes were made and lost in the booths and private dining rooms of the venerable establishment.

Goldman still didn't know why she had ever agreed to come here. This place represented many of the things she hated about Wall Street: the reckless power, the good-old-boy network, the loose money, and the blatant, in-your-face attitude of the self-styled power mongers who felt more comfortable dealing over strong drinks and spicy chicken wings than with telephones and computer networks. The loud, drunken greetings and the hushed, secretive huddles bothered her equally.

Dmitri Ustinov had insisted that she have dinner here

with his team tonight. He refused to hear her claims of too much work and not enough time. If he meant to impress her, to influence her in some way by inviting her here, he could not have made a worse choice.

The rotund young Russian spotted her somehow through the smog. He yelled and waved to her from the bar.

"Cathy! We're over here."

Goldman hated to be called "Cathy." Her name was Catherine. She hoped no one else with whom she might have had dealings on The Street would see her coming into this place.

Still, she returned the wave and wound her way through the milling crowd. A tall, striking blonde stood there next to Ustinov. Catherine had noticed her around the office. Marina Something-or-other. Another Russian. A talented programmer, from everything that Goldman had heard. She seemed very cold, standoffish. She was surprised now to see that Marina Something-or-other was being very cozy with the obnoxious head of testing at OptiMarx.

Maybe it was true. Opposites did attract, after all.

"Cathy, come on over! We have a dining room in back!" Ustinov shouted over the din. "Everyone else is back there already."

When she got close enough, he grabbed her hand along with the Russian woman's and led them both back into the shadowy recesses of the pub. Ustinov plowed through the crowd of boisterous traders, ignoring the hard looks he got from some of them when he shoved them aside so they could get past. They emerged in front of a dark wood-paneled door guarded by one of Harry's waiters. He acknowledged Ustinov's offered tip with a wink and swung the door open for them.

The dining room was dimly lit but quite opulent. She could see the familiar faces of several members of Ustinov's testing team from OptiMarx already seated at the long central table. Silverware and china glinted in the candle-light, reflected by the gilt mirrors that lined the walls, bathing the room in a shower of diamondlike light. Usti-nov led the two women to the head of the table and waved Goldman to the seat at his right and Marina to the one to his left.

Ustinov had refused to take no for an answer when he invited her to come to this place this evening. He pro-claimed that he was entertaining his team, celebrating the imminent approval of the project. In the spirit of teamwork, the SEC team leader should be his guest of honor. Goldman was not sure if the smooth-talking Rus-sian was trying to flatter her, trying to curry her favor for her thumbs-up on the project, or doing all he could to get into her pants. It didn't take keen observation skills to see that Ustinov was a man continually on the make.

Well, whichever it was, Goldman realized one thing was certain. She was ravenous. She had eaten lunch that day out of the snack machine in the OptiMarx break room and couldn't remember when she had last had breakfast. She grabbed a loaf of bread from the cloth-covered basket at the center of the table and ripped off a generous piece. She dipped it into the silver dish of olive oil and took a bite, chewing slowly, allowing the rich taste to fill her mouth.

"How is it, Miss Goldman?" Ustinov inquired.

"This bread is great. Never had better."

"This bread is shit!" he snorted. "Now, back in Russia we have bread. The best bread in the world. Bread to die for. You have never tasted such wonderful bread."

Goldman swallowed before she offered her pointed comment. "Is that the reason the babushkas in Moscow wait in line for days? Because the bread is so wonderful?"

Marina Nosovitskaya choked on her own piece, while those nearby who overheard the short exchange howled with laughter. Ustinov turned beet-red and shifted his attention to refilling Nosovitskaya's wineglass and leering into the deep valley between her breasts.

Despite her misgivings, Catherine soon relaxed, aided more than somewhat by the wine Ustinov kept pouring into her glass. The meal was excellent and the company, save for Ustinov, quite convivial. Maybe this had not been a bad thing after all. She had broken the ice with the OptiMarx team now. The good food, the ceaseless wine, the talk of the project and business in general soon cast a rosy glow on everyone around the table.

Even Ustinov warmed up a bit, losing some of his swagger. He reminded Goldman of a puppy, yipping about playfully, demanding to be the center of attention and to be petted. Somehow, he managed to alternate his attentions between the beautiful blond Russian and Catherine Goldman. She assumed he was being polite to her because of her position. Nosovitskaya had her outclassed on looks.

It wasn't that she felt any need to compete for Ustinov's attentions. He was anything but her type. Still, she couldn't help being flattered by his interest. The seemingly accidental touches, the hand on her arm while he made this or that point, the occasional pressure of his knee on her thigh beneath the table, the whispered asides, all seemed designed to make her feel she was the center of his world, at least for this evening. The obvious fact that he paid equal service to the lovely young lady on his left only heightened the odd attraction she was beginning to feel after the sixth glass of the wonderful wine.

Even as her head spun and she felt her cheeks blush as they had not done since college, Catherine Goldman knew there was no chance at all that any of this would lead anywhere. She was too much of a professional to allow some horny young programmer on the prowl to come between her and her work. Still, it was not an unpleasant way to spend an evening, after weeks of grinding work. No matter the Russian's motives, she allowed herself to relax, to enjoy the food, drink, and male attention.

It was late when she made her excuses. She ignored his protests, got up, and walked a bit unsteadily through the mob that was still in the restaurant, making her way out onto the sidewalk. The cold air felt invigorating and snow gently drifted down through the golden glow from the streetlights.

There were no taxis in sight, not at all unusual for Lower Manhattan this late on a weeknight. They were uptown, hauling theatergoers. Ustinov had insisted on driving her to the hotel, but Goldman politely declined. The walk around the Battery to the Millennium wasn't far at all. It would serve to keep things simple, businesslike. She would not have to summon up some resistance she had not had to call on in years if he tried to extend the evening.

"Very well, Cathy," he relented. "Do be careful out there."

There was something about the look in his eyes when he said it. It could have been disappointment. Maybe worry. Whatever, she allowed him to linger a bit when he gave her a very tight good night hug and a quick kiss on the cheek.

The door to Harry's closed behind her, cutting off the happy laughter and chatter of the people inside. Catherine Goldman pulled her coat around her and turned down Water Street, walking briskly, breathing deeply, allowing the cold, clean air to clear the pleasant fuzz from her head.

She loved the city at times like this, when its ceaseless noise was for once hushed, muted by the new snow as it covered all the grit and dirt beneath a cold, clean, new blanket. The colored lights and exuberant noise from a couple of the late-night bistros along the way poured out into the street, giving the scene a festive, holiday feel. But the street was empty, and she was alone. That was especially true when she turned a corner and entered a block of empty office buildings.

Catherine Goldman never saw the taxicab pull out from the curb a block and a half behind her. Its headlights were off and the street was poorly lit. Besides, she was lost in her thoughts of the evening and didn't hear the vehicle accelerate as it speeded toward where she walked.

Fifty feet behind her, the cab abruptly swerved to its

right, hopped the curb, and rocketed down the narrow sidewalk, gaining speed.

Catherine sensed more than heard the racing auto. By the time she looked over her shoulder, the raging monster was nearly on top of her. Instinctively, she leaped to her right as quickly as she could, diving into an empty, recessed doorway. The cab's operator seemed to anticipate the move and careened in the direction she jumped.

When she hit the cement, she rolled in a heap, trying to get as close to the glass door as she could jam herself, all the while expecting to feel the impact of the vehicle's bumper striking her full force, shoving her against the building, crushing her.

The frenzied cab roared past her, pinned to the building's facade, its sheet metal and side mirror sending a shower of sparks and bits of glass raining down amid the snowflakes as it scraped along the brick wall. Whatever madman was behind the wheel of the thing, he was doing everything possible to get into the nook of the doorway and find her.

The car never stopped, though, as it scrubbed noisily down the brick side of the building. It clipped a row of garbage cans and sent a large blue mailbox spinning out into the street, spewing letters, before it disappeared around the next corner. It trailed blue exhaust smoke and more sparks from the rear bumper that now dragged on the pavement.

Several people who had just stepped from a bar up the street ran in Catherine's direction, attracted by all the noise and smoke and sparks. Two of the men reached to help her up from the doorway, asking if she was okay.

"I'm . . . uh . . . fine," she stammered, and tried to make a weak joke about New York cabdrivers.

With their help, she rose, her knees shaking uncontrollably. Once she was in control of her breathing, of her quaking legs, she assured them that she was all right. Still, they insisted on calling the police and stayed with her until they arrived.

Much later, after the interminable questioning at the precinct offices, the detectives drove her to the Millennium. Once safely inside her room and with the door double-locked behind her, Catherine Goldman collapsed like deadweight onto the settee. The tears she had been suppressing streamed down her face. She had trouble seeing the buttons on the phone as she dialed.

She had riled her share of people along the way—people who had tried to cross the SEC. A couple had threatened to punch her in the nose. No one had ever tried to kill her before. She couldn't imagine anyone hating her enough for that. Now it was clear that someone did.

She had no one else to call. No one else to come to her aid. No one else but her boss at the Securities and Exchange Commission. She tried to regain control of herself before Stan Miller answered.

She didn't want him to hear her sobbing like some hysterical woman.

Chapter 14

Admiral Tom Donnegan dropped the telephone back into its cradle, picked up the single-page message from his desk, and stared hard at its terse Naval-ese phrases. The unimpressive-looking communication did not seem capable of carrying so much bad news in such a few short paragraphs.

First Joe Glass had popped his head up long enough to send an OPREP-Three with the horrifying news, confirming that *Miami* had been sunk by some unknown enemy, its crew lost at the bottom of the Barents Sea. Then, on the heels of that showstopper, he followed up with this latest little tale of high intrigue that seemed to have been lifted from some bad movie script.

"That guy's been reading too many techno-thrillers," Donnegan mumbled to himself as he once again folded the message. He set it back down on his desk before it burst into flames in his fingers.

He knew Joe Glass better than that, though. It was just too wild to believe. The latest person with whom he had shared the news, the person on the end of the call he had just completed, had been just as stunned as he was.

That first message, the news of *Miami*'s loss, had already caused an uproar in the upper levels of the defense community unlike anything Donnegan had ever seen before. The old sailor had seen his share of scrambling, from the fall of Saigon all the way through the balance of the Cold War to the terrorist wars. This was different, out of the blue.

SECDEF had clamped a tight security blanket on any mention of the story. Glass and *Toledo* were still up there under the ice. If someone was attacking U.S. boats, it would be best to wait until *Toledo* was well clear before anyone outside the current small group knew there was anyone up there. That meant they would have to wait a few weeks to announce the loss of *Miami* and to start grieving for her crew. So far it had not shown up in the *Washington Post*. With a story like this, and with all the sudden swarm of activity around the Pentagon in response to it, it was a matter of time.

Donnegan shook his head. That was some PR weenie's problem anyhow, keeping a lid on the thing until they could figure out what the hell had happened and how the hell to respond.

This latest message was now at the forefront of Donnegan's attention. A boat, sunk by an enemy torpedo, as horrible and unlikely a scenario as it was these days, was still something he could deal with. Find out who did it and shoot back. That was simple war.

This last missive opened up a perplexing can of worms.

He shoved the reading glasses up on his forehead and rubbed his eyes to try to ease the pounding headache that had sneaked up on him. The first light of day was just beginning to illuminate the horizon over the stark black limbs of the leafless willows down near the Potomac. Someone was moving about out there. A lone jogger, bundled against the cold, trotted along the river trail.

Seeing the runner reminded Donnegan of someone else he should call: Jon Ward.

Ward would be out running on a morning like this, too. He rarely missed a day. He was probably somewhere along the beach down in Norfolk right about now, pushing his body as hard as he could. The call to Ward could wait a few more minutes. Let him finish his run before he hit him with this latest development and the part he would have him play in it.

Donnegan picked up the message one more time. The words had not changed since the last time he read them. They still told an unbelievable story.

Joe Glass and *Toledo* had been attacked by a probable Russian sub. They had shot back in self-defense. The Russian was sunk and *Toledo* escaped with no damage and only minor injuries.

He had proceeded on his original mission, deploying the DSRV and rescuing the survivors from the wreckage of some new Russian boat, a submarine called the *Gepard*. Now he reported thirty-five survivors on board, including the submarine's commanding officer. That captain was telling some amazing tale of sabotage, a plot launched by no less than Admiral of the Northern Fleet Alexander Durov.

It was all unsubstantiated. In Donnegan's line of work, proof was usually hard to come by.

They knew some things for sure. Someone had sunk the Russian boat. Someone, likely the same bastards, had sent the *Miami* to the bottom. Someone, again likely the same culprit, had tried to do the same to the *Toledo* but had been blasted to hell by Glass and his crew. If they knew all this to be true, news of some nefarious plot by a renegade Russian naval commander didn't seem too far-fetched after all.

There had been rumors coming out of the Kola for several years about secret buildups. Every time someone checked, all they could get were pictures of those rusting hulks bobbing at the pier in Polyarnyy. There had been signs that raised the curiosity of several analysts. Uncharacteristically for post–Cold War Russia, security at all the bases in Kola was tight. So far, they had not been able to get an operative inside any of the bases, and they had been trying for over a year. Why such a freeze-out to protect a fleet of disintegrating hulks?

Donnegan was familiar with Admiral Alexander Durov, Commander of Submarines, Russian Northern Fleet. He was an irascible old Russian sailor. When his name surfaced, Donnegan pulled his file, just to make sure he was refreshed on the man. The photograph showed a tall, white-haired man, a few years older than Donnegan, born and raised in some small town with an unpronounceable name down on the Black Sea. His father had been a hero of the Soviet Union for actions at the siege of Stalingrad during the Great Patriotic War. The younger Durov went through the Soviet Naval Academy and then submarine training at the Leninsky Komsomol Higher Naval School of Submarine Warfare at Leningrad. He had done well, impressed the right people, and had risen rapidly in the ranks while Sergei Gorshkov was building the Great Red Banner Northern Fleet during the sixties and seventies. His attendance at the Grechko Naval Academy in the late seventies marked him for flag rank.

Donnegan shook his head again. No doubt, the fall of the Soviet Union had been hard on Durov and his submariners. Donnegan could identify with that emotion.

He eased down into his chair and sipped from his cup of coffee. This Durov was an interesting man. From what Donnegan could tell from the dossier, he was not a communist at all, but held very strong patriotic views about Russia. He spoke frequently and boldly about the country's rightful place in the world order. He was strongly opposed to President Gregor Smitrov's economic reforms and appeasement of the rebels who sought to further splinter the country.

The man was driven, but to what end? Could he be mad enough to destroy his own new boat, go after American subs, and risk World War III in the process? Was there something going on up at the Soviet sub base that threatened world peace?

Despite all the sophisticated listening devices, the high-tech surveillance equipment, and the advanced U.S. intelligence-gathering network, there was only one way Donnegan could imagine that they might be able to learn the answers to those questions in a hurry.

The admiral pursed his lips as he grabbed the secure phone on his desk and punched in a set of numbers from memory. It rang once before a strong voice answered.

"SEAL Team Three, Commander Beaman."

"Bill, this is Admiral Donnegan at Naval Intelligence."

"Mornin', Admiral!"

"Hey, I know it's early for you out there, isn't it? I didn't expect you to answer. I was going to get somebody to roust you out of the rack."

"I'm still up watching an exercise we got going. We got a team doing a 'rubber duck' into San Clemente Island. There's a new team leader and I just wanted to make sure everything went all right."

Bill Beaman commanded SEAL Team Three, home-based at the Naval Amphibious Base, Coronado Island, California, near San Diego. It was pitch-black outside and two o'clock in the morning there. Beaman had been up since oh five hundred the previous morning and had spent most of this night so far pacing back and forth between his office and the command center down the hall. He always worried about his teams, and never more so than when he sent in a new platoon leader on some dangerous operation.

Although it sounded innocuous enough, a "rubber duck" was a rather hazardous means of getting a platoon and a rubber raiding craft out of an aircraft and into the water as quickly as possible. If everything went well, the team would be racing toward the shore and their mission mere minutes after jumping out of the plane. If there were any foul-ups, there could be a dozen injured men stranded in the dark in water that was miles from land.

"So, how did it go?" Donnegan asked.

"Just got word they were 'feet dry.' You caught me just as I was heading home for some shut-eye. Admiral, I doubt you're calling to inquire about the comfort of my guys."

Donnegan liked this big, rough SEAL. He was the

type who cared about his men, the kind who could be depended on when the chips were down.

Right now the chips were down.

"You're right, Bill. I got a job for you," Donnegan said, the shift obvious in his voice even from a full continent away. "I need for you to saddle up a small team for parachute insertion into a hostile environment. Winter Arctic weather. Full combat rig. It should be a simple surveillance mission, but if you're uncovered, it could get damn hot damn quick."

Beaman whistled. Nothing much fazed him, but the tone of Donnegan's voice was unmistakable. "Admiral, there are only a couple of countries in Arctic winter right now. Canada and Norway are allies last time I checked, so they're out. That leaves Russia." There was a slight pause, as if the SEAL was considering his next comment. He decided to go right ahead and say it. "I hope to hell you have National Command Authority approval on this."

Donnegan smiled. Beaman was good. Very good.

"I just got off the phone with the national security adviser. By the way, President Brown sends his best and wishes you all the luck. I need you to go in and put eyeballs on some subs at Polyarnyy. Our satellites show all they have there are some rusted hulks, but we have a source that says they have some boats there somewhere that are ready for sea."

"Okay, I'll have the team saddled up and ready to rock in eight hours. I trust you'll have the mission profile out to us before then. Better lay on the transport, too."

"Good! I told President Brown you'd be in the air by noon your time."

Bill Beaman was still shaking his head when he hung up the phone. There was plenty more to this phone call than an eyeball mission to check on a flock of dead subs. The president of the United States wasn't doing the two a.m. party-line thing with one of the head honchos at the Pentagon unless there was grave mischief afoot. It looked as if he and some of his boys were about to get their asses dropped right into the middle of it all, whatever "it" was.

Oh well. He was more than accustomed to finding out where the party was and what they were celebrating when the punch bowl was half-empty already. The SEAL commander knew one thing with certainty, though.

He would get precious little sleep this night.

Admiral Alexander Durov stepped through the great bronze doors, his chest thrust out and his head back as if he owned the place. He had loved the Kremlin ever since his father first brought him here as a young boy. It didn't matter if it was the seat of the Communist government, the haunt of the old Czarists, or the home of the current crop of spineless politicos. This thousand-year-old fortress represented the power of the *Rodina*. These walls had witnessed so much history. His country had suffered the torment of a dozen invaders through the centuries, attackers from both the East and the West, but none had been able to breach this place. It was the beating heart of Mother Russia.

As Durov strode in, President Gregor Smitrov rose from behind the ormolu-decorated Louis XV desk. He leaned across toward Durov, his small, girlish hand already meekly extended.

"My dear Admiral Durov, it is so good to see you. It has been far too long since you have come by to visit."

Durov stopped short, ignoring the outstretched hand. Instead, he came to rigid attention and snapped a crisp salute. "President, it is my reluctant duty to inform you that we have lost two nuclear submarines and the brave men aboard them," he said in stiff, formal tones.

Smitrov dropped his hand and stared wide-eyed at the admiral. His face was blank, the forced smile lost. His usual pallor was even more pronounced. Durov held his salute even as he was certain the president of Russia would topple over in a dead faint.

"But how . . . ?" he stammered. "Admiral, how did this horrible thing happen?"

Durov dropped the salute but still held himself rigid as he continued. "We sent the *Gepard* out on her sea trials. We knew the Americans would try to spy on her and that they might interfere as they have been wont to do in the past. Nothing serious, of course. Merely harassment. At least not until this time. At any rate, I ordered my nephew, Igor Serebnitskiv, out with his boat, the *Volk*, to protect her. I regret to report that both submarines are overdue to report in."

"It could be anything. Weather? Mechanical . . ."

"We analyzed tapes from our remote seafloor sensors. There were several very pronounced explosions in the area where they were operating."

There were no tapes. Durov had created them. Still, it gave the illusion of hard evidence and that's what he needed just now.

The former college professor who now ran the government of Durov's homeland was buying the lie without question. Smitrov put his fist to his mouth in horror.

"Oh my God!" he groaned. "All those brave men lost in some horrible accident. How is that possible? I know the boat was new, but was it not the finest—"

Durov held his hand up to stop his questions. "Mr. President, there is more. Before the explosions were detected, we found the signature of three submarines in that area, our two and an American Los Angeles class. After the explosions, all the signatures were lost. The tapes didn't show any torpedo noises, but our experts believe the American attacked and destroyed our boats somehow. Our naval liaison in Washington reported the Americans volunteered to help with rescue operations for a submarine they said was sunk under the ice in the Barents Sea near Novaya Zemlya. This happened a day after the explosions."

Durov paused to let this information sink in. Smitrov sat in stunned silence.

"One has to question how the Americans knew about the loss if they did not cause it," Durov continued. "There is the fact that this happened in our territorial sea. Mr. President, in case you are not familiar with the law of the sea, our territorial sea is the same as our land. An American submarine operating submerged in our territory is an act of aggression, even if it does not fire a shot."

Smitrov was ghostly pale. Durov wondered if there

was a drop of blood in the little man. He whined, "Are you sure? Could there be any doubt? Is there any other proof?"

"There rarely is with these kinds of things," Durov snorted. "That's why you use submarines, to keep things hidden. Come spring, when the ice melts and we can find the hulks, then, Mr. President, you will have your proof."

Smitrov grew even paler and squeezed his eyes closed in a pained grimace. Durov was more certain than ever that the man was going to swoon. Instead, he slumped weakly back into his chair. When he looked up, his eyes were shining with tears, his expression grim.

"I'll assemble my advisers. I must inform the Parliament. They must know immediately. And the people . . . the people need to know. This is a terrible disaster."

"Yes, Mr. President. It is."

With that, Durov turned on his heel and strode toward the door.

"Admiral?"

Durov stopped and half turned to the president. "Yes, Mr. President?"

"My condolences."

"Sir?"

"For the loss of your nephew."

"Ah yes. Thank you, sir. For the loss of all our brave men."

"Yes."

Durov closed the bronze doors and marched smartly down the long hall, the taps on the soles of his boots echoing off the hard marble floor. When he was well away from the executive office, he allowed a small smile to trace across his weathered face.

It had started at last!

The weak fool back there was falling into the trap and did not suspect a thing. Now, in a few hours, the press would have the story and the Russian people would be screaming for action against the American aggressors. Soon the chaos would be unleashed. When it was over, the glory of this historic place would once again be restored.

If he had been sure the security cameras would miss it, he would have allowed himself a joyous jig right there in the halls of the Kremlin.

Marina Nosovitskaya stormed into Dmitri Ustinov's office without a word and slammed the door shut hard behind her. Her beautiful blond features were crimson with undisguised anger. She stopped, bent forward, and slammed her fists down on Ustinov's desk, then stared hard into his wide eyes.

"Dmitri Ustinov, you are an idiot! Were you born with a death wish?" Her voice was menacing, low and deep in her throat as if she might lose control and come over the desk after him.

Ustinov stared at the one place he could find, the beautiful, rounded tops of her wonderful breasts that bobbed with each word, with each blow on his poor desktop. "I have no idea what you are so mad about, Marina. What is the problem?"

She sputtered and hissed some more, but must have

realized that Ustinov was not a good enough actor to be lying to her with such a straight face. She eased down into Ustinov's side chair, unaware that her skirt had risen high enough to give him a tantalizing glimpse of the garters at the tops of her stockings and her luscious white thighs.

"Uncle Boris contacted me this morning. Someone tried to kill Catherine Goldman last night after she left us at the restaurant. A taxicab tried to run her down on the street."

Ustinov shuddered. The implications were not lost on him. "Are you sure it was not an accident? Is she okay?"

"It was deliberate. The police say that she is all right. The cab got away and was found abandoned over on Washington Street. Alstair McLain is screaming holy murder and the entire staff at the SEC is waiting to descend on us as soon as he gives the word. Do you know what this means, Dmitri?"

The beads of sweat that had already popped out on Ustinov's forehead confirmed that he did. His spacious office seemed much smaller all of a sudden, the walls closing in on him. He didn't even notice the flash of exposed flesh when she shifted her legs.

He felt trapped. Why now? Why, when he was so near the glorious success for which he had worked so long and hard? Trapped by chance and bad luck. Someone was trying to kill one of the SEC director's best inspectors. An inspector who just happened to have been assigned a week before to the OptiMarx project. McLain would doubtless look in their direction first. He would not rest until the guilty bastard was caught. With a much more intense investigation, the chances that someone would find Ustinov's special work on the OptiMarx system were greatly enhanced. Even if they miraculously missed it, he would have to lie low, put everything on hold until the heat was turned off.

His stomach flip-flopped when he realized what would happen. There was no possible way to meet Boris Medikov's ridiculously dangerous schedule now. It could not be done with this latest development. He doubted Medikov would be one bit understanding about the special circumstances.

Nosovitskaya must have been reading his mind. She stood up and stepped back a few steps, as if she wanted to be out of the line of fire should Medikov's bullets suddenly begin rattling around the office.

The morning light broke through the clouds outside and streamed across her figure, illuminating her face, her golden hair. Ustinov thought of a goddess, someone lifted from Greek mythology.

She pursed her lips and screwed up her forehead. "If it was not you who ordered the hit on her, who was it?"

He spread his hands in innocence. "I don't know. Could somebody else be scheming with the system? Somebody else who's afraid she'll find out what they're doing? I can't imagine Smythe or Andretti doing anything like that. They are dirty and incompetent, but even they are not stupid enough to try something like this."

Nosovitskaya nodded her agreement. "That's what I concluded, too. This is what Uncle Boris has said: Nothing changes. Do you understand? This development changes nothing. The plan is under way and we cannot afford a change on this end now. He told me that if I determined that you were not responsible for the stupid attempt on Goldman's life, then you are to proceed without hesitation."

Ustinov blanched, all color leaving his face. "That's impossible. We were behind before. Now it is far too dangerous. We must be even more slow and careful now."

She smiled and shook her head. "No. That is not an option. We continue."

Ustinov dropped his head, his chin resting on his chest. Marina Nosovitskaya turned and headed for the door.

"Wait. What did your uncle tell you to do if you determined that I *was* responsible?"

She smiled coyly and formed the shape of a pistol with her hand and finger, pointing toward the bridge of his nose. "Dmitri, my love, I was to kill you."

Jon Ward had his chair turned one hundred eighty degrees from his desk, staring out the window down at Pier 22. Four of the boats of his squadron were tied to the pier and sailors were already scurrying around on various morning errands. The early mist that had hidden the view across the Elizabeth River toward the broad tidal flats to the west was dissipating now beneath the climbing sun. Fishing boats and pleasure craft plied up and down the busy stretch of river, everyone going somewhere, heading out to the open Atlantic or up one of the broad tidal rivers that fed the Chesapeake Bay. A huge orange-painted container ship slid by, its massive hull a scant few yards beyond the end of the pier. Ward could see the Moldovan flag hanging limply from its stern as it passed.

All in all, it was a quiet morning in Norfolk. The world went on, oblivious of the unbelievable crisis that would inevitably come to light. Soon everyone would know. It would be impossible to keep the events up north from them much longer.

It was surprisingly quiet around his office, considering everything that had happened in the last few hours. Joe Glass and *Toledo* had swapped operational command to SUBLANT, so he and his boat were their problem for the time being. The hotshots over in the fenced-in compound might call him if they decided that they needed something. That most likely would not happen. The jokers over there liked to think they ruled the seas from inside their high-security cell. Any admission that they needed to talk to someone who walked on the waterfront might be considered a sign of weakness.

Ward emptied his coffee cup without even tasting the cold liquid. He stood and walked over to refill it from the carafe on the wooden conference table. As he was pouring the steaming brew into his mug, he heard the footsteps of Steve Smedly, his chief staff officer, coming down the hallway. The man was short, black, and always jovial no matter the level of tension that might permeate the atmosphere in his boss's office. Smedly was on the last tour of his career. He had risen through the ranks from seaman to captain the old-fashioned way, by hard work and careful attention to every detail. He had come to the realization early in his career as a naval officer that he was not equipped to lead, but was superb as a staff officer. In that capacity, he excelled. The Squadron Six staff ran like a well-oiled machine under Smedley's direction.

Ward filled a cup for him and shoved it his way when he stepped through the door.

"Thanks, Commodore. I have Admiral Donnegan on the phone for you. He said he wanted to speak with you for a few minutes. Then you should round up the operations officer and the material officer for a conference call with him. They'll both be here in five minutes." He nodded toward the red light blinking on the phone by Ward's desk. "The admiral is on line one. He's been waiting thirty seconds already."

Ward picked up his own coffee cup and walked over to the desk. "Thanks, Steve. Give me a minute with the admiral. Then get the team in here. If Donnegan wants a conference call, he must have some work for us to do."

Ward sat behind his desk and picked up the phone. "Morning, Admiral. I was starting to wonder when you'd get around to calling. Sounds like Joe has his hands full up there. We'll be pretty busy when he gets back."

Tom Donnegan snorted. "You won't have to wait till he gets back. Gregor Smitrov has been on the red phone with President Brown. He accused us of the unprovoked sinking of two of their boats. I'm told he was very rude and indignant. He has called a press conference in two hours to announce this to the world. It appears that the curtain has risen on Alexander Durov's little production."

Ward leaned back and whistled. "Admiral, this could get real ugly. I'll put my 'no comment' face on. I suspect the pier will be humming with reporters once this thing breaks."

"That won't be our problem, Jon. We've got other things to worry about besides the evening news. I've got a job for you. It'll have you and a lot of your staff out of town for a bit. I just got off the horn with your old friend Bill Beaman. He's heading your way this afternoon. He'll have a few minutes to brief you further when he arrives, but essentially, I need for you to work with SEAL Delivery Team Two over in Little Creek. Get that new Advanced Swimmer Delivery Vehicle loaded on a C-5 and over to Faslane. You're going to get there at the same time Joe Glass does. You'll strap the ASDV onto *Toledo*'s back and send her north again. I need you to set up a command center over there somewhere. I'm making you the tactical commander for this entire operation, Jon. You're the best man we've got for the job."

Ward wasn't sure just what the operation was, and he was flattered by the admiral's compliments. But he sure didn't like being stuffed into some underground concrete command center when his boat was going to where the action was.

Still, it sounded as if he was going to be very busy for a while on what was perhaps the most important mission anyone had seen since the nuclear age had begun. Besides, he was ready to concede that it was Joe Glass's turn on the front lines.

"Thank you, Admiral. I'll do my best."

"Jon, on this one, you may have to do even better than that."

Chapter 15

President Gregor Smitrov almost disappeared when he walked up behind the imposing podium in the Kremlin's great ballroom. Even when he stepped up onto the well-hidden riser that had been built especially for him, he still had to stretch to see over the top. He paused for a moment, looking out on the mass of reporters who were gathered there, all chatting excitedly among themselves. They knew there was something big that had brought them here this snowy afternoon in Moscow. "International military incident" had already been leaked to most of them and they smelled blood.

Smitrov used his handkerchief to wipe the sweat from his brow. The bright television lights were unpleasantly hot, but he knew he was not as uncomfortable as the American Navy and the rest of the U.S. government would soon be. What were those fools thinking, anyway? Just when he was making some real headway in economic rapprochement with the West, just as he was solidifying his own support for his liberal policies here at home, the stupid Americans had done something asinine enough to start up the Cold War all over again.

He was still not convinced the American submarine had fired on his boats deliberately. Not even they were that idiotic. The fact was that something disastrous had occurred. According to the information Admiral Durov was providing him, it was the Americans' fault somehow. Now it was his duty to report it, to assume the proper amount of righteous indignation over it, and then to see which would be the best way to gain political capital from it.

Smitrov leaned closer to the microphone and cleared his throat. The room fell quiet. The gathered media representatives sensed the importance of this summons to the Kremlin. No one wanted to miss a syllable.

"Ladies and gentlemen, it is with great sadness that I speak with you today," the Russian president began. "Today, I must report to you that two of our newest nuclear-powered submarines are overdue and we believe they are both lost with all hands."

The hushed silence in the room was destroyed as everyone tried to shout his question louder than anyone else. Smitrov held up both hands in a vain attempt to quell the near riot.

"Please! Please! I will answer all your questions in good order!" he shouted over the din. Even with the help of amplification, it was as if no one was listening. They kept shouting and waving their arms. A few were bent over, talking into their cell phones.

Smitrov conceded. He stepped back from the podium, folded his arms across his chest, and waited. After a while, the gathered reporters realized that nothing was happening except their own antics. They fell silent. Smitrov again stepped up to the podium and, in his best "schoolmaster" voice, scolded the group.

"If you will be quiet, I will tell you all we know and then we will answer your questions as best we can. But we will maintain order here or we will not proceed."

The international reporters were not accustomed to being admonished in this manner. They considered themselves the anointed ones, charged with interpreting the news into the social standards they alone determined were best. No politician could treat them this way, yet Smitrov had just done so. He had gotten away with it. The room was once again quiet.

"Two weeks ago, our newest, most powerful, and safest nuclear submarine, the *Gepard*, left the Polyarnyy Submarine Base, near Murmansk. The *Volk*, one of our modern Akula-type submarines, accompanied her. Their mission was a routine training and testing mission under the winter ice cap west of Novaya Zemlya. This area is inside the Barents Sea. As you know, this is our historic territorial sea, with our claim to sovereignty well established by historic precedent. Some, and especially the Americans, dispute this, but our claim is certain."

Smitrov paused and took a sip of water while he waited for all this to sink in. The reporters were now scribbling feverishly. None made a sound. Even the representatives of the American television networks had their heads down, writing away, attempting to capture each word the president uttered.

"When neither of the submarines communicated with Northern Fleet Naval Command at the regular time, we became concerned. In addition to trying to establish communications with the submarines, the experts reviewed the tapes of our undersea sensor system. The tapes show our two submarines innocently maneuvering inside our territorial waters. They also show another submarine, an American Los Angeles class, operating very near our submarines." Smitrov took another sip of the water. The room was so quiet now he could hear the scratching of the reporters' pens on their notebooks. "Then we detected a series of loud noises, explosions. After that, the tape is empty. We think the American went quiet and sneaked away."

Smitrov, a grave expression on his face, gazed out over the crowd with his sad brown eyes. No one was moving now. Even the incessant scribbling had stopped. The reporters were staring at him, their mouths open in shocked disbelief.

He waited just long enough for the implications of what he was saying to sink in, and then he went on, speaking with more heat and conviction than he had ever used before.

"I will leave the interpretation of these sounds to you and to our experts. I know this: Two of our finest submarines and their brave crewmen now lie broken on the bottom of our sea while the American submarine is slinking safely home."

Smitrov turned to his right and looked toward the tall, white-haired naval officer who had been standing several meters away, at the edge of the brightly lit stage. The Russian president concluded his portion of the briefing.

"I will now turn you over to Admiral Alexander Durov. Admiral Durov is the commander of the Northern Fleet Submarine Force. He will brief you on the details and answer your specific questions. Admiral Durov."

Durov snapped stiffly to attention for a moment as the camera lights moved his way; then he turned to remove the cover from a chart that showed the Barents Sea. A red line stretched out from a point located two hundred miles north of the Norwegian border across the sea to a spot well north of the island of Novaya Zemlya. Inside the line, close to the frozen island, there were two bloodred crosses. Durov stood ramrod stiff as he began to speak in a deep, booming voice.

"Thank you, President Smitrov. This chart shows the area where our submarines were operating. As you can see, it is well within our historic territorial sea. As the president briefed you, the *Gepard* was conducting routine operations beneath the ice. The nature of those operations is highly classified and will not be discussed here. It is of particular interest to note that she was unarmed. The *Volk* was escorting her, in the unlikely possibility that she needed protection." Durov paused and dropped his chin. His voice was much quieter now. "Gentlemen, my own nephew, Captain Second Rank Igor Serebnitskiv, commanded the *Volk*."

Durov wiped what appeared to be a tear from his eye. Though he would have loved to smile at the scene in the room, he maintained a frown of deep hurt and sadness as the camera flashes exploded all around the room, as the zoom lenses on the television cameras whirred in closer to his face, trying to record an uncle's tear of sadness. The assemblage of international reporters sat on the edges of their chairs, hanging on his every word.

He cleared his throat, as if the grief had stolen his voice, and went on.

"Subsequent analysis of the sensor tapes shows that an American Los Angeles–class submarine shadowed our boats very closely from the time they went under the ice until they disappeared from our sensors. It is quite evident to our experts that the American submarine was on a spy mission very similar to the ones they historically and quite typically perform in our territorial waters from time to time."

One of the reporters, a Frenchman whom Durov knew to be sympathetic, raised his hand to ask a question. Durov nodded toward him.

"Admiral, would it be possible for us to hear the tapes you have mentioned? Will they be released to the press?"

Durov shook his head. "No, I'm sorry, Pierre. Analysis of the tapes would show too much of our monitoring capabilities. I am afraid they must remain classified."

The French reporter nodded. "Of course, *mon Admirale*. We recognize their sensitivity."

Durov went on, ignoring several of the American reporters who now waved for recognition. "As President Smitrov has said, we monitored a series of loud noises. After that there was no one but the American."

The room broke into a tumult of noise as each reporter tried to outshout his colleagues. Durov let the discord build to a crescendo before he waved at one of the reporters, a representative from Reuters, the British news agency.

"Admiral, are you implying that the American submarine attacked and sank your boats without any provocation?"

Durov shook his head and held up both hands to

make his point. "Please understand, to make such an ac-
cusation, I would have to be certain of the analysis of the
tapes. I cannot say that yet with absolute certainty. The
explosions could possibly be from some other cause. Perhaps some horrible accident." Durov stopped, surveyed
the room to be certain he had the complete attention of
each of the scribes there, then leaned forward, his eyes
blazing into the cameras, his voice quavering slightly
from apparent ill-concealed anger. "The one thing I can
say for certain is that the American submarine ran away
from the scene at deliberate speed. In so doing, they left
over two hundred and fifty fellow sailors . . . including
the oldest son of my dear sister . . . to die agonizing
deaths at the bottom of the dark, cold Barents Sea."

With that, Admiral Alexander Durov turned and
stomped off the stage, ignoring the urgent, shouted
questions that erupted from the writhing crowd behind
him.

Stan Miller looked around before settling down on the
bench that was hidden from the street by some un-
trimmed evergreen bushes. He angrily pounded in the
numbers on the cell phone buttons. Afternoon Washington traffic whipped past him but the little park on
K Street appeared deserted. The leaden gray sky illuminated the scene with the dull, depressing glow of a typical
February in the city. A damp cold wind had sprung up,
promising snow later tonight, and it was sharp enough
to deter even the most determined late lunchtime jogger.

The news he had just gotten was impossible to com-
prehend. What in hell was going on?

Still fuming, he mumbled to himself as he listened to the number ring once, twice, then a third time. There was a click and then Mark Stern's voice.

"Stern here. What do *you* want?"

Stern would have caller ID. The SEC deputy director swallowed hard before diving right in. "What the hell are those bastards at OptiMarx doing?"

The financier's voice was soothing when he responded, "Stan, you sound upset. What's the problem?"

"Stern, how in bloody hell do you expect me to help you get that bastardized system of yours through the SEC testing if those idiots are going to try to kill one of my inspectors?" Miller growled.

He could hear Stern gasp all the way across the continent. The venture capitalist was taken aback, caught off guard by Miller's question.

"What are you talking about? Someone from Opti-Marx trying to kill one of your people?"

"It's real simple. You remember that dumpy broad, Catherine Goldman? She called yesterday to say she had found something suspicious in the code. She wasn't sure what it was yet, but it didn't look good to her. She mentioned it to one of your guys there in New York. Well, last night, somebody tried to run her down on a street in Manhattan. It was no accident. Somebody wanted her guts spilled all over the place."

The line was silent for a long time. Miller thought the connection might have been broken. He was about to check the phone's readout when he heard Stern's voice again. He was speaking very slowly and carefully.

"Miller, no way was it anybody from OptiMarx. You

can trust me on that. Now listen very carefully." Stern's voice changed. There was an unmistakable hint of a threat. "I am paying you very good money to ensure that we get complete and speedy approval of the trading system from the SEC. I expect a return on my investment. That's how I feed my family and my wife's rather advanced shopping addiction. The approval better come on time and with no problems. Understand? If not, I know a certain congressional committee that would have considerable interest in a certain SEC deputy director's rather sizeable Cayman Island bank account. Do you understand me?"

Miller gulped. His tongue felt as if it were coated with thick wool. There was now over four million dollars tucked away in that account. It was going to be his ticket out of this rat race and it was so tantalizingly close he could taste it. Sweat covered his brow despite the cold, icy wind that whipped down K Street.

"I . . . I understand, Mark," he stammered, trying to conjure up some amount of confidence in his voice. "There won't be any problem. Goldman is a bitch anyway. It was probably somebody else she's pissed off sometime in the past. There've been plenty of them. Anyway, I suspect she needs some time off after such a traumatic experience. I'll put someone else up there. Someone who understands how things work."

Stern's voice turned cordial. "Now, that's the attitude."

"Still, Stern, you better tell your guys up there to tread lightly. We're almost there and we don't want anything to raise any—"

The line had already gone dead.

* * *

Commander Bill Beaman's plane rolled to a halt in front of the hangar at Oceania Naval Air Station. Beaman spotted Jon Ward waiting on the tarmac as he and his team poured out of the C-17.

After a quick handshake, Beaman hopped in the staff car at Ward's invitation; then they sped off to the special intelligence cell at SUBLANT. During the short drive, they talked of the weather and what various mutual friends were doing. Both men avoided the subject most on their minds.

The headquarters compound sat inside a high-security fence just outside the main base. Elaborate electronic monitoring systems checked every inch of the chain-link enclosure. The gates looked as though they would stop anything short of an all-out assault by an M-1 Abrams main battle tank.

After running their ID cards through a computer search, the armed Marine guard waved them through the fortified gate. Ward swung the car into a parking space and the two walked briskly up the steps to the glass doors of an ugly concrete building. Another armed Marine, this one behind a bulletproof glass window, checked their IDs before he waved them through a metal detector and electronic door.

All this security only gave them access to the routine section of the SUBLANT building. The special intelligence section was upstairs, in the far corner of the windowless building. Another armed, grim-faced Marine checked their IDs once more, and then they faced a small device that scanned the retinas in their eyes before the heavy steel door swung open. They were now in the inner sanctum of the most successful military intelligence-gathering operation in the history of the United States.

Despite all the elaborate security measures . . . the armed Marines, the computer ID checks, the retinal scan, the double-locked doors . . . there wasn't a lot of information to give to Beaman. The two men spent time poring over the latest satellite images of the Kola. Heavy cloud cover obscured the visible light photography, but the millimeter-wavelength radar images were quite clear and distinct. The land was rough and, except for the larger cities and towns, mostly uninhabited. Heavy birch and pine forests covered the rolling hills, deeply cut by river-fed fjords that dumped into the Barents Sea.

Even the pictures of Polyarnyy revealed little. Long piers littered with a few rusting hulks, heavy block buildings looking ramshackle after years of neglect. The gigantic, covered fitting-out shed jutting out over the harbor looked to be the only possible target of interest.

The briefing officer, a young lieutenant, was apologetic but not very helpful. His briefing package was embarrassingly empty.

Later, as Ward cranked the car and pulled away from the parking space, he apologized to the SEAL.

"Sorry, Bill," Ward said. "Looks like we're not going to have a lot of help on this one. Come on. Ellen has a mess of crabs ready for dinner, and I suspect the beer is cold and waiting for us by now."

"Lead the way, Commander. I'm starved."

Bill Beaman leaned back and sighed contentedly. "Damn, Jon. You got the life here." The SEAL commander sat in

an overstuffed chair in the family room of Ward's comfortable Virginia Beach home. A blazing fire burned
brightly in the fireplace, a warm counterpoint to the
choppy, iron gray water of Lake Christopher that washed
up at the foot of the lawn, and the dirty, threatening
clouds overhead. "How did you luck into this place?"

Ward was stepping in from the kitchen, a bottle of
Corona in each hand. He handed one to Beaman and
took a healthy swig out of his before he answered, "Ellen
found it. The one drawback is the commute to the pier.
It's an hour by car. About the same by bicycle, my transportation of choice when the weather permits."

Beaman laughed. "You haven't changed a bit since
you lucked into this cushy assignment. Always working
out. What you training for now? Some triathlon?"

"Oh, the triathlon season here doesn't start for another couple of months. Right now I'm getting ready for
the Shamrock Marathon." Ward winked. "If you want
to, we could go for a run before dinner."

Beaman chuckled. The two men had competed
through innumerable races when they both served in San
Diego. Neither was sure who had beaten the other more
often, but the competition was always fierce, yet friendly.

"Naw, in the morning maybe. Tonight, all I want is
some cold beer and Ellen's good cooking." He toasted
Ward with the Corona. Enticing smells drifted out from
the kitchen and he could hear Ward's wife singing softly
back there. "You are one lucky son of a bitch. You know
that, don't you?"

Ward grinned, returned the toast, and plopped down
on the couch next to his old friend. They both stared

into the fire for a few minutes, listening to its pleasant sizzling, popping, and crackling.

The first bits of sleet were beginning to tap against the large picture window. Pleasant as it was in here, it was already a nasty night out there.

Ward broke the silence. "Bill, why the hell are you on this mission in the first place? Aren't you a little senior to be traipsing around the tundra?"

Beaman took a swallow of beer before he answered. He deliberately used his little finger to shove the lime in the bottle's neck back down into the amber liquid. "Tom Donnegan called and asked me if I'd lead the team in. You know as well as I do that you don't say no to Admiral Donnegan. I guess he trusts me and my guys after that little run-in we had down in Colombia. From all I've seen so far, this deal should be a cakewalk after that one."

Ward grunted. He remembered how tough that drug interdiction mission had been on Beaman. Half his team had been killed in a vicious ambush and the rest badly mauled.

Ward propped his feet up on the coffee table. "I don't know, buddy. Latest from Joe Glass on *Toledo* is that the skipper he saved is talking up a storm. He's telling all about a squadron of Akulas sitting there, ready to deploy, and we don't show any intelligence to confirm such a buildup. And Admiral Durov . . . you saw him on the film clip at the Russian news conference, blaming us for everything but the heartbreak of psoriasis. He's the one that apparently commands the new squadron. Captain Andropoyov . . . that's the sub captain Glass rescued up there . . . he says that Durov is some kind of Russian superpatriot, a real zealot, and you know how dangerous they can be. Andropoyov is certain that Durov has hatched some plot to try to take power."

"You mean, like a coup? Surely the rest of the world wouldn't stand by for shit like that!"

"What if the rest of the world was distracted by the good old U.S. of A. sinking a couple of innocent Russian submarines for no apparent reason?"

Beaman blinked hard. He stared into the fire. "Man! A coup!" He thought for another moment, then turned back to Ward. "There's still something I don't understand. Those Akulas are good boats, from all I know about them. But what good are they to him? They can't have more than ten of those babies up there, and that's not much of a threat to us. If they were Typhoons or Delta IIIs, I'd be worried. These boats aren't missile shooters."

"We know quite a bit about Comrade Durov, Bill. One thing we know is that he's a real student of Russian history. Remember the Bolshevik Revolution? Did you ever hear of the *Kronstadt*?"

Beaman squinted for a moment, then shook his head. "Nope. I must have been sleeping through class when we talked about that."

"Well, the *Kronstadt* was a battleship in the czar's navy. It was tied up at the naval base in St. Petersburg. The crew took over the ship during the revolution and trained its guns on the palace there. The city surrendered. They had no choice. It was one of the key turning points of the revolution. I think Durov means to do exactly the same thing. I believe he will use those new Akulas and their fancy cruise missiles as his *Kronstadt*."

George Wallace and Don Keith

Ellen Ward stuck her head in from the kitchen. "You two warriors finished matching battle scars and ready to eat? These crabs are done and I'm hungry."

The two stood, but neither man was quite as hungry as he had been a few minutes before.

Chapter 16

Alexander Durov paced the hotel room nervously, stomping from one side of the suite to the other. He kept telling himself there was no need to worry. The news conference had gone well. The reporters had trampled each other in their eagerness to rush out of the briefing room, racing to get to a data link or to stand in front of their cameras with the Kremlin as a backdrop as they recorded the story.

Durov smiled. He had just handed them every reporter's dream story. There was death, destruction, international intrigue, technology, and the real threat of war. Within minutes the story was screaming from radios, televisions, and Web sites around the world. In hours it would be the front-page story in every newspaper in the world. No one would be talking of anything else for weeks.

When his pacing took him to the street-side window, he could see the huge crowds heading to join the others who were already gathering in Red Square to mourn their brave dead sailors, to scream for retribution against the murderous Americans. Durov clutched dispatches from Washington, New York, London, and Tokyo in his hand. They told stories of similar gatherings in all the world's major cities.

The Americans had been vague so far in their denials. They would not even confirm that they had submarines in the Barents. They said they had caused no Russian boat to sink.

It was the perfect plot. Everyone believed his story. Nobody would be able to prove anything different, at least until the ice edge receded north. That wouldn't happen for several months yet. By then, it would be far too late.

Now, with the American military checked and "Professor" Smitrov distracted by all that was swirling about him, it was time to put the next stage of the plan into play. There would be a constant barrage of grieving widows and crying babies showing up on television to remind the world of the American treachery, to inflame the Russian people's passion for revenge. Meanwhile, Admiral Durov would personally lead a brave but futile attempt to reach the downed submarines, only to be defeated by the Arctic ice. The Russian people would see the images of the brave old sailor doing all he could to attempt the perilous rescue while their president wrung his hands and called for calm. They would wish someone like Admiral Durov could be their leader in such perilous times.

And while all the furor was happening on the world stage, Boris Medikov's little OptiMarx scheme would be unleashed on the American financial markets. The inevitable crash would spread panic around the world. In all the hue and cry, no one would take any notice of a few military maneuvers inside Russia. Not until it was far too late.

He stopped to check his visage in the room's full-length mirror. He did, indeed, look the part of the strong leader his people deserved.

The pain came so quickly he hardly had time to clutch his chest. It ripped through his upper body as if someone had shoved a sword through him.

Durov groaned and stumbled to the desk at the far end of the hotel room. No time to call for Vasiliy. He yanked open the top drawer and fumbled for the little bottle of pills. The pain was so intense he had trouble sucking in a new breath. This was the worst attack yet.

The doctor promised they would get worse. But the pills would stop the pain. They always did.

He dropped the lid from the pill bottle onto the desk-top. It rolled off, onto the floor. Durov shook out two of the little blue tablets and swallowed them. He shakily poured a water glass full of vodka, splashing most of it onto the desk, but chased the medicine with the clear drink. He was feeling better already, even as the fiery liquid streamed down his throat.

His raspy breath was coming a bit easier as the numbness in his throat and left arm subsided. The specialist said there was an operation to fix his damaged heart, but he also said that it would mean several months of recovery. There wasn't time for that now. The *Rodina* needed him now, not in several months. He had convinced himself that there would be plenty of time for an operation afterward. After the course of history had been triumphantly redirected.

He slumped back into the heavy leather chair. That's where Vasiliy Zhurkov found him sitting ten minutes later. His hands were still trembling and his uniform shirt, normally starched stiff, hung limp and sweat-soaked.

"Another attack, Admiral?" the aide asked, the concern heavy in his voice. "A bad one? That is the third one this week. You must see the specialist again."

Durov summoned what little strength he had remaining and shook his head from side to side.

He growled, "For what purpose, so he can put me to bed like some used-up old man? There is far too much to do right now." He forced a weak smile and lied, "Besides, it was a little twinge. Nothing to get upset about. I am all right now. Forget about this. It did not happen."

Zhurkov knew better than to argue with the tough old sailor. He snapped to attention. "Yes, sir. It is time to leave. Your car is standing by outside and your plane is ready for takeoff for Polyarnyy. Boris Medikov will join you on board shortly."

"Very good, Zhurkov. Very good, indeed."

Durov stood and did his best to walk across the room to the coatrack without crouching over. He ignored the iron-tight band of pain across his chest.

Joe Glass sat across the small table from Sergei Andropoyov. An old, beaten chessboard filled the tiny space between them. The plastic chessmen were chipped from years of use on board the sub. The settee in Glass's stateroom was perfect for these matches. It was quiet and private so they could talk freely, yet it was equipped so he could still run the boat from there.

Glass wondered if Andropoyov found any enjoyment

at all in playing chess with him. It wasn't for the challenge of the competition. Although Glass was a fair amateur player, the Russian submariner was in a different league. Glass soon learned his best strategy was to fight like hell and hope for a draw. That tactic had hardly been successful so far. Still, he enjoyed the play and the discussions he was having with the Russian sailor. Sometimes it was easy to forget how much they could have in common despite their vastly different backgrounds. They were both submariners, after all.

After Glass made his next move, Andropoyov boldly shoved his queen diagonally across the board, cutting off Glass's king. The Russian looked up from the board and smiled.

"Captain Glass, I believe that is checkmate. Another well-fought match, my friend. Your game is improving greatly." He sipped from his cup of tea, then looked Glass in the eye as he spoke. "I was wondering. Have you been informing your superiors of our discussions?"

Glass nodded but remained silent.

"Have they told you what they plan for my crew?"

"No, Sergei," Glass replied. "They haven't mentioned the subject at all."

"You are not taking us back to Russia."

"No. We're headed back to Scotland. If this had been a simple rescue after an accident, you would be home by now. I know you understand, under the circumstances . . ."

"You will ultimately send us home, though."

"Once our people have a chance to talk with you and your crew, I would imagine that they'll return you to

Murmansk just as soon as transportation can be arranged. I bet there will be some very relieved families when you step off the plane."

Glass expected to see Andropoyov smile, or at least show some hint of relief. Instead, creases of worry formed on the Russian's forehead.

"I assume, then, that it has not yet been made public that we have been rescued. Our families still believe we are dead."

"That's right. Again, because of the circumstances. We lost a boat up there, too, and almost lost a second one. I think our people want to see what Durov's up to before we let him know that you're still alive."

Andropoyov smiled but his eyes were still dark. "And, I assume, they want to further confirm our rather unbelievable suspicions as well."

"I suppose so, but it's just a matter of time before you're all back home with your families, Sergei. Until we can let them know that some of you survived."

"Joe, it is not that easy. If our suspicions are correct, Admiral Durov will not allow our stories to be believed, nor will he allow our return alive. If they find we survived the attack, that we are telling the truth about what happened, they will try to silence us by threatening our families. If they are not able to do so, they will claim that we have been brainwashed and will try to get us home as soon as they can. This little complication will make Durov more ruthless in his plan. Many will die, I fear. Should we ever be returned to Russia, we will all disappear for 'debriefing.'" Andropoyov's tone left no doubt that the debriefing would be a very permanent solution to Durov's problem. "Such a thing as that is still quite easy to carry out in Russia for someone with Durov's power and influence."

Glass nodded. He had watched and studied the country enough over the years to suspect that Andropoyov was not exaggerating. Andropoyov and the remnants of his crew were a risk for whatever the Russian admiral was up to. They were a fly in the ointment that Durov could not allow to exist long enough for someone to begin listening and believing what they were saying. They alone knew the true extent of his treachery. Anyone ruthless enough to willingly sacrifice one of his own submarines and crew for a political end would not hesitate to kill again. Glass could understand Andropoyov's concern for the families of his crew.

"What do you suggest, Sergei?"

The Russian leaned back in his seat and stared at Glass. "We must remain dead on the floor of the Barents a little longer, until this is all over. We must disappear before you return to your base. Once we arrive there, once we are seen, it is a certainty that Durov will learn that we survived and that we have alerted you to what really happened." Andropoyov's eyes were afire, burning into Glass's as he spoke. "The rescue attempt was unsuccessful. You found nothing but flooded hulks, both your *Miami* and my *Gepard*. You saw no signs of *Volk*. Can you make that happen? It is our only hope for saving many lives."

Glass thought for a few moments. He didn't know if he could trust Andropoyov. He could be stalling for some other reason. This could all be some sort of elaborate setup, designed to throw them off about what was going to happen in Russia.

He looked across the chessboard at the Russian captain. This game they were playing was filled with too many gambits for him to follow. The potential checkmate would hold far worse consequences than merely the bruised ego of one submarine captain.

Somehow he knew he was not wrong about this man. He knew what his next move should be.

Glass reached and tipped over his king.

"I think we can do that," he answered. "It may take a little doing, but it's possible."

The buzzer beside Glass's head yelped. He grabbed the MJ handset and put it to his ear. "Captain."

"Captain, this is the officer of the deck. We have rounded the North Cape. Coming left to course two-two-zero."

Glass stood. He nodded at Andropoyov as he spoke into the phone. "Very well. Come to one-five-zero feet and clear baffles in preparation for coming to periscope depth. Tell radio to line up for a secure voice patch to Admiral Donnegan."

He put the phone back in the cradle and headed out the stateroom door. He turned, looked back over his shoulder, and winked. "I'm going to see about making you disappear."

Stan Miller sat across the desk from his boss, Alstair McLain. The two men were in the director's corner office, but they were not talking. Instead, they were watch-

ing the large television screen that had been built into the
bookcase on the far wall.

A pair of talking heads were expounding about the
reports out of Russia and the wanton disregard of diplomatic realities by the American military. So far, the U.S.
was keeping quiet about the Russians' charges beyond a
stock denial of any submarine-sinking incident beneath
the ice cap. The United Nations Security Council was
going into emergency session while near riots were
breaking out in many cities around the globe. Still, the
American government and military were oddly silent.
That was fodder galore for the pundits.

Miller set his coffee cup on the saucer that was perched
precariously on his knee.

"This shit'll raise havoc on The Street," he sniffed.

"Yeah, volume is already way up, close to a record,"
McLain said. "The Dow is down way over two hundred
points so far and sidecars are in effect."

Miller grimaced. "Glad I'm not trading today. Can
you imagine how long it would take to get a sell order
executed right now? The systems are already bogging
down. Too much volume for the old junk."

McLain nodded, his eyes following the stock ticker at
the bottom of the television screen. "Yep. Too bad.
That's what the OptiMarx system was meant to fix. Instantaneous trading, no communications or transaction
delays, real-time clearance. It would be great if . . ."

Miller saw the opening he had been waiting for and
interrupted McLain when he paused. "Yes! 'If' is the
right word, all right. 'If' it works and 'if' it is imple-

mented in time. The technology is looking very sound, Al. I think we should fast-track the approval."

There, he had said it. McLain stared at his deputy, digesting what he had just heard. "Stan, someone just tried to kill your head inspector on the OptiMarx system. Now you're recommending a fast track for approval? Maybe you'd better explain. I don't understand."

Miller answered without hesitation. "Look, nobody at OptiMarx would attempt something like that the very week she started on the project. Goldman is a hothead as you well know. She is a real pain in the ass. It could have been any of a hundred people she has pissed off in the past that tried to off her the other night. Remember that Senate hearing last year when the president of Que Trading threatened to punch her in the nose in front of the entire subcommittee?"

McLain chuckled. That had been humorous. The effete little Harvard-educated lawyer getting mad enough to threaten one of the SEC inspectors, and a female one at that, had fed Jay Leno's late-night joke machine for a couple of shows.

"That was one for the books," was all McLain said.

"We don't have any link to OptiMarx except some ill-defined hunch, woman's intuition, from Goldman. You want to face the heat when the NYSE shuts down because it can't handle the volume and we got the solution tied up in red tape? Those guys at Eleven Wall Street play rough. They'll be yelling from the rooftops that it's all your fault because you held up the OptiMarx system on a whim." Miller paused for a beat and then went on. "You think that will help your Senate race next year?"

McLain stared at Miller. Very few people knew that he was planning a bid for a Senate seat from New York. The office was becoming available and the timing was perfect. He would need the support of the New York financial community. His chances were near zero without it.

Miller was right. He needed the NYSE.

"Any possible political implications do not affect my decisions at all," McLain said coolly.

Miller winked when he responded, "Yes, sir. Of course, politics wouldn't affect any decisions from the SEC. We have to think of the greater good of the American investor. What I'm saying is that the American investor needs the OptiMarx system as soon as we can get it approved and get it out there."

McLain smiled. "Yes, I understand. For the good of the American investor. Set up the fast track, Stan. If Goldman can't play, if she has an overactive imagination, move her off the project and get someone in there who can."

The commentators on the TV screen had moved on to a discussion about the threat of a major blizzard in the Midwest and how that would impact the cost of natural gas. They were decrying market manipulation and price gouging. Neither man in the room cared. That was a problem for the Commodities and Futures Trading Commission, not the SEC.

Miller set his cup and saucer on the dainty little Sheraton tea table and scurried out of the office before McLain changed his mind. He couldn't wait to get down to the little park on K Street so he could call Mark Stern and give him the outcome of this meeting.

*   *   *

The Air Force C-17 Globemaster III roared ahead at forty-five thousand feet, flying well above commercial traffic. The flight plan had been filed in Rota, Spain, detailing a transpolar flight with a load of spare parts, the route taking them from Rota to Yokota Air Force Base, just outside Tokyo. Despite what the flight plan said, the nearest this bird had been to Rota was a midair refueling between the Canary Islands and the Iberian Peninsula over four hours before. It would be nowhere near Japan.

Now it was over northern Sweden. The plane would cross Finland and then Norway, just a couple of miles west of the Russian border. Bill Beaman sat in the passenger compartment of the big bird with his six-man team. Johnston, Cantrell, Broughton, Martinelli, and Dumkowski had all been on missions with him before. They were veterans of the terrible firefights in the steamy Colombian jungle that had claimed the lives of many of their comrades. The lone new member of this elite group was Jason Hall. The strapping tall black man was a communications expert, as well as an expert sniper. He had arrived on the team after a tour with the SEAL Leapfrogs exhibition parachute team. Although his quiet, competent manner and likable personality melded easily into the team, he was well aware that total acceptance would come only after he had proven himself on a mission. Had he been one of the other team members, he would have felt the same way.

After sleeping restlessly for a great deal of the long flight, everyone was giving his gear a final check now as they neared their target. It never hurt to be careful. Once they were outside, it would be too late to fix any problems. Check, double-check, then have your partner check, too. Beaman inspected Johnston's rig, and Johnston examined his.

Johnston checked Beaman's jump computer against the jump profile. The success of these HALO ("high altitude, low opening") jumps depended on far more than the jumper's instincts. The idea was to exit the plane at high altitude but not to open the chute until the jumper was close to the ground. This lessened the chance that the jump might be detected by anyone on the ground, even if they were tracking the plane on radar. A proficient jumper could travel over a hundred miles horizontally as he fell. The jump computer combined the technology of a powerful chip with a miniature GPS receiver and an accurate altimeter. By following the directions on the tiny screen, Beaman would leave the Globemaster at forty-five thousand feet over Norway and open his chute at less than a thousand feet above the ground, a hundred miles away, over a small frozen pond on the Kola Peninsula in Russian territory.

As he finished his inspection, Johnston asked, "Ready for this, sir?"

Beaman smiled and clamped his helmet on. "Sure, Chief. Just a little stroll in the park. Let's get everybody back in the bay."

The seven black-clad figures followed the heavily dressed Air Force jumpmaster to the rear of the cavernous cargo bay. It was empty except for the team and their equipment packs. All the lights were out to allow them to adapt their vision to the pitch-black sky outside. The only illumination was from a few dimly lit red bulbs low on the deck.

The jumpmaster yelled, "Two minutes from the drop zone! Depressurizing the bay. Everyone on oxygen."

As each man clamped on his breathing mask, supplied from a small bottle of oxygen strapped to his back, cabin pressure whistled down to the near vacuum of the outside. The huge rear cargo ramp rumbled down to reveal near total darkness. The sixty-below-zero air temperature chilled the SEALs, even through their specially constructed jumpsuits. At this altitude, it would be a real race to see which element would kill an unprotected jumper first, freezing to death from the bone-chilling cold or asphyxiation from the lack of air.

As the ramp rumbled down, a red light high up on the right side of the door flashed on. The jumpmaster held up one finger.

A minute to go.

Beaman cinched down again on his shoulder harness. He could feel more than see the presence of the rest of the team behind him.

The red light flashed out and a green one flashed on. Beaman strolled onto the ramp and took one long step off the back end. He dropped into the inky black void. The only sense of falling came when he saw the running lights of the Globemaster receding above and behind him as he tumbled away into nothingness.

Above him, the sky stretched out with a million stars. Below, a heavy layer of thick clouds, painted silver by the starlight, obscured the ground.

Beaman hated jumping into a cloud cover. There was no way to tell how thick it was. He might break through into good visibility and have plenty of time to orient himself if the computer should happen to pick that particular time to go on the fritz. On the other hand, the clouds might reach all the way to the ground. The first time he would know that the computer was wrong would be the millisecond before he experienced how very hard the frozen tundra could be.

Beaman couldn't see the rest of the team. They were too tiny against the vast expanse of the sky. He knew they were there, spaced out above and behind him, each following the computer to arrive at the same frozen pond over eight miles below and a hundred miles to the east.

There was no sense of speed as he fell. The thick padding of the jump helmet dampened the sound of the wind whistling by. The altitude reeled off on the tiny LCD readout as he followed the jump profile. It read right at fifteen thousand feet when he hurtled into the top of the thick cloud layer.

Instantly, any sense of orientation was gone. His one connection with the real world of gravity and frozen earth was the tiny readout on his left wrist. Everything else was lost in swirling gray mist.

Beaman intently watched the altitude and the countdown timer. Somehow, he knew that it must be time by now to open the chute. It seemed that he had been falling for far too long already.

Damn altimeter had to be busted!

Every sense he possessed screamed at him to reach for the D-ring and yank. His body was telling him the ground was rushing up too quickly. At any second, he would be smashed into an unrecognizable pulp somewhere in the frozen wasteland of northern Russia.

Still, Beaman fought the impulse as he had done so many times before in other HALO jumps. If he opened the chute too soon, he would drift miles from the landing zone, maybe into some camp or village where he would be discovered. At best the mission would be delayed for days or more while the team regrouped. At worst they would be discovered, then killed or captured. With all else that was going on in the world nowadays, SEALs parachuting into Russia would be gasoline on an already very hot fire.

He knew in his gut that he had been falling for too long. Never mind how, he knew it. Beaman realized that his subconscious was taking over, that he should rely on his instruments. He was reaching for the D-ring when the chute opened automatically.

He drifted down the last few hundred feet, using the time to settle his raging emotions. God, he hated jumping into clouds!

Beaman broke through the dense cloud bank a few feet above the frozen lake. He flared out and landed in the center of the body of water. He was just starting to gather in his chute when Chief Johnston fell through the thick, overhanging clouds and landed very near the spot where Beaman had first touched the ground. By the time Beaman had his chute folded, everyone else was on the ground, all landing within a few hundred feet of each other.

The jump gear was folded into weighted bags. They melted a hole in the ice with a thermite charge and sank the bags into the depths. The chance of someone ever finding the gear was very remote.

Twenty minutes after the team landed, the only sign that anyone had been there was a hole in the ice, and it was already covered over with a thin layer of new ice. It would be gone in half an hour.

There were also seven sets of ski tracks heading off to the east. With the light snowfall that had begun and the gusting wind, even those signs were gone within the hour.

Beaman's team was in. Now they could go about their business.

Chapter 17

Catherine Goldman stared hard at the handset before she put it back against her ear. She couldn't believe what she was hearing. It was only a couple of days after her run-in with the taxicab and a mere two weeks after she had started the OptiMarx testing, and now, out of the blue, Stan Miller was yanking her off the project. It didn't make sense!

There he was, as oily smooth as ever, on the other end of the line, giving her the hook. What in hell was happening here? She prided herself on being able to see around corners, but this one had sneaked up on her. So far, she couldn't quite put it all together.

"Catherine, you must take a rest," Miller cooed. "Look, you can just go on down to the Caribbean for a few weeks of taxpayer-paid vacation. I can imagine how bad you must feel after what's happened."

Her first instinct was to protest, to convince Miller the incident with the cab had not affected her work at all. "Stan, I'm all right. I'd prefer staying here. Besides, I'm convinced that I'm on to something—"

"Hold on!" the deputy director interrupted her. "Catherine, for once in your life, don't argue. It's all set up. You have been temporarily assigned as the SEC liaison to the Jamaican Stock Exchange. McLain insists."

Catherine Goldman spun her chair around and looked out the plate-glass window of the office. She could see across the dull gray Hudson all the way to the darkening Manhattan skyline. The sky was a washed-out, cold gray as it turned loose a few drab stray snowflakes. The only bit of color was the dark orange Staten Island ferry, churning downriver past Ellis Island and the Statue of Liberty.

She gritted her teeth. Jamaica sounded very good right now, but there was something about this sudden change of assignment that didn't seem right. Alstair McLain was not noted for great displays of concern for the well-being of his underlings. His reputation was more that of a slave driver, and one who had achieved his lofty position by climbing up the backs of his staff. She couldn't imagine why there was this sudden concern for her state of mind.

"I didn't even know Jamaica had a stock exchange," she said.

"Yep. It trades for two hours most afternoons. The rest of the time, you're on your own. Sightsee, lie around the beach, sip those little rum drinks with the big umbrellas sticking out of 'em, whatever you want to do."

"Stan, I'll admit that sounds inviting right now," she said with a soft chuckle, but then she was once again all business. "Look, I've got a lot of work to do here. You know I've never abandoned an assignment and I don't want to start now. Especially one as important and as complex as this one."

Leaving behind this colorless cubicle and its uncomfortable steel-and-vinyl chair wouldn't be all that difficult. The weather had been cold and miserable for weeks, too. She wouldn't miss Ustinov's crude advances or Andretti's disgusting habits.

There was something wrong here, though. Something she still couldn't quite pin down. There was no way she could walk away until she found what it was. This project was too important to the Exchange, to the whole trading system in the country.

"Damn it, Catherine, you won't be abandoning anything. Barry Sanderson is on this afternoon's shuttle headed your way. He'll replace you at OptiMarx. Just give him a 'turnover' and then you be on the morning flight from Kennedy to Kingston."

Goldman gasped. That was an impossible task. OptiMarx was a very complex operation with a myriad of twists, turns, and alternatives in the code. Even an ordinary turnover on a typical project would take several weeks. There was no such thing as an ordinary turnover to Barry Sanderson. Goldman had worked with him on other projects. He was two shakes to the left of hopelessly incompetent. The Harvard-trained inspector's main talent was that he could talk a great game. He always managed to replace his lack of technical competence with a sense of consummate bureaucracy. He had all the backbone of a reed in a windstorm and he did not belong on something as crucial and convoluted as OptiMarx.

"You've got to be kidding! A couple of hours to turn OptiMarx over to Sanderson? I'm not sure I could do it if I had a couple of years." She tried to keep the pleading tone out of her voice, but it was difficult. "Stan, give me a break here. I'm onto something big. It stinks to high heaven and I know I'm close to tracking it down. Just give me a couple more weeks and I'll prove it."

There was a note of finality in Miller's words when he responded, "Catherine, turn over to Barry this evening. That's final. You are off OptiMarx. McLain is fast-tracking it and Sanderson has the job."

The telephone line went dead in Goldman's hand. She couldn't believe it. McLain was fast-tracking a system that she knew was dirty. She had made it clear to them all that she had seen something screwy going on. She had never once cried wolf before without eventually turning up some hairy beast with big teeth. To top it off, this was one of the biggest projects in the history of the Exchange.

The director must be nuts!

Just as Goldman dropped the phone back into its cradle, a sudden thought hit her. A chill traveled all the way up her spine.

Or Alstair McLain himself was dirty.

"Conn, sonar. New contact on the thin-line towed array," Master Chief Zillich's voice boomed over the 21MC. Some of the crew called him "DeeJay" because he sometimes sounded like a radio announcer. He spilled the rest of his message in a rapid torrent. "Designate sierra four-four and four-five. Ambiguous bearings one-six-two and two-four-two. Holding a twenty-four hertz line on the contact."

Pat Durand grabbed the microphone hanging on the stanchion behind the periscope stand. "Sonar, Conn, aye. Master Chief, we'll get a leg on this course and then come right to resolve ambiguity. Do you think this is our friend?"

"Don't know yet," Zillich answered. "He should have a line at twenty-four hertz, but so do a lot of other people out here. Recommend new course two-nine-zero."

Durand replaced the microphone in its holder and ordered, "Station the section tracking party. Track sierra four-four and four-five."

With Durand's words, watchstanders put aside their normal duties and started the process of solving a submerged puzzle. Crewmen who normally pumped the sanitary tanks or monitored the battery jumped to man the fire control computers or the manual plotting tables, working to find the target's range, course, and speed while knowing only the bearing to it. It was a slow, trying, iterative process.

Durand reached for the MJ handset and spun the growler. It caused a loud whoop in Joe Glass's stateroom and interrupted the thought he was giving to a move he was about to make on the battered chessboard.

"Captain."

"Skipper, Officer of the Deck. I have a new contact on the thin-line array." He punched a series of buttons on the BQQ-5 sonar repeater and read the information from the screen. "Current bearing one-six-four and two-four-zero and drawing aft. Designate sierra four-four and four-five. Received frequency two-four-point-one hertz. I am finishing this leg, then coming to two-nine-zero to resolve ambiguity."

Glass leaned back and rubbed his chin. He glanced across the table at Sergei Andropoyov and smiled. "We have a new contact. It could be our friend. We are working to find out for sure."

Andropoyov nodded as Glass rose to leave. He half looked at the chessboard as he responded, "Good. Captain, I believe it wise that you are using caution and prudence."

Glass pulled the doorway curtain aside and stepped into the passageway. "It is always wise to be careful, Sergei."

He almost bumped into Brian Edwards heading for the control room. The XO was zipping up his blue poopie suit as he rushed down the narrow passageway. His hair was tousled and his face still lined from sleep.

"Pull you out of the rack, XO?"

Edwards grinned. "It's the plight of being second in command. Middle management. These things always seem to happen when the skipper is awake and I'm asleep."

"Yep, rank hath its privileges. Now, let's see if this is our friend swimming around out there. Everything ready?"

"Yes, sir. The COB and I finished up a couple of hours ago. We just got to sleep, in fact."

The two stepped into the control room. Except for a flurry of activity on the starboard side where Pat Durand and his fire control technician were working at a pair of computer screens to find a solution, the room was quiet. Glass allowed himself a slight smile. This was the way a professional crew was supposed to work. The teamwork was smooth and the information flowed quickly. They had learned a lot in a few weeks.

Glass noticed that the compass rose was swinging

around to the right. Durand must have finished gathering information on the first leg and was bringing *Toledo* around to the new course to get the second leg. There would be no information to process until the array had steadied up on the new course. That took at least ten minutes. It was a good time to sort out what they needed to do.

Durand saw Glass and stepped over to stand beside the skipper. Both men watched as Glass analyzed the information on the computer screen.

"Skipper, coming around to two-nine-zero now. Section tracking party is manned. No other contacts."

A cup of coffee materialized as if by magic. Glass took a sip.

"Slow and careful. No reason to hurry," he said, speaking to no one in particular, but to everyone in the room. "Let's slip up on this guy before he knows we're here."

Exactly ten minutes later, the bright little dots began to appear on the sonar repeater.

"Regain of sierra four-four," Zillich reported. "Best bearing, one-five-eight. Received frequency two-three point nine."

Glass absorbed the new information as he watched the display. The expected contact would be coming out of the south and heading toward the north, just as this one was doing. Could be the guy. Now they would need to slip around behind him and hide in his baffles as Glass drove *Toledo* in closer.

Glass was banking on *Toledo* being quiet enough to slip in close to the contact before they were heard.

Against most submarines in the world, other than the modern American ones, that usually worked.

Slowly, carefully, Glass brought *Toledo* in closer to the contact. They still couldn't tell if it was their target for sure, but Master Chief Zillich was now certain that it was another sub. That narrowed the possibilities a good bit.

After an eternity of maneuvering, listening, maneuvering again, Edwards called out, "Skipper, I have a good solution on sierra four-four. Course zero-one-three, speed twelve, range four-two hundred yards."

Just as he finished reporting, the underwater telephone squawked and a happy voice with a pronounced Southern accent rang out in the control room.

"Lima Two Golf, this is Four Tango Juliet. Hold your bearing two-two-five, range four thousand from me. Over."

They had been detected. "Son of a bitch!" Glass growled. "Well, XO, we know who the target is now. That's the *Tennessee*, all right. Looks like he counterdetected before we could get a shooting solution."

Edwards gazed at the deck. They had lost bragging rights on this one. Next time they ran into the Trident boat's wardroom, he and Glass would be the ones buying the beer.

Glass reluctantly pulled the UQC microphone down from its clip. He keyed it and spoke slowly, deliberately.

"Four Tango Juliet, this is Lima Two Golf. Roger bearing and range. Almost had you. Ready to start operations."

The response came back in a few seconds.

"Golf, this is Juliet. 'Almost' doesn't count out here,

Skipper. Y'all owe for the next round. Ready to start operations. On course zero-one-five, depth one-five-zero, slowing to two knots."

Glass glanced over at Edwards. "XO, tell Mr. Perkins to get ready. Have the COB go ahead and send the first group of our passengers into the *Mystic*." He spoke into the microphone. "Juliet, this is Golf. Roger course zero-one-five, speed two, depth one-five-zero. I am coming to course zero-one-five, depth three hundred, will slow to two when range is five hundred. Over."

Glass maneuvered *Toledo* until he was below the *Tennessee* and five hundred yards to the side. Although neither skipper could see the other boat, they steamed in close formation, as if a steel rod connected them.

Dan Perkins climbed up into the deep-sea rescue vehicle's pilot seat. Seventeen of the rescued Russian submariners were already sitting in the passenger sphere watching him. Gary Nichols was already in the copilot's seat and flashed him a thumbs-up.

Perkins keyed his microphone. "*Toledo*, this is *Mystic*. All systems ready for transfer. On internal power. Commencing disconnect sequence."

The locking ring with its power umbilical dropped loose. As Perkins flooded and equalized the skirt, *Mystic* came free from its grasp on *Toledo*'s back and drifted upward. At a top speed of three knots, the short distance took fifteen minutes to cover. The *Mystic* passed along the long, broad missile deck until Nichols saw the engine room hatch. He pointed to Perkins, who nodded, then keyed his microphone.

"*Tennessee*, this is *Mystic*. Landing on your engine room hatch in one minute."

"*Mystic, Tennessee*. Roger. Red carpet is rolled out for y'all. Welcome aboard."

Perkins maneuvered the DSRV until the skirt was above the hatch. He let it settle until it gently touched down; then Nichols started the pump to empty the water from the skirt. In just a few minutes, fifty pounds per square inch of sea pressure was firmly holding them attached to the Trident. Nichols opened the hatch and climbed down into the skirt.

The engine room hatch popped open and he looked down into the smiling face of Charlie "Red" Granger, the *Tennessee*'s skipper. The Russian sailors climbed down the ladder into what would be their new home for a while. *Tennessee* was out on patrol and wasn't scheduled to return to her home base at Kings Bay, Georgia, for another two months. The former *Gepard* crew would be safely hidden here, though, away from the eyes of the world and Durov's reach until things had played out.

Once the Russians were unloaded, *Mystic* lifted away for the return trip to the *Toledo*. The transfer, performed deep under the icy-cold Norwegian Sea, had been completed as though it were no more than a simple bus ride.

When it was time for the last group to leave, Joe Glass stood at the bottom of the escape trunk ladder alongside Sergei Andropoyov. He extended his hand and smiled.

"Sergei, go with God, my friend. You have done your country and the world a great service."

Andropoyov grasped the outstretched hand firmly and returned the smile.

"Joe, thank you for all you have done. We must have a toast together when this is all over. I will look forward to giving you the opportunity to once again capture my king."

With that, the Russian captain turned and climbed the ladder up into the *Mystic*. The hatch shut and he was gone.

Chapter 18

Boris Medikov slapped the final keys to log off the computer and leaned back to stretch his taut shoulder muscles. The encrypted message he had been reading was from his niece, Marina Nosovitskaya, and her report on the OptiMarx project was quite troubling. Someone was interfering with the carefully drawn plan. For a bit, he thought they had located the culprit. As it turned out, it wasn't Dmitri Ustinov overstepping his bounds after all, and now they were back to square one.

The apparent lack of response from the American SEC was a mystery to Medikov. By all rights they should be descending on OptiMarx in force. Instead, Marina reported they were fast-tracking the system. Someone with real power was interested in seeing the system online. That is, unless it was all nothing more than a very clever trap.

Medikov chewed on a thumbnail. He had never seen that level of subtlety by the Americans. He could believe such a plot in Russia, but not the United States. They were too accustomed to relying on raw power. If there was some other plot in the works, he couldn't imagine who was behind it.

Medikov stood and strolled around his suite as he usually did when he felt the need to think. The rooms were in the old state-run Mezhdunarodnaya Hotel. The plush suite occupied the top of the elaborate ancient pile of concrete, looking out over the frozen Moskva River. The hotel squatted near the very center of Moscow, meters from City Hall and the Russian Federation Government buildings. It had proved to be an ideal location for Medikov to make his headquarters when business brought him to Moscow. Besides, he loved the ornate gilded fittings and the deep-piled Persian carpets. There was little that could be considered regal splendor in the Russian capital and he welcomed any he could find.

The fact that the state also ran the security for the hotel was an added benefit, especially since Medikov virtually owned the far-flung MVD security apparatus. They monitored every room in the establishment as a matter of course, both with sound and video. Still, they wouldn't even think of bugging his penthouse. Not that he left that to chance. His people swept the place each day. More important, the MVD kept his competitors far from his lair. Yes, it was convenient to have them bought and paid for.

There were other benefits, too. High on the list was the excellent French chef the Mezhdunarodnaya imported exclusively for his use while he roosted here. Boris Medikov didn't like the standard Russian fare. His tastes had grown far beyond the poverty of his upbringing. Even now the remnants of an excellent coq au vin and the dregs of a bottle of Beaujolais of very good vintage sat on the Louis XVI sideboard.

To help him think, he poured a generous draft of Napoleon cognac into a crystal snifter and walked over to the picture window. Someone was bringing unwanted attention to OptiMarx by trying to kill the SEC inspector. There were two possible motives to consider for such a foolhardy move. Either someone wanted the entire project to fail or someone wanted to hide something going on inside the project, something that the inspector had stumbled onto.

There was only one way to learn which it was, who was doing it, and why.

Medikov turned from the window and stepped back into the suite's drawing room. There, three of his most trusted lieutenants were seated around the silk-brocade-upholstered conversation pit.

"Boris, we must do something and do it quickly," Nicholas Vujnovich growled when he saw his boss return to the room. The heavyset old Mafioso had served Medikov from the very beginning, standing by his side when Medikov was little more than a second-rate thug on the streets of Kiev. He was not all that bright, but he possessed the determined cunning and deviousness of a badger. "If this OptiMarx operation is going to make us any money, we have to deal with this interloper with finality. He must be terminated."

Medikov smiled. Vujnovich was predictable. If there was an obstacle in the way, it must be removed. If that obstacle proved to be a man, bullets were a perfectly acceptable means of accomplishing that end.

"Uncle Nicholas, if we go about wildly shooting up New York, people may talk," Medikov said. "It could have a far worse result than if we merely sat here and did nothing but drink cognac and smoke cigars."

"I hate cognac," Vujnovich growled. "It is a drink for a woman! Give me good Russian vodka. So what if the people in New York talk about us? What do we care, anyway?"

Josef Bogatinoff leaned forward and placed a hand on Vujnovich's beefy arm. "Nicholas, use that thick head for a minute before you start launching bullets all over America. Boris is saying that he thinks someone from OptiMarx is the problem. If this person should mysteriously disappear, or turn up filled with lead, it would raise questions about the system at a time when we would prefer staying below the radar of the authorities."

Medikov knew he could always depend on Bogatinoff. It had been several years before that he found the man, struggling through Moscow University, studying for his doctorate in economics during the day and hacking into computers at night. The man was brilliant! Since he had a beloved sister in the Ukraine with three children who were living under the munificence of Boris Medikov, he was fiercely loyal.

"Precisely, Josef! That's my concern." Medikov gave Vujnovich time to ponder the situation while he threw another log on the blazing fire. Even though the room was comfortable, the fire made a warming counterpoint to the snowstorm that still roared outside. The blowing snow masked the Kremlin even though it rose only a couple of kilometers to the west. "No, my friend, for once bullets are not the solution to the problem. We must dissuade this person with subtlety. Quiet threats are fine, but I suspect bribery might be even better."

Mikhail Gikoytski, the third visitor in Medikov's suite,

was banker for the Russian Mafia. It was his turn to raise a question.

"I agree with what you are saying. Violence is not the answer here. How do we locate this person who threatens our plan? It could be anyone inside the OptiMarx organization, even an investor, or someone on the outside but with a hidden agenda and enough money or leverage to get to someone inside."

Medikov smiled. "That is why you three gentlemen are booked on the next Aeroflot flight to London with connections to New York. Do whatever you must to find out who is shitting in our nest. Then please do whatever you must to eliminate the problem."

The three men stared at one another, then at Medikov's back as he walked to the far window to again stare out at the raging storm. How important was this mission that their boss was sending them to right its course?

After a few seconds they stood and left to do his bidding.

The blinding snow thrashed the seven SEALs as they struggled to cross the rugged, sparsely inhabited terrain of the Kola Peninsula. The howling wind, blowing straight off the ice cap to the north, drove the stinging snow against any exposed flesh, leaving it raw and bleeding. They could hardly see more than a few feet ahead as they skied through the scrub birch and fir forest. The trees sparsely covered the uplands between the fjords that cut the land south to north.

Despite the extreme weather, the SEALs were making

good progress. In truth, the weather was a blessing. Any sane man was inside, out of the storm, seeking warmth before a roaring fire. Bill Beaman and his team were the only ones foolhardy enough to be out on a day like this, but they had a goal, a mission that they had been ordered to perform. It would take more than a blizzard to deter them.

Since parachuting in, they had traveled by night, holing up in snow caves during the day. Otherwise there was always the risk of some hunter stumbling across them or a border guard aircraft spotting them during daylight. The terrain proved even more difficult than they expected, so they had fallen several hours behind schedule. The storm would allow them to extend their travel day, to catch up.

They had built a reliable routine: ski across the empty hilly uplands and then drop down to the fjord. Since the fjords were where they would most likely encounter the few people who lived up here, the risky part was crossing their frozen expanse. There, they were exposed. One at a time, they would scurry across the open ice, then hide in the gorse that grew on the opposite shore. Meanwhile, the others watched and waited with weapons at the ready.

So far they had crossed each fjord in the darkness of the Arctic night, but they were now approaching the first fjord they would cross during what passed for day at this latitude. They were well above the Arctic Circle, and the sun was little more than a golden glimmer on the horizon for a couple of hours each day. Day and night held only a vestigial meaning, but Beaman knew from many training missions in the Arctic that most people living and working here still kept to a normal diurnal routine. The body clock seemed to work most efficiently that way.

Johnston slid up alongside Beaman. His words were muffled by the neoprene face mask and then snatched away by the brisk wind. Beaman had to lean in to hear him.

"Skipper, the topo map shows we drop down here. It looks like a small stream that dumps into a larger river a few clicks to the north. You think we oughta be crossing it at high noon?"

Beaman nodded and shouted back, "Yep. I don't figure anyone else is crazy enough to be out here in this weather. Besides, for high noon, it's still pretty damn dark."

"Okay, Skipper. Just checkin'. It looks like open country for a click before we get to the stream. I'll spread the guys out to combat interval."

Johnston disappeared into the driving snow. Beaman knew that Cantrell and his SAW would soon be a hundred meters ahead of him, followed fifty meters later by Martinelli with the M-60 machine gun. Hall, the new guy, would be fifty meters behind with his satcom radio, followed by Broughton and Dumkowski at fifty-meter intervals. Johnston would be bringing up the rear, covering any trace of their passage.

They cautiously crossed the open ground. If anyone had discovered them sneaking across northern Russia, this would be the ideal place to attack. They would be exposed with no chance of finding cover on this barren stretch of ground. Beaman's every sense was on knife-edge, ready at any minute for the heavy rumbling roar of an AK-47 to drown out the howling wind. There was nothing to do but move forward and pray no one was waiting in ambush.

After an excruciating hour of skiing across the open tundra, they arrived at the bank of the stream.

The team gathered in a small grove of scrub birch at the shore of the little creek and rested for a few minutes. Beaman smiled as a fleeting thought ran through his head. This would be an idyllic site for fly fishing in the summer. The creeks up here were world famous for their trophy-sized salmon. He imagined how it would be returning here some warm summer day to try to snag a big one.

Right now, though, this was one of the most desolate places he could imagine.

No time for idle daydreaming. They weren't getting any closer to Polyarnyy by sitting here behind this poor cover, thinking of fly fishing.

Beaman lifted his tired body off the snow and signaled Cantrell to lead out across the ice. It was only a few meters to the other shore, which rose steeply through a heavier growth of fir trees that would provide them better cover but slow going.

The big SEAL grunted as he rose and slid out onto the ice. He was almost to the other side when there was a loud cracking noise. Cantrell dropped from view, but not before letting out a loud cry that echoed from the walls of the fjord. The ice, normally several feet thick, had somehow given way beneath the SEAL and he was now neck deep in the frigid water, his arms flailing as he tried to swim out of the hole he was in.

Beaman jumped up and peeled off all his equipment. He grabbed a rope from his pack and scooted out across the creek. Barely halfway across, he fell flat on the ice and sprawled out as much as he could to distribute his weight across the weakened surface. He slid forward on his chest until he could throw the line to the thrashing SEAL. He began to haul him back to safety.

The entire incident took less than five minutes, but now they had a real problem: a soaking-wet SEAL, exposed in an Arctic blizzard. Beaman knew he had no more than a few minutes before Cantrell would fall victim to hypothermia. His lips had already turned a deep blue. His speech was slow and slurred. Beaman had to get him warmed quickly before he went into shock. If that happened, the big SEAL was doomed. Medical treatment was too far away.

Chief Johnston moved upstream a few meters and crossed the ice-covered creek. When he reached the far shore, he signaled for the rest of the team to join him while he hollowed out a snow cave in the shelter of a large boulder. In minutes, the team moved the now delirious Cantrell into the shelter of the cave, stripped him of his stiffening clothes, and slipped him into a sleeping bag. Martinelli and Hall climbed in on either side of him, warming their teammate with their own body heat.

Cantrell began to shiver uncontrollably, but slowly, the combined warmth of the team brought him back from the edge. It took hours, precious hours they needed to get to Polyarnyy on schedule, to save him, but no one complained.

While everyone else was working with Cantrell, Johnston slipped back down to the stream. Something wasn't right here. They were in the Arctic. Temperatures were well below zero and had been for months. The ice here should be several feet thick and hold up even a big lug like Cantrell.

When Johnston saw steam rising from the open water, he thought he had the answer. As he got closer, he could smell the rotten-egg odor of sulfur. The salty taste of the water confirmed his suspicion. A mineral hot spring welled up beneath the stream right here in this spot. The combination of the high mineral content and the warm uprising water prevented a thick layer of ice from forming.

They would have to be more careful. Hot springs were common up here. Stumbling across another one like this could prove fatal.

Johnston cursed himself. He should have been watching for this. One of his men was in trouble and the mission delayed because he and the team had let their guard down.

The chief kicked hard at the snow as he headed back to the cave.

Jon Ward waited on the pier at Faslane as the *Toledo* steamed up the loch. He spotted Joe Glass standing on the bridge. His old XO sure seemed to have graduated into one fine skipper. And where Ward was sending him would tax every bit of Glass's skill and bravery.

It was just after nightfall at the British submarine base. Beyond the bright lights on the pier, the world was dark as two big Royal Navy tugs pushed *Toledo* snugly against the rubber camels alongside the pier.

"Welcome back, Joe. Sounds like you've been busy," Ward yelled up at Glass.

"Yeah, a bit. Sure could use a beer. What say you lead the way to the nearest pub?"

"In a bit," Ward answered. "I need to brief you and your XO first. We got a job for you, Joe."

"Might have known! Okay, in my stateroom as soon as the brow is across?"

Ward saw the crane swinging the brow into place just aft of the sail. "Sounds good. Permission to come aboard, Captain?"

Ten minutes later, the three officers crowded into the tiny stateroom. As Glass peeled off the heavy bright orange exposure suit that he wore on the bridge, they exchanged small talk and caught up on the news from home. Glass eased down into the captain's chair at the tiny table.

"Commodore, you didn't come all the way over here to deliver the mail bag. What's up?"

"Joe, we need you to go north again. This time with the ASDV. Bill Beaman is up there now doing a recon of the Polyarnyy Sub Base. We think they have a bunch of Akulas ready and armed to deploy there. Bill is supposed to put an eyeball on them. Then you're going to get him out."

"Wow! That's some story. I take it that the powers back in D.C. are taking to heart what Captain Andropoyov was saying."

Ward nodded. "At least they believe him enough to

risk checking it out. We're going to yank the *Mystic* off your back, slap on the ASDV, and give you a full load-out of ADCAP torpedoes. I want to have you under way again by tomorrow morning at the latest. With the SEALs up there and you loitering off the coast, we aren't saying anything to anybody. I don't know how long the political wogs can hold out keeping their traps shut."

Ward looked hard at his old XO. "Joe, I'm proud of what you've done so far on this mission. I'd love to give you a few days to uncoil, but we're in the middle of something the likes of which none of us have ever seen. God knows what's going on up there. I just want you to know how glad I am that we've got you and your guys on the front line of this thing. I'll make it up to you someday."

Glass nodded and allowed himself a weak smile. "No rest for the wicked, huh? Sounds like the pub crawling is indefinitely postponed."

"Afraid so. The tactical commander for this operation is a real hard-driving and heartless son of a bitch."

"Who is that?"

"Me."

Catherine Goldman watched the dingy waters of the East River zip past out the taxicab window. She knew that what she was thinking of doing would get her fired.

Alstair McLain didn't tolerate insubordination and Stan Miller had never forgiven her for that Que Trade incident the previous year. She was convinced that she was throwing away years of hard work, all that effort building a successful career, and it was all for a hunch.

Still, she knew she was right. OptiMarx was dirty!

She didn't have one shred of proof. What was she thinking? Why didn't she just take Miller's dictate and go on down to Jamaica?

The questions flashed through her mind, but she knew the answers already. There was no way she could turn her back on this, pretend everything was all right while she baked on some Caribbean beach. While that nitwit Barry Sanderson gave OptiMarx the high sign.

She would have to get busy and search even deeper and harder through the system code. Then she would be able to figure out what was going on. That would take some time. It would also take access to the system, which she no longer had. There was no way she could go back to the Exchange Place office. Not after her boss had yanked her off the project and reassigned her. If they had not yet changed the access codes, she might be able to log on to their remote access server and work remotely. If they had, she would have to get the new passwords somehow and make sure she didn't show up on the server logs if somebody bothered to check them.

Well, Chuck Gruver over at NYSE owed her a few favors. Maybe it was time to call them in.

The plan was forming up in her head already. It was risky as hell, but it just might work. Besides, there was no alternative right now.

She reached through the partition and tapped the cabby on the back. "I've changed my mind. Take me back to the Millennium."

They were barreling up FDR Drive, almost to the Triborough Bridge that would take them over toward La-Guardia, making good time despite heavy traffic.

"You sure, lady?" the driver yelled back.

"Yeah, I'm sure. I've never been surer of anything in my life."

The cabby shook his head and veered across two lanes of traffic for the next exit.

Chapter 19

Carl Andretti leaned back in his big swivel chair and swirled the Scotch around inside the crystal glass. He gazed at the amber liquid for a few seconds before downing it in a single gulp.

He deserved this treat. Things were going well. Very well. That troublesome bitch from the Securities and Exchange Commission had been canned and had disappeared from the face of the earth. All in all, it turned out to be a far better solution than having her eliminated in the far more drastic way he had attempted.

Andretti stood, strolled to the window, and gazed out toward the Lower Manhattan skyline. The buildings were stacked on the far side of the river like some kid's Erector Set project. The sun was setting behind him, painting the structures where the World Trade Center complex had once stood a deep golden color.

The fat CTO smiled. He couldn't imagine how or why Goldman had gotten herself fired off OptiMarx. It didn't matter. Sometimes it was better to be lucky than good.

Now the system was progressing through the SEC testing procedures at a record pace. This new guy, Barry Sanderson, seemed more interested in checking the boxes on his list than in looking at anything in depth. Better still, the guy was clueless when it came to technology. They would be able to hide anything they wanted to from him.

Andretti offered a toast to the Big Apple across the river. At this rate, the Exchange would be trading using OptiMarx technology by the end of the week.

He stepped to the sideboard and refilled the goblet from the nearly empty Dewar's bottle. They seemed to be making these bottles smaller anymore. One barely lasted through the day. No matter. A few more weeks and he could say good-bye to this rattrap.

That villa in Sicily was getting closer and closer. Plenty of sun and *vino*. He eased back down into his chair, tipped his glass this time in the general direction of the sunset, and imagined how it would be to watch the sun go down from a warm Mediterranean beach.

The jangling phone broke into his reverie. He snatched the handset up and jammed it to his ear. "Andretti. What the hell do you want?"

"Not very hospitable," Alan Smythe answered. "In keeping with your spirit of camaraderie, let me phrase my request this way: Get your ass into my office! Right now!"

Andretti stared at the now silent receiver, his ears still ringing from his boss's screeching command. He couldn't imagine what the hell was bothering the old fag now.

He pulled himself out of the chair and slipped the bottle back into the refrigerator. Might as well ensure that what little was left would be nice and cold when he got back. Maybe it would help extinguish the sudden fire that had flared up in his gut the last half minute.

He stumbled as he stepped out the door and made his way shakily down the hall to Smythe's office.

Catherine Goldman stepped out of the middle of the pedestrian traffic on the sidewalk and slipped into the doorway of the little deli at the corner of Hanover Square. Harry's Bar stood across the tiny square, a brick-and-stone reminder of the night she almost died along this very same street. Deli patrons passed in and out of the shop. None took any notice of the middle-aged well-dressed woman who studied the menu on the wall behind the counter.

The old Vietnamese lady behind the cash register impassively watched her television set as Goldman selected a pastrami sandwich on rye and a cup of coffee, black. President Adolphus Brown was on the TV screen, his face long and sad as he talked. He was saying something about a sunken Russian submarine. Goldman didn't quite catch it. She paid for the meal and found a booth in the back corner of the eating area.

Charlie Gruver walked in just as she sat down. He glanced around the dim interior, his shock of blond hair and his tall good looks giving no hint at all that he was the head computer geek at the New York Stock Exchange. He spied Catherine, sitting in the far corner, well concealed from any casual observer on the street outside. He walked over and plopped down in the booth, taking a seat across the table from her.

"I got your voice mail, Catherine," he said. "Sorry I missed you. I was out on the floor checking with the specialists." He reached across the table and snatched a half of her sandwich, bit off a chunk, and chewed for a moment. "Now, what is this about? You sounded awfully mysterious on the phone. You been reading those trashy novels again?"

She grinned as she watched him chew. "If I had known you were hungry, I'd have gotten one for me, too." She pushed the coffee cup across the table in his direction. "Here's your coffee. I think you take it black." She paused for a second as Gruver took a swig. "Charlie, I need a favor."

He chewed some more and swallowed before answering, "Lemme guess. OptiMarx?"

"Yeah."

"I heard you'd been replaced by Sanderson. Something told me that would grate on you just a little, tiny bit."

She nodded and looked him squarely in the eye. "Damn right it bothers me. What really bothers me is why. I shouldn't be saying this out loud . . . and especially to you . . . but I'm convinced that someone is trying to manipulate the system. I've got no proof of anything, but I found hints while I was testing. They canned me before I could get the goods or even figure out if I was definitely onto something. Giving me the heave-ho is enough to raise plenty of red flags. At least, it is to me."

Gruver took another sip of the coffee while she nervously folded her paper napkin into as tight a cube as she could manage.

"So, Catherine, your woman's intuition tells you that

the system is dirty. You know there's an awful lot of support for it on the floor. Especially with all the shit going on with the Russians and whatever that whole thing is about. It's putting a humongous strain on the old system. The traders are pushing for OptiMarx to go live. They've been waiting on this thing for a long time, you know. You throw a monkey wrench into the works right now, when we're so close to rollout, you will not be the most popular person in this town."

Darkness was descending outside. The glow from the streetlights softened the hard edges of the street. People hurried past, on their way home or out to the local bars for a stiff one after a hard day. Across the street, a young couple walked arm in arm into an Italian *ristorante*.

Goldman picked up a plastic mustard packet and seemed to be studying its label for a moment. She looked up at him again, her eyes hard and her mouth firmly set. "Charlie, I need access to the OptiMarx system so I can continue to test it. I need protected access so no one else knows I'm there except you. Not any of your IT people even. Will you help me?"

Gruver reached across the Formica table, took the mustard from her, and covered her hand with his.

"We've been friends for a long, long time. Of course I'll help. You will have to be careful just the same. There's a lot riding on this thing getting passed and online. There are some very big players wrapped up in this thing, and they play rough. Hell, you, of all people, should know that after what happened the other night." His eyes showed sincere concern when he looked into hers. "Cath, I don't want you to get hurt."

She lifted what was left of the sandwich and took a big bite.

"Don't worry about me," she said as she chewed. "I can take care of myself."

Cold, dark waves slipped back over the periscope as the *Toledo* returned once again to the deep. Joe Glass slapped the handles upward and reached to roll the red operating ring to lower the scope into the well. The lights of Scotland at the mouth of the Firth of Clyde faded away behind them until they were lost in the mist. The black sub slipped through the dark depths of the Irish Sea, heading north.

Glass stepped back from the periscope and glanced around the control room. The crew was dead tired after spending the last twenty-four hours back in Faslane loading torpedoes and supplies and strapping the ASDV to *Toledo*'s back. The normal banter he heard when heading out to sea wasn't there. The crew needed rest. The emotions from the last time up north had taken their toll on these men. The crew, like Glass, had expected to return home to Norfolk after their harrowing trip. They expected the debriefing on their little adventure to take weeks. Instead, Jon Ward was sending them north again, back into danger. They would need to be extra sharp where they were going.

There was already speculation among the crew about the mission. There was no disguising the ASDV. At sixty-five feet long and fifty-five tons, it was a little hard to hide. The black mini-sub was designed to be transported by a mother sub to the mission area. From there, its two-man crew used a lithium-ion polymer battery to propel them and a combat team of up to ten SEALs miles into shallow water. Everyone aboard would be housed in two dry, atmospheric-pressure compartments for protection from the frigid water. The ASDV was equipped with sophisticated sonars and navigation equipment so she could penetrate deep into a hostile harbor. There, she could deliver a combat team who exited through an airlock in the bottom of the mini-sub. It could settle to the bottom to wait, ready to recover the team when their job was done.

This crew had worked with the ASDV before. They knew it meant they would be running in close to the Russian coast. Probably very close. The ASDV didn't have either the range or the speed to be deployed from the safe, deep water that the submariners preferred. It had to be carried up close and personal.

Toledo's skipper walked back to the navigation plot. Edwards was going over the planned voyage track with Jerry Perez and Dennis Oshley. The pile of charts filled the plot table and spilled over onto the deck. Oshley was banging away on a laptop computer, figuring distances and speeds, while Perez programmed the GPS receiver with coordinates Oshley was feeding him. Edwards was double-checking everything the two men were doing.

"XO, when you three are done, I want to get all the officers together in the wardroom to discuss this op. Then tell the COB I want to have a 'rope-yarn Sunday' for the next twenty-four hours."

"Rope-yarn Sunday" was an old nautical term, left over from the days of the sail. It was a time for sailors at sea to take care of personal concerns rather than ship's work. This crew needed a day's break from normal shipboard routine.

"Yes, sir. I'll get everything set up."

"I'll be in my stateroom, talking to the SBU lieutenant," he tossed back over his shoulder.

Specially trained SEALs, members of a SEAL Delivery Team, operated the ASDVs. The mini-sub required a two-man crew as well as a three-man maintenance team that would remain behind on board *Toledo*. They had boarded just before departure, but in the rush of getting under way, Glass had not yet had a chance to properly greet his new passengers.

Lieutenant Hector Gonzales, the SBU team leader, waited in the passageway outside Glass's stateroom. Short, blocky, dark, and extremely fit, Gonzales looked the picture of a Navy SEAL officer. He snapped to attention as Glass stepped out of the control room.

"Stand easy, Lieutenant," the sub captain said with a wink. "There's not much room on one of these boats for all the formal military courtesies. Come on in and let's talk." Glass plopped down in his desk chair. "Okay, Lieutenant. How do you suggest we go get Bill Beaman's chestnuts out of the fire?"

"You know Commander Beaman, Captain?"

"Yep. We had a bit of fun together a couple of years ago down south. We had to bail him out then, too."

"You were on the Colombian op against de Santiago's druggies?" Gonzales asked. "Man, that one is a classic. They teach it at Coronado now."

"Makes me sound ancient," Glass replied with a grin. "I was XO on the *Spadefish* with Jon Ward. Anyway, the weather this time will be just a bit cooler."

Gonzales sat up straight and looked into Glass's eyes. He spoke in a low, straightforward voice. "Skipper, I want to be up front with you from the start. This is my first mission. I finished BUD-S and swimmer delivery school and showed up at the unit six months ago."

"Jon Ward told me that," Glass said with a nod. "He also told me that your skipper claimed that you were the best man he had."

Gonzales smiled wanly and went on. "There's more. My crew is inexperienced, too. We formed up three months ago, as soon as our boat rolled off the assembly line and showed up at Little Creek. We've worked very hard getting mission-ready, but we're real green."

"Hector, I appreciate what you're telling me." Glass cocked his head sideways. "I won't kid you. Where we're going will not be a cakewalk. You and your guys will do fine. Besides, we're just about even."

"Huh?"

"This is my first mission in command, too."

The young SEAL smiled some more and visibly relaxed. "Thanks, Skipper. Don't worry about us. When the time comes, we'll be ready."

"Come on down to the wardroom," Glass said as he rose from his chair. "It's time you met everyone and we let them in on what's going on."

When Glass and Gonzales stepped into the crowded wardroom, the skipper took his traditional seat at the head of the table and waved Gonzales to the one on his left. The assembled group waited, anticipating what their commander might have to say.

"Gentlemen," he began. "As you have probably figured out, since we have a rather large black wart on our ass and five passengers dressed in cammies, we are headed north for a little playtime with the SEALs. A couple of nights ago, a SEAL team parachuted into the Kola. They are doing a recon mission against the sub base at Polyarnyy." He glanced around the table. No one seemed to be breathing. Every eye was fixed on him. Every man knew Polyarnyy was Russia's most closely guarded submarine base and suspected what was to come next. "We are going into the mouth of the Murmansk Fjord to launch the ASDV. They will rendezvous with the SEALs and bring them out."

Doug O'Malley whistled. "Wow, this all sounds like a James Bond novel. I can't wait for the movie. I want Brad Pitt to play me."

Edwards swatted the engineer and retorted, "You'll be lucky if Drew Cary would take the part." He turned serious. "Now listen to what the skipper said. Nav, I want the charts for the fjord updated with all the intel we have, particularly their fixed ASW monitors and minefields. Weps, make sure the underice sonar and the secure fathometer are tuned. Have the weapons and fire control systems double-checked. Eng, you go over the power plant and the ship's noise signature. I want this boat to be so quiet that fish bump into her."

Glass stood when his XO had finished. He nodded at Edwards.

"All right, gentlemen," he said. "If there are no questions, you heard what the XO said. Get a good night's sleep and hit the decks running in the morning."

The Mi-8 Hip transport helicopter, painted in the dark gray color scheme of the Russian Navy, flared to land just beyond the collection of rough, shabby huts and settled down onto the ice. The side door slid open and Admiral Alexander Durov stepped out. He shielded his eyes from the wind-driven ice particles as he walked out from beneath the rotor blast. He marched right past the clutch of officers formed up as a greeting committee and headed for the large central hut.

Vasiliy Zhurkov, following in his trail, shrugged to the ice station commander as he walked past. The group trailed behind, confused and disturbed by the admiral's lack of traditional formality.

Durov trudged across the snow-covered ice, heedless of the covey of confused officers trailing in his wake. The noontime sun gave the southern horizon a pale golden color against the eternal gray of the Arctic winter night. A frigid wind out of the northeast blew ice crystals so that they rattled like hail on the flimsy metal sides of the huts.

Durov glanced around as he approached the sorry encampment and shook his head in disgust. The place was a pigsty. Spare equipment and leftover building materials lay where they fell, much of it scattered over the snow by the wind. Frozen garbage was piled up outside the door to the mess hut. The cooks hadn't even bothered to carry the refuse away from the building entrance. They had just tossed it out and let it freeze there.

Durov stepped up to the central hut's door and jerked it open. He stepped up into a small vestibule, facing another door. He yanked that one open, as the one behind him slammed shut. A burst of Arctic air accompanied the admiral into the stiflingly warm enclosure.

"Hey, shut the friggin' door!" The shout of indignation came with a decidedly American accent. "You born in a barn?"

Durov stopped and stared at the rotund man seated at a metal table, typing at a laptop computer. Smoke circled his head and the remnants of a large lunch and several empty beer bottles, along with a well-used ashtray, littered the table. The seated man looked up and saw who the newcomer was. There was very little change in his sanguine features when he recognized Durov. He rose and stepped unsteadily toward the admiral. He squinted through the cloud of smoke from the cigarette between his lips as he extended his hand. His words were slurred when he spoke.

"Mornin', Admiral. Or evenin', I guess it is. That damn sun up here! I can't tell one from the other. Harry Miller, stringer reporter for Reuters."

Durov ignored the outstretched hand. His face darkened as he looked at the man and his disheveled workspace with distaste.

"What are you doing here?" the admiral demanded.

"I got lucky, I guess. I drew the assignment to come up here and report on your valiant attempt at a rescue. Your government would allow one pool reporter and I drew the short straw."

Zhurkov stepped up behind Durov and whispered in

his ear, "Don't worry, Admiral. This one is on Medikov's payroll. Besides that, we are bringing in the beer by the helicopter load."

Durov nodded curtly. "Very well. Mr. Miller, you will stay out of the way. I will brook no interference with our operations. Time is not on our side right now and you cannot distract our men. Either Vasiliy or I will answer all your questions in due time."

Miller smiled and sucked another lung full of smoke from the cigarette. "Okay by me. Long as you keep me fed and I get a story out of this, I'm as happy as a pig in shit."

Durov couldn't help snorting as he spun on his heel and marched toward his private quarters. Zhurkov was hot on his heels.

"Keep that slob full of beer," Durov muttered to his aide. "Tell him how we are fighting the elements, risking our lives, all to try to rescue our men. Put a tear in your eye every once in a while if you can manage."

"Yes, Admiral."

"Vasiliy, I trust the crew you gathered for this operation is just as incompetent as I ordered."

Zhurkov smiled. "This bunch couldn't drill through this ice if it were melted and sitting in a bowl on their mothers' laps."

"Very well. Very well. Let's begin our desperate mission, my dear Vasiliy."

Chapter 20

Carl Andretti sauntered down the hall to Alan Smythe's grand office, in no particular hurry to answer his boss's summons. He couldn't help wondering what Smythe could be so upset about, but the CTO was certain of one thing. There was no way Smythe or anyone else could pin the failed hit against Goldman on him. That little scheme was far too well hidden. Not even Smythe knew of his ties to the New Jersey mob.

He winked at one of the young programmers as he passed her cubicle. What the hell? He probably was unhappy with the delivery schedule. Miffed that he was over budget on the QA salaries.

Or maybe it was just that his panty hose were riding up on him.

The flabby chief technical officer pushed open the door to Smythe's office without knocking and strolled right in. He stopped, surprised to see Mark Stern seated there on Smythe's sofa, huddled with his boss. Now, what in hell was "Old Moneybags" doing here? The two men seemed to be deep in a heated conversation, but the chat stopped the instant Andretti swung the door open.

No doubt about it. They were talking about him.

Even if they weren't, he wasn't privy to whatever they were saying.

A large-screen television set was blaring away on the far side of the room, with some reporter doing a stand-up in front of the United Nations complex. There were some kind of anti-U.S. demonstrations going on behind him, people yelling, waving signs, surging against a line of police in riot gear. The reporter was babbling on about some submarine accident.

Andretti's eyes swung back to the two men on the couch. Smythe glanced up and growled at him, "Most people knock when they enter a private office. At least they do in the civilized world."

"Hey, you called me and ordered me down here in one hell of a hurry. You sounded pretty upset. I thought you wanted to talk to me," Andretti retorted. He spun on his heel and headed back out the doorway. "When you're ready, I'll be in my office."

Stern jumped up and grabbed him by the elbow. "Hey, hold on a minute. Carl, sit down. We need to talk."

He waved Andretti to the chair across the coffee table from the couch.

Smythe reached for the remote and muted the TV. The crowds on the screen now ebbed and flowed in silence, seething around the U.N. Plaza while mounted policemen tried to keep them from spilling out into the traffic on busy First Avenue.

Andretti stood there for a moment, then held out a hand to Stern. "Good to see you again, Mark. What brings you out to the right coast?"

Stern shook the offered hand but maintained the grim, stony look on his face. "That's what we're here to discuss."

Andretti plopped down in the offered seat. He snagged a couple of candies from the dish on the coffee table.

"Okay, so where's the fire?" he said as he chewed.

The room was deathly quiet for a moment. Outside, night had fallen. The skyline across the river blazed with lights, reflecting with an orange, fiery glow off the deck of snow clouds overhead. It appeared traffic was at a crawl on West Street. A chopper lifted off from the pad just north of the New York Mercantile Exchange Building and swung upriver. Some hotshot executive was in a hurry to get to Westchester.

Stern cleared his throat and spoke. "Several things need to be taken care of, Carl. First off is the matter of the hardware we're using for the project and some reports I've been getting about your attitude concerning it. Frankly, I'm getting very tired of hearing complaints about the Bund System's equipment. That will stop right now. We're using their gear, and that's final."

Andretti started to register a strong protest, but Smythe was faster on the trigger. His voice was low and stone cold when he spoke. "Just sit there, shut up, and listen. This is a one-way discussion."

Stern nodded in Smythe's direction, slid back on the couch, and continued. "You are hereby elected the president of the East Coast branch of the Bund Fan Club. Anyone asks about Bund, you will sing their praises from the rooftops. I want that understood. Am I clear, Carl?"

Despite his thick appearance, Carl Andretti was quick enough on the uptake. He comprehended his position here perfectly. Stern wanted that Bund shit used on this project for some very compelling reason. It didn't matter what that reason was. Stern held the purse strings and Smythe had bought in. The CTO knew that he had nothing to win in this fight. He didn't want to ponder what he might stand to lose.

"Perfectly, Mark." He nodded his head meekly and snagged another couple of candies.

Stern's face twisted into a wicked little smirk. "Good, glad to see some cooperation. Now on to this SEC thing. I don't know who tried to whack Catherine Goldman and I really don't care. I want you to understand that the next SEC inspector that even so much as stubs his toe in the shower will result in the untimely disappearance of a certain CTO and his family." Stern paused for effect, his smirk now an intensely evil grin. "Carl, you aren't the only one around here with connections. Am I very clear on this point as well, my friend?"

Sweat had already popped out on Andretti's broad forehead at the mention of Catherine Goldman's name. Now his wrinkled dress shirt was soaked through. Rivulets ran down his jowls and onto his loosened collar. What the hell was happening here? Why was he now the focus of all of Stern's heat? Something was very wrong. Had the venture capitalist somehow discovered his mob connection? He seemed to be implying that he had. He was more than willing to play a game of "mine's bigger than yours."

Carl Andretti nodded meekly. A bit of the candy had

found its way into a loose filling and was beginning to hurt like hell. The rest of it had rekindled the fire in his belly.

Stern's wicked smile melded into one of satisfied triumph. "Good. Very good. Glad to see we understand each other. Nothing like a little man-to-man talk to clear the air." Stern reached and snagged one of the candies for himself, inspected it, then popped it into his mouth. "Oh, and there's one final point I'd like to bring up for both of you." Smythe had been still, watching his CTO get the tongue-lashing he had long deserved. He was enjoying the pained look on Andretti's shiny, fat face. His head snapped around to look at the VC, not sure now where he was going. Stern still had the broad smile on his face, but his eyes were hard. "That little scheme that you two thieves have cooked up? The one that screws around with the transaction times on the system? Quite clever. Of course, I'll be taking a fifty percent share of the proceeds."

Smythe's jaw dropped. Andretti stared in disbelief.

Mark Stern had just pulled the pin on a grenade and dropped it in their midst.

The room was quiet as a tomb. Below them, on the plaza, life went on as normal. People rushed and jostled to catch the PATH home.

Here, the floor had just fallen out from beneath the pair of computer executives.

Stern rose and headed for the door. He grasped the doorknob, but then turned and looked back at Smythe and Andretti. "You won't have any more problems with the SEC. Sanderson will play ball. I expect the system will be up and running, ready for launch by the end of the week."

Both Smythe and Andretti opened their mouths to protest, but their words would have been directed to a closed door.

It was an intense, agonizing pain that yanked Quartermaster Dennis Oshley from a deep sleep. It knifed through his gut, the blinding flashes of distress doubling him into a fetal lump. His tormented cries woke Bill Dooley, a torpedo man who was sleeping in the bunk above Oshley's in the tightly packed bunkroom.

"Hey, Dennis," he called out. "You okay, man?"

The only reply was another groan. Dooley hopped out of his bunk and stood on the deck, then yanked back the blue curtain to see Oshley, deathly pale and bathed in sweat. The quartermaster was bent double, squirming as he clutched his stomach.

Dooley turned and ran out of the bunkroom, bumping into Sam Wallich, the COB, in the passageway.

"COB, it's Oshley," he panted. "He's real sick. In his bunk."

Wallich rushed into the darkened bunkroom to find Oshley hunched over and groaning in the center of the narrow passageway. Even as Wallich approached, another wave of pain seemed to course through the quartermaster's body. He screamed and fell to the deck, writhing in agony.

"Go get Doc," Wallich cried to Dooley. "He's sleeping in his rack in the goat locker."

Dooley disappeared, heading for the Chiefs' Quarters

to roust the ship's corpsman. "Doc" Halliday dispensed medicine and fatherly advice for the crew of the sub, and, like most submarine corpsmen, he was specially selected and trained to do his work all alone and far from any medical facilities. He could handle most medical emergencies that might arise, or at least be able to stabilize the situation until the boat could get to a location where the patient could be transferred to a better-equipped facility.

Halliday had over fifteen years of experience treating people. That included combat duty with the Marines during the Iraq War. He knew when he could handle a problem and he also knew when he was in over his head. One look at Oshley and he knew he was outclassed by whatever was causing the quartermaster's agony.

He yelled over his shoulder to Wallich, "COB, tell the XO I need him right now and tell the CO we need to do a medevac real quick."

Wallich didn't question the corpsman or hesitate for a second. He disappeared in search of Edwards and Glass.

Halliday persuaded Oshley to lie down. He tried to question the suffering patient, but the sick man was in no condition to answer him. He moaned and held his stomach, oblivious of everything but the pain. When Halliday tried to palpate Oshley's abdomen, the sailor screamed louder.

There was something terribly wrong. Gallbladder? Kidney stones? Duodenal ulcer? Halliday didn't know and he didn't have the test equipment aboard *Toledo* to find out. There was nothing to do but make Oshley as comfortable as he could and get him to a hospital as fast as possible.

Halliday was still taking Oshley's blood pressure when Edwards walked in.

"He going to be okay, Doc?" the XO asked.

"Not unless we get him to shore real quick," Halliday answered. "There are half a dozen possible causes of these symptoms that I know of and who knows how many more I don't? I can't treat any of them. Almost all are fatal without treatment."

Edwards gulped. He had never been in a situation like this before, one where the life of one of his crew depended on his decision. The bulkheads of the already confined space seemed to be closing in around him. After everything they had been through already on this trip, he couldn't believe this was happening now.

"XO, I need you to unlock the controlled medicinals locker," Halliday said. "This man needs a painkiller pretty bad."

Edwards grabbed the key from around his neck as he headed for the medical corpsman's office. On the cramped *Toledo*, most space had to be dual purpose. Doc Halliday shared his tiny examining room with two mini-torpedo tubes, called signal ejectors, designed to shoot flares and evasion devices. Their plumbing protruded well into the closetlike room. Just aft of them, welded to the bulkhead, was a small locked cabinet that contained the various narcotic medicines that might be needed. Edwards had the key. He opened the lock and removed the vial that Halliday had asked for, and wrote on the inventory sheet that he had removed the drugs and why. Then he headed back to the bunkroom.

Halliday took the vial from him and measured out a

dose. He reached over and injected the suffering sailor. Oshley relaxed as the shot took effect.

Edwards looked on with noticeable discomfort. For all his cockiness, the young executive officer hated needles.

"XO, nothing more you can do here," Doc said under his breath. "Why don't you go help the skipper get us to somewhere for a medevac? I'll take care of Oshley."

Edwards nodded and headed toward control. Joe Glass was waiting for him at the periscope stand.

"How is he, XO?" the skipper asked.

"Not good, Skipper," Edwards answered bleakly. "Doc says we need to medevac him as soon as we can."

"Okay, let's go up and talk to the boss. Iceland looks to be the closest place. Last I heard, NATO still kept an SAS detachment at Keklivek Air Base."

The young XO fell to and got to work, plotting out the track to Iceland. At least he was doing something to help now. That relieved the frustration of seeing one of his crew suffering and not being able to do anything about it.

He felt better, but not much.

Catherine Goldman sat in front of the computer screen in her hotel room, waiting impatiently for the laptop to boot up. She opened the slip of paper Chuck Gruver had given her and tapped in the special IP address. When the screen changed and requested it, she added the user ID and password. If this didn't work, she had no idea what to try next.

The screen blinked a few more times and the familiar

OptiMarx logo appeared. She was in! A few more keystrokes and Goldman was staring at the jumble of source code for the elaborate trading system. She dove in and began trailing threads through the labyrinth of complex symbols, making notes on the pad on the desk next to her right hand. The outside world faded from her consciousness as she sank deeper and deeper into the complicated computer code that made up the system.

She had been digging for at least an hour before she spotted a line of code that didn't seem to make sense. She followed it as the logic led her to another subprogram. There the code sent her to a kernel in a different functionality. There didn't seem to be any rhyme or reason to it. It was leading her all over the massive system, from one unrelated module to another.

She couldn't imagine why someone would deliberately write code like this. The system was supposed to be optimized for speed. Jumping all over creation for no apparent reason just didn't make sense.

Slowly, she began to put all the pieces together. A pattern was starting to materialize out of this convoluted jigsaw puzzle. When the errant lines of code were ultimately assembled, they would perform a function that someone had taken great strides to keep well hidden. Now it was a matter of determining what that mysterious function was. Maybe then she could figure out who was behind it.

Catherine Goldman rubbed her stinging eyes, then stood and walked over to the little dresser. Her mind still on the strings and variables she had been studying, she tore open a packet of hotel coffee and brewed a pot in the little urn that rested there. She talked to herself, argued with herself as she worked. She poured herself a cup of the brew as she eased back down in front of the laptop. She was oblivious of the sun rising, to the first determined rays of sunlight that found their way through the thick curtains that covered the hotel room windows.

Admiral Alexander Durov sat at the conference table in his office at Polyarnyy Central Command Building, sipping hot tea as he glanced at the morning copy of the *London Times*. Sure enough, there on page one was a picture of the ice camp and a sad, detailed story of the admiral's brave but tragically futile efforts to rescue his lost nephew.

Quite good copy from that drunk American, Miller, Durov thought. He could write despite his disgusting personality.

He tossed the paper aside. The world was busy screaming at the Americans, demanding that they admit their responsibility for the tragedy. President Brown's weak protestations, his ineffectual claims that the United States was in no way involved with the tragedy sounded shrill, disingenuous. Deny as he might, he still had no explanation for what had happened, and the world was buying the Russian version.

The scenario was heating up nicely. Now it was time for the next step in the plan.

Durov stood and looked at the other men who were seated around the table, talking among themselves. These six men would soon lead his half dozen Akula submarines to sea. They were the heart of his plan. They would be the heroes of the restored and reinvigorated Russia!

Durov smiled as he allowed his gaze to pass along the faces of each of the men. He had handpicked them years before, after determining their loyalty, nurturing their dissatisfaction with the sickening decline of their beloved country, and bringing them along to this moment. They were schooled in the most arduous submarine training he could devise. Lesser men would not have survived the strain. Indeed, the "class" had once been over twice this size. This group had come through the fires, tempered like fine steel. The weaker ones had burned like dry wood.

"My sons, we have waited for a long time for this moment," Durov said, his voice as strong and firm as it had been in years. "All our careful preparations and plans are in place. The clock is ticking. It is time for action."

The six men sat on the edges of their chairs, watching their admiral with rapt attention. There wasn't a sound in the room except Durov's voice and the loud ticking of the antique mantel clock.

"You will start your deployments tomorrow night. Captain Vivilav, you will get *Vipr* under way at twenty-two hundred, just after the American KH-11 spy satellite passes overhead and drops beyond the horizon. You will travel down the fjord and submerge as soon as possible. You will then proceed as follows."

Durov stepped over to a map of Russia and northern Europe that covered one wall. He pulled a laser pointer from his pocket and traced a route around Norway and down the Skattegat into the Baltic Sea.

"Very well, sir," the tall, thin submariner said, his eyes glowing with pride.

"Captain Vivilav, you have the honor of taking station off St. Petersburg and most closely duplicating the *Kronstadt*'s heroic exploits. You will have seven days to be on station. You will not be detected by any naval force, including our own. Is that understood?"

Anatol Vivilav smiled and nodded. "It will be as you ordered. My boat and crew are ready."

Durov smiled and answered, "Good." He then went on to station the others around the northern flanks of the homeland from the White Sea to the Kara to the Barents. They would each be getting under way on subsequent nights, starting with the ones that had to travel the longest distance to their stations.

Durov stepped over to the heavy, ornately carved sideboard and clutched the bottle of vodka. He moved around the conference table, pouring a glass of the *Rodina*'s finest "warrior's milk" for each captain. He filled his crystal shot glass and held it upward in an outstretched arm, saluting his men, his country, the revolution.

"To Mother Russia!" he shouted hoarsely, his lips flecked with foam. "May her sons defend her honor!"

The sound of chairs scraping on the hardwood floor filled the room as the six submarine captains jumped to attention. They answered Durov's toast with "To Mother Russia!"

Each of the seven sailors downed the fiery liquid in a single gulp.

*   *   *

Bill Beaman pushed hard, working his way up yet another wooded hillside. These hills seemed like an endless
series of obstacles. Push up a mount, cross the ridge, only
to be faced with the next. The wind blew endlessly, too,
pelting them with snow and ice crystals. The fir branches
seemed to reach out to slap them, while the birch scrub
tried its best to maliciously trip them.

Just after they crested the latest slope, he signaled for
a five-minute rest stop in the lee of a wind-cleared rock
outcropping. Johnston skied up alongside the SEAL
commander, unbuckled his pack, and sat down on a large
stone. The rest of the team deployed around them, setting up a quickly constructed defense perimeter. Anything less than a well-armed battalion would be in for a
very nasty surprise if they stumbled across this hornet's
nest.

Johnston stretched his back and grimaced.

"Damn, Skipper," he complained. "I'm too old for
this shit."

Beaman chuckled. He had heard the same complaint
from Johnston at least a dozen times a day for the last
four years. They had served together for so long and
shared so much danger that they often thought alike, like
an old married couple. Sure enough, Beaman was opening his mouth to tell the chief to make sure the team took
time to eat when Johnston spoke up.

"We'd better make this a half-hour stop. Guys need
chow and time to fill their CamelBaks." The SEALs had
forgotten canteens years before. Instead, they carried
water-filled soft bladders on their backs, always ready to

give them liquid through a hose that they could suck on. The bladders needed to be refilled with melting snow.

Beaman nodded as he reached for his topo map and GPS receiver. The little device locked on to three of the constellation of satellites high above them. The LED readout gave their position within a couple of meters. His best estimate was that they would be above Polyarnyy in two more days if they maintained this pace. The time spent treating Cantrell after he fell through the ice had cost them.

They were way behind schedule. There was no way for him to know how short the fuse on the international crisis had burned by now. Beaman pursed his lips in deep thought as he studied the map. It showed a road just a couple of kilometers to the south of where they were now. Though it was nothing more than a rough stretch of access road, it ran right up to the sub base's main gate.

Then he saw another line just to the south of the road. It was a railroad track that ran past the base and crossed the fjord, heading to Severomorsk.

Beaman stared hard at the chart for a few more seconds. He motioned Johnston back over close enough for him to be heard without talking loudly.

"Chief, what say we head south a little and see if we can play hobo? We could hop ourselves a freight. We might just pick up a little time."

Johnston winked back. "Now you're using your head for more than a hat rack."

Nicholas Vujnovich and Josef Bogatinoff stepped off the British Airways flight together and walked into the JFK International Terminal. There was only the two of them.

Mikhail Gikoytski was on an Air France flight scheduled to arrive in an hour. Two Russians traveling together were no more unusual than a couple of businessmen. Three might raise suspicions, and especially with all the tension gripping the planet nowadays. They split up in Heathrow right after they stepped off the Aeroflot flight from Moscow.

The pair passed through customs without a problem and walked out to the curb. Less than an hour after they landed, they were in a cab headed for Brighton Beach. As they wound along the Shore Parkway, Bogatinoff watched Jamaica Bay flash by out the taxi window while Vujnovich pulled a cell phone from his pocket and punched in a number. He listened as it rang twice. A female voice answered.

"Marina, my dear, it is Uncle Nicholas. We have arrived. Let's meet for supper at the usual place."

He smiled as he hung up and then nodded to Bogatinoff. Marina Nosovitskaya now knew that they were in New York and the meeting place was confirmed. It would be Murphy's Bar on Third Avenue. It was so crowded and loud that no one could monitor any meeting that took place there.

First they had to meet their contact in Brighton Beach, to gather their weapons and arrange for a place from which to operate. It was so much easier to get weapons in the United States, no worries about having to smuggle them in. Renting a place required nothing more than easily acquired papers and some cash. Everything was so much easier in such a free country.

He winked at Bogatinoff and turned on the first smile he had used since leaving Moscow.

"It is a great country, right?" Vujnovich asked the cabbie in the best English he could muster.

The driver didn't seem to understand his question. Vujnovich studied the man's unpronounceable name on the driver's ID placard. He likely spoke less English than the Russian Mafiosi.

The cabbie shrugged and kept his attention on the tangle of traffic ahead of them.

Chapter 21

The weather during the helicopter ride out from Thurso, Scotland, was as rough as any Jon Ward had ever experienced. Strapped into the *Sea Hawk*'s passenger seat, he was pitched around violently. The SH-60 didn't seem to mind the weather, though, as it rushed across the dark sky, six hundred feet above the storm-tossed Norwegian Sea.

This is no fun, he thought. The way to traverse seas like this is down six hundred feet below the surface in a nice, smooth-riding nuke boat. Far better than up here in this contraption, a machine that somebody had once described as ten thousand spare parts flying in loose formation.

Had to hand it to the SH-60 pilot, though. The guy unerringly located the cruiser they were aiming for in the turbulent gray sea. He kissed down on the tossing, postage-stamp helo deck the first try with barely a bounce.

Ward was glad to jump out of the helicopter and down to the deck. He was almost blown off by the wicked crosswind as he exited the chopper and dashed across the platform toward the hangar. Two of the deck crewmen grabbed the grateful submarine commodore and helped him into the shelter of the hangar.

The skipper of the *Anzio*, Commander Bob Norquest, was waiting there to greet the new visitor. He held out a hand and Ward took it.

"Glad to have you aboard, Commodore. Admiral Donnegan called and gave me a quick brief on what you need. Crusty old bastard, isn't he?" Norquest smiled. "We're happy to help out. Sounds like a lot more interesting stuff than what we were scheduled to be doing today. We're heading for the Norwegian coast now."

Ward nodded and returned Norquest's smile. "Yep, that's Donnegan, all right. You won't find a nicer guy or anyone better to have in your corner when the going gets rough."

As if for emphasis, the cruiser made a sudden roll to starboard as both men braced themselves against a bulkhead. Ward tossed the "brain bucket" cranial helmet and survival vest to a waiting deckhand. He turned to Norquest and said, "Skipper, if you don't mind, I'd like to get to work right away. Let's get up to Combat and find out what's going on."

"Right this way, sir," Norquest said. He stepped through a hatch on the forward port side of the hangar deck and down the passageway.

Ward was right behind him.

There was something comforting about the efficient hum of activity in the big, darkly lighted room. The banks of computers and screens flashing with a myriad of complex images were on the cutting edge. Sailors sat in front of the screens, analyzing the displays, or scurried between stations. Conversations were hushed. The room had an atmosphere of quiet professionalism.

Jon Ward had occupied the battle commander's seat in the Combat Information Center since arriving on board two hours before. The Aegis cruiser, USS *Anzio*, still pitched and rolled, bucking the rising seas north of the Hebrides. Nobody in the CIC seemed to take notice.

Ward had already familiarized himself with the complexities and capabilities of the Aegis combat system. The three huge flat-panel displays on the bulkhead in front of him could be set up to show any bit of information available to the U.S. military. It could all be directed by the trackball that rested under his right hand. Just in case the three screens weren't enough, two fifteen-inch ones were mounted on either front corner of his desk console. Just above his left hand was a switch bank that hooked him up to listen to twenty-four different audio circuits. What's more, he could pipe a different circuit to each ear while talking on a third if he wished.

Talk about information overload! Ward thought.

Still, there was no doubt that this was the perfect command post for this operation. If he couldn't be on the front lines with his boats, at least he would be at sea, and the Aegis CIC was the perfect place to gather information and direct his team. It was better than being aground in some stationary blockhouse back in Norfolk.

"Commodore, message from *Toledo*," the watch officer said, breaking into Ward's reverie. "They need a medevac. Got a crewman with a real bad internal problem. Gall-bladder's probably gone gangrenous, but the corpsman isn't sure. Skipper reports he's heading for Iceland at top speed."

Ward nodded and took the sheet of yellow paper. He read the words. They were pretty much what the watch officer had said. Joe Glass had a seriously ill quartermaster and was afraid the guy wouldn't make it if he didn't get him to a hospital. Glass would not have diverted if the seaman's condition had not been critical.

"What's *Toledo*'s current position?" Ward asked. "Someone plot it?"

"It's up on the center screen. Contact sierra one-eight-seven, the little blue inverted arc."

Ward moved the pointer over to the position. It was a good four hundred miles to the Iceland coast.

"It'll take him at least eight hours with that ASDV strapped to his back. Get me Keklivek on the phone."

"Button six," the watch officer said. "CO of the British air-sea rescue unit stationed there is already waiting to talk with you."

Ward nodded acknowledgment with a slight wink as he punched the button. These skimmers were pretty good!

Catherine Goldman sat back, massaged the bridge of her nose, and stared at her notes. The sun outside was setting behind the OptiMarx building across the Hudson, but she hardly noticed. She had just spent twenty-four straight hours hammering away at the OptiMarx code, but the convoluted jigsaw puzzle had fallen into place. The picture was disgustingly clear.

It had been there all along. Her intuition had proved correct once again. As happy as she was that she had found it, she still mentally kicked herself for taking so long.

The key proved to be in the short sales, that unique Wall Street practice that allowed traders to sell stock they didn't own. They borrowed it instead. Traders "shorted" stocks when they believed the security was going to fall in price. Then they could buy the stock later at a lower price to replace the shares they borrowed, pocketing the difference.

Someone working on the OptiMarx code had spent a lot of time and talent to get around the rules for these short sales. Wall Street discovered back in 1929 that if there were no restrictions placed on when short sales were allowed, unscrupulous traders would drive the price continually down, generating widespread panic while they reaped enormous profits on the mayhem they set loose. Rules were put in place to prevent such manipulation, and those regulations were even more important today when communications and trading were virtually instantaneous. A short-sale panic would be devastating on The Street now. It could even lead to a market collapse.

Catherine took a long swig of her lukewarm bottled water. She even had a tad of admiration for the intricacies of the plan itself. There was a lot of money involved here. No wonder someone had tried to kill her when they thought she was getting too close to their little scheme. People with the resources to set a ploy like this in motion had a lot at stake. They also wielded considerable power and wouldn't hesitate to use it.

Goldman paced from one end of the little hotel room

to the other. She wished she still smoked. A cigarette might help her think. She grabbed a six-dollar Snicker's from the room's mini-bar instead and chewed absently as she pondered her next move.

The decision would be a big one. She had to make the right choice on how to handle this information. She could tell Alstair McLain, her boss, or Stan Miller, the second in command. Maybe she should confide in Chuck Gruver at the Exchange. She trusted him.

She sat back down in the chair in front of the computer and stared hard at the blue-white screen.

McLain was out. He was, after all, the one who wanted to shut her up and ship her off to Jamaica. She still couldn't fathom that the head of the SEC Market Reg Department would be a party to such a brazen plot, but something was fishy there. She didn't want to risk going to him if she could help it.

Chuck Gruver was not a good idea, either. At least not yet. She didn't want to put an old friend in danger when there was little he could do at this point.

That left Stan Miller.

It was well after normal business hours down in D.C. and Stan wasn't the type to stick around to work late. Most likely in one of those Georgetown bars he liked, seeing if he could grab one of the thousands of interns who gathered in D.C. like moths around a flame. Miller had a wife and kids out in McLean somewhere, but his exploits in the bar scene were the office gossip.

Miller was the best bet to call. Despite his playboy reputation, he seemed to be a straight shooter around the office.

Goldman hesitated a moment, tossed the candy wrapper on the rumpled bed, ran the list one more time in her head, then grabbed the phone and punched in Stan Miller's cell phone number.

Marina Nosovitskaya pushed her way through the crowded bar, ignoring the stares she got from most of the men as only one accustomed to such attention could do. The Midtown business crowd was celebrating the end of another hectic workday, drowning minor frustrations or celebrating small achievements at the center of the business world in an ocean of Irish beer. She rebuffed more than one lewd advance from bleary-eyed, middle-aged Lotharios as she made her way through the smoky room. That, too, was the usual course.

She spied familiar faces there in the back corner. The three Russian Mafiosi rose as one to greet her, smiling, bowing in her direction, kissing her hand in turn. Marina lowered herself into the offered chair, demurely smoothing the skirt of her smart gray suit over her long, slim legs. None of the three men seemed to take any notice of her body at all. They were nothing more than the elderly honorary uncles greeting a favored niece. A chilled glass of white wine sat there awaiting her arrival, drops of condensation running down its stem onto the table.

She smiled as the stocky, tough criminals bustled to make her comfortable. It was heady to be able to wield such power over men with no more than a smile or an inch of revealed flesh. Or to have a real uncle as formidable as hers.

Nicholas Vujnovich spoke first once the pleasantries were finished.

"Marina, your uncle Boris sends his affection and greetings. He is looking forward to the day you return to the homeland once and for all."

Nosovitskaya sipped her wine. She set the glass down before she answered, "Yes, Uncle Boris would expect that. I must tell you that I am having far too much fun here in New York City. America is not such a bad place as we have been led to believe, Nicholas. I may stay here. The men here are so much fun and so very sexy. Oh, and I am sure I could continue to help my uncle in his business ventures here as well."

Vujnovich chose to ignore her comments. He sipped at the dark brew in the glass he held. He looked at her for a moment before he shifted the topic to the one that was on all their minds. "Marina, we need to discuss the operations of the OptiMarx system. Your report about the attempted execution of the SEC inspector caused a great deal of alarm in Moscow. You know we can't afford for such an act to risk the plan at this crucial juncture. What do you know of this?"

Nosovitskaya thought for a moment; then she answered, "I don't trust the senior executives there. Especially the CEO and CTO. Smythe, the CEO, is a smarmy little shit, English. He prances around in fancy clothes, pretending he is an important man. Lords it over everyone. He is a possibility for this stupid attempt."

She took a taste of her wine. "Then there is Andretti. He is the most disgusting man I have ever seen, fat, a real slob. He thinks he is a genius, but I have not seen any sign of it. Usually drunk by noon. I'd start with those two. They spend a lot of time together with the door shut and I would wager they are involved if there is some type of conspiracy. Yes, it is likely one or the other or both of them."

Mikhail Gikoytski grunted, his eyes squinted and his jaw set. Even Marina Nosovitskaya, who had grown up amid the Mafiosi, shivered at the look on the man's face.

"We will start with the fat one, the pig. We will squeeze him a bit and see if he squeals. I suspect soon we will know who threatens our plan. That threat will be eliminated."

Bill Beaman watched from where he lay on the frozen ground beneath a scrub birch as the train rumbled up the steep grade, plowing snow out of its way as it came in his direction. The ancient diesel could barely tow its heavy load and push the snow aside at the same time. It groaned and complained as it tried. A long line of flatcars stacked high with oil pipes stretched out behind the engine, down the slope and across the bridge below.

The rusty diesel reached the top of the grade, turned the bend at the crest of the hill, and disappeared from view. Beaman flashed a hand sign to Johnston, who was hiding lower down the bank, closer to the tracks. The rest of the team members were hiding at ten-meter intervals coming up the steep slope.

With the train's crew now out of sight, the SEAL chief rose to a crouch and dashed from his hiding place to grab the short ladder on one of the flatcars as it passed. He swung himself up onto the car and then reached to grab

Dumkowski, running right behind him. Then Cantrell clambered up, followed by Broughton.

Martinelli tripped over the scrub he was hiding behind, but managed to reach the ladder with a lunge. Cantrell grabbed him and hauled him up to join the rest. Hall followed and leaped up onto the car as well.

Beaman saw that the last of his team was aboard the car. Time for him to go. He broke from his hiding place and dashed across the open ground. The train was starting to pick up speed as more of the cars topped the grade and headed down to the other side. Beaman had to run all out, moving as fast as he could in the heavy gear to try to catch the ladder.

It was right there in front of him. He reached out to grab it and made ready to leap up onto the bottom rung.

He never saw the rock before it broke loose under his foot as he tried to push off for the jump. He tripped and started to stumble. The heavy steel wheels squeaked as they turned mere inches away from where his feet were dragging. Beaman tried to keep his grip on the ladder, tried not to lose his hold and sprawl beneath the wheels.

Someone reached down and grabbed the big SEAL commander by the collar, hauling him up to safety by sheer strength.

Beaman rolled onto the car platform, gasping for air, more from the realization of how close he had been to getting himself sliced in half than from the exertion of the run. He nodded his thanks to Hall, the SEAL radioman. Hall waved him off.

"Wasn't anything," he mumbled.

"You just saved my ass is all," Beaman said.

"Hell, I just didn't want to have to explain to the chief why I let you get run over," Hall growled, then turned to join the others stowing their gear amid the stack of pipes on the swaying flatcar.

Joe Glass braced himself against the pitch of the sea. The icy spray poured over the top of the sail. If it weren't for the bright orange survival suit, he knew he would already be soaked to the skin and numb from the cold. The suit at least kept him more or less dry. It was still damned cold and so dark he couldn't see the bow of the *Toledo* fifty feet ahead of him.

It had been sixteen hours since he had sent the message for help. They had raced across the Norwegian Sea to arrive here, just outside the twelve-mile territorial limits of Iceland. Doc had done everything he could for Oshley, but it was easy to see that the quartermaster's only hope was to get to a hospital.

Glass and Doug O'Malley stood shivering in the bridge cockpit. The low steel coaming provided little protection from the crashing seas and none from the biting cold. The hatch at their feet was shut to keep the cold seawater out of the control room below. They were alone out here on the wind-driven sea, connected to the warmth below by nothing more than the thin thread of a microphone.

He couldn't imagine how they were going to do a medevac in seas like this. The dark gray waves tossed the *Toledo* around like a tiny bit of flotsam on a very big and rough ocean. There was no way he could put men out on the main deck for a normal transfer. The only way possible was the risky procedure of doing it from the top of the sail, assuming the chopper that was on the way could find them on a night like this.

Couldn't call it off, though. Dennis Oshley lay down there on the deck just below the hatch in intense pain, clinging to life. The only thing they could do for him out here was to ease the pain a little with Doc's painkillers. If he couldn't pull off the rescue tonight, Oshley might not be around in the morning.

It was decision time for Joe Glass. He could risk the lives of several of his men and a helicopter crew, and put this vital mission in jeopardy, all for the medevac of a single sailor in this weather. Or he could call it off and hope to make it to Norway. He didn't know if Oshley could hold out that long.

Glass grinned and shook his head inside the cover of the survival suit. That's why they give me the command pay, to make the hard decisions, he thought.

Just then a Super Puma chopper dropped through the cloud bank a thousand yards off the port beam, its searchlight stabbing through the darkness, looking for them. O'Malley popped Glass on the shoulder, pointed excitedly, and hollered over the wind, "There it is, Skipper!" The bellowing blow snatched his words away but Glass knew what he was saying.

A wave, higher than most, rose up above the sail and broke over them, filling the cockpit with bitingly cold seawater. The two men stood there stoically while the swirling water drained away.

"Brisk," Glass commented drily.

"Yep, damn brisk!" O'Malley shouted back, smiling.

The bridge-to-bridge portable radio crackled. The voice coming out had a distinct British accent.

"Alpha Sierra Six, this is Romeo Five Bravo. You ready to transfer, Yank?"

Glass grabbed the radio and crouched down into the protection of the cockpit, trying to find shelter from the bawling wind. He pressed the push-to-talk button and yelled, "Pretty rough weather down here! What do you think?"

"Bit of a blow," the Brit pilot answered. "Best get on with it, don't you think?"

Glass smiled. There was nothing like British understatement when the going got rough. He was right. No sense making the rendezvous out here in this storm if they weren't going to go ahead and try to get their man to the help he needed.

"Roger that!" Glass yelled into the radio microphone. "Coming to course zero-one-five to head into the wind. Making five knots. Taking fifteen- to twenty-degree rolls."

"Roger. Coming around now. I'll hover fifty feet above you and lower the basket when you are ready."

"Have them open the hatch and lift Oshley up here," Glass yelled over to O'Malley. "We'll only have a few seconds to get him hooked up."

The engineer nodded and used the microphone to speak to the men below. The access hatch popped open and Wallich's head poked through. He handed O'Malley the clear Plexiglas grounding rod. Shaped like a short shepherd's crook but with a copper core, it was designed to pass the high-energy static electric charge that the whirling helicopter had built up. Anyone who grabbed the cable from the chopper without first grounding it could receive a very nasty, even crippling, shock.

The COB climbed through the hatch and leaned back down to help lift Oshley's basket stretcher up into the cockpit. Doc Halliday stood a little farther down the ladder, easing the stretcher past him, all the time watching his patient. The quartermaster was mercifully unconscious, oblivious of the maelstrom happening around him. Even farther down the ladder, Bill Dooley pushed upward, lifting his friend up to safety and treatment.

Bill Edwards watched it all from the bottom of the ladder, coordinating the work in the access trunk with the team that was driving the ship. Because of the helicopter hovering overhead, the periscopes were housed. That meant that the people in the control room were flying blind. The XO stood there watching everything, doing all he could to make sure the transfer went smoothly from his end.

The Super Puma hovered over the pitching, tossing submarine. Glass saw the crew chief lean out the chopper's side door and begin lowering the cable. O'Malley tried to catch it with his hook, but the wind whipped it about, making it seem to leap away each time he reached for it, jerking it just beyond his reach. It swung past once more and he tried another time. No go. Again and again he tried but failed to grab it. Desperately, he reached out one more time, and came within millimeters of falling over the side into the roiling sea.

Joe Glass grabbed a handful of survival suit and hung on. When O'Malley turned to Glass, there were tears in his eyes.

"Doug, it's no use," Glass yelled. "It's just too rough, too much wind. You'll never get hold of it in this."

O'Malley started to insist that he continue trying, but the radio sizzled again.

"Yank, we'll lend you a hand. Got a rope that'll reach from the sail to the water?"

Glass grabbed the radio and answered, "Yes! It'll take a couple of minutes to get it up here. Hold on."

"No trouble," the pilot answered. "Already missed happy hour at the officers' mess, I'm afraid."

Edwards had eavesdropped on the exchange on the control room receiver and had already sent Dooley running down to the torpedo room to grab a rope. When he got back with it, they fed the line up to Glass in the bridge cockpit and he tossed one end overboard. As the rope dangled down over the smooth side of *Toledo*'s sail, he grabbed the 7MC microphone and ordered, "All stop. Rig out the outboard and shift to remote." They needed to slow for the swimmer who was preparing to drop from the chopper. Even at *Toledo*'s slowest speed, they would race away from anyone in the water. Besides, Glass couldn't risk getting the line fouled in the screw. The outboard would allow him to maneuver the boat to keep the line in the lee, partially protected from the wind and seas by the bulk of the submarine.

The Super Puma hovered fifty feet above the water and fifty yards from the sub. While Glass and O'Malley watched, the black shape of a wet-suit-clad swimmer appeared in the open door of the helicopter. He dropped out, into the black, frigid water. With seemingly little effort, the man swam the short but choppy distance over to the sub and grabbed the line. Hand over hand, he hauled himself up the side of the boat as if he were climbing the ladder from the pool at the YMCA.

O'Malley whistled. "Now that's balls. The water temperature is twenty-eight degrees. We're over twelve miles from land and it's dark. You sure as hell wouldn't catch me doing that!"

"You can be assured that guy's been through worse," Glass answered. "He's with the Brit SAS. It's their answer to the SEALs. Some swear they're even tougher, but I'd never say that to a SEAL."

Within moments, the swimmer was standing beside Glass in the cockpit.

"Afternoon, Yank." The SAS man handed Glass a sealed plastic bag. "This morning's *Daily Mirror*. Thought you'd enjoy page three." The *Mirror* was world famous for the semiclad beauties featured each day on the inside page. "Sorry we didn't deliver before breakfast."

The SAS swimmer reached down to his belt and unclipped the light line that arced upward and still had him tethered to the helicopter. Handing the line to O'Malley, he said, "Just pull this line to reel in the cable. Should help get everything connected up, Bristol fashion."

O'Malley reeled in the line, all the while watching the cable pay out, coming down until he could reach out and grab it with the hook. Seconds later, Oshley's stretcher was attached. The swimmer grabbed the line, attached himself with a D-ring on his harness, and motioned up to the chopper pilot. The pair lifted up into the air and into the waiting chopper.

Minutes later, the helicopter dropped its nose, spun around, and disappeared into the clouds and darkness.

It would take O'Malley and Wallich a few minutes to rig the bridge before they could once again slip below the waves and proceed at all due speed to whatever it was that fate and the Russians held in store for them.

Glass dropped below, shaking his head as he went. He never did have a chance to have his chat with Dennis Oshley, the superserious young quartermaster.

Chapter 22

Admiral Alexander Durov accepted the snifter of dark amber brandy that Boris Medikov offered him. Both men stood at the window, considering the Moscow skyline.

"Beautiful view from up here, is it not? You fail to see the grime down there."

Durov grunted. "No time for admiring the view, Medikov. It's time for work. You may be assured that those dimwits over in the Kremlin are not passing their time gazing out the window." He took a sip of the brandy. "We would all be better off if they were."

A television set chattered away from the far corner of the room. Some minor politician in the *Dumas* was on his feet before a lectern, his face red with anger as he demanded that President Smitrov take stronger action against the murderous Americans. He screamed for a formal denouncement, for the breaking off of diplomatic relations unless the Americans admitted their fault and turned over the assassins for a war tribunal. He called for war if they did not. The camera panned until it found President Smitrov, sitting stolidly, eclipsed behind the president's dais. He studied papers in front of him, ignoring the rabid speaker.

"The tension is building," Durov muttered with what

passed as a smile. "Our leader is showing his true colors, mostly a rather pallid gray."

Medikov nodded, turned, and walked over to the long couch that rested in front of the fireplace, close enough for anyone seated there to feel the pleasant warmth from the crackling flames. The Mafioso had no interest in the polemics of revolution. Fine if Durov and his cadre wanted to win back some ancient, idealistic way of life they believed had once existed. Medikov and his partners were after one thing: profits. There was money to be made in upheaval, but only if one were quick and decisive.

Medikov set his brandy down on the end table and plopped down amid the plush cushions of the couch. Durov took a seat in an upholstered straight chair, crossing his legs and adjusting the crease on his immaculately tailored uniform trousers. The admiral was not comfortable in the decadent opulence of this penthouse suite. It did not seem right that his plan would somehow help support this lifestyle. He assuaged his conscience by reminding himself that he was restoring his country to its rightful place in the world order. It was necessary that he consort with Medikov and his type long enough to achieve a glorious return to power. He would deal with the man and his plunder later.

Medikov opened an ornately carved cigar humidor and offered it to Durov before he took a smoke out for himself. "You should try one, Admiral. They are the finest that our old ally in Havana produces. Try one. You will find them to be sweeter than the kiss of a virgin."

Medikov puckered his lips and held the humidor toward the admiral, but Durov shook his head.

"No, no, Boris. Such a luxury is much too rich for an old sailor's taste. We need to discuss our progress."

"Very well, then," Medikov said with little more than a nod. Then he was occupied with his elaborate cigar-lighting ritual. He snipped the end with a gold clipper, then rolled the cigar through a lighted taper while he sucked gently on it. Satisfied, he leaned back, his head wreathed in pungent, sweet cigar smoke.

Durov squinted at him through the haze and har-rumphed. "If you are quite through, perhaps we could find the time to plan the salvation of Russia."

Medikov's jaws flexed and there was a brief flash of anger in his dark eyes. He held his temper, though, as he leaned forward and gave the admiral his attention. He held the cigar in his hand like a pointer. "Of course, Admiral. You are right. We need to coordinate our efforts now." He drew on the cigar and exhaled a perfect ring, watching it drift slowly toward the room's high, ornate ceiling. "I will take care of my end. I am pleased to report that my operatives in New York tell me we are ready with the OptiMarx project. It will go live by the end of the week. That will give us one full week of pure profit before we crush the American financial system. Our actions should bring the proud American capitalist system to its knees in a few days."

Durov watched the smoke rising toward the ceiling, a wistful look in his eyes. "Then the time is very near. The first of my submarines goes to sea tonight. In a week, they will all be in place, ready to launch their missiles. We must be in a position to move within a few days of then.

Longer and we run the risk of them being discovered and raising suspicions."

Medikov nodded and waved the cigar, ignoring the thick ashes that fell onto the clean white carpet. "I will leave the grand strategy to you and your people, Admiral. One thing does bother me, though. As you know, I am quite fond of the comforts I find here in Moscow. You will not be firing nuclear missiles, by any chance, will you?"

Durov half smiled, baring his teeth. The look gave his face an evil cast, like an animal glaring at its prey. His eyes were dead cold. "Oh, but is it not a dreadful question? How would you know if I lied to you? I could say no, and be lying. I could say yes, and still be lying."

Medikov sucked on the cigar and sent another cloud of blue smoke upward before he replied, "Well, that is hardly an answer. With the truth, I would be able to properly plan which way to move."

Durov's voice was flat, devoid of any intonation. "Now you see the problem that our great leader, President Smitrov, will soon face. You can be assured that I will not tell him any more than I am telling you. Maybe yes, maybe no. Take a chance. How lucky do you feel?"

"Admiral, there is a difference. We are partners, you and I, in the revolution."

"Even the right hand must have some control over the left, my friend," Durov said, then stood and went back to the huge window.

Medikov rolled his eyes.

The smoke from the Cuban cigar had gathered ominously in the far corner of the room's ceiling. It looked ever so much like a dark, brooding thundercloud.

Admiral Tom Donnegan was not having a good day. General Ward Tambor, the national security adviser, had been on the phone a dozen times since noon the day before and had not been in a good mood at all. The sun was just starting to peek over the horizon again and the admiral still had not come up with an answer that would satisfy the politico.

President Brown was being painted into a very tight, uncomfortable corner and Ward Tambor had the job of getting him out. Unfortunately for them all, Donnegan couldn't give them a good out without endangering the SEAL team he had dispatched into the Kola. Or risk giving too much information about the submarine he had sent up there to extract them once their mission was complete. They all knew that Donnegan was not likely to give even a hint to anyone, including the president, his commander in chief, if it might endanger any of his people in the slightest. The risk of any of the media getting wind of what was going on was too great.

No, Brown and Tambor would have to ride out the storm. That sort of shit came with the job!

The desk phone jangled again. Its ring even sounded angry, impatient. Tambor again! The answer would be the same: "I'll tell you all I can when I can."

Donnegan almost let it ring itself out, but there were too many other calls this could be. He snatched it up. It was his aide, handling the phones in the outer office.

"Admiral, Commodore Ward is on the secure IM-

MARSAT line," the young lieutenant said. "He wants to talk to you."

I sure as hell want to talk to him, Donnegan thought.

He punched the lighted button on the phone and heard the scratchy hissing of an encrypted satellite phone line. He smiled, picturing Jon Ward on the other end, seated in the command center on the cruiser. Donnegan would always see Ward as the gangly Navy brat of a kid who practically grew up on his own back porch. Or as the brave-faced but grieving teenager after Donnegan became a substitute father when Jon Ward Sr. was tragically lost. Ward's old man had been Donnegan's best friend since college. The families had grown up together over the years and it was natural for the younger Ward to turn to Donnegan when things were tough.

Donnegan sighed as he listened to the hollow sound of the phone line. That was all a long time ago. Jon Ward was now a captain, commanding a submarine squadron, but right now he was out there somewhere in the Norwegian Sea watching over one of the most crucial operations in modern time.

"What do you have, Jon?" The admiral spoke into the phone's mouthpiece. "How did it go?"

Donnegan heard a dry chuckle on the other end. "Good morning to you, too, Admiral. Nice of you to inquire about my health." Donnegan's inability to make small talk was a standing joke between them. "The medevac went well, given the weather. The crewman is in the hospital at Keklivek. The doctors there say it's a damn good thing they got him there when they did. Another hour or so and they'd have lost him."

"Good. Glad that turned out. How are Glass and the *Toledo* coming?"

"The diversion cost them ten hours. There's not much chance of making up that time. He can't rush around the North Cape at flank and expect to stay undetected for very long, and I imagine everybody . . . friend or foe . . . is just a tad skittish right now. I still haven't heard anything from Beaman, but we'll let him know about the delay when he calls in next time."

"Okay. Things are starting to heat up on the political and diplomatic fronts, Jon. I've never seen anything like this. Russia is in one hell of an uproar and they're getting plenty of guests joining their little party. Tambor told me that Smitrov is trying to keep a lid on things, based on some of the snippets we've been feeding him, but he's in real danger of losing control. We've given him precious little to help our case, either, until we confirm what's going on up there. We could tell him we think there's going to be a coup, but he's not going to believe us unless we can point to something solid."

Ward grunted. "Not good. I don't like the sound of any of this at all. I hate to think about all those nervous fingers on the launch buttons all over Russia. After what we learned from Andropoyov, it sounds as if Durov's plan may be in play."

"That's the way I see it, too. We need that eyes-on information, Jon. If we can get some kind of clue of what Durov might be going to do, then we can figure out how to respond. Give Smitrov a heads-up before all hell breaks loose. Meantime, we pretty much have to sit here on our asses while those bastards call us everything vile and putrid. And while even our friends . . . what few we have left . . . wonder out loud why we don't just fess up and take our lumps. I'm afraid now that President Brown and his guys are about to recommend we ignore the coup threat and cop some kind of plea. Maybe admit we might have collided accidentally with one of their boats or some such damned foolishness, just to get the heat turned off for a while. Anything to get most of the world and the opposition party off his ass."

"They can't do that, Tom. We're getting close to having a look-see and I'll still bet my dolphins that we'll get proof of what Durov's up to when Beaman and his guys get to Polyarnyy."

"Well, don't worry about all that political crap. You just do your job. You'd better be ready for anything up there, Jon. Pray Beaman can get us something we can go on."

"We're going to head north on *Anzio* and wait in the vicinity of Vestfjorden. I figure we'll put out the SQQ-89 and do a little fishing."

The SQQ-89 was the sister of *Toledo*'s thin-line sonar array. It was designed to be deployed a mile behind one of these Aegis ships and to detect very low frequency tonals from submarines. Carefully employed, it was as good as a submarine at finding another boat.

"Jon, I don't even have to say it, I know, but I'm glad you're going to be up there. Son, you better be damned careful."

Donnegan hung up the telephone without waiting for Ward's reply.

"Thanks, Dad," Jon Ward said to the dead circuit.

*   *   *

Bill Beaman peeked over the top of the ridge. The SEAL team had jumped from the flatcar as the old diesel chugged its way up the last hill before reaching Murmansk Fjord. Once they were back on foot, the climb to the top of the ridge had not been too difficult, except for crossing the highway. They were a lot closer to civilization now. Roads were plowed. Cars and heavy trucks whizzed past at dizzying speeds. Getting the entire team across the two-lane road without being discovered took the better part of an hour.

The sprawling Polyarnyy Submarine Base was only two kilometers to the north of where they now hid, but it might as well have been on the moon. The giant covered submarine dock hid the piers from view. Several layers of menacing defenses stretched between here and there. The perimeter road was heavily patrolled. In the hour Beaman had spent watching, at least eight BTR-80 armored personnel carriers had slowly driven down the road. There seemed to always be at least one of them visible.

The BTR-80's gunner had a clear field of fire for two hundred meters away from the road. He could chop anything short of a main battle tank to pieces with his 14.5mm KPTV machine cannon or mow down any person silly enough to get in his sights with his coaxial 7.62mm machine gun. The BTR-80 could carry seven additional fully equipped ground troops protected inside its armored sides. Odds were these were manned with troops ready to charge out and mop up any bits and pieces that might be left lying around after the fireworks stopped.

The ground between Beaman's position and the perimeter fence was clear down to the snow, with not even a bush or a rock for cover. A jackrabbit would have trouble sneaking past. Even if they were able to crawl low enough to try to get across the barren ground, there were probably buried motion detectors and video cameras, too.

Beaman squinted but he still couldn't see any way across the open space. Even if there were a way, it would not help much. The other side of the perimeter road butted up against a four-meter-tall chain-link fence topped with some very wicked concertina wire. Another ten meters inside and there was another matching fence. The space between was mined, according to the briefing documents Beaman had seen. The guard towers at every corner had a clear shot down at anyone caught between the fences.

Chief Johnston slid up to the ridgeline alongside Beaman. He had been scouting farther to the east.

"Shit, Skipper," he grunted. "That place is guarded better than Fort Knox. Any ideas how we're going to get through all that crap?"

"I was thinking of calling the Starship *Enterprise* and having Scotty beam us over there," the SEAL commander said with a humorless smirk.

Johnston didn't show any amusement, either. He rarely cracked a smile.

"Or maybe we can sprout wings and fly on over there," was all he said. At least the chief's sardonic sense of humor had survived the rough transit in.

"Chief, if it was an easy mission, they would've just

sent the Marines to do it. We'll find a way inside that mother. And some way back out again. Let's wait and see what Martinelli and Hall found over to the west. They should be back in an hour or so."

"Maybe they found us a nice, flower-lined path through the woods," Johnston said, but there was still no hint of a smile on his face.

The early morning sun illuminated the street below Catherine Goldman's hotel room window, but it would be several hours before it swung around enough so it could spill inside the cramped room. Down below, the West Side Highway was crawling as the clotted traffic moved in spurts and fits in both directions. Faceless people poured into the world financial center, scurrying along at a hurried pace.

Remnants of a room service dinner vied for space on the tiny dresser with a used-up breakfast tray. The bed was littered with sheets of paper, notes from another night's work.

Goldman wrinkled her nose. She had to get this place cleaned up. It was starting to smell. Not wanting the distraction, she had sent away any maid who had knocked on her door over the last two days.

Goldman took a deep breath, eased down on the bed, punched in the well-remembered phone number, and then listened as it rang. She expected it to go unanswered yet again. Maybe he was gone somewhere on business. Maybe he was taking a few days off.

Someone on the other end picked up and happily answered, "Securities and Exchange Commission, Market Regulation Division, Stan Miller. May I help you?"

She took another deep breath. "Yes, Stan, it's Catherine."

"Catherine! Great to hear from you!" Miller's voice was jovial. "I expected to have a postcard and a bottle of authentic Jamaican rum from you by now."

"Stan, to be honest with you, I missed the flight."

Miller didn't miss a beat. "No problem. I know it was short notice. We'll get you on the next one. The Jamaicans'll never have to know that you partied for a couple of days before you decided to show up down there. We won't tell McLain, either. No reason to get him upset."

"I don't think I can take that flight, either. Stan, listen to me. I missed the flight to Jamaica on purpose. I wanted to spend some more time checking out the OptiMarx system. I just spent the last two days tracking through the code." She paused for a moment, listening for some kind of reaction. Any kind of reaction. There was none. There was only the soft hum of the long-distance line. "I found exactly what I suspected. Someone went to a lot of trouble to hide a routine in there. It's a busy little bit of code designed to bypass the short-sale rules."

Surely that bit of news would get a rise out of Miller, she thought, but there was only silence on the other end. Goldman was expecting an outburst of some kind, anger at the effrontery of the crooks who would meddle with the trading system in such a daring way. Or maybe a grateful gush of relief that she had uncovered the plot before it could be put into disastrous play. Even a scolding for disobeying orders.

Silence was the one response she didn't expect from Stan Miller.

"Stan, did you hear what I said? The system is dirty! Someone got in. If it goes live that way and whoever wrote in those routines begins to use them, the panic could collapse the whole market in no time."

Miller cleared his throat and answered, "Jesus. Yes, Catherine, I heard you. I hear what you are saying. That was great work. Damn good work. Listen. Here's how we'll handle it. E-mail me all your work. Use my personal address. You know it? Good. Less chance we'll panic somebody here who might be doing server maintenance at just the wrong time or something. I'll get a task force to work on it right away. Don't worry about that. Now, listen. You tell me where you are and then you stay right there and don't move. We already know that whoever the bastards are behind this . . . uh . . . this scheme like to play for keeps. You understand me? Don't let anybody see you. Stay there. I'll send a team of agents to get you out of there and take you to somewhere safe until we put an end to this nonsense. You understand what I'm telling you, Catherine?"

Goldman fought back tears. She could relax. The tension of the last few days, the thrill of the chase, had kept her going. Now she was overwhelmed by blessed relief. And just as much by awful, numbing fatigue.

Thank God Stan believed her. That he was moving on it based on little more than her word.

"I'll get the stuff to you as soon as I hang up. If it's

okay with you, I'm going to take the world's longest hot shower."

"Great idea. I'll have somebody there to get you as quick as I can."

"Thanks, Stan. I knew I could count on you."

Carl Andretti pulled himself out of the limo as soon as it stopped in front of the Exchange Place door. It seemed to him that they were making these damn cars smaller and harder to get out of every year. The driver shut the door behind him, waited for his tip, got none, sneered at his portly passenger, and got back behind the wheel. His tires squealed angrily as he pulled away.

Andretti paid him no mind. He had stopped on the sidewalk, breathing in the cold air and watching the rather fetching rear end of a young woman in a short, tight skirt as she entered the building ahead of him. He didn't notice the second limo that pulled to an abrupt stop at the curb behind him. Nor did he see the two men who hopped out and stepped up on either side of him as he followed the tight skirt up the short flight of steps to the revolving door.

He was about to try to cram himself into the same compartment of the revolving door with the woman. That's when two sets of hands, one on either shoulder, grabbed him and jerked him backward.

"Hey, wait a minute! What the hell . . . ?"

A voice from behind his left ear growled in a heavy Eastern European accent, "Mr. Andretti, you vill shut up and come quietly with us or I am afraid you vill be quite dead."

Something hard was poking him low in the ribs. The fat CTO shivered with fear. This couldn't be happening to him. No one would dare threaten Carl Andretti. He was connected. This pair didn't seem to care.

A nearly identical voice on his other side growled, low and deep, "Into the car. Ve are going for a ride, you and us, Mr. Andretti. Ve vant to talk."

The strong hands pushed him down into the backseat of the waiting limo and onto the floorboard. The pair jumped in on either side and shoved his head downward to the floor as the car cruised away. Andretti heard no cry of alarm from anyone on the sidewalk. Either they were all too busy to notice he was being kidnapped or too busy to care.

Andretti struggled, tried to get up, to get a glimpse of the two men who would doubtless soon kill him. "Godammit! Let me up. You sons of bitches are in a world of hurt. You don't know who you're messin' with. I have friends who—"

As the limo swung off Mall Drive onto U.S. 1 heading west, Andretti's face was shoved even harder into the carpeted floor. That shut him up. The car headed south on the New Jersey Turnpike. Just before the I-95 intersection, the limo drove off the turnpike onto a little road that wandered through an expanse of swampy wetlands.

The car eventually eased into an abandoned drive, piled high with garbage, and ground to a halt.

The rear door swung open and Andretti was yanked from the floor, then shoved hard over the hood of the car. He started to sputter, to give them a piece of his mind, but the ugly automatic weapon was now shoved hard up his left nostril. He hushed.

The black-suited man who had been driving the limo now stood in front of him, his thick lips inches from Andretti's face as he spoke, his accent also heavy and Eastern European.

"Mr. Andretti, I must insist that you listen very carefully to what I have to say. If you do what we say, you may well live to see your grandsons. If you cross us, you will never have any grandsons to see. Do you understand?"

The CTO nodded meekly. There was no doubt at all that the man meant what he was saying.

"Good. We suspected you would see it our way. Now, what we want from you is very simple. You and your partners will quit screwing with the SEC on your Opti-Marx system. You will have the system launched and running by the end of the week as the Exchange has contracted for you to do. There will be no more tricks, no funny business whatsoever. And nothing more that might arouse the suspicion of your SEC. Should anything happen to delay the launch, you will cease to live. You can tell Mr. Smythe that what is left of him will be buried in the hole next to you."

The two men who had been holding his arms now shoved him forward, forcing him to kneel facing the murky water, amid the piles of putrid garbage.

Andretti was certain now that they were going to execute him, that he was to die right here in this cold, stinking place. He started to blubber, begging for mercy, but someone kicked him hard in his right side and all the breath left him. As he recoiled, another toe caught him flush in the ribs on his left side and he sprawled in the mud, gasping for air.

He heard the car doors shut and the engine roar to life. The limo's tires spat gravel and mud at him as it raced backward, out onto the road, and then swung around to disappear around the turn, lost from his sight behind the weeds and piles of refuse.

Carl Andretti managed to pull himself painfully to his feet.

"Goddamn you, Stern!" he screeched, and a pair of gulls flapped away from the rubbish pile they had been rummaging through.

The son of a bitch venture capitalist hadn't needed to go through all this gangster bullshit. There was no reason to have those dime-store goons rough him up as if they were all playing parts in some low-budget gangster movie. He and Smythe were playing ball now. Everything was on track now that the Goldman woman had been pulled off the project.

As soon as he could breathe normally again, Carl Andretti found the distant Manhattan skyline over the tops of the reeds. He got his bearings and staggered down the desolate, muddy road.

He cursed Mark Stern with every painful, raspy breath.

Chapter 23

Alan Smythe stared hard at Carl Andretti, a mixture of astonishment and disgust on the Englishman's face. The CTO had been whining ever since he burst into Smythe's office. His trousers were muddy at the knees. He held his ribs and blathered away with some wild story of abduction and near assassination. The two executives faced each other in a pair of modern black leather-and-teak chairs on either side of a glass coffee table in one corner of Smythe's office. Andretti reeked of sweat and garbage. Smythe kept moving his chair back farther from him a little at a time.

A large tumbler half-full of Scotch sat on the chrome-and-glass side table beside Andretti's seat, a bottle of Dewar's next to it. Andretti was pale, still terrified by his involuntary tour of the scenic Jersey wetlands. His voice was high, strained, and it quavered when he talked.

"I'm telling you, Alan, those bastards were going to shoot me dead. Liked to a' scared the shit outta me." His hands shook as he used them both to bring the glass to his lips and took a large gulp. "I don't understand. Why would that son of a bitch Stern go to all the trouble of kidnapping and trying to scare the piss out of me now? We're clean. We've done just what we said we were going to do. Everything is a go!"

Smythe adjusted the hang of his hand-tailored Savile Row blazer so that it draped smoothly from his narrow shoulders while Andretti slouched even farther down in his chair. The corpulent CTO had an odd thought as he watched Smythe. Though they had worked together for three years, he had never seen Smythe out of his jacket, never seen him loosen his tie or roll up his shirtsleeves. The man was never out of uniform.

The Englishman pulled his rose-framed reading glasses from an inside jacket pocket and twirled them about absentmindedly. He was trying to pull together what Andretti was saying. He studied the spectacles for a bit. His designer had assured him that the rose frames were perfect for him, for his perpetually suntanned complexion. His skin tone was a "spring," after all, and rose was perfect for a "spring." It was a fact that a man in his position must always be perfectly groomed. Dress as if he was successful or he never would be.

He looked hard at Andretti. Droplets of sweat marched through the grime on the CTO's wrinkled forehead and pudgy cheeks, down over the multiple chins before disappearing into the dirty yellowing collar.

The man was a pig, Smythe thought, trying to keep the conclusion from being so obvious on his face. If Carl Andretti weren't vitally necessary for this scheme, he would have been dumped long ago. He still needed him for a few more days, until the end of the week when all their hard work would pay off so very handsomely.

"Take it easy, Carl," Smythe said, his voice soothing. "Whatever the reason, whoever sent them, their mission was to scare you. To scare you and me. If their intention was to kill you, I assure you the gulls would be picking at your carcass right now."

Andretti swallowed hard.

"Gee, thanks a hell of a lot! That's a comfort!" he bellowed, and took a gulp so big from the tumbler that some of it spilled from the sides of his mouth and streaked the front of his filthy dress shirt. His face was transforming from pasty pale to an unhealthy blotchy color. The alcohol had started to take effect, his mood segueing from terror to anger.

"Tell you what, then," Smythe said obligingly. "Let's ring up Mark Stern and get this straightened out once and for all."

"Rather have my hands around that slimy little bastard's throat in person and be squeezing real hard while I asked him a few pointed questions." His words were slurred now. He took another swallow, emptying the tumbler, then leaned over and grabbed the bottle for a refill, almost tipping over his chair and the end table in the process.

Smythe reached for the phone resting on the coffee table, but it jangled before he touched it. He frowned as he picked up the receiver. "Cheryl, I thought I told you we were not to be disturbed, no matter—"

Cheryl Mitchell, his assistant, interrupted. "Mr. Smythe, Mark Stern is on the phone, line one. He sounds very upset, as usual, and demands to speak to you immediately. Shall I tell him you're in conference with Mr. Andretti?"

Smythe raised his eyebrows, his frown deepening. "No, no. Put him on."

He punched the button to switch them to the speakerphone, swallowed once, and somehow managed an ingratiating tone when he spoke. He might just as well have been talking to a valued client.

"Mark, talk of the devil. We were just getting ready to call you. Carl is here with me and we need to discuss something with you."

Stern bellowed through the phone, his voice shrill as it spilled from the speaker. "No shit we need to talk! I just got off the phone with my source at the SEC. What are you bastards trying to prove now? I thought we had an understanding after our little visit the other day, Smythe. Are you stupid bastards still trying to sneak something past me?"

Carl Andretti slammed his fist down hard in the middle of the coffee table, sending a spidery pattern of cracks through the glass. He half rose from his chair, weaving, spit flying from his lips as he screamed at the speaker, "Just you wait one goddamn minute! You send some Russian thugs to grab me and rough me up and threaten to cut my nuts off for no goddamn reason and then they leave me in the middle of a goddamn swamp, and here you got the balls to come at us screaming about some cover-up? We ain't hidin' nothin'. You know everything. If you don't believe me, Daddy Warbucks, then you can take OptiMarx and the Stock Exchange and the whole goddamn thing and shove it up your ass."

Stern didn't hesitate. He fired right back, "What the hell are *you* talking about, you fat dumb-ass? What 'Russian thugs'? I don't know anything about any Russians and I sure as hell don't know what you are talking about, you drunken—"

Smythe had to shout to make himself heard above the pair of enraged bulls. His words came out as high-pitched squeaks, but they still served to shut up the two angry, screaming men.

"Gentlemen! Gentlemen! Please. Shrieking at each other is not going to help us get to the bottom of this. Listen to me. If you will stop calling each other vile names for a moment and think, we might be able to figure out what's going on. I'm starting to see a pattern develop." Andretti was back in his chair now, sprawling precariously, on the verge of sliding right out onto the floor. Stern's raspy breathing could be heard over the speaker, but he, too, seemed yelled out. "Let's look at what we know, both the facts and the claims. Let's do it calmly, like the reasonable businessmen we all three are."

"'Kay," Andretti muttered, but his face was still crimson. Stern was silent except for his breathing. Smythe leaned forward, waving his spectacles, as if he were making a sales pitch for some major new deal.

"First, we know for a fact that Carl was kidnapped and roughed up this morning. Carl thinks his abductors were Russian. God knows we have enough of the bastards around here that he would recognize the accent when he hears it. Still, it could have been anyone with an Eastern European accent. The abduction and the threats are a fact. Mark, you maintain that you didn't have anything to do with it, that you weren't just reinforcing your little performance you gave for me the other day?"

"Damn straight I am, although I have to admit that it sounds like a good idea right now. Believe me when I tell you that I can make something like that happen with one phone call. Don't you sons of bitches ever forget it."

Stern's voice rose higher and higher as he went on and he was screaming again by the end.

"Mark, Mark! Settle down and listen for a moment, please. We're trying to piece together the facts now, okay?" Stern grunted but hushed. Andretti was staring longingly at the empty Scotch bottle. "Now you're telling us that someone at the SEC . . . someone you have planted there . . . found something you believe we were hiding from you. You must tell us what that bit of information might be before we can confirm or deny that we know anything about it. Sound fair enough, Mark?"

Stern, still steaming, bit off his words one at a time. "The Goldman woman. The one some stupid asshole tried to whack and shit in our nest in the process? Seems she didn't take the Caribbean vacation we arranged for her after all."

Smythe's mouth popped open and he dropped his glasses onto the shattered table. "Of course she did. The other guy . . . what's his name? He's been here since the other day, rubber-stamping everything we put in front of him as you said he would."

"That's right," Andretti confirmed. "We haven't seen the Goldman bitch in several days and there's no way she could get in here or into the Exchange without somebody seeing her and letting us know."

"Well, I don't know how the hell she did it but she managed to break into your system and she's been traipsing all over your precious code." There was a pause. Andretti stifled a belch. Smythe held his breath. "Guess what. She found where you bastards bypassed the short-sale rules."

Smythe was stunned. Andretti was the first to squeal.

"What the hell are you talking about? We haven't touched the short-sale module. They follow the Exchange business rules to the letter. You found where we played with the trade timing, but that was the only bogus stuff that we stuck in there. We figured that would be plenty enough to make us rich. We didn't dare try anything else for fear of getting caught."

"Well, someone sure as hell jiggered the system and they did a good job of it," Stern yelled right back. "It had to be somebody inside, somebody greedy, somebody stupid enough to get caught, and that points at you two!"

Alan Smythe's voice was surprisingly calm when he responded, "Mark, I can promise you it wasn't us. You know what that means? That means somebody else was playing with the code. I'd wager they are the same ones who are putting the strong arm on Mr. Andretti and me."

"What the hell are you saying?" Andretti asked.

"I'm suggesting that we have competition here. It's all starting to add up. The Russian Mafia has been moving into the financial markets for years, anyplace they could find a toehold. We all know that. Then we have what are apparently Russian thugs pushing Carl around, threatening me, making sure we don't do anything to get the SEC curious before we go live. The simple fact of the matter is that we've got a bunch of Russian programmers working for us, any one of whom could have tampered with the code, stuck in whatever routines they wanted. They're smart enough to hide it well if they wanted to. That's why we use them. They're rather good at what they do."

Stern's voice was quieter now, more distant. Smythe could imagine him leaning back in his big chair, rubbing his chin as he talked. "Smythe, for once your candy-assed chirping is starting to make sense. That means you have to get rid of all the Russian programmers right away to make certain you purge the right one . . . or ones. Then get somebody on the job looking for the dirty stuff. If Goldman can find it, you got some propeller-head there who can, too. I've got the damage contained for the moment, but who knows what other bright-eyed bureaucrat might stumble onto this shit?"

"Hold on, Mark. Let's not charge off half-cocked now. First, we don't know how far along the changes are. They're probably already finished, ready to go when we go online this week. If that's the case, they can make a killing and be gone before we can track down the screwy routines. We won't know who did it until they disappear with the loot. I suspect the market will be a shambles before we could get it debugged. Remember, we all take a bath if that happens. We need those programmers to fix it once we find it. Second, we don't know what kind of horsepower is behind this scheme. If it is the Russian mob, we could be stepping into a hot, steaming pile of some very nasty shit." Smythe was studying the web of lines on the broken coffee table as if they might form a map that could lead them out of the mess in which they now found themselves. Stern couldn't see the slight smile on his face, but Andretti could. He was a wheeler-dealer, and he was moving in to close the sale. "There's one more point, Mark. With the information your contact has provided us, we may just be able to gain an advantage. We may even be able to use that little ticking time bomb in OptiMarx to make the three of us even more magnificently rich. If it is one of the Russian programmers, he may have done us a rather wonderful favor."

"Okay, I'm with you," Stern said, his voice a whisper after all the yelling he had been doing. "What do you have in mind?"

"You've done plenty of business in Eastern Europe, I'm sure."

"When they tore down the Berlin Wall, they might just as well have given me the key to the bank."

"Then I assume you have effective contacts who can help us learn all we need to know about this Russian Mafia?"

They could almost hear the moneyman smiling now on the far end of the telephone line.

"Smythe, you're still a fruit, and your partner there is a dumb lard-ass, but I like the way you're thinking."

SEAL commander Bill Beaman huddled with his team under the scrub birch and jagged rock that sheltered them from the windblown snow. Martinelli and Hall were back from scouting the western perimeter of the Russian sub base. Their report had not given them any ideas for getting inside.

"Skipper, I don't get it," Hall said. "The Russians are usually sloppy with internal security. We should be able to stroll right in through the main gate at high noon without anyone seeing us. What's with all this patrolling?"

Beaman bit off a chunk of energy bar and chewed. He downed it with a swig of water before he answered, "Yeah, that's been bothering me, too. We shouldn't be surprised. That's why they sent us up here to this pleasure spot in the first place. Someone has a bee in his bonnet about security on this base all of a damn sudden. That confirms that there's something important happening here. Otherwise, Ivan would be sound asleep in his nice warm guard shack over there and the only traffic would be your occasional reindeer herd."

Chief Johnston nodded his agreement. "I sure as hell wish we had the blueprints of that place to study before we left. That would've made this a lot easier."

Beaman didn't say anything. He chewed on another chunk of the energy bar as his mind turned over and considered all the possibilities. The rest of the team stayed quiet as they hunkered down eating while they waited. They knew Beaman would come up with something. He always did.

He swallowed the last of his food. When he spoke, his words were strong and sure. "We came all the way up here to see if the Russians had subs ready to deploy out of that big shed over there. We're damn sure going to find out. Here's what we'll do. Hall, you and Martinelli scoot around the perimeter and get up on that ridge to the northeast." He pointed off in the distance, across the sprawling base from where they now sat. "You get caught and you'll answer to me and the chief first, then the Russians later if there's anything left of your hides. I want you in a position where you can look down into the covered docks from the water side and see anything that might come floating out of there. Take one of the satcom radios and report back to home base if you see anything bigger than a sunfish. You'll be on your own over there. If we get split up, remember to get to the extraction point in two days." He tapped Hall and Martinelli on their shoulders and smiled. "Boys, it's a long, cold walk home if you miss the bus. Better get moving. It looks like you've got twenty clicks to cover pretty quick."

The two SEALs shouldered their packs and disappeared into the thick evergreens on the protected side of the ridge. It would take them at least two hours, more probably three, to get in position.

Beaman turned next to the other three SEALs who were squatting in the little circle. "Cantrell, you, Broughton, and Dumkowski set up an observation post right here. I want to know if anything unusual happens. Set up the other satcom radio ready to talk to home base. Chief Johnston and I are going down to see if we can crash their little party without an invitation. We'll stay in touch on the line-of-sight radios."

Beaman and Johnston shouldered their gear and checked their weapons ready.

"Sir, what if you two get caught?" Broughton asked.

"We won't," Beaman answered, and then he and Johnston disappeared into the darkness.

Captain Second Rank Anatol Vivilav sat at the little table in his stateroom, smoking a cigarette, as he read his secret operational orders for what had to be the hundredth time. The *Vipr*, his Akula-class submarine, hummed with activity all around him, but he was alone with his thoughts for the moment. The words on the paper had not changed since their first reading:

Depart Polyarnyy when directed. Submerge before leaving Murmansk Fjord. Proceed by direct routing to take station in Patrol Area "Igor."

Remain undetected from all sources, including Russian naval assets, at all times.

When in patrol area, remain in constant radio communications with Northern Fleet Central Submarine Command on satellite circuit Kommalsat.

No electronic emissions, including both radio and radar, are authorized.

Upon arrival Patrol Area "Igor," maintain weapons system ready to answer launch control order within five minutes.

All forces encountered in patrol area are to be considered hostile and engaged if judged a threat to own ship.

Vivilav knew the meaning in the words, the obvious and the hidden. In a few hours, when he slipped the lines from the pier this time, *Vipr* would be at war. It was a war neither he nor any of his crew ever expected to be fighting. They would not be trading blows with the Americans, with NATO, with the Chinese. They would be opening fire on their own countrymen, on the ships with which they had exercised, on the brother sailors with whom they had sung and drunk, and they would be launching cruise missiles that would pierce deep into the heart of the *Rodina*.

This was no exercise. The shooting would be deadly real.

The veteran Russian submariner glanced up at the clock on the bulkhead above his desk. Most of the boats nowadays had bright red digital time readouts, but he still preferred the warm comfort the old brass mariner's chronometer gave him. The faint ticking of the ancient mechanical mechanism somehow instilled in him far more confidence than all the high-tech wonders that had been built into the *Vipr*.

He could see the minute hand moving. Four more hours, four more trips around the face of the chronometer, until the American spy satellite dropped below the horizon and could no longer look down on this place. That's when they would slip out into the dark, cold Barents.

The first officer stuck his head into Vivilav's stateroom door. "Captain, the reactor is online. It is supplying ship's power. The engines will be warmed and ready in an hour. All weapons systems are tested and ready. We are ready for sea when you are."

"Very well."

The first officer paused for a moment, waiting for anything else his captain might have to say. There was nothing more. He backed out and shut the stateroom door behind him.

Captain Vivilav opened the large safe under his desk and removed a rolled-up chart. Stepping over to the small table at the after end of the cramped space, he uncoiled the chart, spread it out smooth, and studied it. A bright red line showed Vivilav the route he was expected to follow. The circuitous course extended due north from the mouth of the Murmansk Fjord well out into the deep waters of the Barents Sea. From there it bent northwest, passing just to the south of Svalbard to stay far away from the listening station at Tromso, Norway. Next, the line headed to the southwest, for Greenland. He was ordered to hug the Greenland coast until he passed south of the secret NATO listening station on Jan Mayen Island. Once the high headland at Unarteg passed abeam, he was to turn south-southeast and make for the Norwegian coast near Bergen, then ultimately into the Baltic Sea.

He scratched his head as he studied the long, curving, red line. Taking a set of navigator's dividers, Vivilav walked off the distance and calculated the time it would take *Vipr* to arrive at the mouth of the Baltic Sea. He removed his spectacles and rubbed his eyes. If he went slowly enough to stay hidden, there was no way the sub would arrive on station on time. If he took this route and went fast enough, he would be detected. Some idiot in Central Submarine Command didn't understand the complexities of navigating one of these big, new boats.

Vivilav pulled another cigarette from the pack lying on his desk and lit it. He sucked deeply, drawing the acrid smoke into his lungs and holding it before exhaling.

There had to be a way around this. It would take a full day to wind through the tortuous, heavily traveled passage of the Kattegat and the sound between Norway and

Zealand. Then two more days to travel the length of the Baltic to get to Patrol Area "Igor."

There was nothing to be done to shorten that part of the journey. His best option was to try to shave three days off the transit across the Norwegian Sea.

Taking a red pencil, Vivilav drew a line that skirted the Norwegian coast all the way down to the Kattegat. Just have to risk it. No choice. Besides, the NATO sailors listening at monitoring stations were probably sleeping. They believed that all the Russian subs were rusting at the pier these days. There was little other noise for them to listen for except the occasional amorous whale.

Vivilav measured the distance. At normal cruising speed, and even with the far riskier course, they would still arrive half a day late. He would have to travel faster, at least thirty kilometers per hour. *Vipr* could make the trip at twice that speed. It wasn't a matter of how fast the submarine could go, but rather how fast she could go quietly. Every extra kph above her quiet cruising speed equated to an increased risk of being detected.

Vivilav idly scratched his ear. *Vipr*'s maximum quiet cruising speed was fifteen kilometers per hour. They needed to go twice that fast.

He stared hard at the chart as he ground out the cigarette and lit yet another one. He had to travel fast, but still not be found. It was all a risk, but that's what he was trained for. He would stay at quiet cruising speed until he rounded North Cape. That would get *Vipr* past any American submarines that were lurking in the Barents. Then he would take his chances and dash boldly down the Norwegian coastline.

As Anatol Vivilav rolled the chart and stuffed it back into the safe, he heard a quiet knock at the door. It was the first officer again.

"It's time, Captain. *Vipr* is ready for sea."

Vivilav nodded and reached into a locker for his heavy bridge coat and fur hat. The winds would be cold out on the fjord tonight.

Chapter 24

Jason Hall laboriously worked his way upward, using brute strength to pull his body up the sheer rock face. The heavy equipment he carried threatened to drag him down, and it was a long, long fall back down the steep slope. Even in the frigid Arctic night, sweat washed into his eyes and soaked his shirt inside his white parka as he fought to reach the ledge he was climbing for. It was still just a couple of meters farther up. He got a good grip on a crevice and glanced back down. Tony Martinelli was just below him, working over the rocks. Hall knew if he slipped now, he would take his team member down with him.

"Just a little more, M. Almost there. I can see the ledge."

"Gee, thanks. You said that a half hour ago and I'm still looking at your ass."

It had taken longer than they had estimated to make their way around the sprawling submarine base and up to this perch, high on the headlands. It was midnight, four hours since they had left the little temporary command post and the rest of the team. The light wind below was gusting up here. The thick cloud cover scudded high overhead, doing its best to erase the starlight.

Hall pulled himself up to the narrow rock shelf and lay there, gasping for air. Minutes later, Martinelli rolled over the edge and joined him.

"Damn, that was more work than I expected," Martinelli grunted. "Next time you get a yen to take a midnight stroll, why don't you invite Cantrell or somebody else besides me?"

Hall smiled. "Yeah, he could use the exercise, but you'd better do your bitchin' to the chief or the skipper, not me. They're the ones pulled your name out of the hat. Now let's get to work."

Hall pulled the miniature satcom transceiver from his pack and set it up. He pointed the tiny parabolic antenna at a communications satellite twenty-three thousand miles overhead, in a geosynchronous polar orbit. As he worked, he thought how different his life was now. It had not been that long ago that he was a linebacker at the University of Alabama, playing his last game in the Sugar Bowl. Now here he was, on top of some Russian mountain, wrestling highly technical gear into place so he could relay back intel that might help avert a nuclear catastrophe.

Meanwhile, Martinelli unpacked the low-light sniper scope and set it at the edge of the shelf. He aimed it down at where he suspected the open mouth of the cavernous covered dock would be. He looked through the lens and saw the shimmering, green-glowing image of the huge building. He whistled low. "Wow! Have you ever seen anything so big? That thing must cover the better part of fifty acres under one roof."

Hall scooted over beside Martinelli. The night was so

dark they wouldn't have been able to see across the water without the help of the sniper scope. "Intel says they can hide a whole squadron of Typhoons in there," he whispered. "You could play a helluva bowl game inside a barn that size. See any sign of activity in there?"

"Nope. Nothing. Not even cheerleaders or a marching band. I can't see very far inside, either, because of the angle, but I've got a good shot of all of Polyarnyy Sound."

Hall yawned. "Okay, since you got your eye on the scope already, why don't you take the first watch? I'm going to get some shut-eye. Wake me in a couple of hours when the bacon and eggs and grits are about ready."

"All right, but just don't go snoring. Some Russian bear might think it's a mating call and come looking for us."

Hall chuckled as he unrolled his sleeping bag and tried to find a comfortable position on the stony, frozen ground. Martinelli hunkered down and watched the building, the black water of the sound, forcing himself to stay awake and alert. Soon all he heard was the gentle, rhythmic sound of his sleeping friend's breathing. SEALs learned early how to find deep sleep no matter where they had to make their beds.

Martinelli jostled around, trying to find a way to see through the scope while avoiding the sharp rock that was digging into his side. After a few minutes he took a quick break from watching the building. He rustled through his rucksack, found a half-eaten energy bar, and chewed on it for a few moments, occasionally taking a sip of water from his CamelBak. Even up here, on this rocky crag with a biting wind chapping his face and the might of the Russians arrayed just below him, there was no other place Tony Martinelli would rather be. He had been a sophomore in college, floundering, not knowing where he wanted to go with his life. One night when he was supposed to be studying for a final exam, he saw a program on some cable channel about the SEALs. He was hooked, then and there, and, even through Hell Week and BUD-S, he had never regretted his decision. Where else could some kid from Queens have more chance to make a difference in the world?

He was still chewing the last of the energy bar the next time he looked through the sniper scope. He stopped, his mouth open. Something had changed. A massive black shape was just beginning to emerge from the building's cavernous maw. He looked again, harder, squinting, trying to make sure he wasn't imagining the dark form, or that he wasn't being tricked by an errant shadow in what little light there was.

No, it was real, all right, and it was growing larger.

Without removing his eye from the scope, Martinelli reached back and shook Hall. The SEAL awoke instantly, tense and ready to fight. That was something else SEALs managed. Coming awake from a deep sleep, fully alert and set for whatever they had to do.

"We've got activity," Martinelli whispered as soon as Hall slid up next to him. "Looks like an Akula coming out of the barn. You better get on the horn and give the boss a traffic report."

Hall was already fiddling with the satcom transceiver. Martinelli watched the low black shape of the Russian submarine emerge into Polyarnyy Sound, turn to the east, and then disappear around the headland into the Murmansk Fjord.

"Son of a bitch was turning north as he went round the headland," Martinelli muttered. "I do believe he is heading out to sea."

"Yep, that's the way I see it," Hall said. "Message is sent and receipted for. Everybody that needs to know knows now. Let's see if any more of them want to come out and play."

The two SEALs exchanged a silent high five, then hunkered down for a long, cold night.

Captain Anatol Vivilav watched the other submarines of his squadron, still moored inside the covered piers, as his boat slid past them. The *Vipr* moved toward the huge, open door, toward the sweeping sound and eventually the sea. They were on their way at last.

Vivilav knew that when he returned to his northern home, everything would be changed. Mother Russia would be freed from the yoke of the weak-willed government and he would be hailed as a hero of the new revolution. Admiral Durov promised this, so it was true.

Vipr slowly emerged from the building into the inky black night. Wind blew into Vivilav's face. It was still bitterly cold, but it also carried the refreshing, salty tang of the sea. The captain felt the familiar gentle throb of the ship through the deck beneath his feet. This was where he belonged, driving a sleek ship out to meet the wild tempest of the northern seas.

Vipr's rudder swung over, bringing her bow around

to pass between the headlands that separated the quiet waters of Polyarnyy Sound from the Murmansk Fjord. The lights of Pol'narj, the little town that most of the crew called home, seemed dim and subdued this night as they reflected weakly off the inky, dark waters. Even the stars were obscured by darkening clouds that would doubtless begin dropping more snow soon.

Vivilav turned to the officer conning the ship. "Verify that the boat is ready for submerged operations. As soon as we are lined up with the outbound leg, we will dive."

The officer stared back at him, his eyes wide with amazement. He started to protest. "Captain, Harbor Control standard procedure requires—"

Vivilav held up his hand. "This is not a mission for standard procedures. Harbor Control has not been and will not be informed of our departure. We will submerge in the fjord and enter the sea underwater. That way the American spy satellites won't see us and we will slip past their submarines without them even knowing we have left home. Now, do as I order and be prepared to dive immediately."

The young submarine officer scurried to carry out the unexpected command. Vivilav dropped through the hatch and made the long climb down the ladder to the control room below. *Vipr* was already swinging around to the north, to the open sea, as she slipped beneath the placid surface of the shadowy fjord.

Dmitri Ustinov couldn't help grinning as he plugged the flash drive into the USB port of his laptop computer. How naive could these Americans be? He had planted bugs in both Andretti's and Smythe's offices weeks ago. Neither executive had become even the least bit suspicious that someone was hearing his every word, as if the eavesdropper were in the room. No one attempted to sweep the offices for bugs, either. Ustinov couldn't imagine a Russian business being so lackadaisical about these basics of security. Especially one that was engaged in the high-level chicanery that Smythe and Andretti were trying to pull off.

The office was empty this late. Even the hardworking programmers had called it a day and made their way to the neighborhood bars and pizza joints. Dmitri loaded the contents of the memory stick onto his hard drive and donned a headset to listen closely to the raw audio files. The digital recording was remarkably clean, and he was able to hear everything that had been going on in the room. There was Carl Andretti's gravelly voice, his words slurred, as if the drink he was pouring himself had not been his first of the day.

"I'm telling you, Alan, those bastards were going to shoot me dead. Liked to a' scared the shit outta me. I don't understand. Why would that son of a bitch Stern go to all the trouble of kidnapping and trying to scare the piss out of me now? We're clean. We've done just what we said we were going to do. Everything is a 'go!'"

Ustinov leaned back in his chair, his hands behind his head as he listened. So the Americans were still confused and fighting each other. Good! It would keep them too busy to bother him and the scheme he and his friends were about to enact.

He heard Stern talking about Goldman, the SEC

woman, and what she had found. Shit! The bitch had somehow stumbled onto his code in the system. She had unraveled the whole thing.

This was not good news. At least they still had no idea who was behind it, and from what he was hearing, the idiots had at least been able to stop the bleeding, to keep Goldman from telling anyone else besides their insider what she had found.

Ustinov chewed on his lip. The American fools might be confused, but it wouldn't take long for someone as smart as Goldman to backtrack to him. The whole plan would fall apart. Boris Medikov would not accept any excuse for that happening.

The smile was now gone from Ustinov's face. The only thing to do was to get Goldman out of the picture before the information got out. He couldn't count on the OptiMarx fools or the moneyman from California to do that job.

He pulled his cell phone from his jacket pocket and punched in a number. A woman answered on the first ring.

"Marina, my love, I have a little errand for your new uncles."

After relating what needed to be done and hanging up, he brought up his e-mail program on the computer screen. He needed to contact Catherine Goldman now that she had been fired from the project.

Catherine,

You are in great danger. Stern has a mole in the SEC. They know that you have discovered their

plot. They mean to take you out of the picture. I am
sending friends to protect you. Go with them,
please. They will identify themselves as Marina's
uncles.

                              Your friend,
                                 Dmitri

That should do it. The smirk was back on his broad
face as he clicked the mouse on the SEND box.

Admiral Tom Donnegan read the little yellow sheet of
paper with great interest. So, the Russian, Captain Andropoyov, was right. He had been telling the truth. It
appeared that Admiral Alexander Durov's unbelievable
scheme was a reality after all and it was already in progress. Beaman's SEALs had caught one of the mysterious
Akula boats, the subs that were supposed to be rusting
alongside the pier ready for the scrap yard, trying to slip
out of the covered dock. Its treachery was confirmed
when they saw it diving before it ever entered the open
sea. They still needed to know where it was going and
what it would do once it got there. They also needed to
know how many more would emerge from the covered
pens behind it.

Damnation! The clock was ticking now. Amid the
confusion over a contrived international incident involv-
ing Donnegan's submarines, that old fool Durov was going to attempt a coup! It would not be a bloodless one.
Of that they could be assured. One of Donnegan's worst
nightmares was coming true. A rogue Russian with enough

military might to be able to pull it off was about to set loose something that could blow up into Armageddon if it went unchecked!

The admiral yelled out the open door of his inner office to his aide, "Get this out to Jon Ward and Joe Glass right away. Use the SpecOp Intel channel. The ocean up there is about to get real busy!"

Joe Glass stepped up onto the periscope stand. He had just spent a very trying ten minutes wrestling with the geographic realities of the navigation charts. The little detour to medevac Oshley had cost them twelve precious hours that they couldn't make up. They would have to run hard, directly to Murmansk, just to get there in time to rescue the SEALs. No time for fancy maneuvers, just a straight run in.

Pat Durand stood at the forward port railing, watching his ship control team handle the complex task of driving the sub.

"Pat, you ready to go to periscope depth?" Glass asked.

"Yes, sir. Just finished a baffle clear. The only contact is sierra two-four-seven, bearing one-six-nine. He's slowly drawing aft at point-one-degree-per-minute bearing rate. Sonar classified him as a tanker. I'd guess that he's heading down to the south from the Norwegian oil fields. The contact is distant."

Glass nodded and walked over to the sonar repeater to see for himself. He flipped through the displays. Yes, there was sierra two-four-seven on the passive broadband display, just where Durand said he would be. No one else out there. That was one of the few advantages of being in the Norwegian Sea in the winter. Not many people were foolish enough to be out here, cluttering up the open ocean this time of year.

Glass turned to Durand and ordered, "Officer of the Deck, proceed to periscope depth and copy the broadcast. Get a GPS fix and ventilate the boat for twenty minutes while you are up there."

"Proceed to periscope depth, copy the broadcast, get a GPS fix, and ventilate, aye, sir," Durand answered smartly. "Seas are from three-four-two. Coming up on course zero-six-zero.

"Rig control for black," Durand was saying. "Make your depth one-five-zero feet." The lights blinked out, making the room almost pitch-dark. The only lights were the dim red, green, or yellow ones of the instruments.

"Make my depth one-five-zero feet, aye," Sam Wallich responded. "Depth two-two-zero feet, coming to one-five-zero."

He directed the two planesmen sitting on either side of him as they pulled back on their control columns, determining the boat's angle of ascent. The *Toledo* slid up to the shallow depth.

"At one-five-zero feet," Wallich reported.

The sub had begun to roll as it responded to the churning of the sea above them.

Durand reached up and rotated the control ring for the number-two periscope. He shouted, "Number-two scope coming up!"

"Speed seven," Wallich answered.

The chief of the watch chimed in with "Number-two scope indicates 'up.'"

Durand stuck his eye to the eyepiece and started to walk a circle as he rotated the scope. He shouted, "Dive, make your depth six-two feet."

"Depth six-two feet, aye. One-four-zero feet, coming to six-two feet."

Wallich turned to his team, watching the planesmen as they worked to control their depth. He ordered, "Chief of the Watch, flood forty thousand pounds to depth control." The extra weight would help keep the boat from being sucked to the surface in the heavy sea.

"Depth one hundred feet, coming to six-two feet." The rolling increased noticeably now. A coffee cup slid off a shelf and crashed to the deck. No one seemed to take notice.

"Depth eight-five feet."

Glass braced himself in his seat and held on to the railing as the rolling increased. The boat started to pitch, giving them a lurching, unpredictable roller-coaster ride. One minute she would roll over to port and pitch down. The next she would roll to starboard and pitch up. It was enough to send several of the submariners, accustomed to the calm ride in the deep, searching for a convenient trash can in which to bury their heads.

"Depth seven-six feet. Chief of the Watch, flood another ten thousand pounds."

Something heavy went scooting across the deck in the dark and collided noisily with a bench locker. Still, nobody seemed to hear it.

"Depth six-two feet and holding."

"Scope clear!" Durand shouted. He swung the periscope through two complete revolutions, trying to see if there was anything up here that was an immediate danger to the *Toledo*. "No close contacts," he reported.

Everybody in the control room breathed deeply. They were out of danger and could now go back to their normal duties.

Durand swung the scope around more slowly, still looking for anything that might be out there. He could see nothing but the pitching, tossing winter seas and the star-studded sky above.

They were completely, utterly alone out here.

The 21MC blasted out, "Conn, radio. Copying the satcom downlink. Traffic on the spec-op channel. Request the captain come to radio."

Glass made his way through the darkened room, rolling with the boat as he went off in the direction of the radio room. As he stepped inside, the leading radioman handed him a small sheet of paper. Glass was still studying it when Edwards stepped through the door behind him.

"Well, XO, it's started."

"Sir?"

"Bill Beaman's boys report one Akula is out of the barn."

Chapter 25

Catherine Goldman stared in disbelief at the e-mail message that glared back at her from the computer screen. She shivered. Dmitri Ustinov might be a skirt chaser, a bona fide pervert, but he had always been honest with her as far as she knew. If he said she was in danger, she had no choice but to believe him.

Her mind raced as she studied the cryptic message. Only one person knew what she had uncovered in the OptiMarx computer program: Stan Miller at the SEC, the same person who was supposedly sending someone to take her to a safe place. She felt the blood drain from her face. Miller had been her one hope in helping to stop the plot at OptiMarx. Now there was no doubt that he was sullied, too.

There had to be someone she could trust. Someone she could turn to now, both for protection and to see that the corrupted system did not go online and do irreparable damage to the stock market.

The phone on the nightstand jangled, interrupting her racing thoughts. She snatched up the receiver but said nothing. It was a strong male voice that spoke.

"Miss Goldman, this is Special Agent Gorton. Listen to me. This is important. Stan Miller sent us over to move you to our protected safe house. We're just pulling into the hotel garage. Please have everything packed so we can move quickly and get you to a safe place."

She shook her head from side to side and fought the urge to cry. This couldn't be happening! It sounded like something she had seen in some cheap movie. The heroine kidnapped from the fancy hotel by imposter FBI agents. She clenched her fists and made up her mind. Now, more than ever, she had to stay alert, do the right thing. Otherwise, she might not live to tell anyone else about the dirty trading system.

She bent over the laptop and tapped out a reply to Dmitri Ustinov's e-mail.

Need help. Meet me at Andy's Bar on Washington. Hurry.

She pushed SEND before she changed her mind, made certain to delete both messages from the e-mail server, jammed the laptop into its carrying case, then turned and dashed out into the hallway. The elevator door was sliding open as she rounded the corner. She couldn't afford to take a chance. She ducked into the stairwell, just catching a glimpse of three large, dark-suited men as they emerged from the lift and headed down the hall in the direction of her room.

She was faced with a decision. Something in the far recesses of her mind, some plot from a long-forgotten spy novel or television show, bubbled up into her subconscious. It told her to run up the stairs, not down. She charged up the staircase to the next floor landing, then tried to get as close to the cinder block wall as she could.

The door on the floor below her burst open and she

heard the clatter of someone running down the stairs. Only then did she move, exiting the stairwell into the hallway, the door sighing shut behind her. She headed straight for the elevator, her breath already coming in great rasping gasps, as much from fear as exertion. She looked both ways, up and down the long hallway, then reached for the DOWN button.

She stopped. They might halt the elevator on her old floor when they saw it coming down. Or have someone watching the elevators on the lobby and garage levels, assuming she would be naive enough to use one of those ways out. She'd be trapped inside that little cage.

Instead, Goldman turned and ran down the long hall toward a stairway sign she could barely make out at the far end. A door swung open near the end of the corridor and she pulled up short. There was nowhere to duck out of sight. They would have her dead to rights before she could back down the length of the hall.

It was a maid, pushing a large laundry bin.

"Are the stairs down there?" Catherine asked, pointing down the hall.

The woman looked at her blankly. Catherine realized how she must look, her hair askew, face red, eyes wild with panic.

"Exercise," Catherine said. "I use the stairs for exercise."

"*Lo siento. No inglés,*" the maid said with a shrug, and shoved the laundry bin on down the hall past her.

Catherine breathed a sigh and headed for the doorway to the back emergency stairs. Please, no alarm, she thought as she shoved the handle downward and stepped onto the landing.

There was no sound.

She forced herself to take the stairs as quietly as she could manage. She hugged the wall as she went past her former floor and then stooped as she passed the little wire-and-glass window in the door. She stopped on each landing, listening for footsteps following her, coming to meet her.

There was nothing.

Fifteen minutes later, she slipped out a back door of the hotel, hopped down off the loading dock littered with cardboard boxes, bottles, and cans, and headed down Dey Street. Trying not to look too obvious as she looked over her shoulder, she stepped from Dey out onto the much busier Church Street and blended with the other pedestrians.

She should be safe out here. She prayed that Miller would not have had a chance to get a photo of her to the men he had sent. They would be operating on his description. After two days in front of the laptop, she was hardly the neat, well-groomed SEC inspector Miller knew. Her hair was down from its usual tight bun, she had no makeup on, and she wore a sweatshirt and sweatpants beneath her coat. That jerk Miller had never seen her in anything but a business suit.

She turned left on Ann Street, then south on Trinity Place. She walked past the old dark Gothic church that dominated the way. Thankfully the crowds were thick in the early evening, people rushing to the subway or waving to hail a cab. No one paid even the slightest attention to anyone else, just the way New Yorkers typically did.

She allowed herself to breathe. She felt safer here, being jostled by the moving mass of people.

Right on Carlisle and then down to Washington. Wait. Was that one of the men ahead, on the corner? He wore a dark suit, was heavyset, and seemed to be tarrying as he tried to light a cigarette in the blustery wind that whistled down the canyon of buildings. She slowed, looked for a doorway to enter, but the man threw up his hand, caught the attention of a cabbie, climbed into the taxi, and was gone.

There was Andy's, right on the corner of Carlisle and Washington. She had made it.

Goldman stopped and looked through the glass-and-wood double doors. The place was packed, as usual. At first glance, she didn't spot anyone she knew, anyone acting suspiciously. Nobody seemed to take notice of her at all. Just the normal evening crowd.

She shoved the door open, blinked at the instant burst of noise, and slipped inside. She pushed her way through the crowd, seeking the anonymous protection amid the seething mass of raucous people. There didn't seem to be an available chair in the whole place. Then she was in luck. A group of three stood to leave, emptying a table just as she made her way past. Catherine grabbed a chair and, keeping her back to the wall, scanned the faces of everyone who came in through the door.

She ordered a glass of white wine and fought to clear the terror she knew showed on her face. A man came in, a big man who wore a black suit. He could have been one of Miller's people from the hotel hallway.

Did he look her way? Yes. Then waved nonchalantly. A woman at the table next to Catherine's waved back and motioned her friend over.

Catherine was so intently watching the door that she never saw the three men until they stood around her table, casting shadows on her. She jumped, startled, and started to stand. One man put a hand on her shoulder. "Miss Goldman, Dmitri Ustinov sent us to be of assistance to you." His accent was so much like Dmitri's, but much thicker. "We will take you to a safe place now."

"Where did . . . ? Where did you come from?" she blurted out. "I was watching. You didn't come in the door."

Nicholas Vujnovich answered, "We've been waiting for you. Now hurry. We don't know how long it will take the OptiMarx goons to catch up. We have a car outside."

Goldman realized that she didn't have any choice. She was alone and defenseless against forces she had no idea how to fight. This wasn't some CEO inflating his earnings report to buffalo the stockholders or a board of directors trying to pull some insider-trading scam. This episode had already generated far more excitement than she had ever expected to experience as a simple SEC geek.

She looked from one face to another. They were all older than middle-aged, all dark, all expressionless. Their eyes were like ice, without warmth. She hesitated, but what was the use? Right now this was her next best chance to get out of this mess alive.

Catherine grabbed her computer bag and followed the big Russian, not to the front door but toward the back. The other two trailed behind to guard their retreat and so she would not have had any opportunity to turn and bolt, even if she had been so inclined. They passed through a swinging door into the kitchen. The staff looked the other way, pretending they weren't there.

The four stepped into another dark side street. They hopped into a black Ford sedan waiting there, its engine running. Vujnovich sat in the driver's seat while the other two slid in on either side of her in the backseat. The windows were tinted so dark she could hardly see out. And, she realized, no one could see inside, either. The doors slammed shut, cutting off the cold wind. It still seemed frigid inside the car. Catherine Goldman shivered again as she realized once more just how helpless she was.

The car pulled out into the street and merged into the traffic headed uptown.

Alexander Durov sat in the study of his Polyarnyy apartment and did something he rarely, if ever, did. He watched television.

The news anchor was reciting stories of more unrest in the vast outlying regions of Russia. Food was in short supply in central Siberia. Famines and food riots were inevitable now. The little food available was priced far beyond the means of most of the people. The local population was demanding Moscow's assistance. They threatened armed rebellion right there on television if government aid wasn't forthcoming before their families starved.

Durov snorted. There was a time not so long ago when anyone foolish enough to challenge the government would find himself in a gulag. That is if he were lucky enough to stay alive. Any reporter who dared to mention the story would soon find himself in the very next cell to the agitator. Those days were gone. Unrest was rampant, fomented by the restless rabble and encouraged by the reckless media.

It was outrageous, an insult to the *Rodina*!

Normally Durov would have risen and angrily snapped off the television before stomping out of the room. Tonight he merely smiled.

The scene on the screen changed. He recognized London's Trafalgar Square, crowded with teeming masses of angry protesters. The cameras panned over large placards demanding an American explanation for the bloodthirsty sinking of the two Russian submarines in the cold Barents waters. A young reporter thrust his microphone into the face of a protester with wild purple hair, sporting nose, lip, and tongue rings. The angry young man screeched something about the imperialistic Americans who were threatening to start World War III for no other reason than to rub salt in the wounds of the crippled former Soviet Union.

Vasiliy Zhurkov was sitting in another of the room's ornate chairs, staring at the television. He glanced up and caught Durov smiling broadly.

"This is good, Admiral, this mayhem in the streets of the world's capitals?"

"Yes, Vasiliy, very good. We can thank our friend Medikov for the story concerning Siberia. His people control the markets out there and he owns the television station. Another few days of this boiling turmoil and we will be ready."

Durov rose from his seat, stepped over to the small sideboard, and poured himself a glass of vodka. He sipped it as he stared into the fireplace, lost in thought.

He turned away and said to his aide, "Vasiliy, it is time to up the ante a little. Please get President Smitrov on the phone for me."

Zhurkov walked across the wood-paneled study to the large teak desk and dialed the phone. After several minutes and numerous short, whispered conversations, he looked up and nodded. "Admiral, the president is coming on the line now."

Durov took the phone. When he heard Smitrov, he said, "President Smitrov, I fear that I must report our failure to rescue our courageous sailors who have been lost beneath the Barents Sea. The time is past when they could possibly still be alive. Conditions at the ice camp are such that even our best professionals have been able to make little headway."

Smitrov's weak, high-pitched voice came back at him over the crackling line.

"My dear admiral, all of Russia mourns with you for your great loss. Your nephew died a hero of the motherland. If there is anything I can do, just name it."

Durov could barely suppress his glee. Smitrov was an even bigger fool than he thought. This was too easy. The admiral forced a hurt, sorrowful tone to his voice as he replied, "Thank you, President Smitrov. For myself, I need nothing. My sailors, they need solid assurance. If you could come here and speak with them and mourn with the widows, it would mean very much to them. To them and to the people of Russia."

"Of course. I'll fly there the first of next week. My staff will schedule it immediately. Is that adequate?"

"Yes, that would be very much appreciated," Durov

answered. "We will have a memorial service that Russia will never forget. We have much to mourn these days, Mr. President. Much to mourn indeed."

Bill Beaman lifted his head as much as he dared, just high enough for his eyes to see above the snow. He stared across the empty, open ground toward the perimeter road. Nothing disturbed the barren white stretch of land, not even a shrub to hide anyone crazy enough to be trying to sneak across. A BTR-80 chugged noisily down the road, belching blue smoke into the cold air. Its ugly machine cannon was pointed straight ahead, while the tank commander sat up in the turret, surveying the terrain. This one was the third troop carrier Beaman had seen in the last twenty minutes. None of them left a sufficient gap for anyone to slip past them all the way to the perimeter fence.

He slithered back into the protection of the forest, his white camouflage cloak blending in with the snowy terrain. It took an hour to retreat the hundred meters back to the heavy undergrowth where Johnston waited.

"Damn, Skipper! I've seen glaciers move faster," Johnston whispered as Beaman rolled over the log Johnston lay behind.

The SEAL commander grinned, his tanned face starkly outlined by the white hood. "That's just the point. You saw the glacier. You didn't see me."

They both lay low, nothing visible above the little log as they conferred. Beaman had been searching for a way into the submarine base along the perimeter fence while Johnston had been scouting the gates. There were three entrances, all heavily fortified and well guarded. No way to get in through them, short of driving through in an M1A1 Abrams main battle tank, and the SEALs didn't have such a machine at their disposal at the moment.

"Sure a lot of hardware for them to be guarding a bone pile, ain't it?" Johnston said.

"Damn right. We know now that something's up."

"Okay, boss, then what the hell do we do now? I don't know about you, but I don't want to be the one who calls up Donnegan and tells him we found a real beehive but we came up empty on a way to get in and take a better look."

"I'm with you, Chief." The SEAL commander scratched his chin. "You know, the only way we haven't thought about is coming in from the water. Wanna try that?"

Johnston looked at him sideways. "What do you have in mind? We ain't packing any diving gear. I don't figure we can just put on our trunks and swim right in."

"Let me think while we head back up the hill. They can't slip a boat out without us seeing it, but the problem is that we don't have any idea how many more boats they have ready in there. The one that floated out could have been the only one they have in the whole fleet. Or there could be a dozen more sitting there inside that barn. Chief, I think it is incumbent on us to find out or Admiral Donnegan will have our frostbit hides. Come on, let's get moving."

Beaman started crawling. He stayed low and kept silent as he slipped like a hunting predator through the depths of the forest. Chief Johnston was little more than a silent wraith several meters behind him.

Anatol Vivilav stood in the submarine's control room as the *Vipr* swam through the cold Barents. The passage out of the Murmansk Fjord had been without incident. Its tall hillsides had faded into the distance at the sub's stern and then disappeared altogether. The crew of *Vipr* had not seen it. They had been beneath the surface since first entering the fjord.

So far there was no sign of any American submarine or any other warship. Vivilav was relieved. The Americans were playing it safe, not risking any kind of showdown with the Russians during such tense times. Their usual pack of observing submarines was standing off at a safe distance.

The Russian submariner watched with pride as his crew steered the big boat. They were good, well practiced in the trainers, but they lacked sea time. The captain would gladly have sacrificed weeks of work in the trainer for the opportunity to drill his men for just a day of real time at sea. He envied the American submariners, with all the time they spent sailing the world's oceans. Vivilav knew that, as good and faithful as his men were, they were no match for the American submariners' practical, oceangoing experience.

Despite the lack of any American presence so far, he would be very cautious until they were beyond the Barents. If he could guide *Vipr* out into the Norwegian Sea without being discovered, the odds would be in his favor to make it all the way to the Kattegat. He would worry about navigating that treacherous narrow body of water later, when they were much closer. One problem at a time.

First Officer Anistov Dmolysti stepped over to stand beside him. He kept his voice low when he spoke. "They are doing well, Captain. They are learning quickly."

Vivilav glanced around the cramped control room before he answered. The men sitting there, driving the submarine, seemed little more than boys, fresh from some youth camp or university classes. There was no way to know if they were ready for the trials that lay ahead. Vivilav knew that could not be determined today. "Yes, but they will have to."

"Do we know our mission?" Dmolysti asked.

Vivilav nodded. "Yes, and it is time now that we discussed it. Please have all the officers muster in the wardroom in ten minutes."

The submarine captain turned on his heel and marched out of the control room. He needed a few minutes to think about how he would present this most unusual mission to his officers. They had no knowledge of Durov and his plans, but they were loyal Russian sailors. They would follow Vivilav into hell if he asked them.

He pulled the chart from his safe and unrolled it once again. The red-pencil-line track drew his attention, mutely giving a detailed picture of the dangers ahead. He followed its snaking path until it ended in the Baltic Sea. That was enough for his men to know for right now. They were headed for the Baltic and they must make the journey without being discovered.

Vivilav grunted at the sound of a quiet knock at the stateroom door. Dmolysti entered and looked over Vivilav's shoulder.

"Is that where we are going?" he asked.

"Yes, Anistov."

Dmolysti traced the path with a finger. "Why are we staying so close to the coast? This track has us inside Norwegian waters most of the way. That is an act of war. If they detect us, they may well attack."

Vivilav nodded and answered, "That is true, but of little consequence. Our mission is very highly classified and of extreme importance to the motherland. The Americans and probably the British will be hunting us, too. If they find us, they will not hesitate to attack, either. We will stay close to the coast to hide from their listening devices and their ASW searches. We will be safer hiding in the clamor of the inshore noise."

Dmolysti stared at his captain with disbelief. He could not imagine what was happening here. The Americans and the British would be trying to destroy them? The Cold War was long since over, a dim memory far better left forgotten. All was supposed to be peace and prosperity now.

But Dmolysti had heard the rumors of plotting in the Navy, dissatisfied senior officers threatening to overthrow the government in Moscow. He had disregarded them as someone's overactive imagination. Surely such carrying-on was nothing more than idle gossip, invented by cold, hungry officers in a lonely outpost, working hard trying to eke out a meager existence for their families in the bleak north.

He looked at the plot on the chart again. There was no other explanation for the foolhardy course around Norway and into the Baltic, for the odd secrecy on this mission so far, for the unorthodox way they had dived so early after leaving the covered dock.

The realization rolled over Dmolysti. From inside the tiny Baltic Sea, they would be no threat to America. They would be in a position to strike deep into Russia with the missiles they carried.

He felt his stomach drop. The rumors had to be true. There was no other logical explanation.

Dmolysti smiled and looked his captain in the eye. "I understand, Captain. I am with you. Come, the officers are ready to hear from you."

Vivilav smiled back. Dmolysti was a good, smart first officer. He had recognized the true mission as soon as he saw the chart, just as Vivilav knew he would. The only question was his eventual reaction. Vivilav hadn't been sure what Dmolysti would do or where his true loyalties lay. Now he was. His first officer stood with him. That meant that the upcoming task would be much easier.

Vivilav tucked the chart under his arm. The two men stepped out of the stateroom together and headed for the briefing.

Chapter 26

The *Anzio* plunged into the onrushing swell, burying her bow deep into the cold gray water. The flood streamed back along her sleek foredeck, only to pour frothy white over the sides. As each wave passed down her length, the bow reared high out of the water, ready to stab relentlessly into the next swell. A flock of cormorants flew in loose formation astern of the gray warship, looking to snatch any food that might be churned up by her passage.

The officer of the deck watched the agitated sea, scanning the gunmetal gray sky, from the enclosed bridge. Sheets of rain spattered against the broad glass windows. Nothing, not even another ship, broke up the monotonous drabness of the winter sea and sky. Norway was fifty miles away over the horizon to the east, but its mountainous coast was hidden in the clouds. Down below, the crew was just finishing lunch and starting the afternoon routine.

Jon Ward was no exception. He pushed back from the table, patted his stomach contentedly, and sighed. "Excellent meal, Bob."

Commander Bob Norquest sat across from him. The remnants of dinner were still on their plates. The two were alone in Norquest's sea cabin, one deck below the *Anzio*'s bridge and one above the Combat Information Center. The little stateroom included a desk and chair, a broad leather couch, and a small eating area. Though the room was cramped and Spartan by most standards, it still looked palatial to an old submarine sailor like Jon Ward. He was more accustomed to closet-sized submarine staterooms.

"The cooks do a pretty good job. It's tough on them in this weather, though," Norquest answered, then shifted gears. "Any idea how long we're going to be out here?"

As if to emphasize her captain's remarks, *Anzio* took a sharp roll to starboard, sending the crockery rocketing across the table. The two officers reacted, grabbing plates to prevent a messy disaster. They caught most everything, but one errant plate skittered across the table just beyond Ward's grasp and crashed to the deck.

"Sorry. I'm a little slow, I guess," Ward said, and shook his head. "I don't know for sure how long this'll take. I'm guessing two more days for *Toledo* to run into the Kola, a day to recover the SEALs, and then a day to get them out to safe water. After that, we're done." Ward grinned and tossed a good-natured gibe in Norquest's direction. "Think you skimmers can hold out for another five days without a liberty port?"

"You bubble-heads!" Norquest countered. "The sea kicks up a little bit and you guys start looking for a port."

The buzzing of the captain's phone interrupted the repartee. Norquest grabbed the receiver. "Captain."

"Captain, Combat. The ZBO shows Captain Ward

has a message coming across the spec-op channel." The watch officer in CIC held the schedule of incoming radio message traffic and read the listing for one addressed to the submarine commodore. "Should I route it to your cabin?"

Norquest told him to go ahead and then pointed Ward toward a small computer terminal on his desk. Ward grabbed his coffee and moved over there. He typed in his password and the message appeared. Ward read for a few seconds and hit the DELETE key to obliterate the words from the screen.

"I haven't had occasion to use these new shipboard LANs before. I assume it's cleared for SCI?"

Norquest laughed. "I'd say it's too late now if it isn't. The answer is yes. We had a bunch of spooks all over the boat just before we left. They certified the network for everything up to 'rumor.' Judging from that cat-that-ate-the-canary look on your face, that message must have been something interesting."

Ward nodded as he slid back to his seat at the table. "Yeah, real interesting." He scratched his chin as he considered what he had just read. "It looks like Joe Glass on *Toledo* is about to be a little busier than we thought. The SEALs haven't been able to get a good look into the covered pier at Polyarnyy yet. Beaman's come up with a wild idea. He wants to use the Advanced Swimmer Delivery Vehicle *Toledo*'s carrying up there so he can drive in for a peek."

Norquest whistled and shook his head in amazement. "Now, that's not anything I'd be interested in doing. How are they going to pull it off?"

Ward rose and headed for the door. He answered over his shoulder, "That's what I'm going to find out. I need to send a message to Joe and let him know what we're thinking of doing with his little ASDV."

Catherine Goldman stared out the window at the snowy New Jersey countryside, seeing a broad, empty field cut off by a low rock wall at the far end. Anything beyond that was obscured by a dense growth of evergreens. It was an altogether desolate and lonely view, very different from the city.

She was alone in an upstairs bedroom, the door locked from the outside. She had tried it several times during the night and as recently as an hour before. The windows were sealed, but there seemed to be no one outside guarding the place. She hadn't seen a sign of life since she awoke from a fitful sleep, except for a few black crows off in the distance, hovering, looking for carrion.

Her stomach growled, reminding her that she had not eaten since lunch the day before, and that had only been a room service Caesar salad.

The drive from the city had been quick, but it had been hard to judge their speed and, thus, the distance they might have traveled. The combination of the tortuous route, the darkened windows, and her cold, icy fear had left Goldman confused and disoriented. She had no idea where she was, although she had recognized the Holland Tunnel and assumed she was somewhere in New Jersey.

The Russians had taken her cell phone and computer

when they first arrived and then pointedly showed her to this room. Despite what they had told her about taking her to a safe place, it seemed that she was more a prisoner than simply being guarded by Dmitri Ustinov's friends.

Goldman's thoughts were broken by a heavy knock at the door. Before she could even say anything, she heard the lock click, the door swung open, and the one called Mikhail walked in carrying a tray covered with a cloth napkin. The smell of coffee drifted past her nose and she felt weak with hunger.

Mikhail was a large man, powerfully built, with a bull-like neck and upper arms that seemed to strain at the fabric of his suit coat. He had heavy, Slavic features and a thick mane of black hair that showed a few speckles of gray. Last night, he had seemed the youngest of the trio. He was also the friendliest.

He managed what would pass for a smile. "Good morning. I hope you rested comfortably." His accent was so thick Goldman had trouble understanding his words. "Here is some breakfast for you."

Mikhail placed the tray on a small table by the window. As he turned to leave, Goldman grabbed his arm.

"Why am I being held a prisoner here?" she asked.

He gently but pointedly removed her hand, keeping his smile the entire time. "Is for your safety. We protect you from harm. The OptiMarx people would have you killed. You are to them a threat."

"Okay, so why can't I have my phone and computer?" she demanded. "I could at least be getting some work done."

Still smiling, Mikhail shook his head. "That is not to be allowed. You are to have no outside contact. Those are our orders."

"Surely I can have my computer. You can monitor my calls. I have to let the authorities know what's happening."

"Is not possible. Our orders are very clear. I am sorry."

"But—"

He stopped her with a beefy, upheld hand. Now the smile was gone. "Is not for discussion."

Mikhail turned and marched out of the room. The door swung closed hard behind him.

Catherine Goldman heard the lock click shut with utter finality.

Commander Anatol Vivilav stood in the control room staring at the sonar screen before him. The green circle was cluttered, but it was all the noise of the heavy winter seas above them. The Russian captain could not believe his luck. Not a sign of the Americans! They normally shadowed any of the old Russian boats that left the fjord. Maybe the tension in the world over the submarines that had been lost had made them skittish, made them pull back to avoid any other confrontations. Still, the Americans' sonars were better than his. They could be tracking *Vipr* at a distance. He had been maneuvering constantly in an attempt to unveil anyone trying to follow him.

There had not been a sign so far. Either someone very good was following them or they were all alone.

Vivilav moved from the sonar display to look once again at the navigation plot. Anistov Dmolysti worked to map their position on a large-scale chart of the Barents. It showed them about to turn the corner into the Norwegian Sea.

Dmolysti glanced up and nodded at Vivilav.

"We are making good progress, Captain," he murmured. "Still, we are behind schedule. We are using too much time searching for trailers."

Vivilav stared at the chart. Dmolysti was right. As it was, they would be required to set a pace well above *Vipr*'s best quiet speed. They would be going dangerously fast past some of the best antisubmarine warfare forces in the world. If Admiral Durov was correct, those forces would be out looking for them, more than ready to destroy *Vipr* if they could.

"You're right, First Officer. We will stop the evasive maneuvers."

The shrill scream of an alarm interrupted their conversation. Both men jumped and looked around, but everything in the control room looked normal.

Just then, the announcing system blared, "Fire! Fire in the engine room!"

"Anistov, go aft and take charge," Vivilav shouted as he rushed over to the command center. Dmolysti was already running toward the engine room.

The first officer rushed through the compartments until he came to the watertight door leading to the engine room. It was shut. He pulled his air mask into place over his face before opening the door.

He was engulfed in a dark, billowing cloud of black smoke. Visibility was almost nil. He could barely see to make his way down the passageway, deeper into the room. The air mask was cloying, uncomfortable, but it fed him lifesaving clean air and no man would last more than a minute in this thick fog.

He pushed forward, trying to find the source of the fire and the crew who should be fighting it. The smoke grew even thicker. Dmolysti dropped to his knees and felt his way forward along the walkway. After a seeming eternity in the blinding darkness, he bumped into the crewmen who were battling the blaze. Dmolysti could hardly make out the shape of one man through the smoke, but there was no way to see who it was.

He shouted to be heard through the mask, "Where is the fire?"

"In the switchboard!" the crewman shouted back. "It is turned off now, but the wiring insulation must still be burning."

"You will have to get the cover off so you can spray the chemicals inside," Dmolysti ordered.

"We can't," the sailor protested. "It's still burning."

Even through the smoke and haze, Dmolysti could see that the young sailor was quaking with fear. He reached out and grabbed the sailor's fire extinguisher from him, then pushed past him and confronted the switchboard.

The normally dull gray panel glowed cherry red from the heat inside it. Smoke poured out of the vent fins. No wonder the *michman* couldn't or wouldn't open the panel. He would have burned his hands and been blasted by the flames when the panel fell free. But there wasn't any choice. The fire had to be extinguished before it spread. If it reached the highly flammable hull insulation, the whole engine room would be engulfed. Then they would lose the sub.

Dmolysti 'ripped off his uniform shirt. Wrapping it around his hand, he reached out and tried to spin the nuts on the switchboard cover free. The heat was intolerable. Sweat poured from his body and then sizzled as it dripped to the deck. He kept working, jerking back his hand when the heat got too intense to bear. The nuts finally spun free. As the panel fell away from the switchboard, a blast of flames shot out, seeking air, threatening to devour anything in its way.

Dmolysti had fought submarine fires before. He ducked to the side as the panel fell away, escaping the hungry, licking blaze. He stared into the center of hell. The inside was engulfed, a roaring inferno. Molten metal dripped down from the incandescently glowing bus bars. It was so bright, Dmolysti had to shield his eyes and the heat singed his eyebrows and beard.

He grabbed up the extinguisher and pointed the nozzle at the heart of the blaze. The purple chemical poured into the heat, smothering some of the fire before the last of it spluttered out, empty before the fire was knocked down. He dropped the canister to the deck and someone shoved another one into his hands. This one made more progress against the blaze. Another one and the fire was starting to give way. The fourth extinguisher killed the last of the flames.

Dmolysti fell to the deck, exhausted, his breath coming in great heaving gasps. *Vipr* was saved, but the job was not yet done. They still had to remove all the toxic smoke from the sub. Then they would face the daunting task of repairing the damage.

Though his muscles ached and breath was hard to find, he shoved himself erect and stumbled toward the hatch. He yanked it open and stepped out into air that was clean and clear. Once he had removed his air-breathing mask, Dmolysti sucked in great gulps of the smoke-free air. As soon as he found the strength, he stood and hurried toward the control room to report to Vivilav.

The captain stood at the periscope, guiding *Vipr* to periscope depth. He knew they would have to reach the clean Arctic air to clear the smoke from the engine room. The deck was already rolling and pitching as they headed up to the surface.

Dmolysti wiped the sweat from his face with the remnants of his charred shirt.

"Captain, the fire is out," Dmolysti reported. "The engine room is filled with smoke. The port main switchboard is destroyed."

Vivilav nodded and replied, "This will set us back even more. Let's hope no one is up there to see us while we ventilate."

Vipr continued to move up from the depths. They passed through the thermocline, the invisible demarcation line between the very cold waters of the deep ocean and the slightly warmer waters near the surface. Above the thermocline, all sound waves were bent upward. Below it, they were reflected down. That meant that below the thermocline, *Vipr* was shielded from surface ship sonars that might be above her. Once she had climbed above the thermocline, though, she was vulnerable to surface sonars but shielded from any submarine that might be listening from down below.

The sub's periscope broke the surface. Vivilav looked out on a world of gray. The sea churned, shoving the submarine around like a cork bobbing on the ocean's surface. They appeared to be alone. Waves tumbled and crashed over the periscope, momentarily blinding the captain.

They would have to come up farther. They couldn't snorkel at this depth with the waves rolling over the periscope. It would drown the snorkel.

"Make your depth fifteen meters," he ordered. *Vipr* moved up a little higher in the water. At last they were clear enough of the waves for the snorkel to operate. Vivilav shouted, "Raise the snorkel mast!"

He watched as the large black pipe slid upward, clear of the tops of the waves. As soon as he was sure it was high enough, he ordered, "Commence snorkeling."

The grumbling roar of the diesel generator vibrated throughout the boat. The noisy machine sucked in great quantities of clean air and vented out the choking smoke that had filled the engine room.

Vivilav winced. The noise of their diesel would carry for many miles through the water, and he knew that there was no way to disguise the distinctive sound. If anyone were looking for them, they would come running now.

The smoke dissipated, but the stench of the fire remained. Men removed their air-breathing masks, fighting the impulse to gag, and started the slow task of trying to repair the damage.

No one on board *Vipr* was aware of another large submarine, this one traveling below the thermocline on a reverse course, twenty miles away. On board *Toledo*, the narrow sonar trace they saw was classified as a fishing trawler.

Intent on reaching its destination, *Toledo* ignored the brief blip as it passed astern.

Chapter 27

The *Toledo* moved through the cold waters of the Barents. Traveling deep and fast, she felt nothing of the turbulence that raged up above them on the sea's roiling surface.

Master Chief Tommy Zillich sat perched on a high stool in the back corner of his beloved sonar shack. The dim blue light played across his face as he nursed his "boys" while their high-tech electronic "ears" searched out the far corners of the depths. They were doing their best to hear anyone out there long before the other guys realized *Toledo* was in the neighborhood.

He sat back, yawned, and, as he reached up behind his head in a big stretch, he flipped a switch to start a tape in a small playback unit. It was time to test his team and, at the same time, interject a little excitement into an otherwise boring watch. The tape turned as Zillich scrutinized the backs of his watchstanders.

Sure enough, the passive broadband (PBB) operator jerked up straight in his chair as if someone had sent high voltage through it. He began frantically pushing buttons on his stack with his left hand and slewing his joystick to the bearing with his right. His eyes were wide. The displays in front of him shifted through several modes until he finally looked up.

"Chief, new contact!" he shouted breathlessly. "Sierra four-seven-one. Possible Sierra-class Russian sub. Bearing one-two-five. Best range two to three thousand yards."

Zillich frowned. He reached to cuff the young sonarman sharply on his shoulder.

"How many times do I have to tell you blockheads?" he growled. "First thing you do is you report the contact as soon as you detect it. *Then* you classify it. In the time it took you to fondle your joystick, that Russki could have shot your ass off. You better thank your lucky stars that Sierra was on tape. If he'd have been real, he'd have eaten our lunch, Levi."

Zillich reached back and flicked off the training tape.

The chastened operator turned away, his head down. His fellow sonar men threw quiet gibes his way.

Tommy Zillich cleared his throat and looked at them through his eyebrows. "Hey, the rest of you rocks, pay attention. Next time, it may be your turn and—"

"What's happening, Master Chief?" the deep voice behind his shoulder interrupted Zillich's reprimand. Joe Glass was standing there in the sonar room doorway.

Zillich rose from his stool and scooted over toward the door. "Just a little on-the-job training, Skipper. These quiet watches, you don't throw in some OJT every once in a while, this motley bunch'll start taking naps on company time."

Glass leaned down to look at the PBB display. The waterfall didn't show anything except the trace from the taped submarine contact. The only thing disturbing the display was the distinctive chevron pattern of a storm raging away up above. "Agreed. Been quiet, huh?"

"Yes, sir. Only contact was a distant fishing boat a couple of hours ago. That had to be one damn fool to be out trying to snag some fish in that weather up there."

Glass nodded, imagining what it must be like riding out the icy turbulence of a winter storm in the Barents in nothing more than a fishing boat. That was one hell of a way to try to make a living.

He shook his head, then changed subjects. "Master Chief, I need you to attend a briefing in the wardroom in ten minutes. Get yourself a relief and hop on down there."

Zillich replied, "Yes, sir," but he was talking to empty space. Glass had already disappeared out the door.

By the time Zillich arrived in the wardroom, most of the seats were already claimed. The room was full. Glass sat in his customary chair at the head of the table, flanked by Edwards on his left and Hector Gonzales, the ASDV driver, on his right. A sheet covered the bulkhead behind the skipper. The other four crewmen on the ASDV occupied the next four seats. Most of the officers sat in the remaining chairs or on the brown Naugahyde couch that was built into the outboard bulkhead. Sam Wallich was seated on the couch as well. He was the only other chief in the room.

Zillich plopped down on the couch next to Wallich. "Evening, COB. Any idea what's going on?"

"Nope, but I reckon we're about to find out."

Glass stood, cleared his throat to quiet the chatter in

the room, and started the briefing. "Gentlemen, we received a change in plans with the last message download. It seems that Lieutenant Gonzales is going to take himself a little sightseeing trip into the heart of the Polyarnyy sub base."

He ignored the dropped jaws in the room as he reached up and pulled down the sheet to show a small-scale chart of the Murmansk Fjord and several satellite images of the sub base. The chart had a green line extending from the open sea to a location well inside the fjord's mouth. There was a blue line traveling farther down from there until it took a left turn into the Polyarnyy Basin. It ended there.

Everyone in the room leaned forward to stare at the blue line, knowing instantly what it meant. They also knew approval for such an operation in such a screwy world situation had to come from the highest level, one that resided in the White House.

Doug O'Malley put his coffee cup down and whistled long and low. "Wow! I for one am damn glad I'm not riding that little bucket of bolts in there. Talk about stepping right into the bear's mouth."

Glass nodded and allowed a slight smile to play at his lips. "Eng, that's putting it pretty succinctly." He picked up a laser pointer and aimed its red dot at the spot where the green and blue lines met. "Desperate times call for desperate measures. We don't know what these so-and-sos are up to and we have to find out for certain. We'll deploy the ASDV right here. Our job on *Toledo* is to get it to that point and then wait around to pick it up again when it gets back." He traced the blue line with the pointer. "Lieutenant Gonzales will drive the ASDV down into the Polyarnyy Basin and then into the entrance of the covered submarine docks. There he will take periscope pictures of any boats he finds inside. He'll then detour over here to the extraction point and pick up the SEAL team. After that, it's just a matter of turning around and scooting back here."

Every man in the room was thinking the same thing: "Damn sight easier said than done."

Glass turned to Gonzales, the Special Boat Unit lieutenant, handed him the laser pointer, and sat down.

Hector Gonzales rose and stepped to the head of the table. "Thank you, Captain." He stood, half facing the chart, and continued. "Gentlemen, as the skipper said, we will deploy from just inside the mouth of the Murmansk Fjord. We expect a two-knot ebbing current as we head up the fjord. That will limit us to six knots over the ground."

Gonzales turned to face the satellite photos and pointed the laser to a small building near the water. "Intel says this is the command center for harbor control right here."

Sam Donlan, Gonzales's copilot on the mini-sub, piped up. "Hey, Hector, do we have any details on what kind of defenses they may have up there?"

Gonzales glanced over at the dark-haired Irishman, pursed his lips, and shook his head. "Nope. All we have is what we can hypothesize."

Again every man had the same thought: "We have a SWAG. A scientific wild-assed guess!"

The SBU lieutenant's voice was steady and sure as he

went on. "There are most likely some submarine sensors and certainly command-detonated mines. From what we've heard from the SEALs already up there, they have the place wrapped up pretty tight." He turned to the chart again. "Hydrographic surveys show there's a sheer granite wall on this side of the fjord and it drops down to a thousand feet. We'll snuggle up as close as we can to that wall. If we can stay close it'll give us our best protection from both the sensors and the mines, but we'll have to be slow and deliberate. It'll take a couple of hours for us to make it to the Polyarnyy Basin."

"Yeah, I hear you, boss," Donlan said. "We play it by ear. Have we heard anything about what might be inside the basin?"

"Nope. Nothing on that. All we know is that one new Akula has come out of there in the past forty-eight hours. That's the second one we know of, counting the one that ended up on the bottom. We aim to find out if there are any more in that shed and if they look like they may be readied for sea duty. You're right, Sam. We'll have to play it by ear. Once we've grabbed the pictures, we'll pick up the SEALs as planned. Then we backtrack home the same way we snuck in and meet *Toledo* out here."

"How's the surface ice?"

"Shouldn't be a problem. They broke it up for the first sub out and it looks like just a skim now. We should be able to punch a scope through it. Any more questions?"

No one said anything. Glass stood and nodded toward Jerry Perez. "Nav, your turn."

Perez stood. "Well, from our viewpoint, this is an easy

operation so long as they don't start flooding subs out of that place and head them our way. We have to get into the fjord's mouth and hang around, waiting while you guys have all the fun." Perez glanced at the page of notes he held. "The important thing is to sneak in real quiet-like. Nobody is sure what the Russians still have available for close-in ASW. Estimates vary from 'not much' to 'everything still working.' We'll have to assume the latter and be as quiet as we can. COB, that's what you and Master Chief Zillich are here for. We need a real good self-noise monitoring and then be careful about our housekeeping as long as we are in there."

Wallich nodded. "Don't worry, Nav. We got a handle on it. Old *Toledo*'ll be so quiet the fish won't even know we're there. Right, Tommy?"

Zillich winked. "Right, COB. We already have the sonar search plan drawn up. There'll be lots of biologics and surf noise in close to hide in."

"Very well," Glass said, ending the meeting.

As they filed from the room, Jerry Perez mumbled to himself, "Oh, if it were only as easy as it sounds!"

Catherine Goldman searched the room once again, but still she could find no way out. The windows on the old farmhouse wouldn't budge, having been painted shut long ago. Getting one open would do her little good, as it was at least a fifteen-foot drop to the frozen ground. She was resigned to making the leap if she could get outside. A broken leg might be preferable to whatever those dark, heavy men might have in store for her.

There had to be a way out of here! She needed to find

it quickly. It wasn't just that she needed to get to safety. She also had to let someone know what was going on with the OptiMarx system before it went live. She felt queasy every time she considered what the modifications she had found might do to the market if it went online in less than two days.

She sat down on the side of the bed and tried to order her thoughts. She had no idea how all this fit together. No way of knowing who were the good guys and who were the bad in this unseemly little drama.

She fell back hard, frustrated, and rolled over onto her side, pulling her knees against her chest, just the way she had done as a little girl when things disturbed her. She pulled the pillow under her head and fought to keep the tears from coming to her eyes. She didn't have time to cry. She had to stay calm, keep her wits about her, find a way out of this place.

That's when she noticed something in the dark corner of the closet. She had left the door open after looking for a doorway to the attic or some kind of crawl space into another room. A dim shaft of light emerged from the far corner of the closet. She had not noticed it before.

She rolled off the bed and stepped softly on bare feet to the closet, making sure no one in the room below could hear. Scooting a couple of boxes aside, she found an old-fashioned metal grate that looked through to the floor beneath. Crouching, Goldman peered through the opening. Nothing was visible down there but the dusty top of some piece of furniture, maybe a china cabinet or bookcase.

She was about to tiptoe back to the bed when she

heard voices. Men's voices. The deep, guttural tones were clearly in Russian.

For the first time in a while, Catherine Goldman smiled. Russian just happened to be the language she had learned at her grandmother's knee. She said a silent prayer of thanks for the long-departed old lady who had doggedly insisted that the family learn her native language, even though she had fled the pogroms as a teenager.

"It will stand you in good stead someday, my child," she had said. Catherine had doubted it until this very moment.

She recognized the voice. The one she knew as Mikhail was speaking.

"Nicholas, what are we going to do? Sit here and babysit that SEC bitch until the end of time?"

That was the one she believed to be the polite one. He didn't seem so polite now. She heard the disembodied voice of "Nicholas" as he answered him rather heatedly. She struggled to understand his rapid-fire Russian. She was rusty, but still could make out most of it.

"If that is what Boris Medikov orders, that is what we will do."

"Why don't we just kill her?" Mikhail shot back. "We could bury the body and go back to the city and make certain the balance of the plan is carried out properly."

She breathed in sharply and closed her eyes, forcing herself to listen harder.

"Simple. Because Boris Medikov says that we should keep her alive until after the plan is put into effect. She may be useful in dealing with those OptiMarx idiots. Medikov said the time is very soon. At the best, we will only have a few days to make our profits before Admiral Durov puts his plan into effect. From then on, we have to disrupt the U.S. market to divert their attention . . . from us and Durov as well."

Goldman's eyes opened wide as she listened in amazement. Durov? A Russian admiral was involved in this thing somehow. Could this all be tied to the international incident over the missing Russian submarines? Goldman had put all that aside as she concentrated on the Opti-Marx problem. As big an international incident as it was, it couldn't have impacted her investigation. It had never occurred to her that they might some way be entangled. Now, from what she was hearing, it was all part of the same plot!

A different voice, one she had not yet heard, spoke.

"It had better happen soon, before the old bastard's heart gives out."

Nicholas chuckled in response. "No matter. We will still make money either way, Josef. Anyway, it is time for you and me to go deal with that Smythe guy. Mikhail, you will stay here and take proper care of our guest."

Goldman heard the rough scraping of chairs on a hardwood floor and, quickly afterward, the slamming of a door. She hurried from the spot where she had been kneeling in the closet and looked out the front window. She was just in time to see the big Ford blast away down the driveway.

Her head was spinning wildly as she fell back onto the bed.

*   *   *

Admiral Durov stood beside his black Zil, parked at the head of the pier, and watched the scurry of activity down by the black hull of a submarine. The huge expanse of the covered dock was bathed in the dim golden glow of the overhead lights. He pulled his heavy bridge coat more tightly as a bitter-cold wind blew in from the open seaward end of the building.

Vasiliy Zhurkov noticed.

"Are you cold, Admiral?"

"Just the breeze. It brings a chill."

The old man did not look well. The constant tension and effort of the last few months had carved deep lines on his ghostly-pale face. Zhurkov worried his mentor would work himself into a grave before he could ever see his bold plan to fruition.

"Is everything ready for President Smitrov?" Durov asked his aide.

"Yes, Admiral. The memorial ceremony is all planned. The families and all the local dignitaries will be at the chapel, as will select members of the international news media. The president has approved the agenda."

Durov smiled, but the strain of the effort to do so was obvious. "That is good. And after the ceremony?"

"Your special security team will take Smitrov prisoner."

The *Kuguar* was the next submarine scheduled to sneak out into the Barents, and it was ready to depart. The crew hustled to cast off the lines that bound the sub to the pier. The crews of the other four boats stood and watched as one of their brothers headed out to war. As the *Kuguar* began moving toward the open end of the building, the boats bid their good-byes with prolonged blasts of their horns. The sound reverberated around the building, the harsh echoes exploding from all sides.

The black submarine slipped away from the pier, easing through the water. Except for the slow churning of the screw, it barely disturbed the oily smooth surface of the icy water as it moved forward, fading into the blackness as it headed through the door into the open basin.

Durov raised his arm to snap off a sharp salute of farewell to one of his charges, but dropped it to clutch his chest.

"My pills," he groaned.

Zhurkov ran to his side, fumbling to open the bottle that contained his little blue pills. He gave Durov two of them to swallow, all the while chiding him like a misbehaving child. "Admiral, you have put off seeing a doctor much too long. Please allow me to take you to the clinic this instant. The next attack may well kill you."

Durov shooed him off with a wave of his hand. "No, no. Not yet. There is still too much to do. Plenty of time for pampering later."

Zhurkov shook his head. The old admiral's face was deathly white, his lips blue, but not from the cold. Something lurked in the man's eyes, though, something that burned white-hot and bright. Something that made the aide hush his scolding for the moment and trot off to tend to the details of the president's impending visit.

Tony Martinelli rubbed the sleep from his eyes and tried to focus on the yawning mouth of the covered submarine pens. Two nights had passed since the Russian submarine had sneaked out, and ever since it had been boring duty up here on this windswept cliff, dodging snowflakes and staring down at the Polyarnyy Sub Base. Nothing down there but ice, snow and the occasional rusty truck slipping and sliding along on the rutted roads.

"Hey, Jason," he whispered. "Got any water? I'm out."

"Damn, Tony," Jason Hall grumbled. "What did you do all the time I was on watch? I had to crawl out to fill my own CamelBak. Didn't you?"

"Oh, come on. I'll fill yours when I finish here. Just give me a drink."

Hall handed his CamelBak to his teammate. "Okay, but I expect a gentle, unassuming Chardonnay. Not too oaky."

Martinelli took a big swig and wiped his lips. "Right. You'll get melted snow, just like always. I'll try to stay away from the yellow snow, but I ain't guaranteeing anything."

Just then, a ghostly black shadow blocked some of the light at the end of the pier where they had both been staring just moments before. Martinelli almost missed it but then caught the motion out of the corner of his eye. He was all business. He rolled over and pressed his eye against his sniper scope eyepiece. The green shape of the Akula-class submarine came sharply into focus.

"Hey, Jason. Call home and tell 'em we have another one of the bastards coming out of the barn."

The other SEAL was already activating his satellite radio.

Chapter 28

Anatol Vivilav watched with great interest as the young *michman* poked around inside the charred mass of the burned-out switchboard. The diesel had removed most of the smoke, but the acrid smell still hung heavy in the air. It would be a long time before that sickening odor dissipated. The hull insulation and most of the nearby equipment were scorched and darkened by the heat of the conflagration. The bulkheads and overhead were blackened from the smoke.

Vipr had rounded North Cape and was already beginning the long run south, down the Norwegian coast. Even so, they stayed near the surface, snorkeling to clear the smoke from inside the submarine. No effort had been made to repair the damage from the blaze. Heavy pitching and rolling from the winter seas had made any efforts to work futile and dangerous. Instead, the crew could do little more than grab on to any available handhold and wait until *Vipr* could return to the calm of the deep.

At last, when the air was cleaner, they were able to dive, long hours of agonized motion at an end. Just in time, too. They were now starting the most dangerous part of their journey, out here in the Norwegian Sea where the Americans or British would be most likely to catch them. They had to be alert and ready to fight.

The fire meant they lost half of their seawater cooling pumps, limiting them to half of the reactor's full power. They had no chance at all of outrunning any pursuers, at least until they could repair the damage. They would have to depend on the old submariner's two favorite tools: stealth and cunning. Vivilav had already ordered the torpedoes made ready for instant launch in case they had to defend themselves.

As he considered the disarray in his engine room, the captain shook his head in wonder, realizing how close they had come to disaster. But for Dmolysti's quick thinking and bravery, they might well have lost the *Vipr*, and their own lives as well, in the inferno.

The *michman* emerged from inside the switchboard, sweat streaking his face and his cheeks, his arms blackened with soot. He shook his head mournfully.

"I'm sorry, Captain. It is hopeless. The insides are completely consumed, melted copper everywhere. We will not be able to fix it out here."

Vivilav wasn't surprised. He nodded in acknowledgment, turned, and slowly walked forward. Dmolysti met him at the engine room hatch. He saw the downcast look on Vivilav's face and asked, "Not good news?"

The captain leaned tiredly on the bulkhead. His voice was heavy with resignation when he spoke. "No, the switchboard is a complete disaster. I would say that the bus bars were not properly tightened when the shipyard was working on them. That caused a short circuit that arced into a fire. Everything inside is burned or melted.

We are just lucky it did not jump to the hull insulation. We were likely within seconds of that happening."

The first officer nodded without saying anything. As experienced submariners, both knew how close they had come to an agonizing death. Fortunate as they were, they also understood the real consequences of the disaster. Every piece of electrical equipment powered from that switchboard was now lost. They would not have any backup to run if equipment powered from the other switchboard failed. Firing their missiles would take at least twice as long as normal. More immediately important, they would need to operate the lone remaining sea-water pump in fast speed. It would limit their top speed some, but more problematic was the fact that the *Vipr* would now be noisier as she tried to sneak down the Norwegian coast. Their chances of being detected had just ratcheted up considerably.

"Is there anything we can do?" Dmolysti inquired. "We are risking too much already."

Vivilav scratched the graying stubble on his chin and thought for a few minutes.

"There might be a way," he grunted. "I heard a story about one of the old Yankee missile boats back in the Cold War days. They were off the American coast when the missile fire control system lost power. They rigged jumper wires from a spare breaker on another switch-board. That bit of creative electrical work allowed them to stay on patrol instead of returning home in disgrace."

"You think it might work?" Anistov Dmolysti asked. "Do we have anyone on board with the skill to do this work?"

"We'll have to find out. We have no other option. There is a spare breaker available on the starboard main switchboard. We can strip wiring from the port side that we won't need anymore. I would guess that it will take two or three days to rewire everything. Longer if we do not get to work. Every minute we run with the one pump wide-open, the more likely we are to be heard. I want the seawater pump ready before we get to the Kattegat."

The first officer watched as his captain walked away down the narrow passageway. Somehow, Captain Vivilav was going to see that this mission did not fail. Dmolysti could not ignore the gnawing ache in the pit of his stomach as he headed off to look for someone skilled enough to do his captain's bidding.

Jon Ward sat up high in the command seat in the *Anzio*'s CIC, bored out of his seagoing mind. He yawned as he watched the intelligence picture develop on the large-screen display in front of him. Their best estimate of the position of Joe Glass and *Toledo* and the precious ASDV they carried showed up on the screen as a green, inverted U, the symbol for a friendly submarine. Two similar symbols, only these glowing red, gave the intel weenies' best guesses at where the two escaped Russian subs could be.

Ward shook his head and smiled. He knew what a guesstimate those were. The actual positions of the Russian subs could be anywhere within five hundred miles of that symbol, and they could be getting farther away every hour.

The western boundary for the first Russian sub had passed beyond *Anzio*'s current location several hours ago. That's why Ward was sitting here in this seat while the *Anzio* steamed back and forth with her long SQQ-89 towed-array tail deep down in the cold Norwegian Sea, fishing for Akulas.

Besides that, there wasn't much else to do right now. Joe Glass had his orders and the *Toledo* was running off to the Barents to carry them out. Glass didn't need any long-distance coaching from his old captain.

Bob Beaman was flat on his stomach on some frozen mound of dirt above Polyarnyy, no doubt freezing his ass off while he watched the occasional Russian submarine slink out to sea. Everything was in motion. Now all Joe and his guys had to do was to sneak in close, send the mini-sub off to take a nice, long look into the barn, then pull Beaman and his Boy Scout troop out of Russian territory.

That's all.

Ward sat back and took a sip from his cup of coffee. He spat it back.

Damn stuff was cold! He stood, stretched, and sauntered over to the coffeepot. As he dumped the cold joe in the sink and poured fresh, steaming liquid into the china mug, Ward decided to step across the passageway and take a peak inside *Anzio*'s sonar shack. He could justify leaving his post for a moment. He knew it always seemed to improve the guys' morale when they knew the boss was taking a personal interest in what they were doing.

He stepped out of the darkened CIC and blinked several times in the bright light of the passageway. The sonar shack was a few steps forward. Ward walked into a room much larger than what he was accustomed to from his time in cramped submarine sonar spaces. But the banks of equipment looked very familiar. Young sailors stared, trying to pull information out of waterfall displays on CRTs, hoping to see the broadband noise from a submarine painted on the screens. Others watched wavy lines build on the narrow-band displays, trying to find the telltale discrete frequency signature of an Akula-class Russian submarine.

One of the men watching the SQQ-89 narrow-band display noticed Ward standing at the door. He stepped briskly over to greet him. The short, slight man wore the anchors of a chief petty officer on the collars of his blue jumpsuit and a name tag that said STROUD.

"Captain, welcome to sonar," he greeted Ward. He paused for an instant. "Can I help you, sir?"

Ward smiled. He recognized the proprietary attitude that he had observed in most of the best submarine sonar chiefs he had dealt with. This was *his* space, thank you very much. The rest of the ship might belong to the captain, but sonar was the chief's territory.

"Just stopped in to see how things were going, Chief," Ward said. "Any activity out there at all?"

CPO Stroud stepped back toward the narrowband display. Ward followed. The chief pointed to a peak on one of the squiggly lines. "We've been getting some intermittent hits at fifteen-point-two hertz. Not enough to call it a contact yet."

Ward rubbed his chin and thought for a bit. "Hmmm, if that were a closing contact, making, say, fifteen knots in the line of sight . . ."

Stroud smiled, nodded, and continued Ward's thought.

"Yeah, take the Doppler effect out and it puts the base frequency right at fifteen hertz, one of the best tonals for an Akula. That's why we've been watching it so hard. The problem is, it builds for a couple of minutes and then we lose it. Fifteen minutes, a half hour later, we get another hit on it."

Ward watched the display with great interest for a minute. Just as Chief Stroud had predicted, the peak disappeared.

"Damn," Stroud muttered. "Lost it again."

"Chief, why hasn't that tonal been reported to CIC?" Ward asked.

Stroud looked hard at the former submarine captain for a moment before he answered, his jaws working as he considered his reply.

"Ship's policy, sir," he answered. "The officers over there don't want their displays all cluttered up with possible contacts that eventually turn into biologics or fish farts. We have been told not to report until we are sure it is a contact of interest."

The chief's tone left little doubt that this policy was something with which he didn't agree. It was clearly a battle he had lost somewhere along the way.

Ward smiled and winked. "Chief, while I'm on board your fine ship, could you humor an old salt? Send over every possible contact so I'll have something to play with. It gets real boring looking at that big screen and I need to justify this pleasure cruise somehow."

The beginnings of a smile creased Stroud's craggy face. "Yes, sir. I sure wouldn't want you to fall asleep in CIC. Bad form. We'll start sending this guy over for you to play with." The CPO glanced back at the display. "We just need to get him back first, though."

"Oh, we got time to wait for him. We got time."

Alan Smythe, the CEO of OptiMarx, stood proudly at Alstair McLain's right shoulder. It was, indeed, a great day. As soon as this little ceremony concluded, someone would ring the bell and OptiMarx would go live. He smiled a little as he pictured the massive amounts of money that would soon begin rolling into his offshore account.

Television lights burned down on the high platform where he stood with the Securities and Exchange Commission official and other dignitaries looking for face time on all the financial cable channels. Smythe felt the sweat build on the back of his neck, then trickle down his spine. He couldn't wriggle or stop smiling. He stood mere inches away from the chairman of the New York Stock Exchange, looking out over the waiting trading floor.

The crowd below milled about, ready to get the day going, while McLain droned on about the foresight and wisdom it had taken to conceive a project as revolutionary as OptiMarx, as if the colorless bureaucrat had conjured up the entire idea himself and built it with his own hands.

Smythe smiled benignly. Let the bastard have his moment in the sun. He could take full credit for building the system for all Smythe cared, so long as Smythe ended up with the bounty that was about to come.

McLain folded the pages of his prepared speech and grabbed the lanyard. He gave it a sharp yank. The crowd cheered as the bell rang, signaling the start of another trading day there in the center of world capitalism. The floor was transformed into a scene of bedlam as the specialists rushed to clear the opening trades. The ceremony was forgotten, old business. There were profits to be made, losses to be avoided.

The chairman led the group from the balcony and down a corridor to his office. A sumptuous spread of lobster, fresh fruits, and cold cuts of all kinds lay ready on a large antique buffet in the spacious outer office. Bottles of champagne were iced and ready. Several dozen dignitaries, Exchange executives, and OptiMarx staff stood around in small groups, making mindless small talk while they waited for the official party. It was only a few minutes past nine thirty in the morning, but everyone seemed remarkably hungry and thirsty.

Mark Stern was there, a broad, uncharacteristic smile splitting his face. From the color of his cheeks, it was clear he had not waited on the officials before sampling the champagne. He raised his glass in salute as the group stepped through the door. The crowd clapped and cheered, then moved in earnest toward the food.

Stern eased over to stand next to Smythe and waited for the others to move along. Even then, he talked in a near whisper so that no one but Smythe could hear.

"So, you and your Keystone Kops got it finished, huh? I hope you plan to wait a few days before you start using the . . . uh . . . special features."

Smythe glanced at the venture capitalist and took a sip of the bubbly. "Yes, of course. We figured we'd wait a week, and even then we'll start slowly."

Stern nodded his approval. He sidled off to chat with the chairman, who happened to be an old college chum. Another cheer went up in the room as they watched the first OptiMarx trades appear on the stock ticker. Trade volume was building nicely and everything looked to be going perfectly so far.

Carl Andretti walked across the room, an empty champagne flute in one hand and his cell phone in the other. The legs of his slacks pooled around his scuffed shoes, and a prominent button on his dress shirt had come undone. The rest were pulled taut by his bulging girth. He was talking animatedly to someone on the phone. When he caught Smythe's eye he winked and smiled to let him know all was well. He snapped the phone shut with a flourish.

"The ops center is reporting that we are doing over forty percent of the listed stock trades on the system already and the volume is building." He sounded like a teenage boy bragging about his first hot rod. "At this rate we should be doing all of the trades on the Exchange by the end of the week. The system is performing beautifully. Less than a tenth of a second's transaction time."

Andretti grabbed a bottle from a passing waiter and refilled his glass, spilling the champagne all over his fist. He leaned over to fill Smythe's flute as well and whispered, "We're ready to use *all* the system whenever you're ready."

He leaned on the word "all." Smythe nodded.

"Okay, but by all means, keep it off the books. Our friend from California doesn't need to know about this."

He nodded toward Mark Stern, now exchanging secret fraternity handshakes with the chairman of the Exchange. Andretti followed his gaze.

"Don't worry. Don't worry about a thing," the CTO said, and downed most of the wine in his glass in a single gulp.

Boris Medikov watched the formal ceremony play out halfway around the world on the sophisticated satellite hookup in his penthouse apartment. A fire crackled in the fireplace. The sun had already dropped below the horizon. Outside, a cold drizzle was developing into a snow squall as the temperature dropped with the darkness. The mixture of rain, snow, and sleet tapped against the picture windows of his apartment, obscuring the view toward the Kremlin.

Medikov snapped on some lights in the room and poured himself a generous snifter of brandy. It was time for a little celebration of his own.

So they had done it! Marina's last report had been quite heartening. She said the testing had been completed successfully, the system worked the way it was supposed to do, and no one had found even a hint of their hidden code after the Goldman woman's disappearance. The new SEC man, Sanderson, was as promised, a complete dolt who couldn't find his ass with both hands. That had been Medikov's niece's precise words. "His ass with both hands." He passed through every test procedure as quickly as he could and then merrily signed them off as if he was in a hurry to catch a plane home.

Medikov smiled as he watched the television screen. A government official who was pontificating on and on ended his spiel and rang the bell to begin trading. It was now time for the payoff. He had invested years of time and billions of rubles in this operation. Now he had to milk as much out of it as quickly as he could manage before Durov's plot threw everything into a downward spiral.

The view of the trading floor faded out, replaced by some reporter trying to explain how the latest fluctuation in the Dow was caused by a lack of market confidence in the forecasts for economic growth of the euro. It all sounded very scientific but was little more than bullshit. Medikov ignored the man's words, graphs, and charts, his eyes remaining on the stock ticker that played across the bottom of the screen. Each OptiMarx trade was printed with a little 0 in subscript. The 0's were showing up with growing regularity.

He walked over to the Louis XIV desk and typed out an e-mail to Dmitri Ustinov. In a coded shorthand, the message instructed the OptiMarx programmer to start the special system as soon as possible.

Now was the time to reap the considerable rewards of his rather bold venture.

Nicholas Vujnovich waited in the driver's seat of the limo, subtly surveying the rear ends of secretaries as they passed by. He was parked, along with a dozen other limousines, at the intersection of Broad and Wall streets, half a block from the Exchange Building. Cement barriers had restricted vehicle access to the old granite pile years before. Security had allowed them to park just inside the barriers while they waited for their charges.

He glanced over to see Josef Bogatinoff standing just outside a nearby deli. He sipped from a paper cup of coffee as he watched the rear ends of the same secretaries, but not quite so subtly. Vujnovich checked his watch. His mouth watered as he saw the steam rise from Josef's coffee. A cup of the brew, with cream and two extra sugars, was the one thing about this city for which he had developed a fondness. He knew there was no time to go get coffee for himself now. As much as he wanted to taste the dark brew, to be warmed inside by it, he knew he could not signal Bogatinoff to get one for him. There was too much chance someone would see them and later remember the two big Russians, loitering a block away from the New York Stock Exchange.

A bustle of activity at the side entrance to the Exchange caught his attention. People were spilling out of the building, walking briskly down the cordoned-off street to where the limos waited, their official appearances at the morning's ceremony completed and anxious to get to their offices to confront the day's work. Vujnovich checked his watch again. Eleven-oh-three a.m. When he looked up again, he spied Alan Smythe strutting along with the crowd, his nose up in the air, proud as he could be of what he had accomplished this day.

Vujnovich snorted. The OptiMarx CEO looked just short of ridiculous with his black felt fedora and those feminine, rose-framed glasses. The crimson and gold ascot put him right over the edge.

Vujnovich grabbed the signboard from the passenger's seat and stuck it in the window. He hopped out to open the rear door and waited at attention.

Smythe chatted with several people as he walked toward the line of limos. When he saw his name on the signboard in the big car's window, he folded his frame into the seat without hesitation and waited while Vujnovich shut the door and scurried around to climb into the driver's seat.

As the security guard waved them through the checkpoint and out onto Broad Street, Nicholas Vujnovich stole a quick look at his passenger in the rearview mirror. The swaggering fop was already chatting away on his cell phone, oblivious of his surroundings or what might be happening.

The Russian swung the big limo through the heavy traffic and around the turn at the next corner, then slowed with the backup in the right lane. Josef Bogatinoff stepped off the sidewalk and yanked open the rear door of the limo. As he slid in beside Smythe, he jerked the cell phone from Smythe's hand and tossed it through the grate of a streetside gutter. The big Russian shoved the wide-eyed executive across the seat and slammed the door shut before Smythe could utter a sound. With the door closed, no one on the street could see anything inside the big car through the darkened glass.

Vujnovich moved into the left lane and swung the limo back into the flow of traffic, headed down Broad, just another of a mass of black limos and bright yellow taxicabs prowling the world's financial capital.

Bogatinoff pulled a large pistol from his belt and pointed it at Alan Smythe's nose.

"Just sit quietly and do not make move," he growled.

"If you blink, I will fix that face so people will run screaming anytime they see you coming."

Alan Smythe looked down the endless bore of the pistol, at the cold, blank look on the big man's dark face, and promptly fainted dead away.

Chapter 29

Catherine Goldman checked her watch for the hundredth time. Five minutes until noon. Mikhail would be on the stairs now, bringing her lunch to the cramped bedroom that had become her jail.

Sure enough, she could hear his heavy feet at the bottom of the stairs as he hummed loudly and off-key. She scurried across the room and into the tiny closet, trying to be as quiet as possible. She closed the door behind her, then knelt down to grasp the edges of the old metal grate with the tips of her fingers. She yanked up.

It wouldn't budge.

She strained, pulled harder, the sweat popping out on her brow. Her fingers bled where the sharp edges of the grate cut them. The stubborn thing refused to move.

She could hear the dull clumping of the big Russian's footsteps as he made his way along the upstairs hallway. He hummed and then broke out into song, Russian words that she didn't even try to translate. She forced herself to ignore the pain in her fingers, the sweat in her eyes.

It was only seconds before she would have to abandon all hope of escape. Who knew what the man would do to her when he found her, cowering in the closet, her fingers bloody, crying like some chastised child?

She had to get out!

With one final superhuman yank, the rusty hinges of the grate gave way. The creaking! Oh, it was so loud, the Russian had to be able to hear it from outside the door. He was now likely balancing the lunch tray on one leg while he found the key to the lock. He was still singing, though out of breath from the climb up the stairs.

She pulled the grate up, swung her legs over and into the opening. She could hear the scraping of a key in the lock.

Goldman squeezed as hard as she could to push her hips through the tiny hole in the floor.

Jesus! she thought. Why didn't I spend more time in the gym? Maybe left off one or two cheese Danishes and the double sugars in the coffee?

She dropped free just as she heard the bedroom door swing open. Goldman landed on top of an old hutch. Easing the grate closed above her, she climbed down onto the kitchen floor.

There, in front of her, was the door to the outside, to freedom. Above where she stood trying to get her breath, she could hear Mikhail shouting and cursing, frantically tearing the room apart looking for her. She ran to the door and flung it open, welcoming the cold blast of wind that greeted her as she stepped out onto the porch.

A couple of hundred yards of open field stretched before her, covered with patchy snow and corn stubble. It would be impossible to get across to the trees before the big Russian spotted her.

Behind her she heard the rapid thumping of frantic footsteps, tearing down the hallway from the bedroom toward the stairs. There was no way she had time to make it across that field in time.

She ducked back inside and looked about for any kind of hiding place.

The footsteps were on the stairs. Only seconds to hide!

She yanked open the nearest door, hoped to God it wasn't a pantry or tiny closet, and ducked inside, easing the door closed behind her. The footsteps thundered into the kitchen just as she pulled the door shut.

He was so close she could hear the rasping of his breath, the thick, angry words he uttered. In midnight blackness Goldman knelt down and felt around with her hands, trying to figure out what kind of space she had entered. She was at the head of a narrow set of stairs. They probably dropped down into the house's basement. It occurred to her that once the Russian realized she was not outside, stumbling across the field, he would come looking for her in the cellar. She wondered if she had left blood from her cut fingers on the basement doorknob.

Sure enough, Mikhail spotted the open kitchen door that led to the outside. He crashed across the room, flinging furniture out of his way, shouting his guttural curses as he ran. The outside door slammed shut and the room fell silent.

She cracked the cellar door open and peaked out through her tears. Empty. She slipped out into the kitchen. She could see the big Russian through the kitchen's bay window. He was halfway across the field already, struggling through the stubble and snow. He jerked to a halt, looking back at the house.

It had dawned on him that she could not have come this way, that he would have seen signs of her passing, just as he could now see his own tracks stretching back to the house. She had to still be in there, hiding.

He turned and made his way back, still cursing at the top of his voice.

Goldman stood there, frozen. The cellar seemed to offer the best hope of finding a hiding place. She grabbed the doorknob and was ready to duck back in when she spied something on the kitchen table. Something she had not noticed before in her haste to find cover.

There were several pistols lying on the tabletop, as if the Russians had been cleaning them, loading them maybe. She grabbed the biggest one, a large revolver. It looked huge and felt too heavy for her to lift.

Catherine Goldman had never handled a pistol before in her life. She had always felt repulsed by them, convinced they were only made for killing other people, and she was opposed to killing other people.

She knew that this brutal piece of cold, deadly steel might be her salvation. But it was so heavy! It was all she could do to hold it horizontal, its ugly muzzle pointed toward the door where the Russian would burst in any second.

She remembered some old movie she had seen. It occurred to her that she would have to pull back the hammer if she was going to convince her captor that she meant business. Maybe she could get the drop on him, lock him upstairs in the bedroom. She could be gone before the others got back.

It was her only chance.

Mikhail crashed through the door. His cheeks were red from the cold, from the exertion. A sudden grin spread over his face when he saw her standing there, the gun in her hand, the barrel wavering as she struggled to hold it pointed in his direction.

"So. You get drop on Mikhail like John Wayne in Western movie," he growled, his breath coming more easily now.

She brought her other hand to the gun's grip, but it was so damned heavy. She was afraid she was going to drop it.

"Just . . . you . . . hand over your gun and—"

In one startling move, the Russian reached across his body, grabbing his snub-nosed pistol from its chest holster, and brought it up and around to shoot.

Catherine's finger found the trigger and yanked it. Her eyes were closed as the big weapon exploded, its awful roar reverberating around the room, bouncing off the walls, deafening her. The recoil jerked her arms up, tore the pistol from her grasp and sent the thing crashing down somewhere behind her. She could smell the burning odor of the gunpowder.

Goldman gasped, ready to feel the bullet from the Russian's gun tear into her flesh. She realized that she now stood defenseless in the middle of the kitchen. She steeled herself to die.

She opened her eyes.

The evil grin on Mikhail's face was frozen. His hands were clutched at his chest. His pistol had dropped to the floor. Deep crimson blood was already dripping from between his fingers.

Like a giant oak, he tottered slightly and then crashed backward to the floor.

Goldman didn't wait to see if he was just wounded. He might all of a sudden rise like all those wounded bad guys in the movies and chase after her. She ran as fast as she could manage, hopping over Mikhail's bulk, out the door, and across the pasture.

She didn't stop her mad scramble or look back until the house was obscured by the tangle of cold, lifeless trees.

"Commodore, wake up, sir."

The messenger was shaking Jon Ward's shoulder as forcefully as he dared. From experience, he knew to be ready to stand back, duck a fist. Some sailors came up fighting when their dreams were interrupted.

Ward blinked himself back into consciousness. He lay stretched out, fully clothed, on the bed in his stateroom. It seemed like only minutes before that he had fallen back, ostensibly to rest his eyes for a second. The operational order that he had been reading lay where it had landed on the deck and his watch told him he had slept for over two hours.

The messenger stepped back as Ward swung his feet off the bunk onto the deck. He ran his hands through his hair and shook his head to try to clear the haze inside it. The messenger smiled as he handed him a cup of coffee.

"Here, Commodore. This stuff'll jolt you awake."

Ward took a swig and swallowed. "Okay, now, why did you come in here and ruin a perfectly good dream?" he asked.

"Commodore, Captain Norquest sends his respects. He requests that you come to CIC. Chief Stroud has found an Akula."

Ward's eyes grew wide as he jumped up, fully awake. He charged out of the stateroom and up the ladder, heading toward CIC as fast as he could without spilling his coffee.

The darkened room was buzzing with activity. People were busily plotting bearings coming from sonar, trying to squeeze every bit of information they could get out of the faint signals they were detecting. Over in a corner, a group was working on getting *Anzio*'s SH-60B Sea Hawk helicopter up in the air. The twin-engine chopper's APS-124 radar extended the cruiser's eyes over the horizon while the 125 sonobuoys that the helicopter carried sharpened *Anzio*'s ears considerably. All this was tied to the ship's Aegis computer by a secure, high-speed data link.

Bob Norquest hopped out of the commander's seat and hurried across the CIC to meet Ward as he stepped though the hatch. He grinned. "How did you know, Commodore? How did you know that rascal was out there?"

Ward answered with a sly smile, "An old submariner's trick, Skipper. I just guessed where he had to be and how he had to go to get there." Ward walked across the room to look at the large display. "What do you have so far?"

Norquest nudged the trackball at his desk so that the cursor moved over to the same red inverted U Ward had been watching before. It now had a much smaller ellipse drawn around it, one hundred and fifty miles along its major axis and twenty miles wide on the minor one. The area around the target submarine seemed like a small bit of ocean on this scale, but in reality, it covered over five thousand square miles of stormy Norwegian Sea.

"That's sierra two-seven," Norquest offered. "I put a ninety-five percent probability ellipse around our best guess of where he's hiding. As soon as we get Foxtrot Three Two in the air, we'll be able to triangulate the bearings and get a lot smaller ellipse."

Ward grunted. "We'll need it. That guy will be a bitch to track. Have you called the P-3s yet?" It was time to call in the airborne ASW assets. The P-3C Orion was the best way to find and track a submarine if there was no other friendly sub that could be used.

Norquest shook his head. "Not yet. We're waiting to get the Akula localized first, get him pinned down just a bit more."

Ward stared at the cruiser skipper in amazement, his head cocked sideways. He clenched his fists and fought to hold himself in check.

Nobody who claimed to be an expert at antisubmarine warfare could do something so stupid. Not unless he was trying to lose this guy.

Ward gritted his teeth and, when he spoke, used a low, slow voice. "Hunting Russian subs ain't the same as tracking airliners with that big fancy radar. You only get little sniffs of the bastard. You have to act on them right away. If you wait to get solid contact, that Akula will be long gone and you'll be left sitting out here holding your ass in your hand."

Norquest winced but shook his head stubbornly. "No, sir. If I call the P-3s and there isn't any contact, I'll look bad. Our ship will look bad. We'll just wait until Three Two makes contact, narrows the window down, and then we'll—"

Ward slammed his fist down on the table. The room was instantly quiet. "Captain, I've sent envelopes to a lot of skippers with periscope pictures of their ships when they had no idea where we were. They thought exactly the way you are thinking now. The difference was, we were doing that in war games. This, Captain, is for real. Deadly real." He went on in a low, quiet voice, one that only the two of them could hear. "This is not a democracy, Skipper. Nothing we are doing is for show or to save face. Get that damn P-3 and get it now."

Alan Smythe struggled to try to sit up, but the big Russian slapped him and shoved him hard back onto the car's floorboard. In his terror, the OptiMarx CEO had lost track of time and direction, but one thing was clear. These must be the same Russians who had roughed up Andretti.

They were going to kill him. Kill him on the very day of his greatest triumph. Smythe couldn't help sobbing and his body shook uncontrollably. He felt a warm, wet sensation spreading from his crotch as he lost control. He didn't even care.

"Damn!" Bogatinoff yelped. "The girly man, he has just pissed his pants."

Vujnovich chuckled as he yelled back, "Just be glad he didn't shit them."

The limo barreled down the New Jersey Turnpike, mingling with all the traffic. It appeared to be nothing more than another carload of executives headed out of the city for some important meeting somewhere in Jersey.

They took the first Princeton exit. Within a few minutes, they were roaring down a lonely country road and there was no more traffic. Twenty minutes later, they swung into the drive leading up to the isolated farmhouse.

The big car slid to a stop with a spray of gravel. Bogatinoff grabbed Smythe by the collar and lifted him out of the car, then tossed the quaking man to the ground. He winked at his partners as he kicked the mass of quivering flesh and growled, "Get up, you piece of shit. I will not dirty my hands by carrying you."

Smythe pulled himself to his feet and swayed in the general direction of the farmhouse's back porch, toward the open kitchen door.

Both Russians stopped, instantly alert. Smythe stopped, too, wondering what was going on.

The door gaped open, its frilly curtains dancing in the chilly breeze.

Vujnovich was the first to react. He reached into his belt and pulled out his 9mm Glock.

"Wait here with him," he growled. "Something is not right. If Mikhail has stepped out and left the door open, he will be sorry."

"Maybe he is upstairs, mounting the SEC bitch," Bogatinoff offered with a nervous laugh.

"Even Mikhail is not that desperate," Vujnovich said.

The big Russian was already moving low and quick to the side of the kitchen door. He waited a few seconds, listening, crouching even lower, and then dove through the door. He landed on his knees, ready to fire.

He was on the floor beside Mikhail Gikoytski's lifeless form. The pool of blood had expanded around the body and had already started to congeal.

"Son of a bitch!" he yelled. "Josef! Get your ass in here now!"

He got to his feet and ran up the stairs to the bedroom where Goldman had been a prisoner. He was not surprised to find the door open, the room empty, the furniture askew.

Bogatinoff ran up behind him, his Glock out and ready for action. "Now what?"

Vujnovich turned and headed back down the stairs. He was at the bottom before he answered the question over his shoulder. "We find the bitch and we kill her."

"We had better tell Medikov that she is on the loose."

Vujnovich turned and stared at Bogatinoff as if the man had just sprung a second head. "Are you totally daft? Do you want Boris to feed his dinner guests our nuts? We do not tell him a thing until she is dead."

"What about Smythe?"

"Tie him up and inject him with enough heroin to keep him dreaming until we get back."

Smythe shivered in the chill of the kitchen. He didn't understand what either of the men was saying. He almost vomited when he saw the man's body in the pool of blood on the floor. He shut his eyes and tried not to think about who it might be, how he might have died. When he opened them again, he saw one of the men was taking a syringe from what looked like a doctor's bag. He would have turned and run then, but the other one grabbed him and shoved him across the kitchen table. That's when he knew for certain that the needle and whatever was in it was destined for him.

That's when Alan Smythe shit his pants.

Dmitri Ustinov leaned back and reread the coded e-mail. It had worked! They had done it! Now it was time to reap the profits.

He stood, checked his reflection in the office window, and then trotted out to find Marina Nosovitskaya.

The beautiful young programmer was in her cubicle, watching the stock ticker as it played across the screen of her monitor. Ustinov leaned against the wall and turned on his best practiced smile.

She ignored him for the longest time but eventually looked up and smiled in response. Her bright blue eyes danced in the light. "What is it? Or are you just going to stand there and ogle my breasts?"

Ustinov blushed but joined in the lighthearted banter. "That sounds like a very good idea to me, but they are too well hidden by all those clothes to properly ogle."

"That's the way they will stay, I assure you." The smile disappeared as if she had thrown a switch. "Now what do you want?"

Ustinov handed her a copy of the e-mail as he answered, "From Uncle Boris. It is time to start." He rubbed his hands together in eager anticipation. "It looks as if it will not be long until I have enough money to treat you in the manner you deserve."

Nosovitskaya seemed to not hear his clumsy flirtation as she punched in a series of coded passwords on her keyboard. A screen popped up that looked very much like many others in the OptiMarx system. However, this particular screen did not appear in any of the volumes of operating manuals, nor was it referenced in the mounds of documentation.

She typed in several more commands and hit a button marked EXECUTE.

Turning back to Ustinov, she said, "It's working. I set the system so that it would short-sell on any stock if it had two down ticks within five minutes. It will automatically buy when the price drops another nickel."

"A nickel!" Ustinov snorted. "It will take forever to make any money at that rate."

Nosovitskaya looked up and smiled, but it was a smile she might use when talking to a dim-witted child. "Impetuous, greedy boy. Think for a minute, or has all the blood pooled lower in your body?" She dropped her gaze to his crotch for a long second before going on. "At a nickel a share for a million shares, we make fifty thousand dollars in five minutes. Even you should be able to calculate how much that adds up to in a day."

Ustinov shook his head in wonder. "Wow! That comes out to real money. How do we make sure no one catches on?"

Nosovitskaya groaned. "You should have thought of this earlier. It is a good thing that I did. We do what we do in lots of little thousand-share transactions. We use hundreds of different accounts. There is no way to trace them back to any common source. Then, to make it even more difficult, we do a lot of the transactions out on the regional exchanges. No way to put it all together."

Ustinov nodded. "Smart, real smart. Beautiful, too. Marry me and make me happy forever."

Nosovitskaya ignored him once again while she watched the numbers dance happily across her computer screen, the pixels reflecting in her deep, dark eyes.

Carl Andretti had waited as long as he could stand to. There was money to be made and that damned uppity Brit was off God knows where. Smythe had told him in no uncertain terms that he wanted to be there for the initial launch of the "special feature." Smythe was the boss.

Well, he was going to miss it after all. Besides, there was a good chance that these trades would be so far off the books that Smythe wouldn't ever know about them anyway. If that was the case, there would be no need for splitting those proceeds two ways.

Andretti looked over his shoulder several times as he entered the system and watched the ticker as the trades occurred. This particular ticker was just a little different from the one that everyone else saw. This one came directly off the output of the OptiMarx matching system. These were the trades at the instant at which buyers were being matched up with sellers. The numbers everyone else saw came from the stock exchange floor.

Theoretically . . . and according to the plans everyone else had seen . . . those numbers should be identical and be displayed milliseconds apart. Suppose someone could see the trades immediately as they came out of the matching system, but before they made it to the exchange floor? What if that person had the ability to make changes on the fly?

That was the capability that Andretti had secretly built into the OptiMarx system. He was able to move trades around so that sales that should have happened at a lower price showed up at a higher one. He could also manipulate it so that buys that should have been more expensive were accomplished much more cheaply. He knew that if he didn't get greedy and changed only a few trades at a time, there was little chance of their operation being detected.

The fat CTO took a big slug of the Scotch in the Styrofoam cup at his elbow, bent over his keyboard, and started the system. Soon he was directing funds into his own special account, one Alan Smythe had no idea existed. His watery eyes gleamed as he watched the balance begin to grow.

Charles Gruver sat in the big chair in the systems operation center, two floors below the New York Stock Exchange trading floor. From this brightly lit room, hidden behind blastproof doors and protected by some of the most sophisticated security systems outside of the National Security Agency, the NYSE chief technical officer watched warily as the OptiMarx system assumed more and more of the Exchange's total trading volume. The big wall display units showed the system humming along effortlessly, orders pouring in and consummated trades heading back out in seconds, the way they had expected it to do.

Stan Miller leaned over and cuffed him on the shoulder. "Looking real good, isn't it?"

Gruver nodded to the SEC deputy. By experience, Gruver knew that Miller should have been gone long ago. He seemed to be hanging around to watch for something only he knew was going to happen. It was out of character for the prototypical bureaucrat. In all his years with the commission, the man had never shown the slightest interest in this room before. Miller hardly knew how to find the place, although it was the single largest reason for the existence of his job.

Gruver watched the trade volumes play across the screen for a few more seconds and then acknowledged Miller's question. "Yeah, the system seems to be doing just fine. Still, I can't help wondering what Catherine was so worried about. She's usually right on."

Miller shook his head. "No telling. She could go off on wild-goose chases sometimes. Believe me, I know. I work with her every day. You heard from her lately?"

"No, not a word. At least not since just after somebody tried to kill her."

Miller seemed particularly interested in Gruver's answer to that question. That didn't seem in character, either. Miller never struck Gruver as a "people person," as someone who would care about Catherine Goldman's whereabouts or disposition.

Miller chuckled. The effort sounded forced. "Not surprised. We have her under protection. Hiding down in the Caribbean." He changed the subject, his eyes still locked on the big screen. "So, looks like we've got a success here." He waved his hand toward the scurrying numbers on the wall.

"Looks like it so far," Gruver said, then hesitated a beat. He almost shut up but, for some reason, decided to go on. "You know, Stan, I got a funny feeling. I can't put a finger on it, but something just doesn't feel quite right about all this. I think I'll have to do some more checking."

Miller jumped in. "Damn, Chuck! Between Catherine's goddamn woman's intuition and your 'funny feelings,' you're going to drive me crazy. There's nothing for you or Goldman or any-damn-body else to be concerned about here. We're on it. That's our bag. That's why the taxpayers keep on writing us nice, generous paychecks. We got experts. We'll check everything out. We'll keep an eye on it. Just relax and I'll see you in a day or so."

Miller rose and strode briskly out the door before Gruver could express any more doubts. He watched the SEC man go. He couldn't keep the sarcasm from his voice when he spoke to the spot where Miller had just been sitting.

"Yeah, sure. I feel much better now."

Chapter 30

The lengthy memorial service was drawing to a close. President Gregor Smitrov droned on, drawing endless metaphors for the benefit of the gathered mourners, lecturing like the university professor he had once been. The onlookers who weren't sleeping were yawning openly by now.

Mammoth sprays of flowers and gigantic memorial wreaths took up half of the building's elevated stage. The scent of roses hung heavy in the air, the aroma out of place in this cold, icy climate. The submarine base's huge assembly hall was filled with the worldwide media teams, their cameras set to capture the anguish of the families of the crewmen from the *Gepard* and *Volk*, their microphones ready to record the words of the Russian president, as this ugly international crisis seemed to drag on and on. The television crews and chattering reporters had taken over the center of the room, the places where they could get the best camera angles. Friends and families of the lost submariners had been relegated to seats in the periphery of the vast hall, stuck behind steel girders and roof supports that would obstruct the all-important camera shots.

Outside, another winter storm threatened, its winds

already howling down out of the Arctic to wreak its frigid wrath on Polyarnyy. The windows of the building rattled with each icy blast, but the brilliant blaze from the television lights and the press of so many people added warmth to what would normally be a cold space.

A group of Navy officers, resplendent in full dress uniform, stood apart from the crowd, next to a side entrance several meters to the left of the stage. Captain First Rank Gregor Dobiesz tried to maintain his somber expression as he leaned in and whispered to Vasiliy Zhurkov, "That fool will raise the death toll by boring everyone to death."

Zhurkov nodded and tried to stifle a yawn. "True enough, but we will soon have excitement enough for a lifetime, Gregor."

Admiral Alexander Durov harrumphed pointedly from behind the two naval officers, who quickly quieted.

"Is everything ready?" Durov asked, leaning forward.

"It is exactly as you directed," Dobiesz whispered. "When President Smitrov leaves the service, the media will see him enter his limousine and drive off. A squad of our naval infantry will direct him to the capture point. He will never suspect a thing until he is in our hands."

Durov nodded again. "Good. It had better work out just as you have laid it out. We cannot afford your usual incompetence this time."

Dobiesz bit his tongue and leaned forward, as if he was straining to hear his president's closing words.

Up on the stage, Smitrov ended his speech and basked in the polite applause of the crowd. He spun on his heel and strutted off the stage, heading for the waiting press corps. They clamored around the little man like a flock of pigeons begging for bread crumbs. Smitrov shouted the answers to a few questions as he pushed through to the doorway where Admiral Durov waited. The president condemned the Americans for what had happened, alluded to some vague action against the aggressors, but promised nothing.

When he reached the spot where the admiral stood, he smiled politely and clasped the old man in an attempt at a bear hug. When he spoke, it was loud enough for the bristle of microphones that trailed him to pick up his words.

"Thank you for arranging this, Alexanderovich. I hope in some small way, this ceremony will bring closure to the families and tell the world of our suffering . . . of your own personal grief and suffering on behalf of your nephew, your brave sailors. Maybe the Americans will think twice before their reckless aggression causes them to crash into one of our boats the next time."

Durov nodded and smiled wanly. Several camera crews had now panned lenses in their direction.

"You honor me, President Smitrov," he murmured. "I only do my duty for my country, like any good Russian. America is a mighty country, but they should respect Russia as an equal."

Smitrov pulled back and glanced into Durov's eyes, as if he were reading something there. He started to say something but thought better of it. He shook his head, turned, and hurried out the doorway and into the bitter winter wind. He pulled his heavy fur coat tight around his body as he rushed across the narrow street to his waiting car and driver. He ducked into the limousine's open door, and his bodyguard slammed it shut behind him. The car roared off down the alley, away from the building.

"Let us get out of this barren place before the storm grounds us here until spring," he said to the man in the seat next to him.

"An excellent suggestion, Mr. President," the elderly uniformed man responded, and tapped both the limousine's driver and the bodyguard in the front seat on their shoulders to hurry them along.

The military guard standing at the end of the alley signaled the driver to turn right and then saluted smartly as the car passed. At the next intersection, another guard signaled another right turn. The driver followed the directions without question while the president of Russia sat in the backseat, already absorbed in a discussion of economic policy with the uniformed man, his chief adviser. No one recognized that they were being directed deeper into the submarine base, not toward the landing strip where the president's plane awaited, its engines already turning, warming, ready to whisk the leader away ahead of the looming storm. Nor did any of them notice the guards as they systematically blocked off access to the streets behind the car as soon as they had passed by.

Another guard flagged at them, signaling a left turn. There was a frown on the driver's face now as the limousine made the turn into what looked like a narrow alley between two large, dark warehouses. This was not at all the route he had followed coming in that morning.

He had already made the turn, though, before he saw a BTR-80 armored personnel carrier sitting astride the far end of the alleyway, its machine cannon pointing its snout toward the president's car. The driver hit the brakes and slid to a stop just as a large searchlight, mounted on the BTR-80's turret, flashed on. The brilliant beam of white light blinded everyone in the limo.

The driver cursed, but, being specially trained in combat driving techniques and intensely loyal to his most important passenger, he jammed the big vehicle into reverse and stomped on the accelerator. Blue smoke enveloped the spinning wheels as they screamed, begging for traction on the alley's icy surface.

It was a futile effort. Another APC had already pulled up behind them, blocking their only escape route. The APC behind them flashed on its searchlight as well, filling the car with light from that direction.

The driver jumped on the brakes just as a burst of machine-gun fire from the first APC slammed through the armor plate protecting the car's engine. Armor-piercing bullets ripped into the engine block. The vehicle shuddered to a halt as the motor seized. Thick white steam poured from beneath the hood.

There was no way out. President Gregor Smitrov was trapped.

The driver and the bodyguard were not ready to give up, though. Each pulled a submachine gun from the clips under his seat. The president's chief adviser happened to be a former general in the Russian Army as well. He had never stopped wearing the uniform. He had spent years fighting in Afghanistan and, along the way, had scrapped his way out of his share of ambushes. His first instinct was to grab the president and throw him to the floor. The ex-general pulled a Czech CZ-52 automatic pistol from his shoulder holster, slid back the action to chamber a round, and prepared to do battle. If they could manage enough cover fire, maybe the president could make it out of the car, across the narrow alley, and into one of the building doors.

It was hopeless. They were in a deadly cross fire, but these three would die protecting their leader. Another burst of machine-gun fire from the first APC shattered the car's windshield.

The driver and the bodyguard flung open their doors simultaneously and crouched behind them, using the meager armor plating for protection. They bounced up and opened fire at the APC in front of them. Their bullets ricocheted harmlessly off its armored sides. Its cannon spat another burst of machine-gun rounds just as troops, shooting from windows above and behind them, opened fire. The APC behind them joined in with its own machine gun, shattering the car's rear window. The bodyguard twisted around as he directed a short burst of gunfire upward, toward some movement he had seen at a window across the alley. Someone screamed and a body fell out, landing awkwardly in the dirty snow.

A quick burst from an AK-47 stitched across the bodyguard's back, flogging him, flinging him against the brick wall like a discarded marionette. He slid to the ground and lay there, still, bleeding and lifeless.

A second later, machine-gun fire caught the driver, cutting him in half, throwing him down brutally onto the ice.

The old general raised his pistol to open fire, but Smitrov grabbed his arm and stopped him. The president struggled up from the floorboards.

"It's over, my friend. No sense in you dying for nothing." Smitrov raised his arms high and shouted, "Enough! Enough! We surrender. Don't shoot."

It was a loud, authoritative voice that shouted back, "Drop your weapons and come out slowly. One wrong move and we will open fire again."

Smitrov and his adviser emerged from the battered limousine. They both raised their hands high in the air. Smitrov winced as he stepped over the bloody remains of his driver. The man's open, lifeless eyes seemed to be accusing Smitrov, somehow blaming the president for leading him to his death.

The searchlights still blazed, blinding them so that they still couldn't see their assailants.

"Face against the wall, keep your hands high!"

Smitrov's nose was inches from a bare brick wall. He stood stiffly erect, trying to manage some defiance in such an utterly hopeless position. He steeled himself for the shot in the back he expected.

There was another gravelly voice from behind him. A voice that was so familiar.

"Good evening again, Mr. President. I am pleased you have decided to enjoy still more of our warm hospitality here at Polyarnyy." The man's voice was at his ear, so close he could smell his foul, old man's breath. "You see, Mr. President, I am doing my duty for the *Rodina*. We are, at long last, bringing an end to your cowardly rule, to your spineless, groveling behavior before the entire world, to the embarrassing way you have allowed the Americans to murder our sailors and openly laugh at us. With you under arrest, we will be able to bring Russia back to her rightful place of respect and begin to rebuild our glorious nation."

Even standing there, shivering, his heart still pounding from the near-death experience, Smitrov had no trouble recognizing the distinctive voice of Admiral Alexander Durov. The bastard! So the old nationalist was staging a coup! He must be supremely confident of his power to risk this ambush.

Now, with the clarity of retrospect, it was all so obvious. The incidents with the submarines beneath the ice of the Barents had been part of the plan all along. This place would be the site where he would strike, here at his home base.

Smitrov could not imagine how Durov had advanced the plan so far along without being detected by the Federal'naya Sluzhba Bezopasnosti. The FSB, like the KGB that it replaced as the internal security force inside Russia, had operatives everywhere. Nothing moved inside this vast country without someone in the ugly yellow building on Lubyanka Square in Moscow knowing about it. This plan involved many people.

The president had no time now to ponder the intricacies of the admiral's treachery. Hands grabbed him and spun him around to face the old submariner. He blinked against the brightness of the lights, trying to see the man, to see into his eyes.

"Durov, you are a fool if you think this will succeed," Smitrov said, his voice high and quavering. He knew his words were not very convincing, but he had to speak them. "You will be shot for this, and so will each of your henchmen."

Durov chuckled. "My dear Gregorivich, you do not understand. We have already succeeded, and now you will assist us in the next step."

"I will never help you. You will push our country back into the Middle Ages."

"No, I will be able to push Russia into its rightful place in the world order. We won't cringe anymore in the face of the American imperialists. You can either help actively or you can help from the grave. It is your choice, Mr. President."

"Never!"

A pistol cracked at his ear and the president jumped, expecting a bullet to tear through his brain. It was Smitrov's old friend, his adviser, the general, who fell at his feet in a lifeless pile. Blood already oozed from a small round hole in the middle of the man's forehead.

Durov grunted. "Mr. President, I will give you some time to think and another chance to decide your role in the glorious rebirth of our homeland." The admiral turned and spoke to someone else nearby. "Bring him."

Hands grabbed the president's arms from behind. He felt handcuffs encircling his wrists behind him and a dark hood was dropped down over his head, shutting out the harsh, bright lights from the personnel carriers.

The president of Russia was dragged away, his feet barely touching the skim of ice on the frozen ground.

"Damn!" Joe Dumkowski's eyes were wide as the SEAL pointed down the hill toward the submarine base. He shook his head in disbelief as he once again gazed at the impossible scenario he was watching through the spotter scope. "Commander, take a look at this. Look between the warehouses . . . down there by the waterfront. That limo flying the president's flag drove down in there. See where it's just sittin' there, trapped between the two BTRs?"

Bill Beaman pulled his ten-by-fifty binoculars out and looked in the direction that Dumkowski was pointing. They had been watching all the unusual activity on the base with the dignitaries, the press, the families of the dead submariners all showing up for the memorial service. It had been welcome excitement after the hours of seeing nothing much else going on down there. Now something beyond exciting was happening at the Polyarnyy Submarine Base!

Beaman put the binoculars to his eyes just in time to see the first muzzle flashes from the BTR's machine guns. His mouth fell open. He couldn't believe what he was watching. Armored personnel carriers bearing the markings of the Russian naval infantry were firing on the Russian president's official vehicle.

"Joe, get this on film!" Beaman ordered.

Dumkowski pulled out a small digital video camera and attached it to the spotter scope. He focused on the improbable scene being played out down there below their vantage point.

"Looks like . . . shit! They just wasted two of those guys in the car. Somebody else's gettin' out of the backseat. That's . . . damn! That's Smitrov for sure! Some guy in an Army uniform's climbing out of the car with him. They got their hands up. Looks like they must be givin' up."

Beaman grunted. "That's Smitrov, all right. I don't

have a clue who the other guy is. That looks like naval infantry that has the drop on them. There must be a couple of dozen of them."

Beaman moved his binoculars to the right as he caught a glimpse of someone emerging from one of the warehouse doors. He focused on the man for a second, then nudged Dumkowski.

"Make damn sure you get a shot of that guy, the big, tall one just coming out of that building. That's got to be Admiral Alexander Durov!"

Beaman watched as the old admiral strolled across the alley to where Smitrov and his companion were standing, illuminated by the floodlights. The two men were facing a brick wall as if they were lined up before a firing squad.

"Somehow I don't think Durov called this little meeting just to pay his respects to his president," Dumkowski observed. "Looks more like—"

"Son of a bitch! They just shot the guy in the uniform!"

Bill Beaman shook his head again. What the hell was happening down there? More important for the moment, what the hell should he and his SEAL team do about it? Would Durov's men shoot the president next?

Ideas raced through Beaman's brain. A rogue submarine admiral sending boats out on secret missions was one thing, but now he was ambushing the president of Russia! This ratcheted the whole deal up to a different level. The trap had to have been well planned, had to have some purpose in Durov's scheme, whatever that scheme might be. One thing was clear. The bastard must be ready to go public with whatever he was doing. With

President Smitrov either held hostage or executed, there would be no way to keep his plot hidden from the rest of the world any longer.

Beaman watched, stunned, as the Russian president was handcuffed, blindfolded, and shoved into one of the BTRs. The ugly gray vehicle then drove away down the narrow street before being gobbled up by one of the metal sheds that squatted down alongside the piers.

It looked as if the show was over. At least the part of it they would be able to see. Beaman grabbed the video camera and slid back down below the lip of the hill before standing up. He raced down the few yards to the protection of the trees where Chief Johnston and the rest of the team were hidden. This was news that he had to relay as quickly as possible. Admiral Donnegan and the rest of the brass back in D.C. needed to see these pictures with their own eyes.

Without them, there was no way anybody would believe what Beaman had just witnessed. No way in hell!

Commander Joe Glass checked the chart one more time just to be sure, then stepped up to the periscope stand. Pat Durand was "dancing with the fat lady," watching the mouth of the Murmansk Fjord to make sure no one came zooming out and ran over *Toledo* while they were up at periscope depth.

This would be the last time they could fix their position until after Hector Gonzales and the ASDV had completed their mission and they could head home. For the next day or so they would stay hidden, deeply submerged inside the fjord. Coming up to get a navigational fix or to copy the satellite communications signal would be impossible. Sticking a mast above the surface of that bit of cold, icy water would be an open invitation to getting their asses shot at.

Glass tapped Durand on the shoulder. "Pat, let me take a look around. Make sure we have a good GPS fix and all traffic on board."

Glass took Durand's place at the scope eyepiece and looked out. Sure enough, there were the high wooded headlands marking the entrance to the fjord. It looked exactly like the photos in the intel package he had been studying, pictures taken by some crazy Brit submarine skipper back during the height of the Cold War. That guy had brazenly driven his boat right into the fjord, all the way to the entrance to Polyarnyy, in broad daylight, taking pictures the entire way down. Then turned around and slipped right back out again. Amazingly, he lived to tell about it.

Glass hoped the Russian defenses were no better now than the Soviet ones were then. He would follow the Brit sub's track in to a point where he could launch the ASDV. Afterward, he would wait around until Gonzales drove back, reacquire the mini-sub, and then sneak out again.

If all went well, no one on the Russian side would ever know what they had done. If it didn't go well, their grave would lie somewhere inside the cold, deep fjord.

"Skipper," Durand called, interrupting Glass's reverie. "All message traffic aboard. We have a good GPS fix. Nav is satisfied. We're ready to go."

The commander nodded. He slapped the periscope handles up and gave the red hoist ring a tug. The scope slid back down into the well.

"Very well. Let's get this show on the road. Make your depth three-two-five feet. Ahead one-third. Rig ship for ultraquiet."

With that, *Toledo* slipped down into the hostile depths, beneath the dark waters of the fjord.

Chapter 31

Admiral Tom Donnegan slammed the message down hard onto his desk, word side down.

"Damn, damn, and double damn!" he growled, but not loud enough for his aide in the outer office to hear him. "Now what in hell is that old fool up to? First he sinks two of his own subs and one of ours. Then the son of a bitch goes and kidnaps the damned president of Russia!"

The brass ship's chronometer resting on Donnegan's desk struck eight bells, oh six hundred local time. The admiral spun in his big office chair to gaze out the window behind him. Washington was still asleep across the Potomac, but the Pentagon bustled with activity. The parking lot outside his E-ring office was half-full, even at this hour. With troops and ships spread all over the globe and on high alert, with the precarious international situation since the carnage beneath the Barents, there were even more people than usual here to watch and direct.

Donnegan turned back toward the open door and yelled through to the outer office, "Schwartz, get in here! I've got something for you to do."

The admiral went back to reading Bill Beaman's latest message about what he had seen from his overlook above the Polyarnyy Submarine Base in Russia. Ambushes and firefights inside the base. President Gregor Smitrov taken prisoner. All of it happening in broad daylight with a sizeable contingent of the world press less than a mile away. It was all unbelievable, but the admiral did not doubt Beaman's report. They even had video of most of it that they could bring out with them.

Donnegan rubbed his chin as he pondered what it all meant and what should be done about it.

His first reaction was to assume no one inside Russia knew what was going on yet. He could get on the horn to one of his counterparts inside Russia, get the word to the government some way, and let them take it from there. He dismissed that idea. He would have to reveal how he came to know such a thing had even happened. That would mean admitting he had sent combat troops into Russia. There was no way, either, to know how deep Durov's poison had seeped into the Russian military, who could be trusted and who couldn't.

He could do nothing and allow Durov's scheme to play out for a while longer. The United States could feign ignorance like the rest of the world when the coup was inevitably made public.

No, that wasn't an option, either. There was far too much chance that the wily old fox might get away with whatever it was that he was doing. With someone in charge who was as insane as Durov, the havoc he might set loose in the meantime could be catastrophic.

Only one plausible idea remained, and Tom Donnegan shivered at the very thought of it. He could send Bill Beaman and his SEAL team in to rescue the Russian president from his captors. That would thwart Durov and his coup attempt, help to stabilize the Russian government, and bring some just end to this submarine disaster.

There were complications he did not like to ponder. This mission could fail. Hell, it was a near certainty that it *would* fail! Smitrov could be killed in some cross fire. The SEALs who weren't killed in a shoot-out could get themselves captured. Durov could use all that as still more evidence of U.S. aggression, as justification for whatever unimaginable retribution he might conjure up.

"Damn it, Schwartz!" Donnegan yelled. "Can't you hear? I said I needed you."

The young lieutenant stepped through the door before Donnegan finished, carrying a tray with two mugs of coffee. "Sorry, Admiral. I was making a fresh pot of coffee. I brought you a cup. Now, what do you need?"

Donnegan took the offered coffee and allowed himself a slight smile. "Thanks, I needed this. You'll never know how much I needed this." He took a swig, swallowed hard, and then added, "Get President Brown on the phone. If they say they have to get him out of the rack and try to put you off onto some aide, tell them this is a Code Red Emergency call."

Donnegan's aide hardly flinched. He set the tray down and was off to place the call to the White House.

Nicholas Vujnovich stomped across the porch behind Josef Bogatinoff and then stepped through the door back into the farmhouse. Vujnovich remained silent as he started the coffeemaker, then joined Bogatinoff, who had slumped down into one of the kitchen chairs, exhausted.

The night had been frustrating. They had slogged around in ever-growing circles through the woods and fields for miles around the farmhouse, searching frantically for the escaped SEC inspector, for any signs of her at all. Now they sat glumly, too tired to even talk, waiting for the coffee to finish brewing.

Dawn was breaking over the horizon to the east, illuminating the corn stubble in a gray light. A soft but steady rain had started to fall during the night, washing away the last patches of dirty snow, transforming the sodden ground into a muddy morass. Clumps of mud dropped away from the Russians' feet and the legs of their trousers as they sat there sullenly watching the steam rise from the coffeemaker. Water dripped from their shoes and pooled on the wooden floor. Neither man cared.

Vujnovich shook his head back and forth and stared at his hands as he spoke. "She cannot have gotten away from us that easily."

Bogatinoff rose and stepped over to the kitchen sink, trying not to slip on the muddy floor, hopping over the dried lake of blood from their fallen comrade. The body still lay wedged against the wall where they had dragged it. He avoided looking at Mikhail Gikoytski's unseeing eyes as he grabbed two dirty mugs and rinsed the residue out of them before pouring them full of the hot coffee. He set one cup down in front of Vujnovich and sipped from the other.

Vujnovich took a swallow and looked up.

"You think it is time we told Medikov what has happened?" he asked.

Bogatinoff winced, then gazed at his muddy shoes for a few moments before he answered, "No, not yet. Whether we tell him or not, we will still have to find her, or Boris will feed us to the fish. There is nothing to be gained by giving him bad news just now."

A sudden unholy howling scream startled the pair. Both grabbed their guns and dove for cover. The intensity of the high-pitched keening rose and fell, like some wounded animal snared in a trap. Vujnovich slipped low toward the door. He waved Bogatinoff to the other side before easing the door open with the barrel of his pistol.

The two sprang forward, ready to blast away.

They found Alan Smythe, still bound tightly and curled up on the floor where they had abandoned him when they tore out the door to chase after the woman. He was coming out of his drug haze, screaming with a mixture of blind fear and searing pain.

Bogatinoff kicked Smythe in the ribs to shut him up. The howling increased. Meanwhile, Vujnovich grabbed a syringe and filled it with the clear liquid from a bottle on the nearby end table.

"I cannot take that screaming! I have to shut him up before he drives me nuts."

Vujnovich jammed the needle through Smythe's clothes into his buttock and pushed the drug into the OptiMarx CEO's body. The heroin took effect at once. Smythe quieted and slipped back into unconsciousness.

Bogatinoff shook his head. "Many more shots like that and you will make him an addict."

"I do not care as long as it silences that wailing. Besides, I do not expect he will live long enough for it to be a problem. If he does live that long . . . and if we don't find the woman, then we—you and I—will not have long to live ourselves. Boris will see to that." Vujnovich turned and stomped out of the room. "Come on," he said over his shoulder. "Let us fix some breakfast so we have the strength to get back out and find the bitch."

Hector Gonzales climbed up the ladder from *Toledo*'s engine room and through the hatch into the ASDV. Sam Donlan was already up inside the cramped control space in the forward compartment of the tiny submarine. Gonzales eased past him and settled into the pilot's seat. He glanced over at his copilot as he slipped on his communications headset. "We ready to go?"

Donlan held up the checklist. Most items on the long list were already marked off. "Almost. Nav systems are up and stabilized. Battery is fully charged. Flight control computers checked out." He reached forward and flipped a couple of switches on the instrument panel in front of him. Two CRTs jumped to life. Letters and figures danced across their screens. "Running pre-underway diagnostics on the sonar systems."

Gonzales gave Donlan a thumbs-up and fastened his seat belt and shoulder harness.

Except for the lack of any windows, the space looked like the cockpit of any military aircraft. Switches, knobs, and screens filled the bulkhead in front of the two pilots. Strategically located at eye level in front of each pilot was a multifunctional display screen where he could select the information he needed to "fly" this boat. Centrally placed on the bulkhead was a large flat-panel screen that displayed the forward-looking navigation sonar display and bottom-contour/mine-avoidance side-looking sonar. It doubled as a display for the periscope when they were using that.

Gonzales reached down to the console between the two. His hand danced across the controls for the lithium-ion polymer batteries and propulsion system. Everything looked to be normal. The atmosphere purification system controls, on the overhead above them, also checked out fine.

Gonzales keyed a switch on the communications console above his head and spoke into the throat mike. "*Toledo*, this is *Little Boy*. All systems check. Ready to begin disconnect sequence."

The answer came back immediately. "*Toledo*, aye. Verified electrical power disconnect."

Gonzales glanced over at Donlan. The copilot nodded and gave him a double thumbs-up.

"Verified electrical power disconnect," he answered.

"Roger. Verified hatch systems checked shut and locked."

Gonzales looked over at the hull systems status panel. All the lights were green. "Verify, green board."

"Roger. Begin hull unlock sequence."

Gonzales flipped a pair of switches that started the sequence of operations that broke the mechanical lock that held the two subs together. The metal locking dogs rolled free. The ASDV was ready to float away. Only the communications connection was still in place. It would break as the mini-sub moved upward a few centimeters.

Gonzales heard Glass's voice just before the comms link was broken.

"*Vaya con Dios,* my friend. Good hunting. See you in two days."

The link went dead as the ASDV floated free from the *Toledo*. That was the last contact the pair would have with any friendly voice until they finished the mission, but neither man had time to ponder such things.

Gonzales flipped on the main propulsion motor and steered the little boat clear of *Toledo*. He could hear the faint hum of pumps as the automatic buoyancy control moved water around to balance the sub at neutral buoyancy.

The pilot watched the navigation sonar paint a picture of the route in front of them. He spun the wheel to point the boat south and opened the throttle.

It was time to go to work.

Chuck Gruver sat in front of his monitors in his den deep in the bowels of the New York Stock Exchange. It was time for the opening bell to ring and set off another busy day of trading on the floor. The chairman of the Exchange and the VIP of the day, this one the chief executive officer of some new tech company that was floating its initial public stock offering today, were on the television screen. The grinning VIP rang the bell, waved to the camera, and then tossed a bunch of baseball caps bearing the company's logo down to the floor. Most of the traders ignored the caps, though. The daily frenzy had started.

Gruver watched the ebb and flow of the trading on the various displays before him. The day before had been worrying. He still had a suspicious feeling, nothing he could pin down, but something didn't feel right. That same uneasy intuition had come back today.

He leaned in to one of the monitors, as if taking a closer look at the scatting numbers might make clear to him whatever it was that was bothering him. There seemed to be too much sell pressure on particular stocks that shouldn't have it. Whole sectors were drifting lower for no apparent reason.

Gruver shook his head. Probably nothing to worry about. He had long ago decided that he would go loony trying to figure what made traders do what they did. He laughed softly. If he could ever figure out what made those guys tick, he wouldn't be down here in the basement babysitting a bunch of flickering computers.

The phone jangled, pulling him out of his reverie. He grabbed the receiver and jammed it to his ear.

"Gruver!" he growled.

"Collect call for Mr. Charles Gruver from a Ms. Catherine Goldman. Will you accept the charges?"

"Huh? Yes, of course. Put her on."

The phone went dead for a second and then clicked back to life. He heard Catherine Goldman's voice on the other end.

"Chuck? Chuck, is that really you?"

What the hell was wrong? She sounded awful. Scared and tired.

"Yeah, it's me, Cath. What's the matter with you? Where are you? Why are you calling collect?"

"They may be monitoring my iPhone account. Chuck, I need your help. I don't know where else to turn. I'm so scared." It was clear that she was bordering on hysteria. Gruver leaned forward and pulled the phone closer to his ear. This wasn't the strong-willed, imperturbable New York girl he knew. Something was wrong. He listened as she went on. "Chuck, I shot a man. I think he's dead. They're coming to get me. They're going to kill me."

Gruver had to shout to break the manic flow of her words.

"Catherine! Get hold of yourself! Where are you? What do you need?" The members of his staff who were sitting within earshot looked up at the CTO. He shook his head and covered the mouthpiece with his hand. "Now, slowly and calmly, tell me what the problem is."

He heard her take a deep breath. When she started to speak, the control had been restored to her voice. The fear and hysteria were still out there somewhere, though, just beyond the edge.

"Chuck, OptiMarx is dirty. I knew it and now I can prove it. They may not have activated the code yet. It may not be too late. I told Stan Miller. He sent some goons to kidnap me. Ustinov over at OptiMarx warned me they were on the way and sent some men he said would help me."

Gruver broke in. "Wait. Wait. So, where are these guys?"

Goldman's tears were back. He heard them. She fought to stay in control as she spoke.

"They kidnapped me. Ustinov's men did. They took me to some farmhouse in New Jersey. They said they were going to kill me." By the last words, she was blubbering. She sniffed and seemed to pull herself together once again. "I slipped through a hole in the floor and got out and tried to run. One of them came after me, Chuck. I shot him. I think I killed him."

"Catherine, stay with me. You got to be strong now. Where are you? Are you safe?"

"I . . . I think so. I hid all night in the restroom of a truck stop. A TravelCenter of America. Exit 7 off Route 173. Just west of Princeton."

Gruver already had his car keys out of his desk drawer. "Catherine, stay there. Right where you are. Stay out of sight. I'm on my way."

He slammed down the receiver and ran out of the computer center, his mind racing. It would take him at least two hours to get to Catherine, assuming traffic wasn't a problem. Maybe he should call the police. Report what she had said about OptiMarx to the SEC. No, she said Stan Miller was in on this. No telling who else might be, too. He had to do this himself. Had to at least make sure first that she was safe.

So something *was* wrong with the trading system! Even as he trotted for the exit, his business sense seemed to scream that he stay here until that problem was rooted out.

He could still hear the panic, the urgency, the sheer terror in Catherine Goldman's voice. He left the Exchange behind and picked up his pace as he dashed for the parking garage.

*   *   *

Carl Andretti was having a difficult time shaking the cob-webs out of his head. He tried to remember details of the previous night's celebration, but his recollection became very hazy after the third bar he and his coworkers hit. Must have been a pretty good time, though. His mouth felt as if it were stuffed with dry cotton and his head thumped ominously. It took a considerable party to do that much damage anymore.

He reached into the little refrigerator behind the bar in his office and grabbed the ever-present bottle of Dew-ar's. Nothing like a little hair of the dog to get the blood flowing once again. He poured a water glass full of the cold amber liquid and took a large gulp. It was cool on his tongue but burned as it went down.

Good medicine. His stomach growled and began to ache. Soon he would be better. Much better.

There was still no sign of that damn uppity Brit Alan Smythe. Strange that he hadn't been around since the OptiMarx opening ceremony yesterday. He was usually first in line when it was time to pass around the congratu-lations. Andretti figured he would at least have put in an appearance at the office celebration the previous after-noon. Bad form for the CEO to neglect telling all the staff what a great job they had done. How unlike Smythe to pass up a chance to bask in a little limelight.

Andretti took another mouthful of the Scotch and smiled. Smythe had probably gone off with some of his stuck-up, highbrow friends rather than hang around with the rabble at OptiMarx.

Him not showing up this morning was troubling, though. They had work to do. Andretti needed the effete son of a bitch for once. Mark Stern wanted a report about the progress of the system on its first full day of activation and damned if Andretti was going to talk to the venture capitalist by himself. Not after the chewing-out he had gotten the last time. It was Smythe's job to deal with the moneyman. Let him do it.

The OptiMarx CTO set down the now-empty glass and turned back to his computer. He ignored the throbbing in his gut as he entered a series of digits on the keyboard and watched the screen flash to life.

The market was down, but that didn't matter anymore. With his special "in" with the system, he would make a fortune no matter which way the market was headed. Yesterday had been little more than a taste of what glories were about to come. Over fifty thousand dollars had made their way into his secret offshore bank account. Not bad for a partial day's work. Today promised to be even better.

So what if Alan Smythe was too busy with his snobbish friends to remember to show up for work? If he was not here, then there was no reason to split the profits with him.

Carl Andretti got so busy at the keyboard he forgot to refill his water glass.

The servant whispered into Boris Medikov's ear, "A phone call, sir. The caller is most insistent that he speak with you."

Medikov sat at the head of the huge mahogany dinner table that dominated the massive dining room of his penthouse. Dozens of candles on the table, the twin

Georgian sideboards, and in the crystal chandelier, illuminated the richly paneled room with a warm, glittering
glow. Huge wall mirrors reflected the flickering light as it
danced off the polished silver.

The Russian Mafia leader stared at the waiter. His eyes
flashed when he spoke. "Didn't I say that I did not want
to be disturbed while I entertained my guests? Can you
not follow simple orders?"

"I am sorry, sir. He said I was to mention *Kronstadt*."

Medikov started. It had to be Durov. He couldn't
imagine why the crusty old bastard would be calling now.
Everything was moving along smoothly toward the eventual culmination of the intricate plan. Nothing new was
supposed to happen for another couple of weeks while
the world seethed and surreptitious profits were reaped.

The senile old admiral probably had some minor slight
to grouse about. Like so many of the elderly, he could be
such a child sometimes.

Medikov pushed back from the table. The small group
of close associates and their "escorts" looked at their
host. He smiled and murmured, "Please excuse me for a
few seconds. Go on with your dinner."

Medikov strode out of the dining room and crossed to
his private office. He snatched the secure phone from its
cradle and growled, "*Da*, it is Medikov."

"Boris, good evening." Alexander Durov sounded ju-
bilant. "Mark your calendar. This is a historic day. Your
great-grandchildren will ask you to tell the story of this
night."

"Admiral, what are you talking about?"

"The *Kronstadt* Operation has begun. You are to shift

the OptiMarx operation into full-scale offensive mode immediately."

Medikov held the receiver away from him and stared at it as if it had just grown a Medusa head. When he spoke again to Durov, his words were angry but measured. "What the hell are you talking about? *Kronstadt* will not begin for two more weeks. That was our agreement. Two weeks to make a profit. Then the operation will begin."

Durov brushed the argument aside. "Even the best plans are subject to change. That is the nature of war. Smitrov is now our prisoner. It is vital that we act while this advantage is still ours. Now please go to the offensive. I strongly suggest that you stay there in that decadent apartment of yours if you do not wish to be caught in the cross fire."

Medikov held a dead phone. The old bastard had hung up on him.

Chapter 32

Jon Ward eased back in his chair and watched the tactical display as it played out on the flat-panel screen. The picture was getting cluttered. A dozen merchant ships were tracking up and down the Norwegian coast. The Aegis radar was keeping up with a hundred aircraft, some commercial flights, several military planes, and helicopters moving back and forth between the oil platforms and the coast. It was a lot of information and most of it was extraneous.

Ward concentrated his thoughts on three of the hundreds of symbols crowding the big screen. A P-3C Orion aircraft was five miles out in front of the Akula submarine they had found. It was down low, dropping lines of SSQ-53D DIFAR sonobuoys. *Anzio*'s SH-60B helicopter flew at two thousand feet, monitoring the line of sonobuoys the mystery sub had just passed through. The chopper was data-linking the information the sonobuoys heard back to the computers on the Aegis cruiser.

The two aircraft coordinated their sonobuoy patterns, leapfrogging each other as the mystery submarine tried to sneak down the Norwegian coast. They were being very careful not to spook the sub, circling high up in the clouds whenever they could. They couldn't afford for the skipper of the Akula to see them if he came up to periscope depth. *Anzio* was staying just over the horizon. The Russian boat had no idea they were anywhere close.

The sonobuoys parachuted down to the water and dropped their hydrophones four hundred feet into the depths. The sensitive listening devices were set to catch the fifteen-hertz noise tonal this sub was emitting. They could listen for several hours before their batteries died. When they detected the sub, a tiny transmitter floating on the surface radioed the information up to the circling aircraft. The aircraft relayed the information and it was combined with the data from the cruiser's own SQQ-89 towed array. It was a piece of teamwork that was well planned and often practiced.

They needed to figure out where this guy was going. He was staying very close to the Norwegian coast, trying to hide amid all the coastal shipping and biologic noise.

"Good thing he's got that strong fifteen-hertz tonal or he'd be near impossible to track this near the coast," Ward said to no one in particular.

He punched a few keys on his keyboard and spun the trackball. At this speed, the Akula would enter the Kattegat tomorrow night. If Ward's guess was right, the sneaky bastard would be off the Baltic coast of Russia, near St. Petersburg, in two days.

Bob Norquest stepped through the hatch into the CIC. The *Anzio*'s skipper had been very attentive, if somewhat cool, since their disagreement about calling in the P-3s. He walked over to Ward's command chair and bent down to whisper something.

"Captain, there's an 'eyes-only' message for you on the broadcast. You can take it in my cabin if you want."

Ward followed Norquest out and up the ladder to his sea cabin. He was surprised to see the late afternoon sun was already low on the horizon. It had still been dark, in the very early morning hours, when he last left the dim cave of the CIC.

Ward plopped down in front of the computer and punched in his access code. The screen went blank and then lit up with the text of a Navy message.

BT.

WARNING—SPECIAL COMPARTMENTED IN-FORMATION (SCI)

CODE WORD—STEEL HEARTS

EYES ONLY FOR CAPTAIN JONATHAN WARD

TO: COMMANDER CTG-42.2.3

FROM: COMMANDER, NAVAL INTELLI-GENCE SERVICE

SUBJ: MISSION TASKING CHANGE

1. RELIABLE SOURCES VERIFY PRESIDENT GREGOR SMITROV PRISONER OF ADMIRAL DUROV. BEING HELD IN POLYARNYY SUB-MARINE BASE.

2. SUSPECT DUROV IS KEY MEMBER IN PLOT TO OVERTHROW LEGITIMATE RUSSIAN GOVERNMENT. KIDNAPPING JUDGED TO BE MAJOR STEP IN ADVANCING PLOT.

3. VITAL THAT SMITROV BE RESCUED. USE AVAILABLE IN SITU FORCES TO IMPLEMENT RESCUE.

4. ACTIONS SHOULD NOT BE IDENTIFIABLE AS U.S. IN ORIGIN.

5. PRESIDENT BROWN AUTHORIZES UNDER PRESIDENTIAL FINDING J-2721-32.

6. GOOD HUNTING. DONNEGAN SENDS.

BT.

Ward stared at the screen for a moment. He felt numb reading the words. More important was what the words didn't say. Donnegan, his mentor and surrogate father, was telling him to wage war in Russia. The "Presidential Finding" meant that this was a very highly classified mission that President Adolphus Brown wanted done. He wanted it kept very, very secret. There was no mention that the Russian government was involved. There would be no help from that angle.

Donnegan was telling him to send Bill Beaman out on a very long limb.

Norquest avoided looking at the computer screen as he handed Ward a cup of coffee. "Bad news?"

"Yeah, probably. We've got a tough job to give the SEALs. Timing sucks. *Toledo* just started the mission to deploy the ASDV. Joe Glass won't be able to communicate for a couple of days at best." He logged off the computer, rose, and headed for the door. "Let's get up to radio and give Beaman the good news. Maybe he can come up with something."

Anistov Dmolysti leaned into the *Vipr*'s switchboard and handed the *michman* a screwdriver. Cables snaked across the narrow passageway, making it look like the nest for some giant but very disorderly bird. The back panels on the switchboards hung open, revealing the thick copper bus bars inside. The whole scene was one of confusion, but there wasn't time right now for neatness and order. The work had to get done, and done as quickly as possible. Dmolysti hoped that the technicians were following the plan.

The *michman* backed out of the switchboard, moving gingerly to keep from brushing against the bus bars on his left through which five hundred volts of fifty-hertz power coursed. Touching one meant electrocution. The man's body would be fried as his muscles locked up, preventing him from moving away from the current's grasp. He stood up straight when he was well clear of the panel's innards. He removed the thick rubber gloves and wiped the sweat from his forehead.

"First Officer, it is done," the technician grunted. "All the bolts are tight."

Without reply, Dmolysti grabbed a phone and called Anatol Vivilav. "Captain, the repairs are complete. We are ready to turn it on and test the work."

"Good work, Anistov," the submarine's skipper answered. "Have everyone stand clear and we will energize the circuits."

"Captain, everyone is clear. We are ready."

Dmolysti picked up a fire extinguisher, just in case something might still be wrong. He held his breath, recalling the fire that caused this damage. The green POWER AVAILABLE lights blinked on.

There was no telltale flash of light or puff of black smoke. Dmolysti allowed himself to breathe again. It must be working.

Now they would be able to once again run quieter and faster. He grabbed the phone again. "Captain, the seawater pump bus is reenergized. Everything looks to be normal. Restoring seawater systems to normal silent lineup."

He turned to the *michman* in charge of the engine room and ordered the lineup shifted. Now they would once again be difficult to locate. He silently prayed no one had detected their transit thus far.

"What do you mean you lost them?" Jeff Stroud shouted. *Anzio*'s system had been tracking the Akula flawlessly for hours. It was great to have his sonar boys at the center of everything on board instead of relying on those hotshots that ran the radar system. It had been one of his own boys who lost their contact. "How could you lose a frequency that strong? That looked like somebody beating on a trash can with a baseball bat. The only way to lose it would be to turn the screen off."

He looked over the sonar man's shoulder, staring at the screen. Sure enough, it no longer displayed the tell-tale peak at the fifteen-hertz mark. *Anzio*'s SQQ-89 was not hearing the Akula's noise anymore.

"I don't know, Chief. One second he was there, next he was gone."

Stroud slammed down his coffee cup.

"Shit," he growled. "The bastards changed something. Search every frequency. We got to start all over again. I better tell the commodore. Maybe he can pull a rabbit out of his hat again."

He called over to CIC to speak with Ward.

While he waited for the commodore to answer, his fingers danced over the keyboard. Maybe the aircraft still had something. He watched as sonar signals from the sonobuoy fields, downlinked from the circling P-3C, scrolled across his screen. Nothing but snow. The bastard couldn't just disappear. He was out there somewhere and Stroud vowed he would find him again.

Charlie Gruver eased his old Honda across two lanes to get to the freeway exit. Traffic was heavy for a late morning out in the country. Must be people heading into the Poconos for some late-season skiing. A huge red, white, and blue sign rose high above the trees, advertising the truck stop up ahead. A quick left at the top of the ramp and he was in the parking lot. He steered the little car between a row of big rigs and found a parking spot a couple of rows back from the door to the restaurant.

Tractor-trailers were gathered around the fuel pumps or sat idling in the big parking apron in back. Twenty or so passenger cars were parked in the lot. Gruver glanced around and quickly discounted the cars he could see as holding any threat to Catherine. Out-of-state plates and family groups of vacationers.

He walked into the restaurant and found a booth. The place was half-full, mostly truckers and families taking a break from the road. No one looked up or paid him the slightest attention. There was not a sign of Catherine Goldman. She said she was hiding in the ladies' rest-room. A good place for her to hide, but tough for him.

A middle-aged waitress stopped at his booth.

"What you havin,' hon?" She had an easy, friendly tone.

"Just coffee."

"How you want it?"

"Black."

She leaned in closer. Just above a whisper, she asked, "Your name Gruver?"

He looked up, startled by the question. "Yeah, why?"

She raised an eyebrow, checked to make sure no one was close enough to hear her, and answered, "Lady in back said to watch for a tall, blond guy. New York City accent. Said you would order black coffee."

"Where is she?"

The waitress shrugged. "Just wait here. She's in bad shape." She put her fists down on the table and looked him in the eye. "I had me a husband once who beat me and liked to play mind games. She tells me you been doin' anything like that, I'll kick your ass."

Gruver held up his hands in surrender. "Nothing like that. Just a friend helping a friend in trouble."

She was gone. Five minutes later, she was back with his coffee.

"Wait a couple of minutes, then head toward the men's room. Take the door on the left just beyond it. Sign says 'Employees Only.' Got it?"

"Yeah, got it."

"Sorry about comin' down hard. Girl can't be too careful anymore."

"Not a problem. Catherine's a special person. Really appreciate you helping."

She didn't answer. She just went back to serving her other customers.

Gruver drank half the coffee and then got up. He threw a twenty on the table and headed for the restroom. There was the door, just where the waitress said it would be.

He looked around. No one was in sight. He opened the door, stepped into a storeroom, and pulled the door shut behind him.

Catherine Goldman was sitting on a box, holding her head in her hands, staring at the floor. She had not heard him come in. Gruver was shocked at her appearance. She looked disheveled, her clothes muddy and torn, her hair a tangled mess.

He cleared his throat. Catherine looked up, startled, fear flashing across her face. Then she recognized Gruver and rushed into his arms. "Charlie, I'm so glad you came! I'm so scared!"

He held her close. Her body trembled. "Cath, that's

what old friends are for. You're safe now. Nobody's going to hurt you."

Her trembling turned into a violent shiver. He took his jacket off and wrapped it around her.

"They want to . . . I shot . . . ," she stammered. She was not able to go on.

"Look, let's go. Let's get you out of here. It's best to be moving. Then you can tell me what's going on."

She nodded and allowed him to steer her out the storeroom door. He held a protective arm around her as they stepped out into the smoky bustle of the restaurant. This wasn't the self-assured professional that he was familiar with. Something had frightened her deeply.

As they made their way between the rows of tables, Gruver watched for any sign of trouble, for anyone who might mean them harm. He wasn't sure what he would do if he saw a threat. A young couple with a pair of toddlers came through the front door as he was helping Catherine out. The mother looked at them. Gruver gave a wan smile. "It's okay. She's just not feeling well."

They were out the door and headed across the parking lot. The walk to the car lasted forever, but at last they were safely inside his little Honda.

Neither Gruver nor Goldman noticed the big black Ford pull into the truck stop just as they climbed into their car.

"That's her!" Nicholas Vujnovich shouted, pointing at the couple disappearing into the little green car. The truck stop was the closest civilization to the farmhouse. It made sense that she would get here and try to reach help. "Over there with the tall blond guy. The bitch has found herself a protector." He reached into his belt to pull out the big Glock pistol. "Come on, let's take care of her right now before she gets away again."

Josef Bogatinoff held up his hand and gave his cohort a disgusted look. "Easy, my friend. Your Cossack blood is showing. Try using your brains for a second. If we start blasting away out here, the police will be on us before we get to the freeway. All of these trucks have radios. They will tell the world what they see. We will let them go for now." He tossed the big Russian a pencil. "Get the license plate number. If we lose them, we will be waiting for them when the blond guy gets her to wherever they are going."

Vujnovich jammed the Glock back in his belt. It rankled to see that bitch drive away when they had the drop on her. Especially after what she did to Mikhail. And what Medikov would do to them if they let her get away.

Josef was right, though. Blowing the SEC inspector away in the middle of a truck stop parking lot in broad daylight was not the discreet way to handle the situation.

He found a slip of paper and started writing: New York VXZ-692. Bogatinoff pulled the big Ford onto New Jersey 173. He headed toward Interstate 78 back to the city, keeping the car with the SEC inspector in sight. Vujnovich punched a number into the cell phone.

"Dmitri, find out who owns a car with New York license plates. Number is VXZ-692. We need it right away. Get an address."

"Okay," Dmitri Ustinov answered, then added, "Nicholas, it has started. Medikov has ordered us to start the attack on the stock market. We need you all back here right away."

Vujnovich stared at the cell phone. This couldn't be right. They had at least a week before the attack would be started. The time was meant to allow Medikov to build up profit and it also gave the pair time to clean up the loose ends they faced. Some of those loose ends would be news to Boris Medikov, Vujnovich thought as he watched the little Honda pull away from them.

"Clean up what you are doing so nothing points to you," Ustinov continued. "There is lots of concern around here this morning about where Smythe is. Be real careful what you do with him."

Admiral Alexander Durov looked up at the three submarine commanders who stood before him. They were at attention on the other side of his broad wooden desk from where he sat. Their working uniforms were dirty, stained with grease and sweat. The call from Vasiliy Zhurkov said not to waste time for military niceties, and they did not. The admiral wanted to see the trio right away.

Durov rose and stepped around the desk. He walked toward the sideboard, where he poured four glasses of vodka. After passing a glass to each officer, he held his own drink up as a toast.

"Gentlemen, it is time for action. You sail tonight to glory. For the *Rodina*!"

The old man ignored the twinge of pain in his chest as he downed the clear liquid. There was no time for pain now. All he had worked for, all he had lived for over the last thirty years was about to come to pass.

The three commanders toasted him back and downed their own vodka.

Chapter 33

Bill Beaman didn't believe what he had heard. The big SEAL commander sat on a log and shook his head. A chill wind blew out of the northwest, tousling his short blond hair, depositing bits of gritty snow.

The team had been in place for a week now. They should be concentrating on extraction, not contemplating a new mission. One hell of a mission at that.

Jon Ward had just ordered him to do whatever it took to rescue the president of Russia from the clutches of Admiral Alexander Durov. He couldn't imagine what Jon was thinking. This place was a fortress. The SEALs would need armor to go in through the front door, and so far, he had not found any back doors.

He turned to look for Chief Johnston. The second in command was huddled with Cantrell and Broughton a few meters down the slope. The chief looked at his commander sideways, reading the look on his face.

"What did the boss have for us?"

"You ain't gonna believe this. They want us to amble down there and rescue President Smitrov while we're resting."

Johnston turned his head and gazed down at the sub base where the APCs still patrolled just outside the high wire fence. Both SEALs knew there was no way through those defenses. Not with the equipment or manpower they had.

Johnston looked back at Beaman. "What've you got in mind? I've never seen you without a plan."

Beaman dusted the snow out of his hair and pointed down the hill toward the fjord. "Way I figure it, since there's no way in by land, we'll go by water. After all, we're SEALs, aren't we? Saddle up and let's go find ourselves a boat down there."

Jason Hall lay behind the sniper scope. His head ached from squinting into the thing for so long. This whole mission was getting old. He and Tony Martinelli had been up on this ledge for over a week now, watching and waiting. The cold and the wet were starting to take their toll. Hall could feel the stiffness in his joints and the lethargy building from lack of exercise.

The night was dark up here. Dense clouds obscured the moon and stars. Snow blew past, carried by a bitter wind. Across the harbor, the lights of Polyarnyy Sub Base burned brightly, shimmering through the snowflakes. Trucks and people moved in a steady flow into and out of the big covered dock. Something was up. Hall hadn't seen this much activity since they first staked their claim on this plot of frozen Russian soil.

Hall kept an eye to the scope as he reached his leg back to kick his sleeping partner.

Martinelli grumbled back to consciousness. He slithered out of his sleeping bag and moved up next to Hall to see what he wanted. He checked his watch on the way.

"Hey, what's the idea? You're not due for relief for another hour. I was deep in a good dream, just me and Jennifer Lopez. We were—"

"Good thing I woke you before your groaning gave us away. Get that radio ready to go. There's lots of activity down there. Tonight is when the ASDV mission comes off. They're likely coming down the fjord right now."

Martinelli scooted backward on the ledge and set up the little satellite transceiver. It took a few minutes to put the dish in place on the back side of the hill and aim it up toward the satellite. They were using the hill to help shield the transmissions from any listeners down on the sub base. The system used a very narrow beam, but sensitive intercept equipment that might be close enough could detect side lobes, even as weak as they were. The hill helped to divert those side lobes away, out toward the Arctic.

Martinelli hooked the antenna to the transceiver. The tiny green SIGNAL AVAILABLE LED blinked on. He gave Hall a thumbs-up and hunkered down to wait.

It didn't take long. Half an hour later Hall saw the black shadowy shape of an Akula-class submarine slip out of the open end of the giant covered dock. He turned to tell Martinelli what he was seeing. The SEAL was already on the radio sending the contact report back to Admiral Donnegan.

Just like the two previous ones, the big submarine crossed the harbor, churning up the thin sheet of ice that had formed on the water. As the SEALs watched, it turned into the Murmansk Fjord and then disappeared as it dove into the deep waters.

Hall watched until the last ripple washed away toward the rocky coastline. That would likely be it for the night's activity. They would take one more look at the barn and then they could relax for a few minutes before beginning to pack up and get ready for the rendezvous with the ASDV. He spun the scope back toward the covered dock just in time to see another massive dark shape emerge from its mouth.

"Holy shit!" he gasped. "Here comes another one. Something's in the works, Tony. It's time to ring the alarm bells."

Martinelli grabbed up the transceiver. He hesitated. Transmitting two messages this close together was not a good idea. The radio signal was very weak and the narrow beam was aimed upward at the satellite in its geosynchronous polar orbit. Martinelli's voice messages were compacted into millisecond bursts of radio energy to further decrease the risk of drawing unwanted attention. All that caution was designed to limit the chance the transmissions would be intercepted. Still, two messages in rapid succession exponentially raised the risk. No one could decipher the content, but they would know someone was there, transmitting from this cold overlook.

There was no choice. Donnegan had to know about this, and quick. Two boats coming out together was not a good sign at all. Especially with the mini-sub and *Toledo* out there in their path.

Martinelli passed on the contact report as the second

Akula dropped below the surface heading into the Murmansk Fjord.

Hall swung the sniper scope back to look at the covered dock. His jaw dropped. A third black shadow was emerging. "Tony, here comes another one!"

"Jeez, Jase! If we spend any more time on the radio, those Russians are gonna be on us like stink on shit!"

"Quit griping," Hall said with a shrug. "We ain't got a choice here. Get the message out."

Hector Gonzales sat in the pilot's seat, steering the ASDV mini-sub down the narrow slot of the Murmansk Fjord. So far it had been easy, just like the countless training exercises they had been through. The sonar system worked flawlessly, painting a road map between the granite walls for him to follow. The sonar sent out a high-pitched click that bounced off any solid object, like the rock sides of the fjord. The echoes told the sonar's sophisticated circuitry just what was out there. At the same time, the clicks mimicked biologic noises. Its digital sound library switched automatically among various natural sounds. Any listener would likely allow those noises to fall into the background.

From his perch in the copilot's seat, Sam Donlan gazed around at the array of displays and readouts. They told the pair that the ASDV was operating flawlessly. Donlan leaned back, yawned, and stretched. He unbuckled his shoulder harness and seat belt as he unfolded his tall, gangly frame from his bucket seat.

"I'm getting a cup of coffee. Want one?" he asked, not bothering to stifle another yawn.

"Sure, black and bitter."

Donlan crawled through the hatch and headed past the lockout chamber and into the passenger chamber. Gonzales sat back and eased the wheel slightly to starboard to slide around a rocky escarpment.

The blip seemed to come out of nowhere. One second the sonar screen was blank. The next the image filled the whole screen. Something big was out there, coming right at them. It was coming fast!

Gonzales yanked the wheel hard to the left and pushed downward. The tiny mini-sub heeled over on its port side and nosed down, heading for the deep. The pilot's eyes were fixed on the sonar screen as the depth gauge reeled off the numbers of their screaming dive. This was going to be close. Damn close!

The sonar screen was blanked out. Gonzales could hear the hum of the Russian sub's machinery and the beat of its screw through the hull. He knew it must be right on top of them.

Just as quickly as it appeared, the Russian sub was gone. Gonzales shook his head. Had he imagined the whole thing? The sonar screen was blank except for the rock walls of the fjord that were still showing up.

Donlan came crashing forward, rolling through the hatch. His coveralls were soaked with coffee. "What the hell is going on? You could have just hollered if you wanted a donut."

"Damn sub just came out of nowhere," Gonzales grunted. "It caught me by surprise. Damn near turned us into underwater roadkill." He had another thought. "I sure hope *Toledo* hears that bastard coming earlier than we did. I don't think they can duck as quick as we could."

*   *   *

Admiral Alexander Durov sat across the table from President Gregor Smitrov. The little professor was proving more obstinate than Durov had anticipated. They had been sitting here in this room for four hours, arguing, ever since the guards had brought Smitrov from his cell. Life would be much easier for both of them if Smitrov would just do as he was told. Durov's patience had long since vanished. There were so many things that demanded his attention. Instead he sat here wasting time with the weakling president.

He slammed his fist down. The carafe sitting in the center of the table jumped and splashed great droplets of water onto the mirrored, polished-wood surface.

"Damn it!" he roared. "I am telling you for the last time. Either you cooperate or I am going to lock you up and forget where. You will not even have the pleasure of becoming a martyr."

The jangling phone broke the tirade in midthought, before the president could respond in his maddeningly calm way. Vasiliy Zhurkov snatched the phone from its cradle and spoke for a few seconds before nodding at Durov.

"Admiral, it is Captain First Rank Dobiesz. He reports that they have detected very suspicious radio signals. They appear to be coming from the hills across the bay to the north. He requests orders."

Durov looked hard at Zhurkov. His face flushed a bright red. "For a submarine group commander, the man is an imbecile! Do I have to tell him to wipe his ass after he shits?" He snatched the phone from his aide. "Dobiesz, you idiot. Put together a squad of naval infantry and get them up on that hill to search it. Do it right now. Use one of the armed helicopters to get them there."

He slammed the phone down and returned to face his hapless prisoner. The old admiral tried to massage away the nagging pain behind his breastbone as he hammered away at the mouse of a president, trying to make him see the logic of the solution he was offering.

The little man sat there staring back, his fingertips pressed together, that same coy little smile playing on his lips.

Nicholas Vujnovich fumed as he watched the little Honda drive down the freeway. The big blond guy wasn't stupid. He had tucked in between an eighteen-wheeler hauling groceries and a New Jersey State Patrol car. There just wasn't any way to do anything now, even if they had wanted to. If they spent too much time back here tailing them, they might attract unwanted attention. There were other things that needed attending to right now. The SEC bitch could wait a couple of hours.

Vujnovich swung the big Ford off the interstate and toward the country road. Josef Bogatinoff yelped in surprise.

"Where are you going? The bitch is escaping."

Vujnovich pulled to a stop at the end of the exit ramp. He looked each direction down the long stretch of country road before easing out and heading south. He stole a quick glance at Bogatinoff.

"She is not going to get away," he said in a growl. "We will find her in the city where we can more easily take care of her without notice. Right now we have important business to finish back at the farm."

The wind was blowing in from the west, bringing dark storm clouds with it, blotting out the wan late-winter sun and painting the empty New Jersey farmland with a depressing gray light. There would be rain or snow later in the afternoon. The Ford barreled down the empty highway, bouncing over the potholed macadam.

Bogatinoff sat without speaking for a few minutes, watching the naked maple trees flash by.

"What unfinished business?" he asked, unable to suppress the question any longer.

A huge stainless steel milk truck pulled to a stop in front of them, its left-turn blinker flashing. Vujnovich slowed the car as the tanker moved off the roadway and between a set of gateposts. A dairy farm lay a few hundred yards down a narrow country lane. The muddy field beside the road was filled with black-and-white Holsteins, chewing their cud, waiting for the evening milking. The stink of fresh manure filtered through the car.

Vujnovich shook his head as he accelerated once again. He couldn't believe how dense his partner could be. "Josef, did your mother drop you on your head when you were a baby? We have been in and out of that farmhouse for a week now. That Goldman woman knows where it is located. There is a body lying on the kitchen floor and a kidnapped, drugged corporate executive tied up in the front room." He flipped on the right turn signal and turned down a narrow lane. "Do you think the local police might find that a little suspicious?"

They pulled to a halt in front of the farmhouse. The

pair climbed out of the car and stepped up on the porch. They pulled out their pistols and entered the front door. Nothing had changed since they left two hours before. Mikhail Gikoytski's lifeless body lay on the kitchen floor, his blood long since dried into a congealed, sticky mess. Alan Smythe snored loudly in the front room, still sleeping off the effects of the last massive dose of heroin.

"What now?" Bogatinoff asked.

Vujnovich looked around the room. He rubbed his dark beard as he thought for a few moments. The problem was a difficult one. They didn't have time to clean everything up and dispose of Mikhail's body. Besides, what would they do with Smythe? Two bodies were worse than one.

Vujnovich snapped his fingers. It was just too easy. "Josef, give me Mikhail's gun and get another dose ready for our sleeping friend."

He dragged the doped-up OptiMarx CEO into the kitchen and draped him in a chair. Smythe fell forward, slumped half onto the table. Vujnovich took the pistol the woman had used, and wiped it clean. He wrapped Smythe's hand around the grip and trigger. Without warning, he squeezed off a shot that crashed into the far wall.

Bogatinoff jumped in surprise and dropped the hypodermic onto the floor. It shattered and splattered its contents on the tile. "Hey! What the hell! You scared the life out of me. What are you doing?"

"I had to get powder residue on the murderer's hand. He shot poor Mikhail in a drug deal gone bad. Give him another dose and we will get out of here."

Bogatinoff grabbed another needle and started to mix up some more dope. "Should I make it enough to overdose him?"

"Try to do something subtly for once. Make it look as if he did it himself. He would not OD on purpose. Make it borderline. That way, if he dies, toxicology will say it was accidental. If he lives, no police are going to believe a word he says. He will be trying to kick a major habit cold turkey in the slammer."

Commander Joe Glass sat on the stool beside the periscope stand. So far, it had been quiet. Too quiet. Gonzales and Donlan were a couple of hours into their mission on the ASDV and would be working their way down the fjord. There was nothing for him and *Toledo* to do but sit out here at the mouth of the Murmansk Fjord and wait for their return with Beaman and the rest of his SEAL team.

Pat Durand stood over by the ballast control panel, talking with Bill Dooley. They were trying to figure out why the trim system wouldn't prime. The piping system was built to move seawater between various tanks located around the boat. By moving water between the tanks, they could compensate for weight changes on the sub and keep it at a neutral buoyancy and level. That was called "in trim." The discussion centered on what appeared to be a problem with the priming pump. It wasn't drawing enough vacuum.

Jerry Perez stood back at the navigation plot, stooped over the large-scale chart of the fjord. He was keeping track of *Toledo*'s position. As he did, he listened to the sonar man who was standing by the fathometer, reading off the depth of water under the sub. It would be Perez's worst nightmare to get lost in this very confined bit of water and bump into the bottom.

Tommy Zillich sat just inside the sonar room, talking to Sam Wallich through the open door while keeping one eye on his "sonar boys" as they listened to the surrounding water.

Glass watched the scene. They might just as well have been a hundred miles off Norfolk. There was no sign, except for the chart Jerry Perez had taped to the plotting table, that they were twenty miles inside Russian territorial waters, a few miles north of one of the most closely guarded submarine bases in the world.

One of the sonar men jumped. "Chief, quick! I got a contact! Sub close aboard and dead ahead!"

Glass heard the words through the door and glanced up at the broadband display on the sonar repeater. Sure enough, there was a broad white stripe that had just started. Something was out there. Something big. It was close and coming quick. There was no bearing rate. It wasn't drawing to either side of *Toledo*. If they didn't do something, there would be a mammoth collision.

Not much time to maneuver. Not much room, either.

"Left full rudder," Glass yelled. "Steady course zero-nine-zero. Ahead two-thirds. Rig ship for collision!"

Glass hoped he had guessed right. There wasn't room to do much in the way of evasion here. Couldn't go deeper. Couldn't go more than a mile to the east before he had to turn again. All he could do was dodge and hope that Russian sub was on a straight line to the open water of the Barents Sea. If so, he would pass a few hundred yards astern. If not, they would know the bad news soon enough.

Just had to wait a few minutes and hold on. Beads of sweat formed on Glass's forehead and trickled down, stinging his eyes.

Glass breathed again. The Russian sub was starting to draw aft. If they were lucky, it would pass astern.

"Right five degrees rudder, ahead one-third," Glass ordered.

Pat Durand stood beside him, his face dead white and his breath coming in fearful little gasps. "Damn, that was close. I'm sure glad you were out here, Skipper. I wouldn't have reacted fast enough." He studied the sonar repeater. The Russian sub was drawing aft as Glass turned. The fire control picture showed *Toledo* moving around behind the other sub. "What are you doing now?"

"We aren't clear yet," Glass answered. "I don't want him to detect us. I don't want us to run into the mud. I'm slipping around behind him now."

The little dance proceeded as Glass guided *Toledo* around in a slow circle until they ended up dead astern of the departing Russian sub.

Wallich looked at the sonar room door and shrugged. "I don't know where she came from. One minute, we're all alone and the next she's running over us. Definitely an Akula. She had the right signature."

"Here comes another one!" the broadband operator shouted.

Glass steered *Toledo* over to the side of the fjord, giving the second Russian sub plenty of room to pass. Then he slipped his submarine in behind it. Durand looked at him. Glass answered his unspoken question.

"We'll follow this one out to the Barents long enough to call home and give them the news. It looks like all the horses are leaving the barn."

Chapter 34

Charles Gruver steered his little Honda through the thickening traffic. The farmlands of central New Jersey had given way to the urban sprawl of the northern part of the state. The towers of Manhattan were already a smudge on the skyline. The dark, dreary landscape matched his mood. His mind raced, looking for answers. He had to force himself to concentrate on the knots of cars all around him.

He glanced to his right when he had the chance. Catherine Goldman still sat there, not making a sound. She was drawn into a tight little ball, her knees under her chin, her face buried in her hands, just as she had been ever since they pulled out of the truck stop parking lot. Once or twice, he had noticed her shoulders shaking as she tried to suppress a sob or fought an involuntary shiver. This was not the strong, independent, self-assured woman he knew and admired. He could not imagine what had happened to her, who had hurt her so badly. Those were the questions he intended to get answered as soon as she was safe at his place. Gruver vowed he would make whoever it was pay.

The cell phone in his jacket pocket buzzed. Catherine jumped and looked at him, fear obvious in her eyes.

He smiled at her, then flipped the phone open.

"This is Gruver and I'm busy," he growled. "What do you want?"

"Chuck. Where the hell are you? The world is turning to shit here." It was Bill Molsen, deputy chief technology officer at the New York Stock Exchange. "The market's coming down around our ears."

Gruver dodged into another lane and shot past a slowing line of traffic. "Calm down, Bill. Just tell me what's happening."

His assistant took a telling deep breath, then exhaled before he continued. "The market's been dropping like an anvil all day. Worse than the first day after the Trade Towers. The volumes have been unbelievable, Chuck. I've never seen anything like it. The Dow is down a thousand points. No, better than a thousand now."

Gruver whistled softly. That was a catastrophic disaster. He had never seen anything like that kind of drop in a few hours either. The trading floor would be in absolute pandemonium, even with the curbs in place. He could picture the desperate specialists and floor traders scrambling, wild-eyed, trying to quiet the panic while they attempted to salvage their fortunes. The cable reporters shouting into their microphones, trying to be heard over the pandemonium.

He wondered why Molsen would be calling him. As long as their computer systems were working, the free fall on the trading floor wasn't their problem.

Bill Molsen seemed to read his boss's mind. "Chuck, all the volume is coming through the OptiMarx system. There seems to be inexhaustible sell-side pressure. It's driving the prices straight to hell. Something doesn't smell right here."

"What does the chairman say?" Gruver asked.

"He's an inch away from closing the floor until we get a grip on it. He's been down here three times already this morning. Boss, you've never seen the head guy sweat like this."

Gruver pursed his lips. Molsen's words said a lot. The normally imperturbable chairman of the Exchange rarely felt the need to leave his second-floor executive suite during the trading day. He never saw fit to venture into the bowels of 11 Wall Street, to the systems operation center.

Gruver braked hard to line up for the tollbooth. He asked Molsen to wait while he tossed the attendant two dollars. He hit the gas the instant the gate swung up. "Look, Bill, I'll be there in an hour. Until then, use your best judgment. If you think the system is wacky, shut it down. I'll back you."

"Sure thing, boss. I just hope it's still here when you get in."

Goldman sat upright and looked at Gruver when he flipped the phone shut. The tears had dried on her face. There was now a cold, hard light in her eyes.

"It's OptiMarx, isn't it?" she asked. "I told you. Charlie, we have to stop it."

He did not disagree with her as he stomped the accelerator and tried to will the Honda past the slower traffic headed for the city.

"You think this will work?"

The skepticism was obvious in Bob Norquest's words

as he turned away from Jon Ward and leaned on the *Anzio*'s starboard bridge wing. The ship's skipper was staring out at the low, sandy Danish coast. They were steaming sedately, weaving their way through hordes of fishing boats, past coasters moving goods through the Kattegat. The narrow strip of water separated Denmark from Sweden. It was one of the most congested waterways in the world.

Ward sat in the high Naugahyde-covered bridge chair, the seat traditionally reserved for the commodore. Steam rose from his heavy white china mug. He ignored Norquest's tone as he looked out at the gray-green water. "It had better work. If it doesn't, we're out of options."

The officer of the deck stuck his head out of the bridge hatch. "Captain? Commodore? I have come right to course one-seven-two to conform to the navigator's track. No report of any submerged contacts."

The two senior officers nodded to acknowledge that they heard and the OOD ducked back into the bridge house. Norquest returned to the topic but he still didn't look Ward in the eye.

"Jon, we've been going balls-to-the-wall ever since we lost that Akula. You'd have us at flank right now if it weren't for all this ship traffic. You're betting a lot on a hunch."

When they lost contact with the mystery Russian sub up along the Norwegian coast and then couldn't find the guy again, Ward decided to stop the fruitless searching and go for something else. He had ordered the *Anzio* to race down the coast, through the Skagerrak, then through the Kattegat. The plan was to get ahead of the Russian, then wait for him to emerge into the Baltic Sea, assuming that was where he was headed in the first place. They were almost on station now.

"Well, Bob, it's not really a hunch. Let's call it an educated guess based on what we believe his mission to be. We think he has been sent down here to lob cruise missiles into the old homeland. He can't do that from the North Sea. He has to get into the Baltic to be close enough. That means he has to come through here, right past us. We just need to latch on to him when he does."

It sounded so easy when Ward said it, but both men knew how incredibly difficult finding a submarine could be. That was especially true in these shallow, crowded waters. It was worse than trying to find a needle in a haystack. It was more like trying to find one particular piece of hay.

Norquest turned to face Ward. "The P-3 is reporting that the sonobuoy pattern we left back in the Skagerrak is still cold," he said. "No sign of our Akula coming this way yet."

"No surprise there. If this skunk is making fifteen knots or so, I wouldn't expect to find him for another couple of hours. We'll see him soon, I expect."

Ward hoped his words carried conviction. They were taking a gamble. If the boat they had lost was on its way to do mischief somewhere else but the Baltic, the bastard would have free rein unless somebody else detected him out there. Somebody not really looking for him. Every instinct he had told him they would meet the Russian boat again, and soon.

Jon Ward had learned long before that the best guide

he had, the one thing he could count on, was his well-honed instinct.

Tony Martinelli was the first SEAL to see the big transport helicopter lift off from the Polyarnyy helipad. He had been busy brushing the snow from his eyebrows so he could see better when he looked back down at the base. He saw the chopper gain altitude and swing around. It got all his attention when its nose pointed directly at the little ledge where he and Jason Hall had been hunkered down.

"Hey, Jase. This ain't good news. You may wanna look what's coming our way."

Hall scooted up to the top of the ledge and looked in the direction Martinelli was pointing. He recognized the Mi-8 Hip helicopter at once. It could carry a squad of eighteen fully equipped troops and a machine gun at either side door. He and Martinelli had watched plenty of helicopters moving between the sub base and the military airfield over at Severomorsk, to the southwest. Just VIPs, mostly press and government officials in for the memorial service. They were getting their important asses shuttled to their waiting planes and back to Moscow before the storm building to the north trapped them in this unforgiving, inhospitable outpost.

The Hip was coming right at them. This wasn't some VIP shuttle.

"Tony, it's time we vacated our little penthouse," Hall muttered through clenched teeth. The satellite transmissions. They had detected something and were coming to see what it was. "Let's head for the trees."

The two SEALs grabbed their gear and scurried off the ledge, dropping into the undergrowth just as the Hip breasted the hill. Martinelli and Hall wormed their way through the snow and underbrush, trying to get to safe hiding places before anyone in the war bird saw them and opened fire. They split up and burrowed in like animals hiding from a circling hawk.

The Russian helicopter hovered just a couple of meters above the snow-covered hilltop. A squad of naval infantry jumped out the door to the ground. The armed troops spread out and moved forward, heading in the general direction of the ledge where the SEALs had been. They were being very careful, moving slowly, their weapons at the ready.

A hare, frightened by the helicopter's racket, broke from its brushy hiding place and dashed across the stretch of snow in front of the troops. A fusillade of automatic fire chased the hapless rabbit, then churned it into the ground. There was little more left than bloody snow and a rag of raw meat.

These troops were jumpy. They meant business. That made them very dangerous.

Hall lifted his head and peered out from behind the birch gorse that hid his bulky form. Martinelli was ten meters to the left, lying under a larch tree. Hall could just make out the ugly black muzzle of Martinelli's M-4, pointed at the backs of the squad as they made their way toward the overlook they had just abandoned.

The Hip moved a little farther down the slope to a small, level clearing, not a hundred yards from where the SEALs hid. The rotors slung bits of ice and snow, whip-

ping them into a white cloud as it settled to the ground
and the wheels sank into the knee-deep snow. The pilot
likely figured the squad of naval infantry fanning out
around the hilltop would be adequate protection for him
to take a rest while they searched the bluff.

Hall considered the situation. It was only a matter of
time before the squad noticed the SEALs' tracks in the
snow and came looking for them. A wild thought occurred to him. He shook his head, but the thought was
still there. There was a way out. A way that might just kill
two birds with one stone. If it didn't kill a couple of
SEALs in the process.

He twisted around and flashed a hand sign at Martinelli. He moved out, leaving the protection of his hiding
place. Hall crawled through the snow-covered underbrush, his white camouflaged form barely discernible in
the darkness against the half-buried undergrowth. He
seemed to disappear, enveloped by the snow, then reappeared minutes later, in the ice cloud right behind the
idling Russian helicopter.

Martinelli watched in disbelief as the big black SEAL
rose and swiftly covered the last few meters to the helicopter's open hatch. He was running low and quick. The
open ground was dangerous, and even in the darkness,
there was no hope for cover. If the Russian gunner in the
doorway caught sight of him, it would be over before
Hall could react. Even an all-conference linebacker from
Alabama couldn't outmuscle a barrage of bullets.

Just as he reached the rear of the chopper, the snow
around Hall erupted in dirty little volcanoes. He dove
forward, skidding beneath the helicopter. He hunkered

down, trying to see where the fire was coming from. It wasn't the gunner in the Hip's door. Hall could see him. The man was staring wide-eyed up the slope. He was probably wondering if it was his friends shooting at him or if there was somebody else up there.

Hall could see the squad fanning out on the slope and moving back toward the helicopter. They were firing short bursts as they came, aiming at him but being careful not to nip their transportation back home.

This was hopeless, Hall decided. He was going to get chewed up just as that rabbit did. He wondered where Tony was.

The angry burp of an M-4 and the explosion of an M-79 grenade answered Hall's question. Martinelli was firing at the squad. Three of the naval infantry troopers flew back awkwardly, sprawling on the ground. Their blood spread in dark stains across the virgin snow.

The SEALs were still badly outnumbered and seriously outgunned. This would have to be quick. There was no time for hesitation. Hall needed to end this thing and get them out of here.

The squad dropped and scurried for cover. Their fire shifted from Hall to Martinelli's hiding place among the birch and larch. The Hip gunner opened up as well, his rounds chewing bits and pieces from the trees. Hall knew Martinelli wasn't there anymore, that he had vacated the spot as soon as he finished offering the cover fire. The distraction gave Hall the few seconds he needed.

He leaped up and lunged through the open hatch into the helicopter, taking the gunner by surprise. Hall fired twice, and the lifeless gunner fell out of the bird, hanging a meter from the ground, restrained by his harness.

In one quick move, Hall spun the machine gun around to train it on the troops, who were once again advancing his way. Withering fire from the machine gun on full automatic stopped them in midstride. Several fell while the others dove for cover and returned fire.

The Russians' bullets pinged off the armored war bird, which had been designed to carry Soviet Spetsnaz troops into the mountains of Afghanistan. Armored helicopters had been a necessity there. Otherwise the mujahideen would have made short work of it. That same armor was giving the SEAL a few more moments to act.

The pilot, reacting to all the firing on the ground around him, hit the collector and started to spool up the twin turbines. As the big helicopter shuddered, Hall saw Martinelli coming his way at a dead run. He sprayed the enemy squad with more bursts of machine-gun fire, trying to give his buddy the cover he needed. With a mammoth leap, Martinelli dove headfirst into the helicopter as it lifted off. He rolled through the open hatch, then almost fell right out the other side. Hall grabbed a handful of parka and wrapped him up.

"Come on!" Martinelli shouted. "Let's get out of here!" An odd look crossed his face when he realized that Hall was standing in the hatch and the chopper was lifting away. "Jesus! Who's flying this thing?"

Before Hall could answer, Martinelli decided that was not as important as the Russians who were still shooting at them. He grabbed the chopper's other machine gun and sprayed a few bursts at the troops, trying to pin them down until the helicopter was farther away.

Hall leaped into the cockpit. Before either of the two-man crew could react, Hall reached across, jerked the pilot out of his seat, and tossed him back through the doorway into the chopper's cargo area. The Russian landed in a heap at Martinelli's feet. The SEAL booted the guy right out the open hatch. The pilot fell hard to the frozen ground, ten meters below.

Jason Hall lowered himself into the pilot's seat and grabbed the collector as the helicopter started a dangerous yaw to the left. He steadied the Hip and eased the big bird higher before heading south. The copilot stared at him, eyes wide with fear.

Martinelli stepped into the tiny cockpit and stood between the two seats.

"Okay, Jase," he said nonchalantly. "Now what?"

"I figured you wanted a first-class seat on a flight out of here."

"I didn't know you could fly one of these things."

Hall turned and smiled. "What gives you the impression that I can?"

The radio squawked to life. The Russian air controller was demanding to know what was going on.

"Hotel Flight. Hotel Flight. Report your status."

The two SEALs looked at each other and shrugged. The controller repeated himself, more insistently this time.

Martinelli grabbed the microphone, keyed it, and groaned. In his best Russian, he said, "Accident!" He waited a few heartbeats and grunted, "Explosion! Wounded!"

The sound was a cry of pain. It was so convincing that Hall glanced back to make sure his friend was all right.

"Hotel Flight, understand you have wounded on board. Can you return to the base?"

Martinelli groaned again and cried out, "Wounded! Many dead!"

"Hotel Flight, try to make it to the base. There will be ambulances at the helo pad."

"Good actin', Shakespeare!" Hall shouted over the noise of the turbines.

"Let's just hope those guys on the ground back there don't catch on to what we're doing before we get to wherever we're going."

Hall skidded the Hip around the sky, deliberately flying a clumsy, wobbly course. He needed to convince anyone watching that the pilot was in mortal pain and could barely keep the helicopter in the air.

"Which brings up my next question," Martinelli yelled. "They're expecting us to land. Inside the base. You really wanna do that?"

Hall grabbed the little team whisper radio out of his pocket and tossed it to Martinelli. The whisper radios were made for the SEALs to quietly talk to each other when they were close. Their low power output minimized the risk of anyone detecting their signals.

"Call the boss and tell him to be ready for a pickup. We might just as well fly into the mission. Sure beats trying to sneak in any other way I can think of."

Martinelli shook his head, then smiled and flashed a thumbs-up. "Now, that sounds like a plan. Crazy as shit but a plan nonetheless."

Commander Bill Beaman was halfway down the slope, crossing an open meadow through the deep drifts, when he heard the beating of the helicopter heading their way. He dropped to the ground and tried to mimic a snowbank as the Hip flew overhead. It swung wide and circled slowly back, hovering over their former camp. It was as if the Russian chopper pilot knew precisely what he was looking for.

Beaman took advantage of the helicopter's erratic flight and dashed the last few meters to the cover of a line of trees. When he fell to the ground, he landed on top of Chief Johnston.

"Damn, Skipper! Mind not getting so personal?"

Beaman scrambled off the top of him. "Sorry, Chief. You think he spotted us? He sure seems to know—"

He was interrupted by a low sound from his whisper radio.

"Hey, boss, where are you at? Jase thought you might like a lift over to the base."

Beaman swung the tiny boom microphone in place and answered, "Martinelli, is that you? Where the hell are you?"

The answer was a complete surprise.

"We're in the Hip. Give us a vector so we can pick you up. We gotta be quick before the air controllers get suspicious."

In less than a minute, Beaman, Johnston, and the rest of the team were aboard the helicopter and Hall was once again flying toward the Polyarnyy Sub Base. So far, the air controllers were attributing the helicopter's erratic course to the "badly wounded" pilot. Martinelli reinforced the idea with carefully spaced groans and short reports of pain, death, and general mayhem. He assured them the squad had wiped out the threat on the bluff.

Hall brought the Hip in low and slow over the base. The team took advantage of their unique approach to better orient themselves on the base's layout. The metal shed where they had last seen President Smitrov was a kilometer from the helicopter landing pad. So far, the hijacked chopper was proving to be a godsend. It would have been next to impossible to get this far unnoticed. It would have been even tougher to try to fight their way across the base.

Snow whipped up in blinding clouds as the Hip settled in the center of the cement pad. The wheels had barely kissed the ground when three ambulances screamed out of the hangar, blue lights flashing and sirens wailing as they slid across the open space toward the chopper.

The SEALs sat back in the shadows inside the Russian helicopter. They did not want to be seen until the last minute. Cantrell and Broughton tensed, ready to leap out of the left-side hatch and pounce on anyone driving up on that side. Martinelli and Dumkowski were ready just behind the right-side hatch.

The ambulances skidded to a halt beside the bird, their back doors already flung open. The unarmed medics leaped out and ran to the chopper, lugging stretchers and bags of medical supplies. Seconds later the startled medics were face-to-face with four armed SEALs. They dropped the gear and held their hands high. In minutes, the Russians were bound and shoved into the back of the copter. The SEALs hopped into two of the ambulances and drove off to find the Russian president.

The narrow streets through the submarine base seemed strangely empty. No office workers bustling about on important tasks. No sailors heading off to the bars in town. Even the windows of the buildings along the narrow streets stared vacantly back, dark and lifeless. Durov had locked the base down to keep word of his coup attempt secret as long as possible.

Joe Dumkowski drove the lead ambulance. Beaman sat in the passenger's seat, thinking. They had to find Smitrov and get out fast. If they got held up, all was lost. The entire incident would be very ugly. They would be dead. The rest of the world would hear nothing of what had happened. Or it would add to the international crisis, played up as yet another wanton attack by the Americans on the friendly, innocent Russian people, a treacherous follow-up to the attacks on the Russian submarines.

Smitrov could be anywhere. Unaware that anyone had seen the kidnapping, Durov might have left the Russian president in that shed. Or he could have moved him somewhere else. There was no time to search. They had to trust their luck. Go for the building where they had last seen him and pray. If he wasn't there, they would face the impossible task of getting out of the base and to the rendezvous with the mini-sub.

"Left at the next street," Beaman ordered. "We're going to that warehouse down by the pier."

Dumkowski whipped the wheel over and slid around the turn, straightening up just in time to miss plowing into a brick wall. The vehicle shot down the street. Dumkowski made a sharp right at the next intersection. Down another narrow, empty street and then another screeching, sliding turn. Two more turns and Beaman was looking at the same alley where he had watched Smitrov get ambushed. He looked up at the darkened windows. He hoped they didn't hide another ambush.

"Hey, boss," Dumkowski yelled. "Isn't this the place?"

Sure enough, the metal warehouse stood right in front of them. Beaman answered, "Yeah. Let's go in the front door. We'll see if the doorman has our reservations."

The ambulance slid to a halt, and a second later Cantrell and Broughton tumbled out the back. They rushed across the open space as Tony Martinelli swung the other ambulance around, heading for the warehouse's back door.

Cantrell ran low and hard, barreling through the double doors and rolling across the small lobby space. He came up fast, his M-4 flashing like a cobra ready to strike. The single hapless guard didn't have a chance. He was still thinking about reaching for his pistol when two .225-caliber slugs tore through his forehead.

Broughton was a fraction of a second behind Cantrell. His weapon spat twice, tearing through the guard's chest, boring through his heart before leaving exit holes in his back the size of softballs.

Beaman and Dumkowski sprang past the first pair and rolled through the next door. They were in a huge, empty room. The place was bare. There wasn't even any litter on the deck. Beaman was still looking around, trying to find any threats, when Johnston and Jason Hall stormed through a door across the room, weapons ready to rock and roll.

"Anything?" Beaman asked.

Johnston shook his head. "All clear this way."

Martinelli had moved a few feet away from the rest of the group. He found a small door partially hidden by a large cement pillar. The door hung open. The inside appeared to be a small, windowless closet.

"Hey, guys," Martinelli reported. "Someone has been here. They left their eyeglasses." He studied the spectacles for a moment. "I know enough Cyrillic to see Gregor Smitrov's initials on the case."

Johnston looked over at Beaman and asked the obvious question. "What now, Skipper?"

"Damn good question. Got any suggestions, Chief?"

Chapter 35

Carl Andretti watched wide-eyed as the ticker flashed across the monitor screen. It was amazing! He had never seen the market behave like this before. It was absolute panic. Prices just kept dropping and dropping. There were no bargain hunters. No sign of a bottom. The volumes were incredible. The market was coming apart right before his glassy eyes.

The Dewar's wasn't helping calm his jangling nerves. The special secret feature he had built into the OptiMarx system had been automatically buying thousands of tiny chunks of stock, the way it was supposed to, but now it couldn't unload the shares. It was uncanny. There was always someone in front of him, selling shares a tick lower. Right now he had over fifty million dollars invested in the market. Money he didn't have. Money he wouldn't ordinarily need. He would have to come up with it somehow.

If this debacle didn't reverse itself soon, they were ruined. He drained the last of the Dewar's and then poured another one. His hands shook so badly he spilled some of the precious liquid on his keyboard. He wiped it up with his fingers and licked them dry.

Above all else, Carl Andretti dreaded the possibility of

jail. Even through the dull haze from the Scotch, he realized that possibility was now very real.

Smythe. Where was the bastard? The little Brit should be here to help him take the heat.

Cheryl Mitchell, Smythe's assistant, knocked once. Without waiting for Andretti's invitation, she stuck her head through the door. "Excuse me, Mr. Andretti. Mr. Stern is here and he—"

Mark Stern shoved past her and barged into the CTO's office. He was livid and not in any mood to observe the niceties of corporate protocol. Mitchell backed out of the office and shut the door behind her.

Stern jammed his knuckles down on Andretti's desk and rested his body on his fists. He leaned forward, his eyes little more than fiery slits, and glared down at the obese, drunken executive.

"What the hell is happening with that fancy system of yours? The market is going to shit and I'm getting panicked calls from the SEC. You got any answers?" Stern didn't wait for an answer. He straightened up and glanced around the office, then asked as an afterthought, "Where is that boss of yours?"

Carl Andretti saw a light come on. Here was the perfect opportunity to unload the blame for the losses, the snafu in the system. "Mark, I wish I knew where he was. We're over fifty million in the hole already by following his orders."

"You're what?" Stern gasped. "You told me that this whole thing was foolproof. What are we going to do? How can we keep losses like this hidden?"

Andretti managed a smile as he answered, but he

avoided eye contact with the moneyman anyway. "Mark, calm down. I think I have a plan. All we have to do is set the accounts up so that Smythe takes the fall. We don't show up anywhere. Anybody gets wise to our little operation, they'll find a trail to our flaming friend and nobody else."

Stern collapsed onto the settee at the rear of the office. He stared for a moment at a spot on the wall a foot above Andretti's head. The CTO strained to hear his words when he spoke. "Get it done. Hear me? Get it done. If you screw this up . . ."

The powerful financier seemed to run out of air before he could finish his threat.

Hector Gonzales pulled back on the control stick, and the ASDV eased up from the depths of the icy fjord. According to the navigation plot, they were right outside the Polyarnyy Basin. They could run right on in, but it was advisable to take a look around before trying to sneak in any farther. It would not be a good idea to run into unexpected trouble now. Not this close to their objective. Besides, this would be their last chance to survey the territory until they were well inside.

The little black submarine came up until it rested just a couple of feet below the oily smooth surface.

"Okay, Sam, raise the periscope," Gonzales told Sam Donlan, his copilot.

Donlan reached up and flipped one among the myriad of toggle switches in the overhead between the two. A faint hum started from somewhere a few feet aft of their command cockpit. A little red light flashed on the center control console. It read SCOPE DEPLOYED. Unlike the periscopes on board the *Toledo* or other big subs, this one didn't penetrate through the submarine's hull. There wasn't an eyepiece to stare through, either. It was all electronic. When not in use, the scope hinged down into a stowage locker that faired into the sub's starboard side. When they needed to see out, a small electric motor rotated it up.

Donlan pushed a couple of display buttons on the touch screen of the multifunction display. The display changed from a sonar road map to a video picture, a shot taken mere inches above the surface. Even though it was pitch-black outside, the low-light video camera showed the harbor as clearly as if it were high noon.

"Looks like we're where we're supposed to be. Don't see a welcoming committee, though," Donlan said as he panned around. He zoomed in to look at the sub base in more detail. "Looks quiet as a church at midnight."

"Well, then, time's a-wastin'," Gonzales murmured. "Let's get this show on the road."

The next half hour would be the most nerve-racking. All their intelligence sources claimed the base had no sensors looking for a submarine in this close. They should be invisible at this spot.

But they were on this mission because the same intelligence sources had failed to detect any hint of submarine activity here in the first place.

If they were discovered, the first hint would be somebody coming their way to take a look. Their only recourse would be to back out, hit the bottom, and try to hide in the mud until they could slink back out toward where *Toledo* waited.

The ASDV eased across the open water. They had to get inside the covered dock before they could move up to take another look. The periscope was covered with "RAM," a special radar-absorbing material. It gave a radar return the size of a soda straw. Out in the Murmansk Fjord, one tiny moving return popping up for a few seconds would be ignored. In the glassy smooth waters of the Polyarnyy Basin, though, the observers wouldn't be so lax.

Gonzales leaned back and stretched his shoulders. They ached from the tension. "We're there," he said. "What say we take a look?"

The navigation screen showed them inside the dock, just beyond the large open doors. No reason to go in any farther. Getting too close would increase the chance that they might attract attention.

Gonzales pushed the speed control lever in to stop the screw turning. The mini-sub coasted a few more meters before easing to a stop. Gonzales flipped a switch to engage the depth-control hovering system, which would pump water on or off the sub to keep them on depth without the ASDV moving. For the next few minutes, they wanted to stay stationary. Anything moving across the water, even something small and dark like the periscope, would draw attention.

"I'm game if you are," Donlan answered. "That's what we rode in here to do."

Gonzales eased back on the control column. He could

hear the quiet hum of a pump back in the engineering section. The ASDV moved upward almost imperceptibly.

The periscope broke through the surface. The video picture flashed to show the inside of the huge covered dock. Donlan whistled. "Damn, this place is big! Must hold thirty boats or more when it's full."

Gonzales kept his eyes locked on the display as he answered, "About that. It was designed to hold ten Typhoons. Those things are big mamas."

Donlan panned the video camera around. He cocked his head sideways as he watched the display. "Hector, it's empty. Nobody home."

Charles Gruver eased down Maiden Lane in Lower Manhattan, as close to the Exchange as the afternoon traffic would allow. He glanced over at Goldman. She seemed to have recovered somewhat from her ordeal. The color was back in her face, the flash of determination once again in her eyes. This was one strong woman. Gruver admired her in so many new ways. He recognized something else, too. She was becoming someone he cared about, more than as a college friend or business acquaintance. He couldn't help wondering why, after knowing Catherine Goldman all these years, he had hardly noticed her before her plaintive summons on the telephone this morning.

"World to Gruver," Goldman said, her lips forming the beginnings of a smile. "Come in, Gruver."

He shook his head and said, "Huh?"

"Charlie, you were a million miles away."

"Oh, just thinking about the mess I'm about to walk into the middle of," he said with a dismissing wave of his hand. "Look, I'm going to pull over here somewhere and hop out. I can make it to the Exchange quicker on foot." He paused and looked her in the eye. He continued, speaking slowly and firmly. "Listen to me. You take the car and drive to my place. You remember how to get there?" She nodded. "Key's on the ring there. Don't stop for anything. When you get there, lock the door and don't let anyone in until I get back."

She nodded as he swung the wheel over and pulled up to the curb. The cabby behind him honked, shouted obscenities in some Middle Eastern dialect, and shook his fist.

Gruver ignored him. He swung the door open and jumped out onto the sidewalk. Goldman scooted across the seat and beneath the wheel.

He turned, leaned back into the car, and took Goldman's hand in his. "Catherine, please do as I say and be very careful."

She smiled up at him, but he had already turned and was charging down the sidewalk, dodging pedestrians as he galloped toward Wall Street.

Master Chief Tommy Zillich watched *Toledo*'s sonar screen. Last time they had turned, he thought he saw something. Just a fleeting glimpse. Probably nothing but his imagination. The two Akulas in front of them were keeping him more than busy. Still, something had caught his eye.

Zillich watched the course indicator turn to port as *Toledo* came around to a new course as they followed their two playmates out into the Barents.

There it was again! Just at the edge of the baffles, the blind spot behind the boat. Not his imagination this time. Zillich grabbed the 21MC microphone. "Conn, sonar. We've got someone behind us. Just coming out of the port baffles."

Joe Glass's reply was instantaneous. "You sure, Master Chief?"

"Yep. Another Akula. She's following behind us. Looks like there are three of them and that makes us the meat in the sandwich."

Glass jumped over to look at the sonar repeater. Sure enough, there it was, just visible, the telltale trace of another boat. The image was already sliding back into *Toledo*'s baffles as they steadied up on the new course. Did the Akula know they were there? Or was he blindly steaming out of port, assuming he was behind his friends? There was no way for Glass to know. If he didn't do something quick, the Akula would disappear again in his sub's blind spot astern and he would lose the initiative.

Well, as his old skipper, Jon Ward, always said: "No balls, no blue chips." It was time to take a calculated risk.

"Left five degrees rudder," Glass commanded. If the Akula followed the move, he'd better be ready to respond. "Snap shot! On the Akula behind us. Tube two."

Those words got the gun cocked. Just in case they were the target of the Russian sub's attention, the AD-CAP torpedo in tube two would be ready to go. Glass only had to say a single word to send the big weapon on its way.

He turned to Brian Edwards, his executive officer. "XO, we're going to slowly move around behind this guy. I'm going make a long, sweeping turn until he draws abeam of us. Then we'll let him drive on past if he's so inclined."

Glass drew a little diagram on the chart paper that showed the relative positions between *Toledo* and the third Akula. The diagram showed them moving in opposite directions so that the Akula would slowly disappear back into the baffles.

"With you so far, Skipper," Edwards said.

"When we steady up, I'll let our friend draw aft until he is just at the edge of our baffles. Then I'll come left again." Glass drew another picture that showed the Akula steaming away from *Toledo*. His sub was moving up behind the Russian. "I'm going to dance around behind this guy. Tell me if he zigs. That's the only way we'll know if he has detected us."

Edwards studied the crude diagrams and nodded. "Okay, Skipper. I see what you're doing. We're going to spiral in behind this guy. How close you want to get?"

"Brian, I don't want to get snapped up in his screw, but I don't want to lose contact, either," Glass answered. "Let's stay outside a thousand yards. The further, the better, as long as we don't lose contact." He turned to Jerry Perez, who stood just across the plotting table from the two. "Nav, I'm depending on you to keep us off the rocks. We're still in pretty close. I don't want to kiss the bottom."

Perez nodded. He pulled out the ever-present dividers and measured the distance to shallow water.

"We're good so far, Skipper. Nearest shallows are six thousand yards off the starboard beam."

The two black denizens of the deep performed a slow minuet in the dark, cold Barents Sea. Glass kept his team on a hair trigger as they maneuvered around. If the Russian became the least bit suspicious, they wouldn't necessarily know it until Master Chief Zillich heard the incoming torpedoes. By then, it would be far too late to do anything more than retaliate.

The wait was excruciating. Tension filled the cramped interior of the submarine like a thick presence. Glass felt the sweat trickle down his back. He glanced over at Edwards. The XO was gripping the chart table. His knuckles were white, but he still had that cocksure look on his face.

Toledo steadied up, deep on the Akula's port quarter, back in the Russian sub's baffles. The other submarine steamed on, seemingly unaware that there was company trailing right behind.

Edwards watched the tactical picture develop on the fire control computer screen. Pat Durand fiddled with the knobs a little, fine-tuning the solution. Steaming this close behind a submarine was not a place where errors could be forgiven. The only real information was the bearing to the unseen adversary. His course, speed, and range had to be derived based on that slim bit of data.

Durand nodded, looked up, and flashed a thin-lipped smile. "That's it, XO. We're looking right up her skirt."

Edwards glanced around and caught Glass's eye. He

gave him a thumbs-up. The skipper walked over to look at the solution. He placed a hand on Durand's shoulder. "Good work, Pat. Keep your eyes open. This guy could zig at any minute and we damn sure better zig with him." He turned around to Edwards. "What do you think, XO? Do we have a handle on what he's doing?"

The young officer didn't hesitate. "For the moment, yes. We just don't know enough about the guy to stay in this close for very long."

Edwards had a point. In a normal situation, they could spend many hours at the outer edge of their quarry's detection range, watching how a sub did business before they tried to slip in close. They would have time, for example, to find that the rattle from the stern meant the rudder was moving and he was starting to turn. Or hear a pump with a bad bearing that told them he was coming up to periscope depth. This knowledge gave them a tiny edge, a few seconds to react before things got hairy.

In this situation, they didn't have any of this type of specific information. Nor did they have the time to gather it.

They also had no idea how good this Akula's skipper was or how he might operate. There was no time to map out his sound signature before they had to move in close. The *Toledo* was already there.

Glass knew all this without Edwards telling him. There were times when the risk was necessary. He nodded and half smiled as he spoke to his XO. "You can handle it. We're going to stay here, tucked in nice and snug, for a bit. We don't know if there are just these three or if he has some other playmates coming up behind us. It'd sure be a pisser to get our asses run over." He took a swig of coffee and looked over the rim. "Besides, I'd kinda like to know where this train is headed."

Bill Beaman huddled in a corner of the empty warehouse discussing the circumstances with Chief Johnston. There wasn't much time to figure out a plan. Surprise was still on their side, but just barely. Even if they assumed no one had heard their gunfire when they entered the warehouse, it still wouldn't be long before the Russians figured out they had a missing ambulance. That there were no wounded showing up at the hospital. Or before someone found the crew tied up in the chopper. The troops on the hillside would be sounding the alarm soon as well. Once they figured out that the helicopter had been hijacked. Once the alarm was sounded, life would get very hard, very fast.

The rest of the team was fanned out, guarding the entrances. A pair of SEALs at each door, ready to give a rude welcome to anyone who might stumble into their building. Even the well-armed, highly trained SEALs would be no match for the battalion of naval infantry stationed at the sub base. The best they could hope for was a few minutes of protection.

"We've got to move out," Chief Johnston whispered without hesitation. "Skipper, our best chance now is to get out of this base and head for the pickup point."

Beaman looked his second in command in the eye. Johnston never gave up easily. Beaman had never known him to run without a fight. "We've got a mission, Chief. We have to find Smitrov."

"Ah, come on, Skipper. Look at this logically. We're

surrounded and outgunned and in the middle of one of the most heavily guarded submarine bases in the world. We're inside Russia, for God sakes. Fighting our way out of this place is going to be eons harder than it would have been to fight our way in. As soon as they figure out we're here, we're dead. It was a long shot. We missed. Now let's cut our losses and move out before they call down the wrath of God on our heads. We can still deny we were ever here. That'll be hard to do if they have our hides to prove it."

Beaman leaned back against the wall and thought for a minute, rubbing the stubble on his chin. It was the longest speech he had ever heard from Johnston. It made perfect sense. "Okay, Chief," he said. "Let's saddle 'em up. We need to figure out how we're going to get out of here."

Jason Hall gave a low whistle. He and Martinelli were guarding the big double doors at the rear of the building. "Guys. We got company coming down the alley. Looks like two BTR-80s."

Beaman sprinted across the empty warehouse and peeked out the tiny window. Two of the heavy armored personnel carriers lumbered down the alley, coming their way, their headlights casting ominous shadows on the old brick buildings and dirty snow. This was bad news. The two vehicles and the troops they carried could chew the SEALs to pieces in no time.

Beaman noticed something. The driving hatches on both BTRs were open. The 14.5mm KPTV machine cannons were in their stowed positions. These BTRs weren't ready for combat at all. They were cruising along inside their home base, not worried about any attack.

The pair of ugly gray vehicles ground to a halt outside the warehouse. The side hatch swung open. Ten uniformed troops stumbled out, pushing and shoving good-naturedly as they joked and lit their cigarettes. Their AK-47s were slung carelessly from their shoulders or leaned up against one of the BTR's massive tires.

A small civilian fell out of the hatch of the lead BTR. Someone behind him had shoved him. The little man fell clumsily and rolled over onto his back on the snow-covered cobblestones. An officer wearing the shoulder devices of a captain first rank climbed out, stretched, then bent down and yanked the little civilian to his feet.

Beaman could see the civilian's face. It was Gregor Smitrov, the president of Russia.

Bill Beaman had just enough time to get everyone in place before the Russians sauntered through the door and into the warehouse. They all came in. No one stayed outside with the vehicles.

As the door swung shut behind the group, Beaman called out in Russian, "Drop your weapons and raise your hands. You are surrounded."

One of the Russian troops must have been a little more scared than his friends. Or perhaps dumber. He fell to one knee and blindly opened fire in the direction of Beaman's voice. The heavy rumbling of his AK-47 filled the closed space. The SEALs opened fire an instant later. The light slap from the M-4s sounded trivial in comparison to the Russians' weapons. The Russians dove for cover. All, that is, except the four who now lay motionless on the concrete.

It was a short, vicious firefight, no quarter given and

none asked. Grenades flew across the narrow space and exploded behind a pillar that had shielded four troopers. A burst of stray AK-47 fire caught Broughton in the leg, spinning him around and tossing the heavy SEAL to the floor.

Jason Hall was backed into a corner, pinned down, the object of three troopers' interest. He sent a burst in the direction of two of them and chucked a grenade behind the other. The blast tossed the hapless soldier hard against a rear wall. He sprawled there and lay motionless. The other two broke and ran toward the door. They made it halfway across before they were cut down in the cross fire.

There was a lull in the firing. Beaman heard a shout from across the room.

"Stop shooting. I am coming out."

The Russian captain emerged, holding the little civilian in front of him like a shield. Smitrov was pasty white, shaking so hard the captain had to hold him upright with a forearm beneath the president's chin.

Beaman could see that the captain held a pistol to Gregor Smitrov's temple. The Russian officer's eyes scanned the room, trying to locate the ambushers in the darkness and smoke. He licked his lips nervously, then spoke. His voice was loud, his hearing stunned by the gunfire and explosions.

"I assume this is the man you want. You will let us go and give yourselves up or I will shoot President Smitrov here before your very eyes. Then you can explain to the world how it was you who killed the president of Russia."

From behind the pillar where he hid, Bill Beaman

knew he had seconds to act. He took a deep breath, sighted down his rifle barrel, aimed, and, with a soft exhale of breath, squeezed the trigger of his weapon twice.

The Russian captain jerked backward as if someone had struck him a mighty blow to his stunned face. Two small red dots decorated his forehead just above the bridge of his nose. He was dead before he tumbled hard against the back wall.

As soon as the captain released the grip on Gregor Smitrov's neck, he scurried toward the big American.

He almost made it.

A sudden burst from an AK-47 knocked him hard to the concrete. He lay still as a pool of blood formed around him.

Martinelli fired, cutting down the last trooper. The place fell silent.

Beaman ran to Smitrov's side and rolled the president onto his back. He was still alive, but he was losing a lot of blood from some nasty chest wounds. Beaman could hardly feel a pulse.

Jason Hall ran to help as Beaman ripped Smitrov's shirt open. The three entrance wounds were high up on his torso, stitching from his left shoulder across to his breastbone. Hall held his ear to the wounded man's chest and listened to his shallow breathing.

The big SEAL looked over at Beaman and shook his head as he answered the unasked question. "Not good. His lungs seem okay. I can't hear any rasping or gurgling. The pulse is pretty thready and he's losing a lot of blood. Skipper, we need to get him to a hospital real quick."

Chief Johnston walked over and squatted next to the

pair. "Broughton took a slug through his calf. Passed straight through without tearing up too much meat. The boy'll be okay. Just pretty sore for a while. Those guys were sloppy. Didn't leave anybody outside. We'd better get moving. All that noise has to attract somebody."

Beaman rose and nodded. He looked down at Hall. "Put a quick pressure bandage on Smitrov, then get him in the BTR. Any more first aid, we'll have to do on the run." To Johnston, he added, "Let's go. Everyone in the lead BTR."

They all headed out of the building, spacing themselves out and moving low. Weapons were ready, fingers on triggers. Never could tell when reinforcements might arrive.

The team piled into the lead BTR. Tony Martinelli hopped into the driver's seat and fired up the big eight-cylinder 7403 diesel. Heavy blue smoke poured out of the exhaust as the brute roared to life. The BTR lurched forward as he slammed the drive into gear.

Beaman hopped up into the second driver's chair and pulled the two armored hatches shut while Cantrell sat in the gunner's seat. He moved the machine cannon out of its stowed position and readied the big gun for battle. The little 7.62mm coaxial machine gun was ready as well.

Martinelli steered the awkward eight-wheeled vehicle down the alley, picking up speed as they went. He looked over at Beaman and smiled. "Tony's Taxi at your service. Where to, boss?"

"San Diego, if I had my choice. For now, head for the gate. It's time we got out of town."

The SEALs sat, tensely waiting for any reaction as they

raced down the narrow streets of the sub base. Broughton and Johnston manned firing ports on either side
while Hall worked on the wounded president.

It was anticlimactic when they roared right through
the main gate and headed down the road toward town.
No one fired a shot or even called out in alarm. A BTR
leaving the base was a matter of little curiosity. They were
well down the road and hidden behind a bend before any
of the SEAL team breathed again.

Beaman tapped Martinelli and yelled to be heard over
the howl of the BTR's engine, "Tony, head for as close as
you can get to the rendezvous point. We need to get our
guest some real medical care. I don't think we can trust
any hospitals around here."

Martinelli gave his skipper a thumbs-up, then steered
the bulky, bouncing vehicle on down the rutted road.

Chapter 36

Admiral of the Northern Fleet Alexander Durov slammed down the phone so hard the glass vodka decanter on his desk rattled. This was unbelievable. Somehow, soldiers had shot their way right into the inner reaches of Polyarnyy and had managed to steal President Smitrov right out from under some of the best troops Russia had.

The admiral was speechless, too stunned to even scream at the poor underling whose task it had been to relay the bad news to him. Reports were still coming in, the voice on the phone had said, but it appeared that someone ambushed a squad of his best naval infantry in the hills above the base. The perpetrators had mauled the squad and stolen their helicopter. Then the invaders brazenly flew the thing to the base, shot up another squad, took Smitrov from them, and, in the process, managed to kill that idiot Gregor Dobiesz.

Their mayhem complete, they disappeared into the night, despite the most sophisticated and absolute security of any military installation in the country.

It was astonishing. Who could be behind this bold, improbable attack? No one outside the admiral's own closest conspirators even knew that Smitrov had become his prisoner. Only he and the guards who held him knew of the president's precise whereabouts. Word had just been leaked within the hour that the president's plane was missing on its return to Moscow. There was no way anyone within the government could have any idea of what was going on.

Yet some powerful and well-trained force had been able to carry off this daring attack. The skill and daring meant they were military. They could not have been from the Russian Army. Smitrov kept close contact with the Army. The few remaining specially trained teams were busy down in Chechnya.

The timing was puzzling as well. Smitrov had only been a prisoner for forty-eight hours. Someone found out about the president's capture, then planned and executed the attack in less than two days.

It just wasn't possible. Yet the messenger had been most certain it had happened. Smitrov had been yanked from his grasp. The scheme that had been proceeding so well was now in severe jeopardy.

Durov paced around his office, massaging his aching chest as he marched from one wall to the other. Everything was at risk. Smitrov was an important piece of the plan. Now he was out there somewhere, unaccounted for.

There was much planning to do, contingencies to take into account.

He half heard a phone faintly ringing in the next room. Vasiliy Zhurkov stuck his head in the door.

"Excuse me, Admiral. Boris Medikov is on the phone. He demands to speak with you at once."

That was interesting. Durov's suspicions soared. Per-

haps the Mafioso was somehow involved in the attack at
Polyarnyy. Durov had no illusions. Medikov would have
no qualms about turning against the plot if there was
profit in it for him. The man was only interested in the
money, not the glory of his country's return to greatness.

"Put him through, Vasiliy. And get my medication.
The man gives me heartburn."

Durov picked up the phone and greeted the Russian
crime kingpin with a verve he did not feel. Medikov ignored his greeting. He started right in, going straight to
the point of his call.

"Admiral, we have been attacking the American stock
market all day. It is in panic. Another day or two like this
and it will collapse in total turmoil."

"Good! That will deflect the American attention away
from us, just as we have planned. It will teach them a
much-needed lesson in humility."

Medikov's tone changed. He was speaking like someone trying to explain a simple point to a slow child.

"Admiral, keeping them concerned and off guard is
one thing. Destroying the world economy is something
else. If the American stock market collapses, it will devastate the rest of the world economy in no time. We must
now retreat."

Durov took the bottle of pills his aide offered him and
downed two of them with a quick swallow of vodka.
"What do we care about the world economy? Why should
I care if the British or the French can't afford to buy yet
another fancy automobile? We are freeing Russia. That is
the purpose of our attack on the United States stock
market."

"Admiral, we have billions of rubles invested in the West. We will lose it all. I am ordering our people to back off the attack."

Durov was livid. This underling dared counter his orders! He would ignore the wishes of the next great ruler of Mother Russia. This was insubordination of the worst kind.

"You will do as ordered!" he roared, ignoring the searing-hot poker that jabbed him in the breastbone. "You will press the attack! You will not back off now that victory is so near! I don't care about your filthy rubles!"

The voice on the other end was just as manic when Medikov responded, "You do not order me! I'm not in your silly Navy. The attack on the market will stop. It will stop immediately!"

Durov took another swig of the vodka and forced his voice to calmness. The medicine was beginning to quell the pounding ache in his heart. "Boris, listen to me. If the attack is halted, there are certain dealings you have made that will reach the ears of the FSB. I don't think you would like the consequences should that information be made known to the authorities."

The Federal'naya Sluzhba Bezopasnosti, successor to the old KGB for internal security matters, was not an agency to trifle with. Even someone as powerfully connected as Medikov could disappear without a trace.

With that, he eased the telephone back into its cradle and reached for the bottle of blue pills again. Durov smiled to himself as he worked to control his breathing. He shook out two more of the capsules.

Medikov would get little enjoyment from his beloved

profits. If he only knew how futile it was to worry so over the ramifications of what he and his henchmen had set into motion.

If he only knew how little time he had left.

Anatol Vivilav stared out through his submarine's periscope. Lights on the Swedish coastline illuminated ships steaming in every direction. *Vipr* was moving through the narrow waterway separating Sweden and Denmark. The sub's scope was a tiny pipe, barely making a ripple on the surface as they headed east.

He had spent many hours talking with old Russian submariners, listening to their tales of threading their way through the Kattegat. It was one of the busiest crossroads in the world. Hundreds of ships traveled its narrow passage every day, carrying steel from Krakow to factories in France or wine from Spain to Latvia. All of those ships seemed to be overhead right now, intent on running over his periscope in the darkness.

If the water was a few meters deeper, he could drop down below periscope depth and sneak through unmolested. There wasn't enough depth to separate *Vipr* from the keels of the big, new tankers that plied these waters.

"Captain," Anistov Dmolysti called out. "Sonar is reporting a ship at bearing one-four-three. It has a zero bearing rate. My best estimate is a range of a thousand yards."

Vivilav spun the periscope around to look down that bearing. He saw the huge bow wave of a freighter bearing down on them. He had to maneuver or the freighter would cut *Vipr* neatly in half.

"Right full rudder," he ordered. "Steady on course two-one-zero. Anistov, make turns for thirty clicks, please."

"Yes, Captain. You only have three minutes on that course. Shoal water in fifteen hundred meters."

Vipr swung around as ordered and jumped ahead. Vivilav felt the periscope buck as the sub gained speed. He knew that anyone on the surface who might be watching could now easily see the scope as it kicked up a huge, roiling white feather of water. Nothing to do about that. They had to move or be run down.

The freighter steamed on, oblivious of the submarine hustling to get out of the way. Vivilav could see sailors standing on the bow, leaning on the railing and smoking as they cruised by. The freighter's bow wave was a massive wall of water, filling his view. The knife-sharp ice-breaker bow reached up to the stars.

It was going to be very close.

"Prepare the ship for collision!" Vivilav shouted.

He heard men around him, scurrying, making *Vipr* ready for catastrophe. He knew that the seven watertight doors separating the compartments were already slamming shut. Each compartment would be isolated to minimize flooding when the freighter plowed into them.

He kept the periscope locked on the freighter. It was drawing closer still, but *Vipr* was moving ahead. Maybe, just maybe they would make it. Maybe they would pass clear. Or it would hit them farther aft, back in the engine room. Then they would sink to the bottom, unable to move.

Time seemed to slow to a crawl. Vivilav watched, fascinated by the huge wall of steel bearing down on them. He could make out the individual welds joining the steel plates on the freighter's side. He could see the sailors up on the freighter's bow, pointing toward *Vipr*'s periscope and gesturing wildly. They must understand that there was a submarine below the high feathering wake they were seeing out there ahead of their ship.

Vivilav watched as the freighter's bow passed just a few yards aft of *Vipr*'s screw. They had made it. Made it by a couple of meters.

The captain felt the chill sweat, clammy on his back. His hand shook and he couldn't stop it.

"Captain! Shoal water in five hundred meters," Anistov Dmolysti called out. "We have to turn now!"

Vivilav had forgotten about the shallow, rocky water they were aimed for. It was safe to turn now. The freighter was passing clear, steaming on out toward the Skagerrak.

"Left twenty degrees rudder. Steady course one-zero-five. Anistov, make turns for ten clicks, if you please." Vivilav leaned back and rubbed his tired eyes. "Let us hope there is no more excitement for a while."

Dmitri Ustinov stared across the desk at Marina Nosovitskaya. The rise and fall of her breasts, barely restrained by the taut fabric of her peach-colored sweater, held his attention like some hormonal magnet.

"Dmitri, would you please concentrate on the business at hand?" Nosovitskaya chided. "We have work to do."

Ustinov chuckled. "I am concentrating. The objects of my concentration are quite breathtaking."

"You are incorrigible," she retorted with a disapproving frown. Still, she took a deep breath and drew her arms back behind her chair. The sweater stretched even more tightly across her breasts, the nipples threatening to pierce right through the filmy knit fabric.

Ustinov's mouth dropped open. His eyes bulged as he swallowed hard. The pencil he had been using rolled across the desk and fell to the floor, unnoticed.

Nosovitskaya laughed before returning her attention to her computer monitor screen.

"Show's over," she said. "Now get to work."

The pair was alone in OptiMarx's testing lab. With the trading system now fully operational, there wasn't much need to test anything. It made an ideal command center for their attack on the stock exchange.

Today had been exciting. The short-sale module performed flawlessly. It danced across the lists of stocks and offered selected securities for sale. They were stocks they didn't even own in the first place. Under normal circumstances, they would wait and buy the stocks later, when the prices were lower. Their plan had nothing to do with normal times. They were hell-bent on driving the market to its knees.

To anyone watching, it looked random, but the algorithm kept up a steady sell-side pressure. Wherever it sensed that buyers were available without sellers, it offered stock for sale. The inexhaustible supply drove prices down. Anyone trying to sell his shares had to lower the offering price, and there were plenty of sellers. The market worked on a herd instinct, and now a stampede was on. Panic was in full force. It was simple application of the law of supply and demand. America's own financial empire was being used as a weapon against itself.

Ustinov watched Nosovitskaya's fingers race across the keyboard. She smiled as she spoke.

"We've sold over three hundred million shares so far today. That's ten percent of the total market. This program really rocks!"

The American slang sounded so provocative as it rolled off her tongue. She licked her lips. The glow of the monitor made her big, dark eyes shine. Her cheeks were flushed from the excitement of what she was watching.

Dmitri Ustinov moved closer behind her, put his hands on her shoulders, and bent down, his face brushing against hers as they watched the figures scroll seductively across the screen.

She was so lost in the staggering value of what she was seeing that she didn't even bother to shrug him away. He couldn't tell if his raging erection was from her burning nearness or from the sheer immensity of the dollars he was watching slip across the breadth of the monitor.

"The P-3 reports a scope sighting on the ISAR," Bob Norquest said as he slumped into a seat. He handed Jon Ward a grainy photograph showing a periscope moving through the water, kicking up a large feather behind it. A large freighter filled the background beyond the scope. "Looks like you guessed right again. Your luck is holding."

The two men sat alone at one of the large tables in the *Anzio*'s wardroom. Ward had slipped in here for a cup of coffee and a few minutes away from the hustle and bustle of the Combat Information Center. Three of the cruiser's junior officers watched a satellite relay of an NBA game in the lounge area at the aft end of the wardroom. Their cheering had quieted the moment their captain walked in.

Ward took the picture and looked at it for a moment. "Standard Russian attack scope, all right. Hasn't changed in twenty years. Looks like he's trying to sneak through submerged. I'd bet he just got caught in traffic and was trying to keep from getting run down." He slid the picture back across the table toward Norquest. "You gotta love this improved ISAR technology. That P-3 was probably two hundred miles out when it grabbed the picture. Radar goes right through clouds, rain, or whatever."

Norquest nodded and answered, "That's what he reported."

The 1MC speaker interrupted the conversation. "Flight quarters! Flight quarters! Man flight quarters!"

Ward glanced over at Norquest, his eyebrows arched.

"Just getting a jump on you." Norquest answered the implied question. "That guy will go deep as soon as he's out in the Baltic. We're stationing the SH-60 to set up a sonobuoy field. We'll trap that Akula and hound him all the way across the Baltic."

"Bob, you're starting to think like a sub hunter," Ward said with a laugh.

Norquest acknowledged the compliment with the slightest of nods.

*   *   *

The BTR-80 troop transporter jolted across the rough terrain, knocking everyone around as if they were riding inside a cement mixer. Tony Martinelli kept the throttle as open as he dared. The farther away from the sub base they got, the safer they would be, the less likely they would be to have to fight their way out of this mess.

Bill Beaman tried to read the map, but it was difficult. There was no way to hold the flashlight and the map and still brace against the jarring ride.

"Tony, near as I can see, it's another kilometer," he shouted above the transporter's howling diesel engine. "There should be a ravine coming up that heads down to the beach. We'll be within harking distance of the rendezvous spot there."

Martinelli's eyes were hidden behind his night-vision goggles. He nodded and then, when he saw the ravine, yanked the steering wheel over, pushing the big, lumbering armored personnel carrier off the highway. He followed what looked to be a little-used trail that headed down toward the water. It was overgrown with brush and covered with a coating of crusty snow. The rough trail still afforded a smoother ride than the rugged ravine would.

Beaman looked back over his shoulder to where Jason Hall was taking care of Gregor Smitrov. The Russian president was still unconscious, but he seemed to be breathing a little easier.

Hall glanced up, read the concern on his skipper's face, and yelled to be heard over the noisy motor. "Still touch-and-go. I've got the bleeding pretty well stopped.

Either that or he's about to run out. He needs real medical attention pretty bad, though."

"He gonna make it?"

Hall shrugged his massive shoulders. "Don't know. Right now it's in God's hands."

The BTR lurched to a sudden halt, throwing Beaman against the dashboard. He came up rubbing a knot on his forehead. "What the hell?"

Martinelli killed the diesel. In the sudden silence, his voice boomed. "Sorry. Looks like this is as far as Tony's Taxi goes."

He pointed out ahead of them where the ground suddenly fell away. Twenty meters of sheer drop lurked between them and the rocky beach below.

Beaman popped the hatch open and pulled himself up on top of the BTR. He looked to the left, to the right, and then out at the black waters of the Murmansk Fjord. Good rendezvous spot. The shore was partially hidden by a line of rocks jutting out, forming a protective curve around the beach. Patrol boats would have a hard time seeing into the little cove. The land side seemed treacherous and remote. There was little possibility of anyone stumbling onto them. The problem was getting down the cliff to the water.

The rest of the team piled out of the BTR, grateful to be away from the noise and smell of the hard-riding machine. Johnston tied a rope to the front of the BTR and tossed the end of it over the edge. "Skipper, looks like we rappel down unless we sprout wings in the next little bit. Ready to go?"

"Yep. Let's get down there," Beaman replied as he warily scanned the wide, dark sky. If anyone was looking for them yet, it would be much easier to see them up here. "Make it snappy."

Johnston fastened himself to the rappelling line and dropped over the edge. He bounced and hopped against the vertical rock face until he landed on the narrow strip of beach. Cantrell followed him down.

With two SEALs below and the rest still at the top, it was time for the most difficult maneuver, getting President Smitrov down. Hall fashioned a crude rope basket stretcher to hold the wounded man and fastened it to the rappelling lines. The pair below guided the lines while the team above slowly lowered the stretcher, trying all the while to keep it from bouncing against the rocks. The men were as gentle as possible lowering the wounded man, but the brisk wind kept threatening to send the rough stretcher crashing into the rocks. The cliff was hard enough to do more damage to the Russian president's body. Jason Hall slipped over the top and edged down the sheer drop, using his body to cushion Smitrov from the rock wall. It was slow, tedious work, but in ten minutes, Smitrov's stretcher rested on the beach.

Broughton followed Dumkowski down the rope. The wounded SEAL refused to even grunt from the considerable pain when his leg slammed into the rocks. Beaman took one more look around and followed.

As they gathered their equipment, a small black shape emerged from the waters a few meters out in the fjord and moved toward the beach. It barely rose above the wave tops. The short upright periscope was the only thing that might draw any attention to it.

Dumkowski saw it first. He pointed and said, "Skipper, looks like our ride is here."

The ASDV eased in until it was ten meters from shore and a third of its bulk was above the surface. That was as close as Hector Gonzales could safely maneuver the mini-sub without running into the rocks and risking damage.

Johnston gathered up his gear and headed out into the freezing-cold water.

"Come on," he growled. "Hot chow and a shower's waitin' for us when we get back."

He swam the last few feet to the mini-sub, then ducked under the surface to go into the ASDV through its bottom entrance.

Cantrell and Hall followed, carrying the wounded Smitrov above the surface as far as they could. They, too, ducked under. Hall held his big hand over the Russian president's mouth and pinched his nose shut with his fingers. They entered the sub's underside hatch and handed Smitrov up to Johnston.

As the last four were gathering their equipment, Beaman heard the ominous, heavy beat of a helicopter heading up the fjord. He knew immediately what it was. "Sounds like company coming. Let's get out of here!"

The four SEALs hurried out into the water and swam toward the ASDV as a Mi-24 Hind attack helicopter rounded the headland and moved their way. The ugly wasp was searching the shoreline. It would be, by now, looking specifically for them. Beaman could see the short wing, loaded with rockets. The four-barrel 12.7mm 9A624 machine gun slewed around like an angry cobra searching for prey. If they spotted the SEALs in the water or spied the ASDV while it was still on the surface, the helicopter gunship would chew them and the mini-sub into little pieces.

Abruptly the Hind spun around until its snout pointed directly at the furiously swimming SEALs. Fire erupted from either wing tip as two 9M17P Falanga antitank missiles roared toward them. The missiles passed overhead, slamming instead into the BTR-80 where they had left it on the cliff. The armored personnel carrier exploded with a deep-throated *whoomp!* It erupted into flames, brilliantly lighting up the cold night sky.

"Down!" Beaman yelled. "Get under and swim for it. Don't come up for anything."

He took a deep breath and dove deep. They had to make it to the ASDV before the chopper lost interest in the destroyed personnel carrier and began sweeping the surface of the cove.

Beaman took long strokes and kicked hard toward the sub. The bone-chilling water sapped strength from his body. An iron band seemed to be wrapped around his head and it was being tightened until the pain was unendurable.

Still he swam on. He was at the point of giving up when he bumped hard into the steel shape of the ASDV. With one more lunge downward, the SEAL commander surfaced inside the lower hatch. He gasped for air as the other three came up alongside him.

"If you children wouldn't mind getting out of the water, we'll head home," Sam Donlan hollered.

The men struggled out of the icy water as quickly as they could while the mini-sub sank beneath the waves of the fjord, out of sight of the killer chopper.

Chapter 37

Chuck Gruver stepped into an even bigger maelstrom than he had anticipated. The Exchange was in pandemonium. He had never seen such expressions of raw fear on the faces of the traders on the stock exchange floor, not in any of the assorted panics and sell-offs he had witnessed over the years.

As he turned the corner toward the stairs leading down to the computer control center, he crashed headlong into the chairman of the Exchange going the other way. Sweat poured off the normally imperturbable executive's face. His tie was askew and his usually carefully combed gray hair was mussed. He grabbed Gruver by the shoulder.

"There you are! Chuck, it's coming apart at the seams! I'm calling all the senior executives to an emergency meeting in the conference room in ten minutes. Be there."

That was another sign that something major was happening. The chairman did not rule by committee. He preferred conferring with a few trusted advisers and then sending down a fiat from on high. That modus operandi allowed him to muster support while giving the appearance of total control, keeping himself and his office above the messiness of whatever fray they faced. Nothing ever moved fast. Better to delay a good decision than to hurry a bad one. That had always been the old man's motto.

"Well, sure, but—"

"Chuck, call the SEC tech weenies. See if you can get their take on this fiasco. We need answers if we're going to come to some kind of resolution of this mess."

"Chief, funny you should mention that," Gruver said. "Catherine Goldman just told me that she has found where the system is dirty. She thinks that we should shut it down. I was just on my way to—"

"No! No!" The chairman shook his head vigorously and squeezed Gruver's shoulder even harder. He did not want to believe what he was hearing. "We'll talk about it in the meeting. That's the kind of thing we need everybody to sign off on. Get input from all quarters. Carefully consider all our options. We can't afford to go off half-cocked, do something drastic, and start some kind of a panic."

Start a panic? Gruver thought. The chairman could see the turmoil swirling all around him already. The old man was faced with a true emergency situation this time. A natural political animal, he tended to follow his instincts, and his instincts were telling him the best thing to do was to form a committee, study the problem, and stall for time. Spread the risk around in case things went to hell in a handbasket. Things might just get better by themselves while the group was hashing it over, coming to some kind of consensus.

"Boss, you said it yourself. The system isn't behaving

normally. It's coming apart at the seams. Let's be careful, do the prudent thing, and shut it down right now."

The chairman refused to stick his neck out on this one.

"No, not yet," he answered firmly. "Let's see what everyone else says first. It's just too risky."

He let go of Gruver's shoulder, turned, and scurried up the stairs, headed for the womb of his executive suite. Gruver stared at the rear end of the leader of the free world's financial markets as the man fled the chaos on his trading floor. The CTO shook his head in wonder as he started on down to the computer center to see what the latest damage report was.

Hector Gonzales steered the ASDV out toward the deep water of the Murmansk Fjord. The mini-sub angled downward as he kept it just a few feet above the bottom of the cove. No way of knowing if the Hind chopper saw them slip out from the beach after it attacked the BTR-80. At least there had been no ordnance directed their way. That was promising. If they had been spotted, if there was any suspicion that they had gotten away in the mini-sub, the Russians would be out on the fjord, searching for them. In the narrow confines of the fjord, there wasn't much room to hide. The ASDV wasn't fast enough to run. They would have to try to blend in with the steep, rocky bottom.

The depth gauge clicked away as the tiny sub descended farther into the cold blackness. Their best protection would be the water itself.

The navigation sonar painted the bottom onto the

video screen and guided Gonzales down the slope. The side of the fjord's wall changed from a vertical drop to a gradual decline, and then started to level out. By that point, the sub and the SEAL team were far beneath the surface, separated from whatever danger might be up there by a thousand feet of protective water.

Once near the bottom, Gonzales turned the wheel to the left and headed the ASDV out toward the opening to the sea. The mini-sub hugged the edge of the slope, staying where it was steep, not venturing out onto the broad, flat bottom. Sam Donlan danced through the tactical displays while Gonzales kept his attention concentrated on driving the sub.

"Hmmm," Donlan said.

"Don't make that irritating humming noise without telling me what you see," Gonzales fussed.

"I'm picking up high-speed screws on the passive sonar. Sounds like they're coming from somewhere behind us."

Still, Gonzales did not look up. His gaze was locked on to the navigation display. He nudged the mini-sub even closer to the muddy bottom. "I hear you. Any active sonar?"

"Nothing yet. I'm guessing they're still four or five thousand yards farther upstream. I figure they just got under way from the harbor security pier down by the entrance to Polyarnyy." Donlan shifted so he could see another display and then watched the numbers dance across the screen. "Signal strength is building. They're heading this way in a big hurry. You think we ought to secure the nav sonar before they get wind of it?"

Gonzales squinted at the display in front of him, thought for a moment, and then shook his head. "No way. We won't be able to stay down here in the mud with it turned off." He reached over and nudged a slider on the touch panel display. "I'll drop the signal strength to the minimum, though. I can't go any lower without risking bumping into the bottom. Besides, even if someone up there picks up our sonar, he'll think he's listening to a whale with a bad case of gas."

Donlan chuckled, envisioning some hapless sonar man listening to a whale farting in the depths. That had to be an interesting sound.

"Well, they know something's down here now," Donlan said. "They may not know yet if anybody was in the BTR when they torched it, but they'll figure that was the extraction point and that somebody was running around in their little fjord to grab those guys. They'll be listening real hard."

Bill Beaman had stuck his head through the hatch into the command module. He listened to the two pilots' easy give-and-take but knew enough about what was going on to sense there was a problem. "Trouble?"

"Not really," Gonzales answered, still without looking up. "We just have some company heading out to wish us bon voyage. How are our passengers doing?"

"The boys are destroying the chow you brought out. These new boats are great. I can't imagine hot chow on a mini-sub in the old days. Broughton is okay. Hall gave him a shot for the pain."

"Glad you like our ferry service," Gonzales said, his eyes still on the display in front of him. "Please recommend it to all your friends. Sorry we're all out of champagne. How's Smitrov?"

"Still out. Hall hooked him up to a saline drip. That'll help stabilize things some, but we need to get him some real medical help quick."

"We'll do what we can, but—"

"Guys, our friend is active," Donlan interrupted. "Sounds like an Elk Tail sonar. I'll bet you a buck our friend is a Grisha V patrol boat. He'll be armed to the teeth. Torpedoes, guns, missiles. He'll even have a rocket mortar. An RBU-6000. Nasty little piece of gear. Tosses twelve mortars in a circle pattern around you. It's designed to detonate simultaneously so the effect is additive. It'll ring your chimes. This guy is not someone we want to argue with."

Beaman looked over Donlan's shoulder at the tactical display. The screen showed someone behind them was actively pinging. The 14.7-kilohertz sonar was unmistakable. The signal level was increasing. Every time Beaman heard a ping over the speaker, he saw a bright line shoot out from the center of the display. That line showed a bearing from the mini-sub to the hunter that was quickly coming from above and behind them.

Donlan looked over into the worried eyes of the big SEAL. He smiled and pointed at one of the red numbers on the display. "No problem until the signal strength on that indicator gets up to forty-nine decibels. He doesn't have a chance of finding us so long as it's below that." The readout now showed thirty-two decibels, but it was climbing steadily. "Even then, chances are real good he won't be able to pick us out down here in all this mud and fish shit."

"Sure thing," Beaman responded dubiously. "That's what the owner's manual says. I'll believe it when that guy turns around and goes home."

Gonzales smiled. "At least the Grisha has to go dead in the water every time it wants to use the dipping sonar. That allows us to run some between the dips. Their Bull Horn hull-mounted sonar isn't sensitive enough to pick us up in these confined waters."

Beaman stole a glance at the signal strength indicator. He swallowed hard. The readout had climbed to thirty-six.

Admiral Alexander Durov paced the length of the command center. He reached the brick wall, executed a precise about-face, and paced right back again, as if he was on sentry duty over the seeming chaos surrounding him. All around his position, people ran about, shouting commands into radios or hurriedly typing messages on computer keyboards. It looked like total bedlam. Durov didn't say anything as he continued his pacing, oblivious of all the activity. He seemed lost in his thoughts.

The old admiral suppressed a smile as he watched the frenzied movements of his command staff. It was all so familiar, so comforting. Clausewitz had called it "the fog of war," an apt description. Men were forced to make snap decisions that affected the existence of nations, the lives of many human beings, all based on such little information. Much of the intelligence they did have was conflicting, subject to doubt.

No matter. It was the time for a true leader to shine through. Durov pulled his tired old body up even straighter and ignored the knife-sharp pain in the middle of his chest. The light in the room flashed off the rows of medals and ribbons on his dress uniform. He hoped the men would look his way to remind themselves that he was there and in charge.

"Admiral!" Vasiliy Zhurkov shouted from across the room. He held his hand over the mouthpiece of a telephone. "Boris Medikov is on the secure phone. He reports that the American financial markets are in shambles. The news stories are full with tales of terrible woes. He wants to speak with you."

Durov shook his head and held up a gloved hand. "Tell him I am occupied. Thank him for the report and tell him to keep up the pressure. I want to know the minute the markets are closed for the emergency. They cannot sustain it for much longer."

The admiral resumed his steady march. The large tactical display on the far wall showed the three new Akulas as they moved out of the fjord and toward their assigned positions. The plotting was an educated guess. There would be no communications with any of them. They would do as ordered, though. Durov had hand-selected and trained those men himself. They would not fail him or the motherland. They were where the display said they were.

The admiral allowed himself the slightest of smiles. All the pieces were falling into place. Such a carefully orchestrated plan. Years in the development. By this time tomorrow, the *Rodina* would be well on her way to being safe and strong again.

There was one problem. Smitrov. Durov still could not imagine who had managed to spirit that little weak-kneed egghead away from his captors. Or how they had found out about his imprisonment.

Perhaps he was no longer a problem. Perhaps the president died when the Hind rocketed the armored personnel carrier it found parked on the cliff above the fjord. Maybe the helicopter had caught the rescuers before they had an opportunity to leave the BTR, while they waited for some rendezvous. It would be another half hour before his troops could get there to confirm it.

The pilot had reported seeing something moving on the water as he attacked the troop carrier. The airman could not be sure in his account. Maybe it was nothing more than turbulence below his rotating blade. Still, Durov dispatched a Grisha V patrol boat to find out for certain.

There had not been anything on the surface. Perhaps the pilot had seen a mini-sub, scrambling to dive with the president and his rescuers. He could not be certain.

If so, that meant two things. First, the attackers were American SEALs. That was the one group in the world with the equipment and organization to carry off such a daring and sophisticated attack. Second, any mini-sub would now be heading out to rendezvous with a mother sub waiting somewhere toward the Barents.

The old admiral stopped his marching and rubbed his hands together. Static electricity snapped between his silk-gloved fingers. His eyes sparkled as brightly as the medals on his chest.

Of course it had been the Americans. Certainly there would be a rendezvous.

It was time to set a trap.

Nicholas Vujnovich guided the big Ford Crown Victoria through the thickening traffic. He had to grind the vehicle to a sudden halt as the road headed down toward the gaping maw of the Lincoln Tunnel. A little red Kia darted in front of Vujnovich, cutting him off. The big Russian laid on the horn, wailing his protest. The Kia driver, a pretty young woman, flipped him off and darted on across his path and into the next lane.

Vujnovich shook his head in disbelief. Americans! They are without manners. Such a thing would never happen in Moscow. A big black car was accorded proper respect. After all, only important, powerful people drove such automobiles.

"Call Ustinov," Vujnovich said to Josef Bogatinoff. "See if he has run down the license plate yet."

As the line of cars inched toward the tollbooths, Bogatinoff punched in the numbers. After a short wait, the Russian spoke into the phone. As he talked, he searched in the glove box until he found the stub of a pencil. He wrote on the back of a road map. Vujnovich listened to Bogatinoff as he repeated Ustinov's information.

"Charles A. Gruver, Apartment 3906, 421 East Fortieth Street. Got it."

Bogatinoff listened to the voice on the other end of the line for a moment more and then turned to Vujnovich. He held his hand over the cell phone as he spoke. "Dmitri wants to know when we will be at his office to help him."

Vujnovich snorted and wiped his forehead with a big hand. "Tell him that we will be there as soon as we take care of Goldman and her knight in shining armor. We cannot afford to leave loose ends lying around. Especially now."

Bogatinoff relayed the message and then looked at Vujnovich as he listened to what Ustinov was saying.

"Dmitri says we should forget Goldman," Bogatinoff said. "He says she no longer matters to our plan. He wants us to come to where he is as soon as we can."

Vujnovich reached across and jerked the cell phone from his friend's hand. He punched the OFF button and tossed the thing over his shoulder into the backseat like a discarded soda can. Bogatinoff, eyes wide and mouth still open, looked at him questioningly.

"I'm not taking orders from that wire-head," Vujno-vich spat. "We have unfinished business to attend to, whether he likes it or not."

Traffic eased for a second. He shot forward, tossed a twenty to the tollbooth attendant, and gunned the big car without even waiting for change. The yawning tunnel swallowed up the big black car.

Dmitri Ustinov did not like the way things were going. He had signed on for this project to play with the American stock market. For him, it was one big, challenging video game. None of this had ever seemed quite real to him. They would have their fun, get filthy rich in the process, and then he would ride off to someplace warm where the women wore few clothes and the margaritas flowed from perpetual fountains. No one would get hurt. He would be finished with Boris Medikov and his dark-eyed lackeys, too.

Those goons Medikov had sent over were now out there somewhere trying to kill people. Ustinov wanted no part of murder. Besides, Catherine Goldman was a friend by now. So was Gruver.

He had toyed with the idea of telling Vujnovich that he could not locate the address of the license plate owner. The thug would never have believed that. If Ustinov gave false information, it was certain that even if Vujno-vich and Bogatinoff didn't make him pay, some other heavy-handed hoodlum eventually would.

There was only one thing to do if he didn't want to be directly responsible for the Goldman woman's untimely demise. Though his every instinct screamed for him to let it alone, to allow the whole thing to play out, he still punched a few buttons on his BlackBerry, found Charles Gruver's apartment telephone number, looked over his shoulder to ensure that Marina had not yet returned from the ladies' room, and dialed.

It rang four times. No one answered. He was about to drop the phone back into its base. He had done his part. He had tried.

A distorted, metallic voice came on the line. "You have reached the Gruver apartment. Not here. If you are not a telemarketer, please leave a message at the beep. If you are, kindly drop dead."

He waited for the tone.

"Charles! Catherine! If you can hear me, pick up. This is Dmitri. Dmitri Ustinov at OptiMarx. It is important! Please pick up or call me at the OptiMarx number immediately. I need—"

There was a click and a faint voice. It was Catherine Goldman. It sounded as if she might have been asleep.

"Dmitri? It's Catherine. How did you know where—"

"Yes, it is me." He paused for a moment and swallowed hard. The full ramifications of what he was about to do had just settled on him like a heavy weight. He went on anyway. "Catherine, listen to me. It is very important. Some men are coming to kill you. You and Charles. They know where you are. You must run."

Goldman's voice was much firmer now. She was fully awake. There was steel in her tone.

"Why should I trust you, Dmitri? The last time I asked you for help, they kidnapped me. Who knows what they would have done if I hadn't escaped?"

"You have got to trust me," Ustinov pleaded. "If I know where you are, then you must see that these men do also. Those men, they were only supposed to keep you out of the way for a few days. I swear that was what they told me. Now you are much more of a threat to them. They will not hesitate to kill you. Please get out of there and go someplace safe. Do not tell me where you go. Just go someplace else. I beg you."

The line went dead. Ustinov stared at the receiver. There was no way of knowing if she believed him, if she would obey him.

When Ustinov looked up, he was staring straight into the cold blue eyes of Marina Nosovitskaya. She was not smiling. "What have you done, Dmitri?"

"Fixed something we should never have broken."

She looked at him strangely. Her eyes narrowed. "It is that Goldman woman. Why are you risking everything we have done to protect her?"

Ustinov rose from his desk. Even standing erect, the young computer tech barely reached Nosovitskaya's shoulder. He was close enough to her to feel the warmth of her glorious body. Her perfume almost made him swoon. He fought to maintain his convictions with her standing so close.

"Marina, there is no reason to hurt her. To hurt anyone. By the time she knows for certain what is going on, we will be done and gone. Rich beyond our dreams and back to Russia or wherever we want to go. If she gets hurt, though, the Americans will be relentless. They will hunt us down. Manipulating their beloved stock market is one thing. Murdering a government official and the CTO of the stock exchange is quite another." He reached out and took her hand in his. "I'm doing this to protect us, not the Goldman woman."

He tried to read the expression in her ice blue eyes. There was no way on earth to tell what she was thinking.

Brian Edwards looked across the plotting table at Joe Glass. The submarine captain was measuring out the distances between his boat, *Toledo*, and where they thought the three Akulas were by now.

"Skipper, how long are we going to tail along behind this train?" the young XO pointedly asked.

Toledo had been following the Russian submarines out of the Murmansk Fjord and east along the Kola Peninsula for a little over twelve hours. Safely tucked up against the coast of the motherland, the three were trucking along at twenty knots. They didn't seem to be the least bit concerned about anyone trailing them.

Glass was satisfied with what he saw on the chart. He looked up at the XO and answered his question. "I'd say this is far enough. I'm guessing our friends are heading into the White Sea. Let's break off now and head back. Gonzales and Beaman and the boys may get just a bit touchy if we don't show up to pick them up."

He glanced forward toward Jerry Perez. He was standing on the conn, between the two periscopes.

"Nav, slow to five knots," Glass ordered. "When our friends have opened out to three thousand yards, reverse course to three-one-zero. We'll come up to periscope depth when you get on course. I'd like to grab a quick communications download before we head back into the fjord."

"Aye, sir," Perez acknowledged. "Slowing to five knots."

The big sub slowed as the three Russian boats steamed on to the southeast. After they had traveled away for ten minutes, Perez swung the sub around to retrace their course. As they turned, Master Chief Zillich and his team searched for any other sonar contacts. Except for the fading Russian subs, they had this bit of the Barents Sea all to themselves. Perez guided the sub up to the surface, stopping just as the scope broke free through a bit of skim ice and into the clear Arctic night. Two minutes later, all incoming communications traffic was on board and Glass had transmitted a message to Admiral Donnegan and Jon Ward, telling them about the Akulas and where they had last seen them.

That done, *Toledo* slipped back into the depths. Edwards flipped through the myriad of messages that had accumulated while they were hiding inside the fjord. Glass was busy getting the sub headed back to the Murmansk Fjord as quickly as possible.

Edwards whistled, startling Glass. He looked over to see the XO, his eyes wide as he read the screen on the laptop computer he had perched on the chart table. Edwards waved for Glass to hurry over.

"Skipper, you've got to read this! Things are heating up fast back there."

Glass leaned over Edwards's shoulder and scanned the message. It was a copy of Beaman's orders to do whatever he had to do to get into the Polyarnyy Base and rescue President Smitrov. Glass whistled as well.

"You're right, XO. Let's get back there quick. No telling when they'll be ready for pickup or what kind of shape they'll be in." Glass turned and delivered the orders. "Ahead flank. Nav, get us up there as fast as you can."

Toledo jumped ahead as the throttle man opened the "ahead" throttles. Steam poured into the massive turbines, driving the great bronze screw at a frantic pace. Even with them racing ahead at this speed, it would be six hours before they were back at the rendezvous point, ready to pick up the ASDV.

Glass hoped the mini-sub and SEALs could hold out until he got there. He quietly prayed they would be there waiting for them when they showed up. If they weren't . . . if they didn't show up . . . that would only mean one thing. That was an eventuality Joe Glass did not want to ponder.

Chapter 38

Admiral Tom Donnegan sat behind his old battered oak desk and stared out the window. He had been able to pull enough strings to have the massive desk follow him over the years from one port of call to another, most recently from Honolulu to Washington, D.C. At the moment, his mind was far away from this cluttered office. It did not register the dimming sky or the first lights that flickered on across the Potomac, reflected by the river's oily, calm surface. He was someplace else, thousands of miles to the east and far to the north, at a cold spot off the Russian coast.

This was one of those times that tried anyone in command. He could do nothing more than sit and worry. His team was out there on the front line in a hostile, uninviting place. In actuality, they were way out beyond the front line on this one. They knew their jobs. They were doing them. At least he could pray they were. There had been frequent messages from Jon Ward, but he was as out of touch as Donnegan was. Neither Ward nor Donnegan had heard a word out of Russia since Beaman coolly acknowledged the order to get on his horse and ride right into Polyarnyy to rescue the president of Russia.

Donnegan broke his gaze and looked at the brass chronometer that sat on the far side of the old desk. Couple of hours before dawn in Polyarnyy. He had no idea where Beaman was. No way to know if they had somehow managed to get to Smitrov. Nor if they had found a way out of the sub base with or without the president.

There had been no bulletins on CNN. No urgent telephone call that carried bad news. Those were good signs.

He wished he could hear from Joe Glass and *Toledo*. Such murkiness, such uncertainty was making an old man of him. He envied Ward. At least he was keeping busy, chasing that rogue Russian submarine into the Baltic. Donnegan had to sit here behind this battle-scarred old desk of his and worry his ass off.

He heard the phone ring once amid the swirl of activity outside his door. He didn't answer it. Someone from his staff would. If it was important, they would tell him. Still, he did not breathe.

Tim Schwartz, his aide, stuck his head through the door within thirty seconds.

"Admiral, two things," he said, with his usual calculated efficiency. "First, we just received a message from *Toledo*. They confirm the SEAL report of three more Akulas out of the barn. They were running submerged toward the White Sea. Glass says they will be there sometime today. He is breaking off-trail to head back for the ASDV pickup."

Donnegan nodded and allowed himself a breath of air. His faith had been well placed. Someone out there was doing his job. Glass was showing some healthy initiative. It was obvious that Jon Ward had trained him. His orders were to stay in the fjord to be ready for the rendezvous. The situation changed and Glass marched off to do what he thought was right. He didn't take time to ask permission. He just did it. Just as Jon Ward would have. Good work.

"And the other thing?"

"General Tambor is on the secure phone," Schwartz reported. "NSA has some imagery that he wants to talk with you about."

Donnegan grabbed the red phone from his desk and punched the flashing yellow button. He heard the faint hiss of the encrypted STU-III synching with the one on General Tambor's desk.

"Tom, got some pictures for you," the National Security Agency head said. "Fire up your secure VPN."

Donnegan turned to the PC on his desk and entered a special password. The screen flashed to the NSA high-security home page. "I've got it up."

"Good. We have some radar images from the last KH-11 pass you'll want to look at. Go to today's image page and zoom in on Murmansk."

Donnegan clicked his way through Tambor's directions. The screen transformed into a high-resolution picture of the area. He zoomed in to the territory around the Polyarnyy Sub Base. Everything looked normal, except for the broad white arrow of a ship's wake heading out from the sub base. At the head of the wake was an armed Grisha V corvette, heading up the channel. Tambor heard Donnegan's low whistle. The NSA chief added, "Looks like your boys up there may have stepped into a world of hurt."

Donnegan zoomed in closer and stared at the picture

more carefully. He moved the cursor away from the corvette, over toward the high slopes of the shore. "Ward, do you see the fire burning above that little cove to the left of the Grisha?"

"Yep. Looks like some kind of armored vehicle. It's been pretty well chewed up."

Donnegan zoomed in to maximum. The burned-out BTR filled his computer screen. The image resolution was good enough that Donnegan could make out the individual birch twigs charred by the fire. "That's right above the rendezvous beach. Our team would have been coming out there tonight."

"I see," Tambor said, then thought for a moment. "Either they stole a BTR to get out of the base or one tried to stop them. Anyway, something took the thing out. By the looks of the blast damage, it was a couple of good-sized antitank rockets. I don't see any bodies. Maybe your boys made it out before all the shooting started."

"Hope so," Donnegan grunted, praying they weren't, instead, incinerated inside that thing.

"That's just part of what I wanted to show you," Tambor went on. "Zoom in on the mouth of the fjord. Look over near the coast."

Donnegan panned the picture up until he was seeing where the Murmansk Fjord dumped into the cold, stormy Barents Sea. There, hidden behind a bend in the channel, was what Ward Tambor was talking about.

"Looks like a Udaloy II–class destroyer," Donnegan said through pursed lips. "Where in hell did he come from?"

"He showed up between satellite passes. It's bearing

the side numbers for the *Admiral Chabanenko*, their newest antisubmarine warfare destroyer. Projections show it has a Plinom sonar suite and two Helix ASW helicopters. Its torpedoes will reach clear across the channel and those SS-N-15 Starfish ASW missiles will take out any sub it can find."

"He looks like he's hiding there. Somebody is setting a trap."

"Looks that way," Tambor answered grimly. "Tom, you better warn your boys before they swim right into the jaws of the damn thing."

"Lord knows I wish I could. No way to get hold of them now. They're on their own, I'm afraid."

"Then let's pray that God's with them."

"Ward, I've already been praying as hard as I can."

Catherine Goldman was facing yet another deadly quandary. She had just finished a hot bath and was brewing a cup of tea when Dmitri Ustinov called. There for a moment she had been feeling back to normal, the fear washed away with the soothing bathwater. She had managed to put out of her mind the look on the dark-eyed man's face when she shot him to death. The horror she felt as she ran through the wet snow, escaping the farmhouse. The awful hours, waiting in the back room of the truck stop for Charlie Gruver to come rescue her.

The call had caught her off guard.

She sat in Gruver's thirty-ninth-floor apartment and stared out at the East River. Fear was threatening to take hold of her again. She could sense it creeping around the edges of her resolve. She didn't like the way it made her feel out of control, no longer in charge of her own fate.

She took a sip of the tea and glanced around the living room. This place was definitely a guy's apartment, complete with cheap Crate & Barrel furniture. Some awesome electronics on the shelf at the far wall, though. Even that was covered with thick dust. Magazines were piled on top of the gear, and a couple of empty beer cans rested on the shelf alongside the expensive equipment.

She allowed herself a smile. The place could use a woman's touch.

Charlie had told her to stay here and not let anyone in until he got back. Things had changed. Dmitri Ustinov swore that there were men on the way here already to kill her. The same men who had kidnapped her. Men she feared. She had no place left to run. They seemed able to find her wherever she went.

Still, it was no time to panic. She had to think of a plan.

Maybe calling the police was the right answer. She needed protection from those goons. So did Charlie. She had no idea how she would ever explain all this to some New York City flatfoot. It sounded crazy enough to her when she ran the unbelievable events of the last few days through her head. Stock-trading manipulations. Russian gangsters. Kidnapping. Attempted murder. Killing in self-defense. It all sounded like the plot from some over-the-top movie. The kind she and Charlie had enjoyed so much together the few times they had socialized after work. It had been about the only fun she allowed herself, sitting there in a theater with him, groaning at the convoluted story lines, laughing out loud at some of the silly dialogue. Now here she was, swallowed up in the middle of one of those far-fetched scenarios.

There wasn't a lot of time to ponder what to do now. Goldman searched Gruver's apartment until she found the phone book in a drawer under a kitchen counter. It was hidden by a stack of Chinese takeout menus and pizza delivery ads. Maybe, if she survived this whole mess, she could do something about Charlie's eating habits as well.

She flipped the book open and found the number she was looking for. The phone was answered on the second ring.

"FBI, Special Agent Decker. Can I help you?"

Jason Hall hovered protectively over his unconscious patient. The Russian president remained on the edge, teetering between life and death. Hall was using every bit of knowledge and skill he had learned and honed during his years as a SEAL. He had no idea if it would be enough.

Thankfully the bleeding had stopped and the saline drip was restoring vital fluids to Smitrov's system. Hall felt the man's pulse for the hundredth time. Still weak, but better than it had been.

Bill Beaman stepped out of the command module and stooped beside Hall as the SEAL once again inflated the blood pressure cuff on Smitrov's arm. "How is our patient, Jase?"

Hall checked the readout on the electronic panel and glanced up at Beaman. "Blood pressure is one hundred over seventy. It's coming up. He may make it, despite my best efforts."

Beaman clapped a large hand on the SEAL's shoulder. "If Smitrov makes it, he owes his life to you."

"Maybe, but I sure would feel better if he came around. It's easier to work on a patient who can talk to you."

As if on cue, the Russian president emitted a low moan. His eyes fluttered open. He tried to rise and muttered something unintelligible.

Hall gently pushed him back down and urged him, in Russian, to lie still. As he became more aware of his surroundings, recognition came slowly to the injured man. He coughed once and strained to speak.

"Where am I? What happened?"

Beaman recounted the shoot-out and rescue from Polyarnyy. "You have been shot, President Smitrov. We are trying our best to get you to medical help. You must stay still and not waste your strength. We will give you a shot for the pain."

The little Russian man tried to rise. "No shot! I must stay awake! I need to communicate with the Kremlin. That traitor Durov must be crushed."

Depleted by the effort of his words, he groaned and fell back. Hall was already pumping up the blood pressure cuff.

Chief Johnston squatted down next to Beaman. "Skipper, Gonzales sent me back to fill you in. That Grisha is getting closer. Sam Donlan doesn't think we've been detected yet, though. He does say the guy might get lucky. He said signal strength was up to forty-two."

Smitrov, his eyes closed, overheard the conversation. He forced his words between his cracked lips, his English surprisingly good. "That will be one of Admiral Durov's harbor defense ships. They will be trying to kill us, not capture us. They will have to make sure I am out of the way. How can we escape?"

Beaman chuckled as he answered, "Don't worry. We still have a few tricks up our sleeve."

"I sure as hell wish you'd tell me what they are," Johnston growled. "That Grisha has a playmate on the other side of the fjord. It looks like they're trying to herd us right on out of town."

Beaman rubbed his eyes and blinked. A thought had occurred to him. "Chief, I figure that there must be something waiting for us further up the fjord. Us and our pickup submarine, too. You don't think they're trying to herd us all into a trap, do you?"

Johnston looked hard at him, then down at the president of Russia. The little man grimaced in pain, but he was nodding.

"I know Admiral Durov," he whispered. "That is precisely what he is doing."

Commander Joe Glass sat at the back of *Toledo*'s control room and talked with Brian Edwards. It was time to do a little planning. They had to penetrate into the Murmansk Fjord again to pick up the ASDV, Gonzales, and hopefully by now, his passengers. It would not be as easy this time, after Bill Beaman and his guys stirred up a hornet's nest in the process of trying to rescue Gregor Smitrov. No telling what kind of reception might be waiting.

Toledo was less than an hour east of where they would turn south into the fjord. The Akulas were far to the east by now. They were probably turning into the White Sea, if Glass's guess was right. Zillich reported his sonar screen was empty. There was not another ship in sight.

Doug O'Malley hovered at the back side of the periscope stand. The red-haired engineer had relieved Jerry Perez as the officer of the deck and was waiting for directions from the two senior officers.

"Eng, slow to one-third and do a careful sonar search," Glass ordered.

"Yes, sir," O'Malley replied. He turned and, in his usual staccato voice, ordered the helmsman, "Ahead one-third."

The helmsman turned the engine-order telegraph to the one-third position. It was answered by the throttle man. The submarine began to slow.

Glass returned his attention to Edwards and the chart they were studying. He ran his finger around the long, narrow spit of land that projected from the eastern headlands. It closed the entrance to the Murmansk Fjord down to where it was only a few miles across from the end of the spit to the western headlands. Beyond, the fjord opened into a broad bay of deep, protected water.

"Brian, last time we went down the western side and stayed close to the beach. This time let's hug the eastern side."

Edwards looked at the chart. The entrance channel was narrow and deep, rising sharply on either side. Inside the entrance, near the shore on the east side, the bottom was shallow and gently sloping. Then it dropped vertically to a thousand feet deep less than a mile from the beach.

"Skipper, here is perfect. Go in deep and snuggle up to this shelf. It should hide our signature in the surf noise for anyone out in the basin and make it easy for us to listen."

"Brian, there is hope for you after all," Glass said with a smile. "It's pretty much what I had in mind. Deep and slow. Real quiet-like. We'll follow this shelf around until it heads south." Glass ran his finger around the chart, indicating the general course they would take. "When we're sure we have a handle on any welcoming committee, we head over to the rendezvous."

Edwards nodded his understanding, then asked, "Should we man battle stations and get a couple of fish ready?"

"Man battle stations silently, but no weapons. We'll be inside Russian territorial waters. We send out a fish in there and all hell will break loose. Load a MOSS in tube three. That'll be our protection."

The MOSS, or "Mobile Submarine Simulator," was a small torpedo-like device that could swim out of a torpedo tube and then play a recording of *Toledo*'s sound signature while following a preprogrammed course. The idea was to convince any pursuer that the MOSS was actually *Toledo* while the real submarine snuck off in another direction.

Edwards wrinkled his forehead and shook his head. "Not much protection if ordnance starts raining down on our heads, Skipper."

"Yeah, but if ordnance starts raining down, we haven't done our jobs, now, have we?"

Edwards made another face. "Guess not, but those SS-N-15s are going to hurt just as bad either way."

"That they will, XO. That they will," Glass said, and went back to studying the chart as if there was really any more he could learn from it.

Nicholas Vujnovich and Josef Bogatinoff emerged from the Lincoln Tunnel. The traffic snarl inside the huge tube had seemed interminable. Vujnovich hit the steering wheel with his fist and shouted Russian curses in frustration. He flung the big Ford around the traffic loop and merged into still another mess of rush-hour traffic trying to make it to the West Side Highway.

"This is going to take damn near forever," he raged. "That bitch will die of old age before we get there."

Bogatinoff pulled his Glock from its belt holster and dropped the clip out. He worked the slide to remove the round from the chamber before checking the weapon over. He loaded the round back in the magazine, slapped it into the butt, and slid a round into the chamber again. He grinned viciously. "Not much chance of that, Nicholas."

Traffic came to a complete halt. In front of them was a sea of red brake lights. Vujnovich smashed the horn in frustration. The blast blended with the cacophony of every other driver around them doing the same thing.

"Turn up Tenth," Bogatinoff yelled to be heard over the din. "Maybe we will make better time. The address is way over on the East Side, so we have to get clear across town anyway."

He waved to the right with the barrel of his pistol.

"Put that thing away before someone in this parade sees it," Vujnovich snarled.

He punched the accelerator and twisted the wheel. The Ford lurched through a red light at Tenth Street and roared down the narrow block. The two men ignored the angry blare of horns from the cabbies they had just cut off. They were, at least, moving again as Vujnovich dove into the warren of streets of the West Village, weaving uptown and toward the East Side.

Boris Medikov accepted no excuses for failure. Certainly not a bit of heavy traffic.

Finally they pulled into a parking garage on Thirty-ninth Street, just a block from the address they had for Charles Gruver's apartment. They locked the car, walked up to street level, and looked around to take their bearings. The neighborhood seemed to be all high-rise apartments with shops and restaurants on their ground floors. They could just catch a glimpse of the rectangular steel shape of the United Nations Building, framed by a gap between two cement monoliths. The East River was a couple of streets over.

The two walked down Tunnel Entrance Street to Fortieth. There, just across the street, was 421 East Fortieth. They could see the building's large marble lobby through the glass-and-steel entrance. A burly doorman stood just inside the revolving door and a pair of attendants worked behind the service desk next to the bank of elevators. No way to slip past them without being seen.

"Come on," Vujnovich muttered. "There will be a back way in."

They headed around the corner and back down Tunnel Entrance. It took a couple of minutes to find the service entrance to the building. A quick twenty to the staffer sneaking a smoke and they were inside. The service elevator was just around the corner. Within seconds, they were on their way up to the thirty-ninth floor.

Captain Second Rank Anatol Vivilav sat in the tiny cabin of his new submarine, sipping a glass of hot, sweet tea. His first officer, Anistov Dmolysti, sat across from him, stirring in another sugar cube. *Vipr* was heading across the Baltic Sea now that she was safely deep enough that the crowded shipping lanes above were no longer a danger.

"Well, First Officer, we are almost there," Vivilav said as he watched his friend drop another sugar cube into his tea. "From the looks of your sweet tooth, Admiral Durov is going to need to negotiate another treaty with Comrade Castro when this is over. Just to prevent a sugar shortage."

Dmolysti smiled. "We all have our vices. I will just be glad when we can go home."

"We all will, my friend," Vivilav agreed. "We all will."

They sipped their tea in silence for a few moments. The two submarine sailors relished this precious quiet time. It allowed them to sit and relax together after the tensions of the past few days and before the excitement of tomorrow.

Vivilav broke the moment. "Anistov, our orders are to commence at first light tomorrow. Have all the missiles and the launch system checked tonight. I do not want any mistakes or malfunctioning equipment in the morning. Our job is much too important to allow that. We are the most crucial part in Admiral Durov's plan. The future of the *Rodina* hinges on how well we do our duty tomorrow."

Dmolysti rose and stood at attention. He saluted smartly. "It shall be as you order, Captain. For the *Rodina*."

He turned and stepped out of the stateroom.

Commander Vivilav took another sip of his tea. He did not taste it at all.

Chapter 39

Carl Andretti sank even deeper into an alcohol-shrouded stupor. The worst day of his life was drawing to a close. To make it worse, he had just drained the final precious drops from his last bottle of Dewar's.

He slumped there at his desk, pondering his predicament. Everything he had, his fortune, his professional standing, was wrapped up in making OptiMarx work. His real future depended on that little "special feature" that had been designed to ensure him a bountiful cash flow for many years to come. Even if he and Stern could pull it off, even if they could pin all the staggering losses on Alan Smythe, all he had worked for over the last five years was still in ruins. He might stay out of jail if he played his cards right and he was real lucky. His career was over. His vast fortune was lost.

Even in his drunken state, Andretti knew what he was up against. His reputation on The Street was in shreds. No respectable broker or analyst firm would hire him now. His considerable debts with his "friends" in North Jersey were way past due. Those hard-asses wouldn't wait much longer. Their "collection agency" played rough.

Andretti stared at the bottom of the empty glass.

There was no way out for him there. Running was no good. That took cash. Besides, they would find him wherever he went. Then they would settle the debt in a final and fatal way.

The harried CTO rose and walked unsteadily to the window of his office. He looked out at the plaza twenty-three stories below. It seemed to beckon to him, to offer him a quick and easy way out. Andretti snorted. He knew he was far too much of a coward to end it that way.

He turned from his reflection in the window. No sense staying here, alone in the office, drowning in his own misery. If he was going to consume enough courage to end this, he might as well do it in the company of his old drinking buddies. In the comfort of Harry's Bar. Once the decision was made, he felt better.

He pulled on his jacket, left the office, and made his way unevenly down the long hallway toward the elevators. As Andretti bounced from wall to wall, his shoulder struck one of the horrid modern art paintings Smythe insisted on hanging everywhere. It fell from its hook, its glass cracking when it hit the floor. The bastard would scream when he found that. Too bad. He shrugged and left it where it fell.

As Andretti passed the testing room, he noticed the light was still on inside. Odd. No one should be in there this late. Besides, it didn't make any sense because testing was finished. Cleaning crew probably left it on. He was about to head on down the hall and closer to a double Scotch with his name on it.

That's when he heard voices from inside the testing

room. A man and woman, talking. The female one sounded like Marina Nosovitskaya.

Man, was she a piece!

Andretti grinned. Maybe she was in there fooling around with one of the geeks. That might be worth taking a quick peek at. Watching was the next best thing to doing.

He slipped as quietly as he could through the door and made his way among the cubicles and toward the sound of the voices. Despite his buzz, he managed to keep silent. It was clear that the pair in the testing room weren't paying much attention to anything else that might be going on around them.

Hidden behind a cubicle divider, invisible in the shadows, Andretti stopped to watch.

Dmitri Ustinov was standing close behind the beautiful Russian programmer, his hands inside her sweater as he fondled her breasts and mumbled in her ear. She stood there, accepting his ministrations, entranced by the numbers that danced across the computer screen. She seemed fine with his hands on her.

Andretti heard the excitement in her voice when she spoke.

"Dmitri, we have made over five hundred million dollars today. I don't believe it! We are rich. We have killed the market, exactly as Medikov has ordered us to do. Just us! We have done this all by ourselves! The Exchange will not even open for trading tomorrow because of us."

Ustinov was fumbling with the buttons on her sweater. He answered her, his voice thick and trembling. "Five hundred million. Medikov gets most of it. I managed to siphon off ten percent for us."

"You mean you cheated Boris Medikov out of fifty million dollars?"

"Yes, my dear. It is safely put away. For us. You and me. Old Boris will never miss such chump change. Now that we've crashed the American stock market, it'll be years before he could untangle the records and find us, even if he were inclined to try."

Ustinov had conquered all but the last of the sweater buttons. He pulled it away to reveal her white shoulders and flawless breasts. She sucked in her breath as Ustinov's hands encircled them.

Andretti could not believe what he was hearing. The two were talking about a conspiracy that involved enormous numbers. He had no idea who this Medikov guy was, but it sounded as if he must be the boss of this scheme. Here was his ruination, standing right there in front of him, one groping the other.

It was these two who had killed his system and cheated him out of millions.

Nosovitskaya leaned back against Ustinov and sighed. A look of utter satisfaction flitted across her beautiful face.

"Dmitri, I never thought I would say this, but you are a genius," she murmured. "You deserve a proper reward." She took one of his hands in her own, removed it from her breast, and slid it down her body. "What kind of reward would you like?"

Andretti couldn't help himself. He stepped forward to get a better view, to try to hear more about this plot of theirs. He stumbled, catching his shoulder on the corner of a hanging bookshelf. It fell to the floor with a horrifying crash.

The Russian pair froze for an instant. They spotted Andretti in the shadows. Nosovitskaya was the first to react. She pointed at Andretti and shouted, "He heard us! Dmitri, get him!"

She stood there, breathing fire and pointing toward Andretti like some golden goddess of war. Her sweater hung open to her waist, but she made no pretense at modesty. It was time for action and she was giving the orders.

Ustinov was a second slower than she was. His mind had been targeted on his long-awaited prize. It took a moment for him to shift gears.

Drunk or not, Andretti knew to seize the moment. He had to get out of there, and fast. He dashed out the door and down the hall. No time to wait for the elevator. The stairs were too slow. The young Russian would easily catch him.

He dashed into his office and slammed the door. The lock clicked into place. He was trapped, but at least they couldn't get in.

He heard the crash of Ustinov's shoulder as he slammed desperately into the heavy door. The Russian would never be able to break in. Andretti had had the door reinforced when he first began the skullduggery with Smythe. He did not want anyone breaking into his office to see what he was up to.

Oh God, if he could get a drink. Andretti could never remember being so thirsty. He picked up the empty

Dewar's bottle, looked at it to verify the magic elixir was all gone, then dropped it on the carpet.

He swallowed hard. There was only one thing to do.

Andretti stepped to his desk, punched a few keys on his computer keyboard, and clicked the mouse a couple of times. He saw the entry in his address book he needed. He grabbed up the telephone.

Ustinov rammed his body hard into the door once again, then brutally kicked it. He grunted and swore in Russian the whole time.

Andretti dialed a number. It was answered on the third ring.

"Securities and Exchange Commission, Enforcement Division."

"Hello, this is Carl Andretti, CTO for OptiMarx Technology. I want to report a Russian plot to manipulate the U.S. stock market."

Toledo sank slowly and silently even farther into the depths of the Murmansk Fjord. She was rigged for quiet running. Every piece of gear that wasn't essential was secured. All the vital equipment was operating in its quietest lineup. She was quieter than the surrounding sea. Careful design, years of testing, and constant vigilance had made sure of that.

Glass hunched over the chart, across the table from Jerry Perez. The navigator looked up at Glass. "This is going to a little dicey, Skipper. It would sure be a lot safer if we could move out in the channel a little more."

"Sorry, Jerry. We need the protection. You'll have to trust the ESGN and the fathometer."

The Electro-Stabilized Gyroscopic Navigation System was a marvel of modern engineering. A tiny beryllium ball hung in a near perfect vacuum, suspended by a powerful magnetic field. The same field caused the ball to rotate at over thirty thousand revolutions per second. At that high speed, the ball acted like an extremely sensitive gyroscope. It sensed and acted against every force that caused it, and *Toledo*, to move. Tiny, very sensitive accelerometers detected the gyroscope's actions. The ESGN's computer controller knew its initial position. By continuously adding the accelerometer's output, the computer could tell Perez where they were within a few yards. The whole apparatus, hanging in the overhead just outside the radio room door, was the size of a bushel basket.

The problem with the whole scheme was in the accuracy of the initial position. Any error, even if it was off a few inches, was compounded geometrically as time passed and the mistakes accumulated. Even with GPS, the errors could add up. Normally Perez accounted for these errors by putting an "uncertainty" circle around the sub. He knew they were inside that circle. He just wasn't sure where.

Now Glass was telling Perez to guide *Toledo* without benefit of that uncertainty circle. It was a tremendous risk. If he was wrong, even by a little bit, they could smash into the unforgiving granite wall. The fathometer didn't help. It kept them off the bottom. It didn't show them anything about the cliff that was so close by their port side.

The navigator nodded. Sweat poured off his forehead

and trickled down his back. His hand shook as he grabbed a pair of dividers to measure their speed of advance.

"Yes, sir. I'll do my best. Time for the turn. Recommended course one-seven-three, speed one-third. Thirty-two minutes on this leg."

"Left full rudder," Glass ordered. "Steady course one-seven-three."

The rudder swung over, pushing the submarine's nose around until she was pointed into the mouth of the fjord. Perez plotted the ESGN position as they steadied up on the new course. "Captain, hold us on track. The turn looked good."

Glass had already moved forward. He stopped next to Brian Edwards. The XO stood beside the fire control system, watching as his team probed the dark, cold waters to find any threat. Edwards was scribbling on a notepad and talking on a set of sound-powered phones while he watched the computer screens.

"Got anything of interest, XO?" Glass asked him.

Edwards nodded and held up a hand, signaling his skipper that he heard the request but would have to answer in a second. He held one earpiece of the phone to his ear so he could better hear a report that was coming in from somewhere. He spoke into the mouthpiece. "Sonar, fire control, aye."

He turned to Glass. "Skipper, we have two contacts. Couple of Foal Tail dipping sonars. They're well down the channel and no threat to us." He sketched a crude drawing of the fjord and drew two bearing lines from *Toledo*. "From the bearing lines and signal strength, the best bet is one on either side of the channel. Looks like they are leapfrogging up the channel. One is moving while the other is dipping, so . . ."

Edwards stopped talking and held the earpiece to his ear again. After a few seconds, he again spoke into the mouthpiece. "Sonar, fire control, aye." He looked back to Glass and went on. "Sonar reports they are getting a faint screw beat from the same bearings as the dippers. It looks like we have a pair of Grishas down there."

"Okay, XO. Keep an eye on them, but they aren't much threat yet."

"Yes, sir. I wish I knew what they were up to. You think they have our friends?"

"Not likely. Gonzales will have that thing way down in the mud. Those dippers won't have a chance of finding them there."

Glass hoped his voice sounded more sure than he was. He prayed the ASDV was still down there, and that it was coming his way by now.

He looked up at the active sonar intercept receiver. The Foal Tails were just starting to show up there now. Zillich was right. The signal strength was so low, there was no chance the Grishas were looking for *Toledo*. Besides, Glass and his crew had more immediate things to be concerned about.

Toledo was moving smoothly through the narrow slot. The granite wall was a scant few feet to port, its mass protecting them from detection. It also threatened them with destruction. Nobody breathed easily for the entire thirty-two minutes it took to run this leg of the entry.

"Mark the turn," Perez called out. "Recommend we come right to course zero-nine-four."

Glass exhaled and gave a sideways glance over to where the navigator sat hunched over his chart. "You mean come left, don't you, Nav?"

"Huh? Oh yeah. Sorry, Skipper. I screwed up. Nervous. Recommend come left to zero-nine-four."

Glass ordered the course change and watched the compass rose as the submarine swung onto the new course, parallel to the spit of land and inside the fjord. Once he was satisfied that they were on the new course, Glass stepped back and stood beside Perez. He placed a hand on the young navigator's shoulder.

"Nav, you have to stay calm," he said in a fatherly tone. "Take it easy. Just like you do when you're surfing one of those waves you love so much. I'm depending on you, so you need to stay in control. Get a cup of coffee and take a deep breath, okay?"

Perez nodded his head. "I'm okay, Skipper. That was just too close back there."

"On that point, we agree."

"Captain!" Edwards called out. "Sonar reports picking up auxiliary noises. Bearing zero-six-three. Zillich says they sound like they are pretty close."

"No screw?"

"No, sir. He says he's not picking up any main propulsion sounds at all. Whatever it is, it's sitting still. It didn't show up until after we made the turn."

Glass looked down at the chart. The bearing to the mysterious new contact put it close inshore, on the same spit of land he and *Toledo* were using to hide behind.

He looked over at Edwards. "Zillich have any idea what it is yet?"

"No, sir. Not yet."

The active intercept receiver started beeping madly. The red LED readout flashed a warning that it was detecting a 3.4-kilohertz active signal on the same bearing as the mystery contact. Signal strength was high, off the scale.

"Shit! That answers that question. Horse Jaw sonar. Russian Udaloy tin can!" Glass said. "Son of a bitch! The bastard was hiding there, like he was lying in wait for us. Like he knew we would be coming." It was a Russian destroyer and if the son of a bitch didn't know *Toledo* was there yet, he soon would. "Chief of the Watch, launch evasion devices from both signal ejectors. Reload and stand by to launch again."

Sam Wallich stood up and punched two buttons high up on the ballast control panel. Down in the middle level, Doc Halliday was sorting his medical supplies just in case he might need them after the rendezvous with the SEALs. He jumped and bumped his knee hard on the table as both signal ejectors, mounted outboard in his tiny office, cycled loudly, kicking out their noisemakers. The two NAEs tumbled in the submarine's wake and started to emit a mask of noise geared to blind any sonar operator listening for *Toledo*. The NAEs might hide the sub's location, but anyone out there who doubted that there was an American submarine swimming around in the Murmansk Fjord had just had all question removed.

"Now launch the MOSS," Glass ordered. When he had been Jon Ward's executive officer, Joe Glass was the one who tended to take the more thoughtful route in a pressure situation, pondering any situation thoroughly before acting. Ward was quick to decide and act. Glass had learned that there were times when further study could be fatal. He, like Ward, knew he would have to rely on his training and instincts in those instances. This was one of them.

Edwards had a questioning look on his face. "What's the plan, Skipper?"

"XO, we're going to decoy them off with the MOSS. Then we'll move in real close and hide underneath the bastard."

Edwards shook his head in wonder. "Damnedest idea I ever heard, Skipper. It just might work."

Glass winked, hoping his XO had learned from him the same lesson Ward had taught him. He turned and gave another order. "All stop. Chief of the Watch, keep us on depth with the trim pump."

The screw stopped turning and *Toledo* glided to a stop. The sub was near silent, hidden behind the screen of noise from the NAEs. Wallich would use the trim pump to move water on and off the boat to keep the submarine near the ordered depth. Even though the trim pump was built to operate silently, it was still better not to use it unless it was needed. Especially if they were going to hover beneath an enemy destroyer.

Down in the torpedo room, Bill Dooley checked the launch control panel for the MOSS. The courses and speeds the little simulator would follow were all correctly entered. He checked the tapes to make sure the latest copy of *Toledo*'s signature was loaded. Satisfied that everything was set, Dooley flipped the toggle switch to launch the device on its journey.

Out in the number-three torpedo tube, the end cap fell away from the green tube containing the MOSS, giving the vehicle access to the sea. The battery in the MOSS energized the propulsion motor, starting the little propeller at the aft end. Slowly it started to move down the tube, then out into the waters of the fjord. It swam a hundred feet free of *Toledo* before angling upward to a depth of three hundred feet. While it was moving up, a tiny transponder reeled out behind the MOSS. It stopped when the distance between the MOSS and the transponder was exactly the length of *Toledo*.

Steady on the new depth and the first course, the MOSS was ready to do its job. The tape started playing. Anyone listening to a passive sonar would swear they were hearing *Toledo* heading out into the center of the fjord.

The MOSS emerged from the NAE's noise field with its player serenading at full blast.

The sonar operator aboard the *Admiral Chabanenko* jumped to attention when he heard the new return. He was certain that the American submarine they had been expecting was trying to sneak away behind the noisemakers' screen. He was even surer of it when he faintly heard the distinctive screw beat of a Los Angeles–class propeller.

The operator grinned as he reached down and pushed the button to send out an active sonar ping again.

Three hundred feet below the icy surface of the fjord, the MOSS called up one of its special tricks. The transducer trailing behind the little vehicle and another one in the main body picked up the incoming active ping, processed it, and sent back a sonar return that precisely matched a return from *Toledo* that showed her trying to sneak away.

With the magic of electronics, the tiny MOSS looked just like the massive submarine. There was no way for the Russian sonar operator to know any differently. He disregarded the large jagged return from the noisemakers. Instead, he concentrated on the sharp return he was seeing from a submarine moving away from all the clutter.

"Got him!" the Russian said out loud.

The American was as good as dead. The operator sent the return to the fire control system. It automatically calculated the speed, course, and range of the submarine and fed the information into the SS-N-15 system. The antisubmarine missile system calculated the trajectory for the missiles to land close to the escaping sub. Too close for it to get away.

The doors flew up from missile launchers tucked under both bridge wings on the Russian destroyer. A missile from each side brilliantly lit up the night as they roared out of their launch tubes and raced into the sky. Seconds after the first two were airborne, two more missiles flew into the black night. The flights were short, lasting less than four seconds while covering some five thousand meters. When each missile was over the sub's expected position, the aerodynamic nose cone fell away and the torpedo payload parachuted down. The four torpedoes splashed down around the escaping "submarine," the first directly astern, the next ahead, and the last ones on either side.

The four torpedoes each started a slow spiral search as

they sank into the depths, pinging and listening for their quarry. The sonar returns satisfied the logic circuits on the torpedoes. The four raced in to detonate near enough to their target and more than powerful enough to gouge gaping holes in its pressure hull.

The only damage done was to the mobile submarine simulator. The mangled remains of the MOSS sank to the bottom of the Murmansk Fjord.

Its signal was forever silenced, but it had done its job well.

Brian Edwards watched the scene play out on the sonar screen. He shook his head from side to side. "Skipper, I figured we were dead. That was brilliant."

Zillich stuck his head out of the sonar room. "Screw blade from the Udaloy. He's cavitating like a big dog. Real anxious to get someplace in a hurry."

"Good riddance," Glass said. "Now I think we'll stay right here and wait a bit. That guy upstairs is running over to investigate what he hit. It'll take him a while to figure out that he's been suckered. He'll be hoppin' mad. It's best we be gone by then."

His eyes wide, Sam Donlan looked at Hector Gonzales. Neither one needed the ASDV's sensitive sonar to hear the explosions. The noise reverberated through the mini-sub's hull.

"That didn't sound good," Donlan said.

Gonzales glanced over at the tactical display. "Nope. Sure didn't. I hope that wasn't our ride home."

"I'm with you. It'd be a long, cold swim."

Bill Beaman stuck his head into the command module. His face was gray. "What the hell was that?"

Donlan pointed at the screen. "That was a series of underwater blasts up near the mouth of the fjord. It looks like you were right about the trap. It also looks like something or somebody sprang it."

"Shit! I hope it wasn't *Toledo*."

"Yeah, we were just having that conversation," Gonzales said. "How is our VIP passenger?"

"Still weak, but improving. I'll feel a whole lot better when we get him some proper medical care."

"We're an hour from the rendezvous coordinates. Assuming our bus is still out there and in one piece, Doc Halliday will be working on him in a couple of hours. We'll have him in a real hospital in a couple of days."

"Sounds like a pretty big 'if,'" Beaman said.

"That was a pretty big boom."

Beaman gave Gonzales a slight smile. "Joe Glass is driving that sewer pipe. It'll be there waiting for us, all right. You bozos just make sure we're at the right place at the right time so he doesn't have to troll around for our asses."

With that, the SEAL commander ducked back out of the command compartment.

Chapter 40

Catherine Goldman leaned back on Charles Gruver's sofa and tried to force her breathing back to normal. She expected the FBI to be there at any moment. Special Agent Decker had promised her that they were on their way. So far, though, there was no sign of them and it had been ten minutes already. There was no sign of the Russians, either. Maybe Ustinov had been lying, trying to flush her out so they could get to her more easily.

She checked her watch one more time. A full minute had passed since the last time she had looked at it.

It had taken some fast talking and serious name dropping to convince Agent Decker that the bizarre threat she was telling him about was real. Even then, he had put her on hold while he called the Securities and Exchange Commission to verify her story and confirm that she was who she said she was. He had clicked her off before she could give him a name or two to check with.

A hot flash of fear shot through Goldman when he came back on the line and reported that he had spoken with Alstair McLain. The director of market regulation might have demanded that she be arrested and turned over to the SEC. She had been ordered off the OptiMarx project. She had taken off on her own crusade. McLain had rejected her report of wrongdoing out of hand. Even if he weren't in on the whole thing, he would think she was nuts for what she was claiming. Right now, lying back on the couch in Charlie Gruver's Midtown Manhattan apartment, trying to stave off panic, she had to admit to herself that the whole thing sounded pretty far out. She knew it was all too real.

Surprisingly, Agent Decker reported that McLain had been very helpful. The agent's attitude was completely changed. There was a real sense of urgency in his voice. He sounded very much like Charlie Gruver when he ordered her to stay right there in the apartment and not to let anyone in the door until he and his agents arrived. They were on their way, he said. It did sound as if he was on a cell phone, moving quickly. She hoped so.

As soon as she hung up with the FBI, Goldman tried to call Charlie Gruver again. It was a ritual by now. Call, wait for the ring, listen to the pleasant businesslike voice mail greeting every five minutes. That's what she had been doing since she received the frightening call from Dmitri Ustinov, telling her the Russians knew where she was.

She tried again anyway. The phone rang once, then again. On the third ring, Charlie Gruver answered.

"Charlie, thank God!" she cried, the words spilling out. "I've been trying to get you for hours. Dmitri Ustinov from OptiMarx called. He was trying to warn us. The Russians know where we are, Charlie. They're coming to . . . to kill us."

She couldn't suppress a sob at the end. There was an odd popping on the other end of the line. Goldman realized it was Charlie clicking his teeth together. It was a habit of his. He did it when he was thinking through some knotty problem. She was surprised she had noticed it before. Even more surprised that she was together enough right now to recognize what the clicking was.

"Calm down, Catherine," he said. "You're safe for the moment. Did you call the police?"

"No, I called the FBI. I just hung up with them a few minutes ago. They're supposed to be on their way."

"Good. Good. Catherine, listen to me. You have to keep the door locked and don't let anyone in unless they show a badge with 'FBI' all over it."

Gruver's voice sounded worried now.

"I'll be careful, Charlie. How are things down there by now?"

"It's absolutely nuts. None of us have ever seen it skid like this. Panic selling, huge volumes. The chairman's stonewalling. I think he's into denial. He refuses to close the floor or shut down the system. He's afraid of the political repercussions. I'm positive you were right, Cath. The OptiMarx system is dirty as hell. If we don't prove it to the chairman and convince him to stop trading, the system will crash the Exchange."

Goldman listened. Everything she had predicted was happening. They had to get through to the chairman somehow and make him understand this was all part of some kind of massive, bold plot to manipulate the market.

Goldman had a quick thought. It was a risk, but it might be the only way to avoid a total disaster.

"Charlie, call Alstair McLain at the SEC. Tell him you found the system had been tampered with. I don't think

he's corrupt. I think he's just being a damn fool politician. A bureaucrat through and through. He knows I've
gotten the FBI involved now, so his antenna is definitely
up. Tell him the system has to be shut down and the
person who makes the decision to do it will be the world's
biggest hero in tomorrow's *Wall Street Journal.* He
won't be able to resist the glamour and glory, Charlie."

"Catherine, you're brilliant. I owe you a dinner."

"That works for me. I'm hungry and the only thing
I've found here to eat is a bag of stale tortilla chips and
something in the fridge that might have been a jar of
salsa in a previous life."

"Okay, so it's a bachelor pad," Gruver said with a
chuckle. "Look, I know a nice Chilean place just around
the corner. Candlelight and soft guitars. Sound good
once we save the economy of the free world from the bad
guys?"

Goldman smiled. It didn't sound like real food, but it
sure sounded nice. "Great. Just hurry back."

"I'm on my way as soon as I call McLain."

The doorbell was ringing as Goldman replaced the
phone in its cradle. Good. The FBI was here. She hurried
down the hall toward the front door.

The building intercom buzzed as well just as she got
there. The doorbell rang again, impatiently.

Catherine hesitated. She punched the intercom button.

"Yes?" she said in a whisper.

The voice on the other end had a thick Hispanic accent.
"This is Carlos, at the front desk. There are several

gentlemen down here who say they are from the FBI. I see their badges. Did you call the FBI?"

She stared hard at the apartment's front door. If the FBI agents were in the lobby, who was ringing the doorbell? Only one choice. She pushed the intercom button again. "Send them right up. Tell them to please hurry!"

Catherine sucked in a deep breath and peeked through the peephole in the front door. Two Russians from the New Jersey farm stood facing the door.

She drew back. She was shaking again and she knew she was about to erupt into tears. She had to fight it; stay strong. Otherwise, they would find her huddled there in the hallway sobbing when they broke through the door.

She examined the door. It was a typical New York apartment. Three sliding locks and a dead bolt. It would take even those two burly men a minute to break through.

Catherine swallowed hard, turned, and ran back into the living room. No place to hide here. There was just the floor-to-ceiling picture window framing the East River and Queens beyond. Cowering behind the curtains wouldn't be such a good idea.

There didn't seem to be anything to use for a weapon, either. No fireplace poker or baseball bat. Nothing.

Something heavy slammed dully against the front door. The latches held, but they would not be able to keep the Russians out for long. They didn't seem too concerned about making noise or a mess.

Goldman was near panic as she looked around wildly for anything with which to defend herself. She needed a weapon, something to enable her to hold the Russian thugs off long enough for the FBI agents to get up to the thirty-ninth floor.

Another hard crash against the door. The molding around the door frame began to splinter.

Catherine remembered something. The cutlery drawer in the kitchen. Might be something in there. She ran into the little kitchen alcove and threw open the drawer by the stove. Nothing in there but some plastic forks and carry-out condiment packages. She yanked open another drawer. Empty. She found a few knives in the third drawer. The paring knife was dull, but it was the longest blade in the drawer. It would have to do.

There was a third desperate, forceful crash at the door. The frame was on the verge of giving way. She didn't have much time. God, the FBI should have been up here by now. She didn't remember the elevator being so slow when she had ridden up.

Catherine looked around her again. She couldn't stand and wait for them there, in the middle of the kitchen, with no hope of escape. Even with the knife, she couldn't hope to hold off two ruthless, experienced brutes like these guys. They would be armed, too. She ran across the living room and into the bedroom at the far end of the apartment. The front door crashed open an instant after she shoved the bedroom door closed behind her. She stopped to engage the flimsy door lock.

The Russians tumbled into the apartment, quickly got to their feet again, and looked around for any sign of the woman. Vujnovich pointed Bogatinoff toward the kitchen while he stepped down the narrow hallway to the closed bedroom door.

Goldman was getting her bearings. The bedroom was bare and Spartan with little more than a large water bed and a dresser piled high with clothes. The closet against the near wall wouldn't offer any protection. That's the first place they would look and they would have her cornered with no room to fight back.

Then she spotted the sliding glass door that led outside, onto a small patio. She stepped that way and looked out.

The tiny patio jutted out from the wall. There was an old, rusted portable grill there. Otherwise it was empty. It had a small, waist-high wall around it with a couple of dead potted plants sitting on it. Then there was nothing more than thirty-nine floors' worth of air between her and the early-evening traffic way down below on First Avenue.

There was no place else to go. Maybe she could hide out there until help came. She was determined not to face the cold-blooded Russians again if she could help it.

She slid the glass door open and stepped out onto the tiny platform. A chill wind blew in off the river, cutting through her flimsy dress. She could see down onto the United Nations complex and up First Avenue to the north. She slid the door shut behind her and huddled against the cement wall, out of sight, clutching the feeble little paring knife in her hand. She prayed she wouldn't have to defend herself with such a poor weapon.

The bedroom door flew open, its hinges separating from the jamb, the latch flying all the way across the room to slam hard into the sliding glass door.

Josef Bogatinoff fell into the room. His momentum

was stopped when he crashed into the water bed frame with his shins. He rubbed them and angrily kicked the frame. Nicholas Vujnovich followed behind the other big Russian. He held his Glock out and ready. They looked around the empty room.

"Where is the bitch?" Vujnovich growled. "She had to run in here to have locked the door behind her. She has to be here someplace."

He tore open the closet door. Nothing in there but identical blue suits and starched white shirts. He ripped them off their hangers until he was satisfied no one could be crouching behind them.

Bogatinoff tapped him on the shoulder and pointed at the sliding glass door with the barrel of his pistol. Vujnovich nodded and signaled for Bogatinoff to stand ready while he opened it.

He yanked the door open so Bogatinoff could spring out onto the patio.

Goldman screamed and lunged at the big Russian, burying the knife up to its hilt in the fleshy part of his outstretched forearm. He dropped the Glock to the concrete and twisted away, pulling the knife from Goldman's grasp. Blood was already spurting from the wound as he stood there and looked at the knife in wonder. Then over at the shivering woman, as if he could not imagine anyone like her daring to try to defend herself against him.

Bogatinoff cocked his head sideways, but it was not the pain of the knife buried in his arm that had distracted him. It was the sound of running feet and muted shouting coming from the front doorway of the apartment. Bogatinoff looked back at her again, his eyes burning.

He reached and grabbed her by the throat with his good arm, lifting her feet off the floor of the tiny patio. Even using one hand, his viselike grip cut off her breath. Goldman's vision started to dim, the blackness spreading in from the edges of her sight as she struggled to breathe, to pull away his fingers from her neck.

She knew it was too late. He could flip her over the edge of the patio wall. He would have silenced her, saved whatever their plot was, avenged the death of his partner. Even as she felt the blackness claim her senses, Catherine Goldman knew it was too late.

Somewhere behind her she faintly heard what sounded like someone screaming "FBI!" but she couldn't be sure. The blood roaring through her ears drowned out the sound, so she couldn't tell how close they might be.

She was desperate now, searching for the strength to pry the Russian's hands from around her throat. She thought she heard a couple of pops. The darkness in her head was spreading, taking over her field of vision. She expected to feel herself falling, plummeting down toward the street.

Goldman felt the Russian loosen his grip, felt herself being dropped. It was a blessedly short fall. The concrete floor of the balcony reached up and slammed into her face. At least the fingers around her throat were gone. At least she wasn't tumbling over and over into free space.

She raised her head, shaking it to clear the fog, and looked up just in time to see the big Russian spin around as if some big hand had slapped him hard.

He disappeared over the railing.

She struggled for breath, tried to pull herself to her feet as she fought back against the blackness.

Goldman felt a hand on her shoulder. She jerked away, ready to defend herself with her fingernails and feet if she had to.

"You all right, Miss Goldman?" someone asked. It was a strong voice, yet soft and reassuring.

Catherine struggled to answer. Her throat felt as if it was swollen shut. She forced out a guttural sound that sounded something close to "Yes."

She could see it was a large black man dressed in a dark blue windbreaker. Gold letters on the front spelled out FBI.

"I'm Special Agent Decker. I think you called us."

He helped Goldman to her feet and held her up by her elbows as she walked unsteadily back into the bedroom. He eased her down on the edge of the water bed. The sloshing movement made her even dizzier, but she looked at her rescuer and tried to croak out a question, to ask where the two attackers had gone.

"Don't try to talk, miss. They're both taken care of. Looks like we got here in the nick of time. The big one was fixing to throw you off the balcony. He went over himself when we shot him. The other one is . . ."

He nodded toward the bedroom door. She could see a pair of feet. Someone was lying facedown in the hallway. He was not moving. She looked back to the sliding door. The balcony outside was empty.

There was some kind of commotion with a great deal of shouting somewhere outside the apartment, in the hallway. Decker pulled a pistol from a holster under his Windbreaker and moved toward the bedroom door.

Charlie Gruver burst in, his hands held high. He

stared at the FBI agent and at Catherine, sitting there on his bed.

"I live here! She's my guest," he said.

He rushed over, kneeled down, and took Catherine into his arms. She melted into his embrace, holding on to him for dear life.

Then everything was all right for Catherine Goldman.

"Admiral," Vasiliy Zhurkov said for the third time, trying to break into Alexander Durov's thoughts. "The Captain of the *Admiral Chabanenko* is on the radio. They have destroyed an American submarine that was trying to sneak into the Murmansk Fjord. Destroyed it on their first attempt. You were right, Admiral. Absolutely right."

Durov walked around the desk in the middle of the command center and stood next to his aide, the slightest of smiles on his rugged old face. From here he could see and respond to everything happening in the large room. Dozens of men talked on radio circuits, plotted symbols on huge Plexiglas maps, or bustled about doing a myriad of jobs. Standing here in this spot reinforced for Durov the feeling that he was in control of vast forces, a powerful navy at his beck and call, ready to do his bidding at the slightest word. He had stood in this spot through too many crises to let the illusion become his reality. As much as he willed it to be different, now that all the players were in place and had their instructions, there was little more he could do. He might give a little guidance or issue a few menial orders, but they would have little effect on the outcome of his grand scheme. The die had already been cast.

"Vasiliy, tell him to stay on station and continue his search regardless. The Americans are too wily to die so easily. Even if the submarine has been destroyed, there is a good chance they had not yet rendezvoused with the invasion force which kidnapped our president."

Zhurkov looked at him oddly, nodded, and spoke into the handset.

Durov glanced around the room. "Any communications with our submarines?" he asked, knowing the answer even as the words left his mouth.

"No, Admiral. It is still a couple of hours before they start shooting. The last of them should just be getting into his shooting box now. That would be *Vipr* in the Baltic. Anatol Vivilav had the longest distance to travel."

"Yes, Anatol," Durov said with a thoughtful nod. "We asked much of Captain Vivilav. Sneaking past the Americans and the British out in the Norwegian Sea. Threading through the Kattegat into the Baltic. It is a lot to ask, but Vivilav is a tough submariner. He will be on time. Of that you can be sure."

The old admiral rocked on his heels, with the most contented expression on his face Vasiliy Zhurkov had ever seen.

Bill Beaman stood between Hector Gonzales and Sam Donlan, watching over their shoulders as they maneuvered the mini-submarine. The ASDV was at the rendezvous point. Gonzales was circling the area while Donlan searched for the *Toledo*. Something that massive should have been easy to locate, but so far, there was no sign of the submarine.

The two Russian Grisha frigates intermittently pinged away farther south. Their sonars were gaining strength as they closed in on the spot in the fjord where the ASDV searched. The threat intercept receiver showed a signal strength of thirty-nine.

Beaman pointed to the receiver. "Didn't you say thirty-nine was the magic number? Above that and they would know we were down here?"

Donlan glanced over at the big SEAL and explained, "It ain't quite that cut-and-dried. Above thirty-nine decibels, they have a chance of detecting us, assuming the operator is awake, his gear is tuned, and he can sort our return out of all the other clutter he is looking at down here in the mud."

"Okay, just makin' sure we're not on *Candid Camera* yet."

Gonzales looked up from the navigation screen. "Skipper, to tell you the truth, right now those two guys are the least of our worries. We need to find *Toledo*, if she's still out there in one piece. Our batteries are gettin' a little low and our guest back there needs a doctor pretty quick. If you want to help, go out the hatch, swim around out there, and find that sub for us."

"All right, I read you," Beaman answered sheepishly. "'Quit buggin' us. We got work to do.'"

Donlan started to nod but then grabbed his sonar headset and pulled it more tightly to his ears. "Got the beacon. Real weak." He slewed the cursor around to read the bearing. "Hector, *Toledo* bears zero-three-one! She's still here but not where she's supposed to be."

Gonzales turned the wheel. The mini-sub came around

until it was pointed right at *Toledo*. He looked up at Beaman. "Bill, we need you to get ready for docking. We ain't got time to waste. Those Grishas might not see us yet, but *Toledo* is a whole lot bigger fish."

Gonzales pulled back on the control yoke to bring the mini-sub up to the mother sub's depth. He pushed a button up in the overhead and spoke into the little boom microphone he was wearing. "Mama, this is Baby. Hold your signal. Ready to dock. Depth eight-zero-zero."

The little speaker sounded tinny as the reply came back to them.

"Roger, Baby. Mama at eight-four-five. Course two-one-zero. Speed two. Ready for docking."

"Roger, ready for docking," Gonzales answered. "Coming around now. Suggest we don't dally."

"Agreed . . . in spades!"

Gonzales spun the mini-sub around to match *Toledo*'s course and nudged the throttles so that the ASDV was swimming just a little faster than the big submarine. The homing pulse changed modes so that it fed a constant range, bearing, and glide angle to him, just like the instrument landing system on an aircraft carrier.

Gonzales locked his attention on the navigation screen. He hit a button on his touch screen. The picture changed to show a path sloping down to the landing point. Numbers and symbols aided Gonzales as he steered the mini-sub home. A green ball on the screen represented the ASDV. The optimum approach path was shown as a white box. As long as Gonzales kept the ball inside the box, they were heading safely home. If he drifted out of the box, the ball flashed red, warning him of the danger. The graphics fed by the mini-sub's computers and the homing beacon were all he had to work with.

"Boss . . . uh . . . you're comin' in a little hot, aren't you?" Donlan asked. The ball was flashing yellow and bouncing against the top of the box. The speed showed at six knots. The maximum safe landing speed, by the book, was four knots.

"Yep. We ain't got time to lollygag around out here," Gonzales answered with a quick grin. "Help me get this little pig home."

"TV comin' on!" Donlan called out. He flipped a couple of switches. The central display screen flashed and then steadied out to show nothing but murky gray and flickers of brightness. The low-light TV wouldn't be good for much until they were close to *Toledo*. In these pitch-black waters, there wasn't much else to look at.

"Roger," Hector answered. "Still a thousand yards out and fifty above." The ball was still hugging the top of the box, threatening to break out. "Seven minutes to touchdown."

"Got you, boss. Signal strength on the Grishas is now at forty-four. They're going to see *Toledo* pretty soon if they haven't already."

Gonzales nodded. Nothing he could do about that except to get latched to *Toledo* as fast as possible so they could scram. He was doing that. The mini-sub drifted to the left. He nursed the stick just a hair, adjusting the ASDV's course to compensate for the crosscurrent.

"Current's picking up something fierce. That's going to make this damned interesting," Gonzales said drily. He didn't take his eyes off the screen.

The going seemed painfully, maddeningly slow, but the mini-sub moved unerringly toward its mother sub.

"There she is!" Donlan called out. "Just coming on the screen now."

On the television monitor, the *Toledo* emerged from the hazy gray background. She looked like a huge black whale gliding through the depths.

"Home sure looks good," Donlan commented.

Gonzales grunted. His attention was fixed on bringing the mini-sub over the after hatch on *Toledo*. The crosscurrent was getting worse, pushing him sideways and forcing him to compensate, like an airplane pilot making a landing in a powerful crosswind.

"Mama, Baby holds you visually. Range twenty yards. Stand by for touchdown."

"Roger, Baby. Mama standing by."

Gonzales eased back on the throttle, matching *Toledo*'s speed until he was hovering just above the big sub.

He stole a glance over at Donlan and smiled. "Almost there. Flood down five hundred."

Donlan reached over to the ballast control panel, on the console between the two pilots, and flipped a switch. Water flooded into the depth control tank, forcing the ASDV to sink. The copilot watched the meter count off five hundred pounds of water flooding in. He flipped the switch back, shutting the flood valve.

"Five hundred flooded."

"Good. Almost at touchdown."

The ASDV settled down onto *Toledo*'s broad back.

"Mama, Baby has touched down. Engaging latch."

The mechanical linkage swung into place, locking the ASDV to the mother sub.

"Sam, pump down the transfer skirt."

"Baby, sonar reports the Grishas are increasing speed and still coming this way. We need to scoot. Are you locked down?"

"Mama, Baby is locked down. Let's get the hell out of here."

Chapter 41

Master Chief Tommy Zillich sat leaning against the bulkhead in the back of the sonar shack. His tailbone was sore from hours of sitting. A tension headache was tightening its pincers on a spot just above the bridge of his nose. Pressing a set of earphones to his head, he tried to concentrate harder, to sort out the babble of noise he was listening to outside *Toledo*'s hard shell. His "boys" could play with all their high-tech computer gear as much as they liked. He would use the best tools a good sonar man possessed: his ears and a lot of years of experience.

The rest of his boys were following the antics of the two Russian Grishas. There was not much challenge keeping tabs on those skimmers. They were racing around as if they wanted to be heard and tracked. One would sprint ahead while the other one pinged away with his Foal Tail dipping sonar. Then they would switch places. His concern was what ordnance those guys might launch, or the Udaloy destroyer when it realized it had sunk a dummy.

Zillich glanced up at the threat intercept receiver. The LED showed the signal strength of the Russians' sonar was now up to fifty-six.

Zillich knew that *Toledo*'s thick anechoic rubber coating was a definite advantage when dealing with active sonar. It was designed to absorb the transmitted energy and lower the big sub's sonar cross-section. Still, the coating wasn't perfect. It didn't cause them to disappear like a Romulan cloaking device.

When the signal strength got high enough, *Toledo* could still be detected. It was getting high now. The Grishas should be getting enough of a return to see their shape even if their sonar men were asleep.

Just then, Tommy Zillich heard a sound that made his blood run cold. Multiple splashes, directly overhead.

He grabbed the 21MC microphone and yelled a warning. "RBU-6000 splashes! Close overhead!"

One of the Grishas had shot its rocket-powered depth charges. The hundred-and-twenty-five-kilogram antisubmarine mortars, normally fired in salvos of twelve, would sink until they hit something, or until their timers went off. The twenty-five kilograms of high explosive would detonate with an awesome force. One mortar hitting *Toledo* could damage her severely. A whole salvo detonating around her would be fatal.

"All ahead flank!" Glass shouted without hesitation. *Toledo* jumped ahead as the throttle man whipped open the throttles, pouring steam into the propulsion turbines. Joe Glass was already doing the math in his head. The bombs sank at a rate of twenty feet per second. They had less than a minute to get clear. The deadly race was on.

"Skipper," Brian Edwards yelled. "We can't go above twenty-five knots with the ASDV strapped on! We might rip the latch away!"

"I know. Get the people out of there, quick! We may

have to jettison the thing if we can't get away fast enough."

Jerry Perez's eyes danced between the clock and the needle climbing up the dial.

"Skipper, fifteen knots, coming up fast," he reported. "Twenty seconds since splash."

The *Toledo* raced away from where they had heard the sinking mortars. They were a hundred and fifty yards from where Zillich first detected the splashes. It might not be fast enough. The Grisha might have led them, too. They might be racing directly toward the sinking depth charges instead of away from them. There was no way to know. Despite all the highly technical gear around them and the well-trained crew, sometimes they had to rely on gut instinct.

"Twenty knots. Twenty-five seconds."

There wasn't anything to do now but run and pray they were fast enough. The mindless, death-dealing bombs were sinking down into the cold, dark water. There would be a detonation. It would come in half a minute now.

"Twenty-five knots. Thirty-two seconds."

"Left full rudder," Glass suddenly ordered. "Steady course north."

Toledo heeled over like a fighter plane abruptly banking hard left, trying to gain advantage in a dogfight. Edwards and Glass grabbed the plot table to hang on. The compass dial spun so fast now that the numbers were a blur. The sub's speed dropped to twelve knots as the bow spun around to the new course. Then the boat shot straight ahead again.

Edwards glanced at Glass and asked, "Knuckle?"

"Yep," Glass answered with a grin. "I'm giving them something to keep them busy for a few minutes."

When the boat made the abrupt turn, its huge rudder shoved vast amounts of water into a swirling vortex. The massive eddy would stay there for many minutes after the sub ran away. More important, the tower of moving water would bend the probing sonar pulses from the ships on the surface. That would cause a huge return, one large enough and strong enough that it might convince a sonar operator that he was locked on to a submarine.

"Twenty knots, forty-seven seconds."

"How far?" Glass yelled. He needed to know the distance *Toledo* had traveled away from the presumed splash point. The sudden twisting turn had moved them off in a new direction. The straight-line distance back was what was important. The plot was the quickest way to find out.

Perez glanced at the "bug," the little dot of light projected on the plotting table that showed the boat's position. He eyeballed the distance from the "bug" to where they had heard the splashes. He began his answer.

"Four hundred . . ."

The blast was deafening.

Books and coffee cups flew across the room, their crashes adding counterpoint to the reverberating cacophony of the blast. Dust, shaken out of the nooks and crannies of the overhead, settled to the deck, giving the space an eerie, foggy feeling.

The violent shaking threw Edwards hard into the hydraulic manifold outboard of the plotting table. He fell to the deck, landing on his face, and blood was already oozing from the back of his head.

The violent shaking and mind-numbing noise stopped as abruptly as it started. Joe Glass picked himself up off the deck and surveyed the control room. Around him, everyone else was shrugging off the attack as well.

All except Brian Edwards. The executive officer lay on the deck, not moving.

Glass saw his friend, his alter ego, lying there motionless, but there wasn't time for him to rush to Edwards's aid. Someone else would have to attend to the XO. The skipper had to get *Toledo* out of there before the Grishas fired another round.

"Ahead full, make turns for twenty-five knots," Glass ordered.

He looked at the sonar display, trying to glean any information he could from it. The depth charge blast had filled the fjord basin with reverberating noise. It overpowered the sensitive sonar hydrophones. The screen was a wash of white.

The Foal Tail active sonars still pinged away, lighting up the threat receiver. The Grishas were still up there, still hunting.

Zillich leaned out of the sonar room door and shook his head. "Damn, Skipper! That was close." He pointed at the threat receiver. The signal strength had dropped to forty-nine. "Our friends are still up there, but I think they're looking at that knuckle for the time being."

"I sure as hell hope so. We need for it to keep them busy for a few more minutes," Glass answered. "Have you heard anything from that Udaloy?"

"Not in all that mess out there. It'll be quite a while

before the echoes die down. The granite walls of the fjord are bouncing that blast all over the place."

"Let's use that. If we can't hear them, they sure as hell can't hear us."

Glass turned back to the control room. Jerry Perez was working on Edwards. The XO seemed to be re-gaining consciousness. Sam Wallich was taking reports from around the boat, checking for damage. Doug O'Malley was busy tracking the Grishas, making sure *Toledo* was ready to shoot should Joe Glass give the order. That was normally Edwards's job, but O'Malley had stepped right in to cover for the injured second in command.

"Skipper, I have shooting solutions on both of those bastards," the engineer reported. "Give me the word and I'll be happy to light the fuse."

"Not yet, Eng," Glass answered. "Keep a solution on them, but let's see if we can slip out of here. We're still inside their territorial waters, you know. That Udaloy is still up there, too." Glass turned to Wallich and asked, "What are the damages, COB?"

"Not too bad, Skipper." The chief of the boat read from the Plexiglas status on which he was writing. "Number-two chill water pump breaker tripped open. They reshut it and it works fine. Small electrical fire in number one CO_2 scrubber. Fire is out. Reflash watch is stationed. Atmosphere is normal."

"That all? Any injuries, other than the XO?"

"Bunch of bruises and scrapes is all," Wallich reported. "Nothing serious. Doc Halliday is busy with our new

VIP patient. He reports Smitrov is being taken to the wardroom."

"Everyone out of the ASDV?"

"Yes, sir. Last man, Commander Beaman, was in the escape trunk when the blast happened. I guess he got bruised pretty good. Upper and lower trunk hatches are shut. The ASDV is secured for transit."

Glass could picture his big SEAL friend in the cramped little escape trunk, being banged around by the blast. With all the pipes, gauges, and hand wheels in there, it was most likely the same as being trapped in a clothes dryer. It was a wonder that Beaman wasn't more seriously hurt. Altogether, it appeared they were very lucky. No significant damage to the boat or serious injury to the crew.

Wallich talked on the phone headset for a few seconds. He turned back to Glass and reported, "Skipper, that was Doc on the line. He asked if you could come down to the wardroom. President Smitrov is requesting to speak with you immediately."

"On my way," Glass said. He turned to O'Malley as he headed out the aft control room door. "Eng, I'll be in the wardroom for a few minutes. Run north at full for another ten minutes and then slow to four knots. Stay slow, quiet, and deep."

"Aye, sir. Ten minutes at full, then slow, quiet, and deep."

Glass stopped by where Edwards was being helped to his feet. He had a handkerchief pressed to a nasty gash on the back of his head.

"XO, sit there for a bit," Glass ordered. "Then get

down to see Doc when you are steady enough." Edwards tried to protest, but the skipper raised his hand to stop him. "We've got a handle on this. You get down and get that head looked at. Even a skull as thick as yours can't stand up to HY-80."

Glass slid down the ladder to the middle level and headed forward to the wardroom. He wasn't prepared for what he saw when he opened the door. The place was being turned into a trauma center. The counters were filled with medical supplies. A half dozen crewmen sat on the Naugahyde couches, either waiting to be treated or already being attended to by other crew members.

Doc Halliday was working on Bill Dooley at the far end of the room. The torpedo man sat stoically while Halliday stitched up a nasty gash on his arm. Dooley looked up and smiled wanly when Glass walked in.

Two of the cooks were hanging big stainless steel operating room lights in the overhead above the wardroom table, bathing it with a harsh white light. The table, covered with sterile white cloth, had been transformed into an operating table. President Smitrov lay in the center of it. One of the SEALs, Jason Hall, was inserting an IV needle into the crook of the Russian president's arm. The tubing led up to a plastic pouch of clear liquid.

Glass noticed that several of the people giving first aid appeared to be other members of Bill Beaman's SEAL team. That made sense. They would have had extensive training in emergency medicine. A lot more than his crew would.

Beaman sat in a chair at the head of the table. He was shirtless. Chief Johnston was cleaning a mass of ugly contusions and scrapes on the big SEAL's left shoulder. Beaman jumped up when he saw the skipper and sprang over to greet his old friend. He grabbed Glass's outstretched hand.

"Joe, it's damn good to see you. Thanks for all the welcoming fireworks when we came on board."

"Don't mention it. Least we could do for you guys."

"Hey, it's just like old times. If Jon Ward were here, we'd have the old band back together and ready to go out on tour."

It had been a while since the three men had worked together. That time, they had teamed up to help stop a notorious Colombian drug smuggler, Juan de Santiago, in a steaming jungle. Now here they were, again working together, but this time in frigid Russia.

"Yeah, that would be great. I'm afraid Jon is off playing on some skimmer. He's probably mad as hell he's missing all the fun up here, though," Glass said. He nodded at Gregor Smitrov. "I see you brought along an extra passenger."

The 7MC loudspeaker blared, interrupting the conversation.

"Captain, Officer of the Deck. I have slowed to four knots and come to course north."

Glass reached under the head of the table and grabbed a microphone that was hanging there. He keyed the mike. "Captain, aye. Eng, where are the Grishas by now?"

"Captain, they are still pinging away like a son of a bitch," Doug O'Malley answered. "Best estimate is eight thousand yards astern. We have ten minutes on this course before we need to turn."

"I'll be up in a minute."

Beaman picked up the conversation as if the interruption hadn't happened. "I kept bragging about what a good bus driver you were. He insisted on taking a ride. Let me introduce you." Beaman looked down at Smitrov and spoke in Russian. "President Smitrov, this is my old friend Commander Joe Glass. He is the captain of the USS *Toledo*, the fine submarine on which we now find ourselves."

Smitrov opened his eyes and tried to focus on the two men standing over him. His voice was strained and weak when he answered in passable English, "Captain, I am very thankful for your hospitality." He stopped to swallow, to take in more breath. "I must request to use your radio room. I must talk with my government at once."

The Russian president was pasty white in the harsh light. The pallor of his skin was a good indication of the suffering he had endured. It was clear, though, that the man still had fight left in him.

Glass wondered if he would live, let alone be able to fight for the survival of his country's rightful government.

"I'd be happy to allow you use of the radio room, Mr. President, but I'm afraid a contingent of your countrymen are up there on the surface right now trying to kill us. We're a little busy at the moment trying to lose them."

"Those are rebels, fighting with that dog, Durov," Smitrov growled, his face growing red as much with anger as from the strain of speaking. "They are, in truth, trying to kill me. You are no more than collateral damage. You must help me stop Durov and his evil plot. Sink the miserable traitors. You have my permission! Sink them!"

Smitrov tried to rise, but Hall restrained him. The president fell back on the makeshift operating table. He closed his eyes for a moment and Glass thought he might have passed out. Then he opened them again and looked up at Glass. His words were soft but pleading when he spoke again.

"Please. I must talk to my government. Captain, please get me somewhere that I can. The fate of my country depends on it. Time is of the essence."

The man was clearly drained. His breath came in ragged gasps. What little strength he had kept in reserve was now spent.

Doc Halliday grabbed Glass's arm and spun him around. When he spoke, his words were surprisingly forceful. "Captain, you have to leave my patient alone. He's lost a lot of blood. He's slipping in and out of hypovolemic shock. I've got him on a saline drip to get some blood volume back and I'm giving him epinephrine to get his blood pressure up." The medic reached over and placed Smitrov's legs back up on the stack of books that were substituting for leg rests. "You've got to let him rest."

"What are his chances?"

Doc shook his head sadly. He spoke softly so that only Glass could hear him. "Even if he was in Portsmouth Hospital, I would give him even money at best. Out here, we just have to pray and depend on luck."

Glass nodded. "Doc, give me one second to tell him we'll do all we can. It'll ease his mind."

Glass returned to Smitrov's side. He sympathized with the man's plight. The longer it took for him to rally his forces, to let them know what was going on, the more time Durov had to consolidate his position. There was little that Glass could do. Between the two frigates behind him and the Udaloy destroyer and its helicopters waiting to pounce on them at the mouth of the fjord, there was no way he could go to periscope depth and broadcast a message. It would be suicide.

"President Smitrov, we will do our very best. I've got to get my boat out into open water before we will be able to use the radio. Otherwise, we'll all die soon after I raise a mast, and before we could send any kind of message." Glass looked into the Russian president's eyes. "Mr. President, we may well have to kill some of your countrymen in order to get out of here. Many of them will be innocent pawns."

"I understand, Captain," Smitrov answered, the sadness heavy in his voice. "It must be done. You must do your duty so that I can do mine."

Glass pursed his lips, then turned and left the wardroom.

The fight was on.

Marina Nosovitskaya stood back and watched Dmitri Ustinov run full force again and again into Carl Andretti's locked office door. He was making scant headway attempting to get at Andretti, who hid on the other side.

She knew that time was running out for them. The Opti-Marx CTO had certainly called for help by now.

"Marina," Dmitri called over his shoulder. He grimaced as he rubbed his aching upper arm. "Find something we can use for a battering ram. A fire axe or something."

He took a running go and slammed hard into the heavy door again. It shuddered but showed no signs of giving way.

Nosovitskaya looked around the open office space. There was nothing that looked like a battering ram here. Maybe back in the testing room. She trotted down the hall and disappeared through the door.

The young blond programmer searched the room, but there was no weapon in here, either. By chance she noticed that Dmitri's computer was still online. Normally he was careful to never leave it operating when he wasn't sitting in front of it. He never seemed to mind having to log back on each time he left his workstation. Now she knew the reason. Fifty million reasons.

Nosovitskaya sat down in front of the machine and tapped a few keys on the keyboard. Within seconds she found what she was looking for. She smiled. Dmitri was nothing if not predictable. The code for his secret bank account was there. It was in a file named "Marina."

The sound of pounding feet and shouting male voices interrupted Nosovitskaya as she copied down the numbers on a sticky note. Time was running out. Someone else was here and they were making a lot of noise.

Nosovitskaya slipped over and cracked the door open just a sliver. She peeked out just in time to see four men with drawn pistols charge down the hall toward Andretti's office. Their dark blue windbreakers had FBI written across their backs in large gold letters. Ustinov was already spread-eagled on the floor, yelling for the agents not to shoot.

FBI? Andretti had gotten serious attention in a hurry.

She moved away from the door and walked back across the big room. The red EXIT sign on the far wall marked the door to the stairwell. She slipped through the door, eased it shut behind her, and headed down the metal-and-concrete stairs.

It took her fifteen minutes to climb down to the building's first floor. Nosovitskaya opened the door and stepped out into the marble-lined lobby. She was just in time to see an elevator door open across the way. Two of the FBI agents escorted a handcuffed Dmitri Ustinov out of the elevator and turned toward the huge plate-glass front doors.

Nosovitskaya stood and watched as they crossed the lobby, just as the other curious passersby were doing. Ustinov glanced up, in her direction. He saw her. Their eyes met for an instant. The agents pulled him away, out the door and toward where their car waited at the curb. The plaintive look on the man's face was lost on her.

She turned away, toward the back exit of the building, and walked out into the night.

Chapter 42

Lieutenant Tim Schwartz burst through the door and pulled to a halt before he crashed headfirst into Admiral Tom Donnegan's big desk. The normally reserved aide had not even bothered to knock on the door or straighten his tie before barging into his boss's office in such a hurry. He was breathless, his eyes wide. "Admiral, quick! You've got to see this. CNN is carrying it live."

Donnegan glanced up from his desk and peered over the half-rim reading glasses that rested on the end of his nose. Young Schwartz was never this excitable. Donnegan had chosen him for his aide not only because he was smart but also because he was unflappable. Something important had grabbed his attention.

Donnegan deliberately removed the reading glasses and closed the file he had been studying. He moved it to the top of a tall stack of similar buff-colored folders in his wooden out-basket. The screen on the big television mounted on the far wall flashed on. Schwartz flipped the channel over to CNN. Some talking head reporter was standing in Red Square, using the familiar view of the Kremlin as a backdrop.

Donnegan's attention perked up when he heard the reporter say something about "Durov" and "probable coup." Troops rushed about on the cobblestones behind the reporter. They appeared to be manning a hastily erected, sandbagged gun emplacement. A T-74 main battle tank rumbled to a halt, its cannon pointed out across the broad expanse of Red Square. Someone inside the ancient fortress was frightened enough to take serious, and visible, precautions.

The image shifted to a briefing room. A Russian naval officer, resplendent in an admiral's full dress uniform, stepped to the center of the room and towered above a dark wooden lectern that waited there. The Russian flag and the naval ensign were framed on either side. The elderly white-haired man stood stiffly erect, glaring at those in the room until the hubbub subsided. The imposing figure had the bearing of someone accustomed to commanding and being instantly obeyed. The assembled group of newsmen hushed.

Donnegan recognized the officer at once. He was Admiral of the Northern Fleet Alexander Durov.

The old sailor stood silent for a moment longer after the room had grown quiet, surveying the reporters with an icy glare. When he was ready, he spoke into the bank of massed microphones, his voice clear, cold, and crisp, with not a hint of hesitation or weakness. Even without the help of an interpreter, the old man's meaning would have been obvious, but CNN's interpreter confirmed it and provided the chilling details in English.

"The time has come to free Mother Russia from the bondage of foreign oppression. Our government has failed in its sacred duty to uphold the honor of the *Rodina* and the sovereignty of our nation. Over the last decade, we have endured the insults and slights of the West and have not responded. The puppets of the imperialists have taken control of the Kremlin and have sought to emasculate the mighty forces that have protected the motherland for generations with their bravery and blood."

Donovan could not believe the sheer force and determination in what he was hearing and seeing. Admiral Durov's face was flushed red, his jaw muscles drawn taut, as he glared into the camera. He was not reading from prepared notes. This speech had been well rehearsed.

"The weakness of our so-called leaders has allowed a tragedy to take place. The Americans have preyed on our vulnerability and had the effrontery to brazenly attack our ships in our sovereign waters! They have done so without reason or provocation. They have murdered our brave sailors before our very eyes. All the weaklings in Moscow have offered as a response to their massacre are apologies! It is time for this to stop!" Durov slammed his fist down hard onto the lectern. It shook so violently that a glass of water danced off the edge and crashed to the floor. "The *Rodina* will once again assume her rightful role in the world. We will demand the respect that the free people of our country deserve."

Durov paused and stared into the camera. His icy blue eyes flashed with pure hatred.

"Even as late as today the Americans have blatantly dispatched one of their submarines into the Murmansk Fjord in violation of every principle of international law. We believe we know the reason for that treacherous incursion. I am proud to report that the ships of our mighty

Navy trapped it and destroyed the invader! We will suffer these insults no more!" Durov drew himself up to full height, standing rigidly erect as he went on. "I must also tell you that President Smitrov is missing and we fear he has been kidnapped by the Americans. We believe a special operations team accomplished this unspeakable act. We further believe that the renegade submarine had entered our territorial waters to retrieve that team and the president. We do not know if that retrieval took place before the invading boat was destroyed. Nor do we know if President Smitrov is alive or dead. However, the Russian military, with me at its head, has taken control of the puppet government of our country before the Americans can take advantage of our weakness and further escalate their aggression against us. All officials will immediately swear loyalty to the new government that is being formed or they will be dealt with along with all other traitors and cowards.

"Just like in times in the past, the sailors of the *Rodina* will once again be at the forefront of the battle. The grandchildren of the brave sailors on the *Kronstadt* stand ready to defend the motherland. They are manning the capital ships of this century and training their weapons on those who would falter in reaching our destiny."

Admiral Durov turned abruptly and marched off the stage, out of camera range, ignoring the questions being shouted at his back.

Tom Donnegan shook his head in shocked disbelief and muted the television sound before the reporter could begin his ill-informed analysis. So the old fool had gone beyond the point of no return. Up until this point there was always the possibility that Durov would stop short of outright rebellion. Or at the worst, he would rattle his saber some to demand concessions from the Russian government. The press conference left no room for doubt. Durov meant to establish a new, militarized Russia. One with him in charge. A shiver of dread passed through Donnegan.

"Do you believe that?" Schwartz asked. "You don't think they got *Toledo*, do you? What was all that blather about the *Kronstadt*?"

Donnegan scratched his chin.

"We won't know about *Toledo* for a day or so," he answered. He sat back in the overstuffed office chair and sipped from a cup of coffee. "This is one of the real trials of senior command. We can't do anything but sit here and pray until Joe Glass calls home or we get some verification that *Toledo* is lost." Donnegan set his coffee cup on the desk. "You need to brush up on your Russian history, Tim. The *Kronstadt* sailors bombarded the Czar's Winter Palace in St. Petersburg during the Bolshevik Revolution. It was a turning point that allowed Lenin to consolidate his power. It looks like we have much more serious problems to attend to. I think we now know what Admiral Durov's submarines are up to."

The scenario running through Donnegan's mind was chilling. If *Toledo* had truly been sunk, Durov would use the president's disappearance as another example of American aggression and there would be little to do to rebut him. He would blame everything that happened on the U.S. along with the American-friendly government in his country. The inevitable turmoil would make it all the easier for him to pull off his coup. Meanwhile, the rest of the world would be distracted by all the charges. He had a bunch of nuke subs out there to hold everyone hostage. This was one royal mess.

The phone rang, interrupting his worrying. Schwartz grabbed it before it rang a second time.

"Admiral Donnegan's office. May I help you?" He listened for a few moments while he scribbled notes on a scrap of paper, then replaced the receiver. He stood there, considering what he had written down.

"You going to tell me who that was or you going to keep it a personal secret?" Donnegan asked impatiently.

"Sorry, Admiral. That was President Brown's chief of staff. You are to report immediately to the White House situation room. All the national security team is there already. General Tambor is on his way in, along with the joint chiefs and the director of intelligence." He paused again, squinting at something else on the paper. "They also said Alstair McLain from the Securities and Exchange Commission is going to be there."

Donnegan's eyebrows went to a quizzical arch. He cocked his head sideways. "Considering what we just heard, I expected that call. Did they give you any idea why somebody from the SEC is coming?"

Schwartz hunched his shoulders. "Not a clue."

"It is time, Captain," Anistov Dmolysti said flatly. The two Russian submarine sailors stood at the back of the control room, watching the crew at work. *Vipr* was in the center of the Gulf of Finland. The lights of Tallinn and Helsinki were just over the horizon behind them.

St. Petersburg was a few kilometers ahead. They were in their patrol box. The long trek from Polyarnyy was over. It was time for them to do the job they had been sent here to do.

Captain Anatol Vivilav looked at the large clock mounted on the after bulkhead. As usual, his first officer was right. Everyone was in place already, doing his job and anticipating the captain's next command.

The air in the tiny control room was thick with the sweaty odor of twenty excited men preparing to go into battle for the first time in their lives. The air-conditioning could barely keep up, even though the *Vipr* was submerged in the cold waters of the Baltic. Eager young faces reflected the harsh yellow-green light of a dozen computer screens.

Vivilav felt very old. He was surrounded by children who had been entrusted to his protection. Soon they would usher in a new era of Russian greatness. Or they would die in the attempt.

He shook his head, trying to clear the extraneous thoughts. There was work to do. A battle to fight.

Vivilav looked at the sonar repeater. It was crosshatched with hundreds of traces. The confused picture was expected. Every trace represented a ship that the sonar team was tracking. The Gulf of Finland was a busy maritime highway. He glanced over his shoulder at Dmolysti. "Does sonar report any contacts of interest?"

The first officer grabbed a phone from its holder on the bulkhead and spoke into it for a few seconds.

"*Nyet*, Captain," he answered. "All tracks are merchants or fishermen. No tracks will approach *Vipr* within five thousand meters."

"Well, Anistovovich. Let us go up and take a look around. I would not want to unduly frighten one of those poor fishermen." Vivilav's voice became very serious. "I want to start shooting as soon as we can verify the area is clear."

"Everything is ready for the first salvo," Dmolysti answered. "Alpha cruise missiles are loaded in torpedo tubes one through four for the first salvo. We will reload immediately for the second salvo. All missiles have their target packages entered."

The SS-N-27 Novator Alpha was the latest in Russian cruise missile technology. It had replaced the older SS-N-21 Granat. The Alpha used geographic positioning satellite information and an advanced inertial navigation system to find its target. That eliminated the need for the Granat's questionable terrain-mapping system. The superaccurate Alpha missile was ideal for this mission. The increased accuracy allowed the Russian designers to replace the Granat's two-hundred-kiloton nuclear warhead with the Alpha's four-hundred-kilogram conventional warhead.

"Very good," Vivilav answered.

It would have been much easier if all the Alpha missiles could be loaded and fired in one salvo, but the *Vipr*'s fire control system only allowed the land attack missiles to be fired from four of the submarine's ten torpedo tubes. The design weakness would mean having to wait at least ten minutes between salvos while Vivilav's crew reloaded the torpedo tubes and checked the missiles. *Vipr* would be exposed during that time. They would also have four smoky missile exhaust trails pointing right back to them. There was no other choice. They had to fight with the systems they had.

"And self-defense?" the captain asked.

The first officer glanced at the torpedo tube status board to verify what he was reporting. "Tubes five through eight have torpedoes loaded. ET-80-A antisubmarine torpedoes. Tubes nine and ten have RPK-2 Vi-yuga antiship missiles loaded."

He looked over at the evasion and antiair panel. Green lights indicated all systems ready there as well. Two tubes mounted in the top of the sail housed Strela heat-seeking antiaircraft missiles. The four evasion device tubes, mounted back in the aftermost compartment, would shoot noisemakers into *Vipr*'s wake to hide the sub from any incoming torpedoes.

"All self-defense systems armed and ready," Dmolysti reported.

Vivilav nodded. At least he had weapons to defend his ship and devices to confuse the enemy. Not that there was much chance that anyone would be in a position to attack *Vipr*. As far as he could tell, they had made the run down from the Barents undetected. Still, it was better to be prepared.

He stepped over to the periscope and pushed the button to raise it. The silvery metal tube rose as he crouched and waited for the eyepiece to emerge from the well. When it did, he slapped down the handles and put his eye to the eyepiece. He saw the black darkness of the deep. As he stood straighter, following the scope up, he could make out the rushing flashes of white foam break-ing over the lens. Then he saw the gray overcast night sky.

He rotated around, looking for any ships. Even though *Vipr*'s sonar was tracking multitudes of ships, he visually confirmed that there were none located in the patch of ocean he saw. Just to make sure, he looked around again, rotating more slowly this time, searching every wave top. Still no ships.

"Captain," Dmolysti said, his voice little more than a whisper. "Do you want to search with radar?"

"No, not this time. There is no one up there right now. Using the radar would attract attention from any-one searching over the horizon."

"Very well, Captain," the first officer answered. "We are ready to commence launch. One minute to scheduled launch time."

Vivilav stepped back from the periscope. He was not certain of all the reasons for what was about to happen. He was not even certain how it could possibly be the best thing for his country. But his commander had ordered it done. Admiral Durov was a god to him. He recalled the day he first heard Durov lecture at the Soviet Naval School at Stalingrad. If Admiral Durov ordered it done, Anatol Vivilav was bound to do it.

"First Officer, commence launch sequence," he or-dered without wavering.

The outer doors on four torpedo tubes clanged open. Four deadly missiles were made ready to leap into the night sky on fiery trails.

*   *   *

Jon Ward sat in the command seat in the CIC on board the *Anzio*. The large flat-panel display mounted on the bulkhead in front of him was littered with tracks from the dozens of surface ships that *Anzio*'s advanced Aegis radar was following. Most were shown as white rectangles, telling him at a glance that those ships were positively identified as noncombatants. He could ignore them. Some of the rectangles were yellow. That signified that they had not been positively ID'd yet. Those didn't interest Ward, either.

His eyes were locked on a green triangle with the notation AA275 written beside it. Just to the east of the green triangle was a red box with an open side facing down. Beside it was written AS124. AA275 was the Aegis track number for *Anzio*'s SH-60 helicopter. Its radio call sign was Foxtrot Three Two. AS124 was the track number for the Russian submarine they had been tailing all the way from the north of Norway, through the Baltic Sea, and into the Gulf of Finland.

"Commodore, Foxtrot Three Two reports ceiling at one thousand." Bob Norquest sat right beside Ward, listening to the helicopter pilot on the tactical radio. "One Two Four is at the edge of the sonobuoy field. Three Two is going to drop down to two hundred feet and deploy a new line."

Ward nodded and switched his attention to the outboard flat panel. It was showing the underwater game of cat and mouse they were playing. The Russian sub had slowed to a speed of two or three knots. After charging at high speed all the way from the Kattegat, this guy was slowing to patrol speed even though he was only a few kilometers from Russian soil. It didn't make much sense for him to dally around out here unless he was up to no good.

Twenty thousand yards up ahead, the SH-60 helicopter, Foxtrot Three Two, eased down out of the cloud cover that had been hiding him so well. He was coming down so he could drop sonobuoys ahead of the Russian sub. The sub was too far ahead for Jeff Stroud and his sonar team on *Anzio* to hear him, but the SH-60 and its sonobuoys gave Ward a good set of ears out in the distance. As long as he could keep the helicopter up in the air, the sub would be hard pressed to escape, if he even knew he was being tracked.

The low cloud cover had been a godsend. Three Two could stay hidden up in the clouds while he followed the sub. He could hear the Russian fine from up there, but the sub skipper couldn't see the chopper if he popped up the periscope for some reason. Now Foxtrot Three Two had to drop down beneath the clouds to deploy his sonobuoys. Ward couldn't help holding his breath until he could get confirmation that the SH-60 was back in the overcast again.

"Skipper, loud transient on the bearing of the Akula!" Chief Stroud's voice boomed over *Anzio*'s intercom. "Second loud transient. Sounds like he's shooting missiles!"

At the same instant, the pilot on Foxtrot Three Two screamed into his microphone: "Bird in the air! Contact is shooting! Second bird. I say again, contact is shooting!"

Two red blips appeared on the screen as the Aegis radar picked up the two missiles.

Ward swallowed hard. Things were happening fast. Way too fast.

Captain Anatol Vivilav returned his eye to the periscope just after the second Alpha missile roared off into the night sky. He was shocked at what he saw. An American SH-60 helicopter dropped out of the clouds and filled his field of vision. That meant there had to be an American ship close by. The SH-60 was unmistakable. It was a deadly development. It had to be destroyed before it could drop one of its torpedoes!

"Launch the Strellas!" Vivilav shouted. "American helicopter directly overhead!"

He slammed up the scope handles and punched the button to lower it. He stole a glance at Dmolysti as the first officer pushed the button for the launch of one and then the second heat-seeking missile. The control room shuddered as the two rockets blasted out of the launch tubes just over their heads. The Strellas were "fire and forget" missiles. Once they were on their way, there was nothing for the crew on *Vipr* to do but pray they did their deadly work.

The loud explosion told the story even before the sonar operators could announce hearing the wreckage hit the water. *Vipr* was safe for a few more minutes. The helicopter's mother ship was still out there, though. It would not take them long to realize their chopper was gone. *Vipr* still had to launch the rest of the cruise missiles before Vivilav could give any thought to running.

*   *   *

"SAM! SAM! Contact shooting at us—" the chopper pilot was yelling when the tactical circuit went dead. Aegis track AA275 disappeared.

The helicopter was gone.

"Captain, Bridge. Explosion on the bearing to our chopper. I can see outbound missile tracks on the same bearing. Someone's shot our bird and launched missiles, too."

Ward watched the terrible scene unfold for a split second. Then he acted. It was time to go on the offensive. There was no doubt that the Akula submarine had destroyed the helicopter and had sent lethal missiles out on a mission of death. Now was the time and nobody knew how to fight *Anzio* better than Bob Norquest, her skipper.

"Captain, you are weapons free on all hostile tracks," Ward said.

"Engage the outbound missiles with SM-2s," Norquest ordered without hesitation. "One on each track. Engage the Akula with ASROC. Assign four ASROCs to track Alpha Sierra One Two Four." There was a note of quiet, controlled anger in the man's voice. He had just lost three crewmen out there in that chopper.

To Ward's left, the *Anzio*'s weapons officer bent to the task. His fingers danced across his control panel, assigning missiles and sending them on their way. Out on *Anzio*'s main deck, a piercing siren blared for an instant, warning anyone foolish enough to be topside that they had scant seconds to take cover.

A small square hatch on the ship's main deck, just for-

ward of the bridge, flew open and flames vented upward
from the Mk-41 Vertical Launch System as the first missile leaped out of the forward vertical launcher, riding a
column of flame from its solid-fuel rocket motor. The
SM-2 antiaircraft missile roared vertically upward to a
thousand feet and then arced toward one of the cruise
missiles the Russian sub had launched. The missile followed an invisible radar trail at Mach three as it raced
toward its target.

A millisecond later, another SM-2 from the after vertical launcher roared skyward after its prey, the other Russian cruise missile.

Four ASROC missiles, two from forward and two
from aft, joined the fire trails that already lit up the night
sky. The antisubmarine rockets raced to where *Anzio*'s
computers said the Russian sub should be lurking just
beneath the surface. The four missiles arrived over the
spot within seconds. Each of them dropped a Mark 46
torpedo from its nose. The torpedos parachuted into the
sea as the missile canisters tumbled harmlessly down into
the water.

With over a Mach-two speed advantage, it didn't take
long for the SM-2s *Anzio* had launched to catch up to
the two Russian cruise missiles. The first SM-2 dove on
its quarry. The radar-activated proximity fuse detonated
when the missiles were ten feet apart. The blast shock
wave tore the wings off the little cruise missile. A millisecond later, the continuous rod warhead shredded the
wreckage as it tumbled toward the sea.

The second SM-2 dove toward its target, but it did
not fare as well as its partner. It lost its prey in the radar

clutter. There wasn't enough room for the antiaircraft missile to turn and climb back up to resume the hunt. The SM-2 exploded when it impacted the water. The Russian cruise missile rocketed on and disappeared over the horizon, eastbound toward unsuspecting cities and the people who lived in them.

Ward stared as the cruise missile disappeared from the radar screen. The flight profile was unmistakable. The Russian sub had launched a land-attack cruise missile. It could be nuclear. It was possible that he had just witnessed a nuclear attack against Russia. There was no way to tell. Maybe there was a chance to warn the Russians and save thousands of lives. Maybe millions.

He grabbed a microphone and uttered words he thought he would never have to use. "This is an OPREP-Three Pinnacle Nucflash message. Reporting a possible nuclear attack. Russian submarine launched cruise missile, launched from position zero-two-seven degrees, three-zero minutes east longitude, five-nine degrees, four-seven minutes north latitude. Missile headed east toward Russia."

The emergency report would be in front of the National Command Authority within seconds.

"Sonar, report any warships!" Captain Anatol Vivilav shouted into the microphone. There was no time to wonder how the Americans had known they were here. Or how far they might have been trailed.

"American warship, probable Aegis-class cruiser, bearing two-four-one. Best guess at range, ten thousand meters. Coming up in speed now. Captain, he came out of nowhere."

Vivilav turned to Dmolysti and said, "First Officer, finish the cruise missile launch as quickly as possible. I'll attack the American."

"Yes, Captain."

"Open the outer doors on tubes nine and ten," Vivilav ordered. "Assign both Viyogas to the American cruiser." The captain hardly stopped to breathe as he barked out commands. He had to attack the American before the American could attack him. "Launch both missiles."

Vivilav was too busy to hear the splashes from the American Mark 46 torpedoes when they entered the water. The sonar operators were occupied, too, concentrating on the cruiser. They never heard the motors come up to speed as the tiny twin counterrotating propellers drove the deadly fish toward *Vipr*. The first time Vivilav realized he was under attack was when the threat receiver above his head began alarming shrilly. It was detecting the forty-kilohertz active sonar from the torpedoes as they drove home.

There wasn't time to run. Or even to pray.

The first torpedo hit just under the control room. The shape charge in its warhead drove a half-meter-wide hole through *Vipr*'s steel side. It vented molten metal and superheated explosive gases into the compartment. Fires spontaneously ignited all around the compartment. The ice-cold Baltic poured in.

That's when the other three torpedos hit.

The one that struck in the reactor compartment caused the reactor to shut down and ripped open a weld in the steam piping. High-pressure steam roared out into the engine room, scalding vapor parboiling everyone unfortunate enough to be in the compartment. The temperature was driven up to two hundred degrees and the pressure to six atmospheres before the cold sea temperature started to condense it.

The third one hit the screw, blasting it sideways and destroying the shaft. The bent shaft became a one-meter-thick, forty-ton steel snake as it slammed around the engine room, smashing machinery and people. Water roared in through the massive hole the shaft left in the aft end of the doomed submarine.

Vipr was dying, but the Mark 46 that hit the torpedo room was the merciful coup de grâce. It hit torpedo tube number ten, where one of the Viyogas was armed and ready to launch toward *Anzio*. The blast detonated the missile's volatile fuel and its four-hundred-kilogram warhead. The warhead, designed to sink an American aircraft carrier with a single hit, ripped the bow off the submarine.

Those few crewmen still left alive after the initial blasts died as the *Vipr* plowed into the muddy bottom of the Gulf of Finland.

Chapter 43

Joe Glass stared at *Toledo*'s sonar screen. The noise from the Russian torpedoes exploding in the fjord had died down, and now passive sonar was picking up contacts again. The two Russian Grisha frigates were still pinging, still looking for them somewhere astern. Zillich reported that they had now moved away from the knuckle and were resuming a search pattern. They must have realized that they had been nibbling at the wrong bait.

The Udaloy destroyer was still up ahead somewhere, between *Toledo* and the open sea. He was playing it very cagey. Glass couldn't find a trace of the bastard on any of the sonar screens. He was there, though, waiting to spring his deadly trap. A decoy wouldn't fool him this time.

"Captain, tubes one and two ready in all respects," Doug O'Malley announced, his rapid-fire words spilling out even faster than usual. "Mark 48 ADCAPs. Tubes flooded and outer doors open."

Glass nodded and glanced over at the red-haired young lieutenant commander. With Brian Edwards being attended to down in the makeshift emergency room, O'Malley had stepped up to become the fire control co-ordinator. The engineer seemed to be handling the increased pressure well. It would have been better to have him face this predicament in a series of drills, but that was not a luxury they would have. Besides, there was nothing like a baptism by fire to bring out the best in a man. Somehow, looking at the young officer, Glass knew he would do his best. That's all he could ask.

"Very well, Eng. Have tubes three and four flooded and made fully ready."

Toledo could flood all four torpedo tubes at once, but she could only have the outer doors open on two tubes at a time. Normally this was all that was necessary. In most cases, they would have just one of the million-dollar ADCAP fish in the water at any given time. Occasionally, the skipper might shoot a pair, but that was only if the target was large. With two doors open, the team was able to guide both torpedoes, using hair-thin copper wires that trailed out behind the torpedoes. Once the door was shut, the wire was cut, leaving the fish on its own.

With two frigates and a destroyer up there on the surface, any fight today would be a melee. Glass knew he would have to shoot his way out. There would be weapons, ships, and confusion all over the place. An underwater dogfight was no place to worry about checking out torpedoes or flooding tubes.

While he had a few moments to breathe, Glass figured it was a good time to tell his team what he planned. He sucked in a deep breath. "Attention in the attack center. We are going to fight our way out of this fjord. We will engage any hostile surface ship that we encounter. The Udaloy will be the primary target. The Grishas will be secondary targets."

Glass looked over to see Master Chief Zillich in his usual position, leaning out of the sonar room door. He had a determined look on his face as he listened to his skipper with one ear and to his headset with the other.

"Tube one will be the first fired weapon," Glass continued. "Tube two will be the backup. As soon as each weapon is running normally, cut the wire and shut the outer door on the tube."

Pat Durand nodded and spoke into a sound-powered phone. Glass knew that the team down in the torpedo room would be ready to shoot. Ready to reload another ADCAP into the empty tube once the first had been sent on its way.

"If we are fired upon, we will shoot evasion devices from both signal ejectors and evade toward the open sea at flank."

Sam Wallich gave his skipper a thumbs-up. Both ejectors already had evasion devices loaded and he was ready to shoot them on a moment's notice.

"We will stay deep and try to sneak out. Nav, keep me fifty feet off the bottom and snug up against the east flank of the entrance, just like when we snuck into this little rat hole."

Jerry Perez stood hunched over his navigation charts, sweat dripping off his chin and pooling on the Mylar chart cover. He was feeling the pressure but trying his best to hide it. He nodded his understanding.

Glass paused long enough to look around the cramped space. The young faces of his crew looked back at him with grim determination, each man ready for whatever came. He had told them, straight out, what he planned to do. Every man knew the danger that lay ahead. Whatever was about to happen was left up to chance and the fortunes of war.

"Gentlemen, this is what we have been trained to do," Glass said. "Our country is depending on us to do it to the best of our ability. I know you will. Let's go to work!"

Master Chief Tommy Zillich disappeared back into the sonar shack. The rest of the team went back to their tasks, sifting every morsel of information to try to figure out what the Russians were doing. Quiet settled over the control room, the only sound that of the well-oiled hum of a perfectly tuned machine, a professional team hard at work.

Joe Glass sat back on the little flip-down stool behind number-two periscope and stretched his aching back. Standing for endless hours on the hard steel deck never used to bother him. Now it was torture.

Must be getting old, he thought. He smiled. He used to think that Jon Ward was unspeakably old when they were on *Spadefish* together. Now here Glass was, "the old man" on *Toledo*.

Doug O'Malley clamped his hands to the earpiece, trying to hear. His brow was furrowed with concentration. He glanced over at Glass, his eyes reflecting concern. The skipper jumped up and stood next to his fire control coordinator.

"Captain, sonar reports picking up rotor frequencies on the conformal array. Master Chief says it has to be a Helix. Counterrotating."

Glass nodded. The Russian KA-27 Helix helicopter was designed with one task in mind, finding and destroying American nuclear submarines, and it was damned good at its job. A Udaloy destroyer normally carried two of the seagoing bumblebees, and the destroyer stalking *Toledo* had put one of theirs in the air. This was yet another complication in an already devilishly complicated situation.

There was nothing to do but snuggle close to the mud and try to sneak by.

"Thanks, Eng. Plot him and see if he has any pattern we can use," Glass told O'Malley. He looked back at Perez. "Nav, report depth."

"Depth eight-seven-five," Perez answered. "Water depth nine-two-five feet."

They were as close to the bottom of the fjord as Glass dared to get. Any noise *Toledo* made would hopefully be absorbed and scattered by the mud below them.

Sam Wallich read Glass's thoughts.

"Skipper, all stations rigged for ultraquiet," he reported. "Even a fish couldn't find us."

Nobody breathed, as if even that might give them away. The Helix chopper circled above, his trace now showing up plainly on the narrowband display. Glass expected to hear Zillich cry out a warning any second that there was an incoming torpedo in the water.

The room was quiet, though.

Waiting was the hardest part. The uncertainty and dread built to an unbearable level. Glass stood there in the center of the control room, trying not to let the helplessness overwhelm him. Sweat dripped down the back of his neck and soaked through his poopie suit. His mouth felt as if someone had stuffed it with an old sock.

They had done all they could do. They could only wait.

He reached for his cup of coffee, but his hand shook so badly that he thought better of it. He glanced around. No one had seen his hand shaking. They were all lost in their own tasks, dealing with their fears as best they could.

The *Toledo* inched forward, each turn of the screw bringing them a little closer to freedom. It also brought them a little closer to the warship that was guarding the way out of this mess.

They noticed the change on the display. The circling Helix gradually fell astern. They were leaving it behind.

Maybe they would make it out of here after all. Still, the steep granite walls of the fjord closed in around the sub, giving them even less room to hide from the determined Russians.

O'Malley's shout shattered the hopeful silence in the control room.

"Skipper, the Grishas are picking up speed. Master Chief reports they are both closing." Glass started to answer, but the engineer held up one hand. He pressed the earpiece to his head with the other. His voice increased in pitch as he said, "Contact on the Udaloy. Bearing zero-three-one. Heavy screw beat. He's coming fast!"

The frigates were coming up behind them and they had just picked up the first hint of the destroyer out in front. Looked as if he was charging in for the kill.

As if to punctuate the engineer's report, the threat receiver screamed an alarm. Glass, startled, jumped, and turned to read the alarm. The red LEDs flashed a received frequency of 4.5 kilohertz and a signal strength of sixty-nine.

The Udaloy destroyer's Horse Jaw active sonar had them nailed. Just as Glass had feared, the bastard was waiting at the gate again. He had used the Grishas to herd *Toledo* toward him and the Helix to warn him when they were about to step into the trap. If the American submarine somehow slipped out of the noose, he would send up his other Helix and place it just outside the entrance to the fjord to make sure *Toledo* didn't get away.

Glass had to grudgingly admit it. The SOB was clever. He knew his business.

There was no time to ponder the situation any longer. It was time to act. If they were going to shoot their way out, they had better get to shooting.

"Snapshot! Tube one on the Udaloy!" Glass barked.

Doug O'Malley spun in the best solution he could pull out of the air. The fire control system had to tell the ADCAP torpedo where it should start looking, even if it was little more than a guess. There wasn't any time to get better information. Within ten seconds, O'Malley called out, "Solution ready!"

"Ship ready!" Jerry Perez yelled.

At the same instant, Pat Durand shouted, "Weapon ready!"

Twenty seconds had elapsed since Glass had ordered that tube one be used against the Russian destroyer.

"Shoot on generated bearings!" Joe Glass ordered.

Pat Durand punched the launch button for number-one torpedo tube on the CCS Mark II launch panel. The whoosh-thump of high-pressure air from down in the torpedo room confirmed that the ejection pump was flushing the four-thousand-pound ADCAP torpedo out the tube.

The battle was on.

"Tube one fired," Durand called out. "ADCAP running normally in pre-enable."

"ADCAP running normally in high speed," Zillich confirmed from sonar.

Reports tumbled on top of each other as the team moved.

"Incoming weapon in the water!" Zillich yelled out. "Bearing three-five-five. Second weapon bearing three-four-seven."

Someone, probably the destroyer, was shooting back at them. Shooting two torpedoes. Anticipated or not, that news was still chilling to all who heard it.

"Ahead flank!" Glass ordered. "Launch the evasion devices."

Toledo jumped ahead as the throttle man yanked open the ahead throttles. The sub shuddered as the reactor operator shifted the huge coolant pumps to fast speed, pushing massive amounts of water through the reactor core. The main engines needed every erg of energy to drive the sub ahead.

The evasion devices tumbled wildly in *Toledo*'s wake as they emitted a wall of spurious noise. It was precious little protection, but the noise might throw a little confusion at the torpedos heading their way.

"Incoming weapons bearing three-five-five and three-four-nine! Both active!"

If they were going to go down in these frigid waters,

so far from home, Joe Glass was fiercely determined to go down fighting.

"Snapshot on the closest Grisha. Tube two," he called out.

O'Malley updated the solution on the frigate.

"Solution ready," he reported.

Durand was on his heels. "Weapon ready!"

"Shoot on generated bearings," Joe Glass ordered. Again the roar of high-pressure air signaled an ADCAP torpedo on its way. "Cut the wires and close the outer doors, tubes one and two. Open the outer doors, tubes three and four."

Zillich's voice boomed again over the announcing circuit. "Incoming weapons bearing three-five-five and three-five-zero. Own ship's first fired weapon in active search."

The two enemy torpedoes were out ahead of them and coming fast. One of them was on a zero bearing rate. It was driving directly at them. The first ADCAP torpedo fired by *Toledo* was out there now, and it was actively searching for its target. The twenty-kilohertz active sonar and advanced computer controls on board the ADCAP would find and destroy any target it found in a large patch of water.

"Skipper, both signal ejectors are reloaded and ready," Wallich yelled.

"Shoot both signal ejectors. Reload and shoot again," Glass shot back. "I want as much noise in the water as we can make!"

Toledo was still going all out, making a run for the open sea. In the confines of the narrow fjord, there wasn't any room for error. At this speed, the slightest twitch would result in seven thousand tons of racing steel slamming into the unyielding granite wall of the waterway. The crew would have the barest instant to register what had happened before the frigid Barents filled their tomb with tons of seawater.

"Incoming weapons bearing three-five-five and three-five-two. Both still active. Own ship second fired weapon in active search."

The race was still on. The second ADCAP they shot was awake and looking for something to annihilate.

"Tubes three and four ready in all respects," Pat Durand called out. "Reloading tubes one and two."

The lights on the fire control panel blinked on. They showed that the outer doors for tubes three and four were open. Glass had two more torpedoes to use. They wouldn't do anybody any good sitting there in their tubes.

"Snapshot, tube three on the second Grisha, then tube four on the Udaloy."

"Solution ready on the Grisha. Solution ready on the Udaloy."

"Two more incoming weapons," Zillich sang out with just the hint of a tremble in his voice. "Coming from astern. Best bearings two-six-zero and two-seven-zero. Both in active search."

Jesus! The problem had just gotten markedly more complicated. One of the frigates had sent two torpedos spinning their way as well. The narrow fjord was now filled with hurtling underwater ordnance.

"Weapons ready, tube three assigned to the Grisha. Tube four to the Udaloy."

"Shoot tube three first, then tube four."

Durand punched the launch button for tube three. Its weapon was still roaring down the tube when he punched the button for tube four. Two more fish were on their way.

"Incoming weapons bearing three-five-five and three-five-seven. One is range-gating."

Both of the torpedoes from the destroyer were still out there and one of them had caught a good scent of its intended target. Its electronic brain had found *Toledo* and shifted its sonar to home in on the sub.

"Depth to the bottom?" Glass asked.

"Depth five-zero feet under the keel," Jerry Perez answered.

"Bring me down to ten feet. Do it quick!"

Perez gulped. "But, Captain—"

"Now!"

"Yes, sir."

Toledo charged ahead, speeding along just above the muddy bottom, her screw churning up great clouds of sediment behind the racing submarine. The debris presented the Russian torpedo with a huge target. It shifted its steering vanes slightly to attack the new, larger, more inviting objective.

The second torpedo found the same enticing target. They both zoomed in for the kill.

The near simultaneous explosions erupted on the floor of the fjord just aft of the sub. The detonations shook *Toledo* violently.

As soon as the reverberations stopped, Glass picked himself up off the deck and shook his head to clear it. He expected to hear the roar of water under the crushing pressure of the depth or the reports from watchstanders telling him of a dying ship. Instead he saw his crew also climbing back to their positions, shaking off the blow. Incredibly, they were still alive and fighting.

Then his stomach sank. Their forward speed was dropping down in a hurry.

"Reactor scram. Loss of both turbine generators," the engineering officer of the watch, the officer in charge of operating the reactor plant, reported, right on cue.

The explosions had caused the reactor's control rods to drop to the bottom of the core, quenching its nuclear reaction. The turbine generators, the source of the sub's electrical power, were also off-line. That could have been from the scram, or from some other damage. There was no way for anyone to tell yet.

All Glass knew for certain was that *Toledo*'s run for freedom had been stopped in its tracks. The main engines were useless without steam from the reactor to drive them. The battery could give them a little power and the emergency propulsion motor could push the boat for a few minutes, but at a slow creep.

"Still hold two incoming weapons in active. Bearing two-six-five. Both weapons on the same bearing." Sonar was still working and Master Chief Zillich was on the job, reminding them there were still two Russian torpedoes playing around out there, looking for them. "Udaloy coming up in speed. Own ship weapon on that bearing is in reattack."

In addition to the two remaining Russian torpedoes that were still racing at them, there were four of *Toledo*'s fish heading out toward the Russian surface ships. Glass still needed a way to defeat the incoming weapons. He couldn't outrun them now without the reactor.

He had a thought. Jon Ward had taught him a trick years before on a *Spadefish* training mission when the "enemy" seemed to be coming at them from all angles.

"All stop," he ordered. "Hover at nine-one-zero feet."

Doug O'Malley looked at his skipper, a quizzical expression on his face. Jerry Perez appeared to be on the verge of a stroke. Glass smiled.

"Relax, gentlemen. Those fish out there are looking for a moving target. We're going to do our best impression of a rock on the bottom." He looked over at the ballast control panel and saw that the signal ejectors were reloaded and ready to go again. "Master Chief, shoot both signal ejectors."

The two evasion devices floated upward, enveloping *Toledo* in a shower of noise.

"Incoming weapons bearing two-six-five, still active."

Glass listened to the report, but his mind was elsewhere. He needed to get the reactor back so they could fight on. He grabbed the 7MC microphone. "Maneuvering, Captain. Report cause of scram and status of recovery."

"Captain, Engineering Officer of the Watch," the 7MC blared back. "Commencing fast recovery start-up. Scram was caused by the shock from the explosion. Popped open a scram breaker. Starboard turbine generator will be available when the reactor is back online. Port turbine generator is out of commission until the output breaker is replaced."

Not as bad as Glass had expected. The reactor would

be critical, making power again in a couple of minutes. One of the turbine generators would be available to make electricity, but the other one would not be available until the electricians could repair the breaker. At least the main engines weren't affected. *Toledo* could still run at sixty percent of her flank speed.

Still, for right now, sitting here was the best plan.

"Incoming weapons still bearing two-six-five. Still in active search."

Zillich was tracking the Russian torpedoes' relentless run directly at them. Thankfully, the underwater bloodhounds were still sniffing around. They had not locked on to the sub. At least not yet.

A sudden loud explosion hammered the hull. It was not as bad as the torpedoes a few minutes before. Still, it was hard enough to kick more dust out of the overhead.

Glass looked at the sonar traces. Both incoming weapons were still there. So were the Russian ships. It had to have been one of *Toledo*'s weapons.

Zillich answered Glass's unspoken question, and it was not what Captain Glass wanted to hear.

"Explosion on the bearing to the Udaloy. Looks like our first shots went past him and hit the cliffs on the other side."

"Damn! What about the others?"

Zillich held up his hand and said, "Just a second, Skipper. Inbound weapons passing overhead. Still in active search."

Everyone in the control room could hear the high-pitched whine of the Russian torpedoes. They grew louder for a moment. Then they started to fade.

"Best bearing to the Russian torpedoes zero-eight-two. Torpedoes opening."

The shots had missed! The tension in the tiny space eased just a bit. They would live for a few more minutes, at least.

Somehow, the Russian torpedoes had failed to sniff out *Toledo* where she sat, just above the bottom.

A second loud explosion rocked the sub. Everyone braced himself, then looked around, wondering what it had been. This time it came from the south.

"Loud explosion on the bearing of the first Grisha," Zillich called out. There was a grin in his voice when he said, "Breaking-up noises on that bearing. Looks like we got one of them."

"Detect! Detect! Acquisition!" Pat Durand yelled out. "Third fired weapon acquired on the Udaloy."

Durand watched the computer screen on the weapon control panel as it graphically played out a dance of death from the wire-guided torpedo. The ADCAP torpedo that *Toledo* had sent toward the Russian destroyer at the mouth of the fjord unerringly homed in on the ship. Its sonar shifted from "search" to "attack" mode as the Otto-fueled rocker-plate engine came up to maximum speed. With the torpedo charging toward it at sixty-five knots, the *Admiral Chabanenko* was helpless to escape.

The deadly weapon nosed up until it was running just twenty-five feet below the waves. An upward-looking hydrophone began pinging, searching for a ship as it passed underneath. The magnetic influence exploder sensed a mass of steel overhead just as the upward-looking hydrophone received its sonar returns. The firing circuit was satisfied that the torpedo was under the *Admiral Cha-banenko*. An electric jolt shot through the firing squib, detonating the small squib, which, in turn, detonated the warhead.

Six hundred and fifty pounds of PBNX high explosive created a huge superheated gas bubble beneath the help-less destroyer, brutally ramming the center of the ship skyward. Just as quickly as it formed, the gas bubble col-lapsed, dropping the center of the destroyer into a huge hole in the surface of the fjord.

Even the strongest steel and heaviest construction would have been helpless against the massive forces gen-erated by the mighty explosion. The *Admiral Cha-banenko* broke in half, torn apart by the heaving, twisting forces beneath it.

In less than a minute, the remnants of the warship slipped beneath the waves.

Chapter 44

Admiral Tom Donnegan stepped into the wood-paneled conference room, his hat in his hand. He had been in this place several times before, yet he was still struck with awe each time he entered—and Tom Donnegan was not easily awestruck.

If it had not been for the pair of Marine guards at the door, the room could have been some corporate boardroom in a high-rise on Wall Street. Instead, he was deep in the third basement under the West Wing of the White House.

Donnegan knew most of the people seated around the large walnut conference table. The secretary of defense and the joint chiefs sat to the left of an empty center chair. The national security adviser was whispering something to the president's chief of staff to the right of the empty seat. The rest of the country's key decision-makers for military action and intelligence were arrayed around the room. They either talked quietly with each other or studied papers that had been placed before them.

There was an ominous buzz in the room. The events of the past few weeks had come to a head. Everyone knew that's why he was here.

Donnegan noticed a short, white-haired gentleman,

dressed in a gray pin-striped suit, nervously standing all alone at the far end of the table. That must be Alstair McLain, he thought, the guy who made the rules for the stock markets. He was shorter and heavier than he appeared to be in his newspaper photographs. Donnegan could not imagine why McLain would be called to this particular meeting.

The wall behind McLain was covered with a reverse-projection situation board. A large, finely detailed map of western Russia filled the majority of the screen. It looked very similar to the one the admiral kept in the Naval Intelligence Command Center, but this was even more comprehensive.

Donnegan was still acknowledging greetings from those who had noticed him enter the room when President Adolphus Brown strode briskly through the door behind him. All those gathered together in the room rose. They sat back down after the president had taken his chair at the center of the far side of the table.

Dr. Samuel Kinnowitz, President Brown's bespectacled national security adviser, started the discussion by clearing his throat and pointedly closing the dossier before him.

"Mr. President, gentlemen. We appear to have a problem." A former Stanford law professor, the NSA treated every briefing like a classroom lecture. He looked at the group around the big table over the tops of his glasses and rubbed his chin. He seemed to be considering whether or not to give a pop quiz. "It appears that the Russian government has entered a period of serious and tumultuous upheaval. You have all seen the interview with Admiral Durov, I am sure. He is not only assuming the reins of government of his country by using military force, but he is also accusing the United States of sinking two Russian submarines, and also of kidnapping President Smitrov, precipitating this whole crisis. He is, in effect, blaming his coup on us. We . . . those of us in this room . . . know what has truly taken place. We also know that our operatives near the submarine base have images of Durov's troops kidnapping the president. So far as we know, those Navy SEALs somehow managed to get Smitrov away from Durov's people and were attempting to rendezvous with one of Admiral Donnegan's submarines . . . the *Toledo* . . . somewhere in the Murmansk Fjord. The plan was to use a mini-submarine to extract them. That is, I'm afraid, about all we do know. We do not know if President Smitrov is dead or alive. We do not know if the SEALs were able to escape. We have satellite evidence that they used a Russian troop carrier to attempt an escape from Polyarnyy, but that carrier was destroyed by Russian fire. There is every chance that everyone . . . the SEALs, the Russian president . . . were all killed in that attack and the photo evidence of the kidnapping of President Smitrov was destroyed as well. If that is the case, to the rest of the world, all evidence would now point to Admiral Durov being accurate in his charges against us. In short, gentlemen, we have one royal mess up there!" Kinnowitz turned to look at Admiral Donnegan. He stared at him for a full fifteen seconds before he spoke again. "Tom, what have you heard from your assets up there? Please give us some positive news."

Tom Donnegan rose, but he turned to address his

comments to President Brown. "Mr. President, we don't have any new communications since just before the SEAL team went into the Polyarnyy base to attempt to rescue Smitrov. Dr. Kinnowitz is correct. We did see pictures of the troop carrier they apparently used to escape, and it was in flames. We also have not heard from *Toledo* since before it entered the Murmansk Fjord to recover the swimmer delivery vehicle. We do have a development, though. The latest imagery is showing a good deal of activity from warships in the Murmansk Fjord. We think they are hunting for the mini-sub and for *Toledo*. As we heard in his speech, Durov is claiming they have been destroyed already. Personally, I don't believe a damn word of it. I would prefer to assume they are okay, that they are still fighting for their lives, until we have something more solid than Durov's boasting. I know *Toledo*'s skipper. If there is a way . . ."

President Brown stopped him with a frown. "Tom, that's not a lot to go on. When will you have something more definite for us?"

"Not until *Toledo* is clear of the fjord and comes up to communicate. If she's still alive, she can hardly come up to give us the news headlines when she's busy dodging torpedoes down there."

The president was displeased with the answer. He was being blatantly accused by a crazed military zealot of initiating acts of war and ordering the kidnapping of a head of state. He was being made the fall guy for a coup in Russia. Members of the opposition party were vilifying him at that very moment on the floor of the Senate for his mishandling of the crisis. The president did not want to be told he would have to wait still longer for an answer. He gritted his teeth when he spoke again.

"I assume you don't have any idea where those other Russian subs have gone to, either?"

"Sir, we know where one of them is. We have been tailing it all the way into the Gulf of Finland. The other four headed out of the Murmansk Fjord and down into the White Sea. Sir, we don't have any assets up there to track them." He wanted to editorialize a bit, to remind the president that it was Congress's heavy-handed pork-barrel approach to military spending that left them with so few boats to do this job, but he held back. This was neither the place nor the time. "Those Akulas haven't shown up on any imagery or communications intercepts since then. However, I expect that Durov's reference to the *Kronstadt* incident was a thinly veiled threat to use them in some way."

"What way?" Brown asked, puzzled.

"My best guess—and it is only a guess—is that he has loaded up those boats with cruise missiles. He will lob a few into Russia somewhere and negotiate with the survivors."

Brown's already pale face turned ashen. The others around the table stopped breathing.

"Survivors? What are you saying, Tom? You don't think he would take this nuclear, do you?"

Donnegan looked the president in the eye. He did not hesitate when he answered the question. "It is very possible, Mr. President. The Russians have two types of operational submarine-launched cruise missiles. The SS-N-21 Granat has been around for a couple of decades. It has a two-hundred-kiloton nuclear warhead. We know from our intel that they have a lot of those birds still available if they wanted to use them. Up until now, they didn't have the boats to deliver them close enough to anywhere to shoot them. These new Akulas would have the ability to do that."

"You said they have two types," Kinnowitz said.

"Yes. The other choice is the SS-N-27 Alpha. It's still in development. They are nonnuclear, but they are a whole lot more accurate than the Granat. As I say, they're new, but we do think that they have a few test birds. Some of those may be aboard those submarines. They would use them if they wanted to hit precise targets in an effort to make a statement."

Kinnowitz sat down hard and slapped the table in front of him. "The bastard could make quite a statement with a mushroom cloud over St. Petersburg. Or by putting one of the Alphas right into the ear of Smitrov's second in command."

"Or both," Tom Donnegan added.

"Which missiles do you believe the Russian subs are carrying?" President Brown asked.

"We don't know and there is no way for us to tell. Not until they detonate, that is. The airframes of both missiles are identical, so even if we got a picture of one of them in the air, we couldn't tell if it was a nuke or not."

Adolphus Brown looked stricken, as if he was having trouble breathing. The room fell deathly quiet. Dr. Kinnowitz broke the strained silence.

"So we must wait until we hear from *Toledo*. Or until Durov produces corpses." The NSA pointedly ignored

Tom Donnegan's hard look as the admiral eased back down into his chair. Kinnowitz opened another folder in front of him and was clearly changing subjects. "Now, there are other matters. Matters about which we do have considerably more information, thank God. They appear to be related directly. Mr. President, Alstair McLain from the Securities and Exchange Commission will go over the details."

McLain rose and cleared his throat. Every eye was on the man. Others in the room had the same curiosity about his presence at the meeting as Donnegan had. McLain dropped his bomb with a true flair for the dramatic.

"Mr. President, we have reason to believe that the Russian mob has penetrated the United States financial markets and has made a concerted effort to disrupt the stock markets."

The intake of breath around the table was audible. The president stared at McLain in disbelief. "What? Are you sure? Where's the proof?"

McLain retreated a step. There was a defensive tone in his voice when he answered. He was not accustomed to receiving a frontal assault from the most powerful man on the planet. "One of my best people, under my direction, uncovered the plot. The Russians buried code in the new OptiMarx computer software system, the one that was designed to handle all trading on the Exchange. We now have one of the Russians who worked for Opti-Marx in custody and he has proven to be quite cooperative, in exchange for us guaranteeing him safety from his countrymen. By the way, there appears to have also been a second unrelated criminal compromise of the system as well. The OptiMarx chief technology officer is singing like a bird as well on that score. The system is now off-line and we seem to have everything under control once again, operating under the old trading system, until the bad code can be expunged and the system verified by my agents."

"The Russian Mafia?" Brown asked wearily. He now seemed to be having difficulty fathoming it all.

"Yes, Mr. President. It appears that, while the Mafia was behind this, it was done with the complete knowledge and approval of our old friend Admiral Durov."

Brown turned and looked at Dr. Kinnowitz. A deep furrow creased his brow.

"Sam, what do you make of this?" he asked.

The national security adviser took a drink of water, buying time to formulate his thoughts before he spoke. "Although the mob obviously wanted to make money, I'd say from Durov's perspective it was primarily a diversionary attack. They knew that by having this happen, at the same time the whole world was accusing us of blowing up Russian submarines, it would be much easier for Durov to seize control and solidify it before anyone noticed. Worldwide financial panic seems to have a way of—"

Before Samuel Kinnowitz could continue, a White House communications officer, a Navy lieutenant, burst through the door and into the situation room. His eyes were wide, his face flushed.

"Mr. President! Pardon the interruption, sir. We are receiving an OPREP-Three Pinnacle Nucflash! One of our boats in the Baltic is reporting that a Russian submarine has launched a cruise missile. Launched it toward Russia!"

"Shit! It's started!" Tom Donnegan was startled to hear his own excited voice in the stunned-quiet room. "Anything more, Lieutenant?"

"Only that the message is from some guy named Ward on the *Anzio*."

"Mr. President, we'd better warn the Russians," Kinnowitz said. "Make sure they know it isn't one of ours."

President Brown was already reaching for the red phone, strategically placed inches from his right hand.

The room broke into pandemonium. The men gathered here were charged with defending the nation. They knew the urgency to take immediate action. All the phones in the room were attacked as they tried to get their staffs to work.

Amid the noise and chaos, President Brown did his best to give the message to the high-ranking Russian who answered the crisis phone on the other end of the line. He had to try to convince the man that the impossible was happening, that there was a missile racing at his country at that very moment. And that it was a Russian missile.

The communications officer raced back into the room again. The man was sweating heavily. No one was paying him any attention until he yelled at the top of his voice. The room fell silent.

"I have voice comms with the *Toledo*! President Smitrov wants to talk to President Brown!"

The Russian SS-N-27 missile raced across the Gulf of Finland, twenty meters above the gray seas. At Mach

0.85, the missile reached a point above the brown sand beach a few miles south and west of the old Czarist capital of St. Petersburg ten minutes after it was launched from *Vipr*.

Inside the missile's computer brain, a correction to the course was made. The silver bird rolled slightly as it turned southwest, away from St. Petersburg. The leafless birch forests were a trackless blur below as it raced on toward its predetermined target.

The Alpha followed the contour of the land as it climbed from the low-lying coastal forests to the wooded hills in the south of the Leningrad Oblast. The smokestacks of Novogrod flashed by to the east. The missile flight control algorithm continuously updated its position, courtesy of the American GPS. It made minor corrections as it continued to follow the flight plan that had been programmed into its electronic brain.

The Volga River passed under the deadly bird and then the Moskva River appeared below. After checking its position, the Alpha obediently spun around to follow the Moskva toward the heart of Moscow. As it raced down the waterway, the missile climbed and increased speed until it was roaring toward its target at Mach 0.95, five hundred meters above the cold, snow-covered ground.

Boris Medikov slammed the phone down in disgust. The call had been from his niece in America, Marina Nosovitskaya, and her news was the worst he could have anticipated. She reported Dmitri Ustinov's capture by the FBI, the loss of the OptiMarx operation. She had also been unable to communicate with her "uncles." There was news on the TV of an FBI operation that involved the deaths of two Russian nationals in a gunfight. She was afraid it was Vujnovich and one of the others. She was on the run and would be out of contact while she went into hiding.

Unbelievable! All that work, all the time and money invested in the scheme, and it was busted!

It was all because that idiot Durov insisted that they put the plan in motion before it was ready. The senile old admiral had cost him millions of dollars and several of his best men. All so the old martinet could strut around in his silly uniform and give orders to his adoring submarine sailor boys.

In his anger and confusion, Medikov did not know how he would do it, but someday, some way, he would make the crazy old man pay for this.

He flung his glass against the far wall and then stomped across the large living room to the bar. He needed to get control of his temper. Weighty decisions were best made when rational, not in the heat of a crimson rage.

He sloshed some cognac into another one of the crystal snifters as he contemplated which of his operatives could best be assigned the task of eliminating Durov before he went any further.

He took a large gulp and felt the comforting burn as it went down his throat. That's when the idea hit him. It was so obvious.

It had been decades since Medikov had bloodied his own hands. It had been all business in those days. Murder allowed him to advance his control of the organization. Since then, it had been more appropriate for him to have others do his gory work for him, distancing himself from the act and better serving his masquerade as a legitimate businessman.

No one was better equipped than he for this murder, though.

He would confront Durov. He would explain to the megalomaniac how his irrational lust for power had cost them all so dearly.

Once that had been done, he would kill Alexander Durov with his own two hands.

Satisfied he had arrived at the perfect solution, Boris Medikov turned to stare out the picture window at the Moscow skyline. He felt better already, the calm returning to his mind as he considered the snowy tableau out his window. The city seemed especially alive this bright, cold morning. The sky was unusually clear.

One of the advantages of the penthouse apartment, atop the Mezhdunarodnaya Hotel, was the striking view. He had often relied on this scene in times of crisis to relax him as he considered the steps necessary to solve a difficult problem.

A small flicker of movement across the sky caught his attention.

He looked up just in time to see the moving object take the shape of a silver-gray missile. It was racing directly at him.

The mobster did not have time to duck. He could only stand transfixed for the half second it took the missile to fill the entire sky.

Somewhere in the room a phone was ringing.

The last thought to pass through Boris Medikov's mind was that it was Admiral Alexander Durov calling.

Calling to claim victory in this final skirmish.

President Gregor Smitrov lay on the wardroom table on board the *Toledo*, drifting in and out of consciousness. The slight pitching and rolling of the deck indicated to him that the submarine must be at periscope depth somewhere in the winter waters of the Barents Sea. Doc Halliday confirmed it while fussing with his patient's dressings.

Smitrov dimly remembered hearing the explosions, feeling the boat shaking furiously at some time in his stupor. He expected to awaken to feel the cold inrushing of seawater.

They must have survived. They were surfacing. That meant that his Navy had lost the battle in the fjord. He had never been so joyous over a defeat.

The IV was still dripping saline into his veins as Smitrov took the radiotelephone handset from the American sailor and clutched it to his ear. His voice was weak and it cracked as he spoke. Each utterance taxed him to the maximum. The muscles under his pallid skin tensed in pain with every move. Everything depended on him being able to talk for a few minutes more.

The man fought with all his willpower to stay alert, to overcome the drowsiness from the painkiller he had been given. He had to remember the proper authenticators and code words. He had to be able to prove he was who he said he was, despite the raspy, weak voice. He had to be able to convince those to whom he talked that he had not been drugged or that he might be delirious from his wounds. The fate of his country, even of the world, depended on him staying lucid just a little longer.

Doc Halliday watched his patient. He threw an occasional disapproving glare at Joe Glass.

Glass shrugged. There was nothing he could do. There was too much at stake right now. They all knew that Smitrov had to take command of his armed forces and stymie Durov before the rogue admiral gained even more power. The longer Smitrov waited, the more time Durov had to consolidate his power base and coerce others to join him.

The first communication was to the United States. President Brown related the missile launch and the reaction in Moscow. Smitrov formally requested the Americans provide him with assistance in the battle against Durov and his supporters. After a few minutes' hurried conversation, the two leaders broke away. Each had plenty to do.

"Captain, is it possible to please shift frequencies now so that I may speak with my Security Council?"

Toledo's radios were reconfigured so that Smitrov could be placed in direct communication with the Russian government committee responsible for the nation's defense. When President Smitrov reached the council, they were already meeting in emergency session in a hardened underground bunker, buried under tons of rock and concrete on the outer perimeter of Sheremetyevo Airport. The complex was built to withstand the full might of a total nuclear war and support the Russian government for an extended period. Although rarely used after the fall of the Soviet Union, it was still maintained and was fully operational. The council meeting room could have been one of the ornate chambers in the Kremlin, all gold gilt, red velvet draperies, and mirror-polished marble floors. Only the whisper of filtered air wafting through the space and the concrete walls behind the drapes gave away the location.

At the first word from the United States about the threatening missile attack, the Security Council and the rest of the senior government officials had boarded a special high-speed subway train for the quick trip here. The subway had only two stops, the Kremlin and this bunker. It, too, was a relic of the Cold War, but had also come in quite handy on this historic day.

Just minutes before Smitrov's call, the council had heard confirmation that the missile had hit the upper floors of the Mezhdunarodnaya Hotel. The old pile of cement was heavily damaged and there were casualties. Fires were raging on several floors and the building was in danger of collapse. No one could imagine why the hotel had been the missile's target. Several speculated there might have been an error in the bird's navigation computer, that it was aimed at the Kremlin. Thankfully, the missile was nonnuclear and the hotel was the only building damaged. There had been a collective sigh of relief as the Russian high command realized they had been spared a nuclear holocaust. Though they still held their breath, this attack appeared to have been the only missile launched so far.

Gregor Smitrov's voice crackled through the speaker at the head of the huge conference table. The amplification filtered out much of the weakness in the president's voice. His tone was all action.

Smitrov gave the command to place his armed forces on full alert and dispatched all the antisubmarine forces he could muster into the White Sea. A submarine, even one of Durov's sparkling new Akulas, would have a tough time staying hidden from them for long in that tiny, enclosed sea.

Army divisions, known to be loyal, were swung into place to blockade Murmansk and Polyarnyy. The problem was the immense distances involved and the primitive transportation into the area. By the time the Army had surrounded the trouble spot, anyone inside would have more than ample time to escape.

At the president's order, the director of the Federal'naya Sluzhba Kontrrazvedky swung into action. The FSB was the successor to the KGB for internal security matters and had inherited its reputation for ruthlessness. The director ordered borders, both internal and external, to be slammed shut. Transportation and communications would grind to a halt. Nobody would be able to move without the correct papers, and then only under close scrutiny.

More than one man in the bunker thought how ironic it was that the old ways threatened to be returned. Several vowed out loud it would be temporary, until this crisis could be quelled.

Smitrov told them of his kidnapping by Durov's troops, of his rescue by the Americans. He promised that he would return to Moscow as quickly as he could. He didn't have to tell them why it was so necessary. Even if he successfully thwarted Durov, someone else with an equal appetite for power would step in to fill the vacuum unless he was back at the helm of state, strong and secure.

Smitrov dropped the handset the second he completed his talk with the council. He did not have enough strength to hold it any longer. He closed his eyes for a moment as he lay back.

"Is Captain Glass still here?" he asked.

"I am here, Mr. President."

"Captain, please take me to Pechenga," he said to Glass.

"Where?"

"Pechenga. It is a mining and fishing town on the Norwegian border. I visited there with my father when I was a boy. It is far enough away from Murmansk that it is unlikely Durov would be able to do anything there. They have a hospital and an airfield so I can more quickly return to Moscow."

Glass looked at the chart. Sure enough, there was Pechenga, at the head of the Pechenga Fjord. It appeared to be a hundred miles from *Toledo*'s current location in the Barents Sea. They could be there in four hours, easily.

Glass stood and turned to leave the wardroom. Smitrov reached out and took his hand as he walked past. His grip was surprisingly strong. "Thank you, Captain. You have done much to help save my country."

Glass didn't quite know what to say. He looked down for a moment. "Let's just pray this all works out. Now you get some rest while we get you to Pechenga."

Smitrov closed his eyes again as Glass left the wardroom. He was asleep in a few seconds.

Chapter 45

Alexander Durov listened to each stroke as the old clock chimed the hour. It was time at last. After all his years of planning, working, and scheming, the time to strike had come. It was not the perfect scenario, the way he had envisioned it all this time. That was always the nature of war. That's why contingency plans were drawn and factored into the equation. It was going to work just fine, now that he had shown the traitors that he had the ability to turn them into dust if they did not cooperate.

He glanced around the command center to locate his aide. He found Vasiliy Zhurkov hunched over a communications console, discussing some problem with a young officer who was seated there.

"Vasiliy, it is time," the old admiral growled. "Please stop whatever you are fooling with and connect me with the Security Council on the secure line."

Zhurkov rose, stood erect for a moment, and turned toward Durov, as if he dreaded facing him with the news he bore. There was a questioning, concerned look on Zhurkov's brow.

"Admiral, we are receiving reports that only one missile hit its target in Moscow," he reported. "The only damage report we have is a fire in the Mezhdunarodnaya

Hotel. Something is seriously wrong. There should be a complete salvo . . . all rockets launched from the *Vipr* by now. And, sir, we have not been able to establish contact with *Vipr* to get a report."

Durov stepped back and almost stumbled. He was shocked by the report. He reached out and braced himself against the edge of the desk, drawing strength from the solid feel of it.

This was bad news. Very bad. The attack from the *Vipr* was key to striking fear into the hearts of those spineless lackeys pretending to rule the *Rodina*. The first salvo was meant to take out the *Duma*, the Lubyanka Square headquarters of the FSB, and the Ministry of Defense Building. They might manage to pull themselves together without such a demoralizing show of force. The strike against Medikov was an afterthought, a nice touch, since there was a spare missile.

The old admiral gathered his thoughts for a moment. Even with this letdown, his years of meticulous planning had provided for just such a contingency. He had accounted for every eventuality. Even this seemingly impossible one. The plan would not come together as easily as he had thought and it was much riskier, but all was not lost.

He shook his head to clear the spiderwebs that had crept into his vision.

"Vasiliy, place the call to the Security Council," he ordered, his voice strong and sure. "I will speak with them now."

Young Zhurkov found the Security Council in their underground command center. Durov took the phone from his aide and began dictating terms.

"By now you have felt the first minor sting of my forces. You are now aware that the peoples' Navy can reach into the heart of the motherland." There was silence on the other end of the telephone line. He lowered his voice an octave. "I am sure that you are familiar with the history of our great country. Just like the brave sailors of the *Kronstadt*, my sailors will defend the *Rodina* with the last drop of their blood. Their missiles can reach much farther than the *Kronstadt* cannons. They are far, far more deadly as well. Gentlemen, my patience is growing thin. You continue to deny the inevitable. You insist on negotiating with the aggressors who have attacked our country and kidnapped our president. Listen to me. You will turn over control of all government functions immediately." Durov paused to savor the moment of triumph. He listened to the hollow echo down the phone line of those words he had heard so many times in his dreams. "If you hesitate, the next strike will be much more than a pinprick. Gentlemen, you have four hours to do as your new leader has commanded. After that, you will become instantly irrelevant."

Without another word, Admiral Alexander Durov slammed down the telephone.

The USS *Toledo* plowed through heavy seas as she ran toward the town of Pechenga, hard on the Norwegian-Russian border. It would have been a faster, more comfortable trip if the submarine could have stayed submerged, back in the calm depths. Their very important passenger, though, needed to be in constant communications with key members of his government. That meant a rough ride on the surface of the winter Barents Sea. It was the only way to keep the BRA-34 antennas up out of the water and still make reasonable speed.

Joe Glass sat in the wardroom-cum–hospital ward where Gregor Smitrov still lay. The Russian president was strapped to the wardroom table so he wouldn't roll off during the rough ride. Smitrov was making a valiant attempt to stay awake, to not allow the pain medicine he was being given to cause him to lose control of the situation. Doc Halliday hovered over his patient, trying to convince him that he needed to rest. So far, Smitrov was ignoring the medic.

The radiotelephone crackled and came to life. Smitrov reached out and pulled the handset to his ear. The conversation was conducted in Russian and took a good deal of time. Glass was able to catch portions of it. He heard "Durov" and "Polyarnyy" mentioned several times in the rapid-fire exchange.

Finally Smitrov dropped the handset to the table, eased back onto the pillow, and closed his eyes. For a moment, Joe Glass thought the man had lost consciousness. Then he turned and looked up at Glass.

"Captain, once again I must ask for your assistance," he whispered weakly. "Admiral Durov has threatened more attacks if the reins of power are not surrendered to him within four hours." Smitrov paused and breathed deeply, as if dreading what he was about to say. "I fear his next attack from the submarines in the White Sea will use nuclear weapons. Even with our best antisubmarine search assets, it is not possible to find those submarines in time to prevent such a devastating launch. We must stop him from giving the order in the first place. We must do that immediately. In his present state of mind, the old fool might decide to go ahead with the attack early to prove his might."

Glass nodded in agreement.

"Do you know where Durov is?" he asked. "Can your forces take him out?"

A faint shadow of a smile flitted across Smitrov's face. "Our admiral is a creature of habit. He is in the one place where he feels the most omnipotent. He is in the command center at the Polyarnyy Submarine Base."

"Then it should be a simple matter to send in an air strike."

"That is where I need your assistance, Captain," Smitrov said. "It seems that none of our frontline attack aircraft can reach the Command Center inside the four-hour window. We have anticipated no need to send them to attack our own base, you see. The only strike weapons available that have the accuracy and the power necessary are your Tomahawk cruise missiles." He looked up at Glass. His eyes were clear. "I assume this submarine carries such weapons. I need for you to strike Polyarnyy and remove Admiral Durov."

Glass couldn't quite believe what he had just heard. The president of Russia was asking the commander of an American submarine to launch cruise missiles at his country's most prized submarine base and kill the head of his country's submarine service.

"We do," Glass said.

"My deputy has spoken with your government already," Smitrov continued. "You are to copy something called a 'mission data update.' I pray you know what that means."

"Yes, Mr. President. I know what an MDU is," Glass said with a smile. "It tells the missiles precisely where to fly. We'll copy the message. I guess we need to go to work."

Glass stepped into the control room, where he spotted Brian Edwards standing by the fire control system. He sported a large white bandage wrapped around his head.

Edwards didn't see Glass when he walked in. His attention was directed at Pat Durand as the lieutenant operated the console like a concert pianist in midsonata.

"Nice fashion statement, XO," Glass said with a smile. "How is the walking wounded feeling by now?"

"I got a bit of a headache. That damn pipe was hard."

"It's my understanding that the pipe was slightly harder than your head," Glass chuckled. "What's going on here?"

"Pat is downloading an MDU. It's almost all on board. Any idea why we're getting one now?"

Glass turned serious. "We're going to launch a strike. Man battle stations missile." He turned and addressed the navigator. "Mr. Perez, submerge the ship to six-two feet."

"Aye, sir!" Edwards responded, but he still looked mystified about what he had just heard. Jerry Perez jumped from his seat and started issuing orders.

As *Toledo* slid back beneath the waves, Glass watched the crew move to man their stations. Shooting Tomahawk missiles was a methodical, controlled evolution.

There was none of the mad scramble associated with unexpectedly coming face-to-face with the enemy and shooting at him with a torpedo.

"Skipper," Durand sang out. "MDU is downloaded and verified. We have our mission tasking order, too. I don't need the BRA-34 anymore."

"Very well. Mr. Perez, lower all masts and antennas."

The twelve "vertical" launch tubes that held missiles on *Toledo* weren't really vertical. They were angled backward so that they could be fitted into the confines of the forward ballast tanks. That meant that they fired their weapons back over the sail of the submarine. If the mast or periscope were up when the missiles roared away, it could result in them being damaged by the blast of the rocket booster motor. That was also why the sub had to be submerged to launch the missiles.

Brian Edwards read the launch order on the computer screen. He blinked once, then was all business again.

"Skipper, we are launching a four-bird strike. I have assigned the birds in tubes five through eight to the mission. Tubes nine and ten hold backup birds."

"Very well. Spin up missiles. Begin launch sequence."

Edwards nodded and turned back to his team. They continued the complex task of downloading all the flight information to the cruise missiles out in the ballast tanks. They checked every system on each of those birds. Nothing was left to chance. They were sending a million-dollar missile out to do a job. Once it left the sub, it was on its own. The systems had to work.

"Captain, tubes five, six, seven, and eight are ready for launch," Edwards reported.

"Open tube doors on tubes five, six, seven, eight. Launch Tomahawk missiles, tubes five, six, seven, eight."

Pat Durand flipped the switches on the launch console. Out in the ballast tanks, the doors opened at his command. Each missile roared out of its tube, powered by a rocket booster attached to the back of the bird. The rocket shoved the Tomahawk up to fifteen hundred feet in the cold sky. As the engine burned out and dropped away, a sequence of events began that transformed the missile into a small robot airplane. An air scoop dropped open beneath the missile and two small, stubby wings scissored out from inside the missile's body. The turbofan engine, supplied with air from the scoop and ignited by a small explosive squid, came up to speed to give the missile power. The bird then dropped down to wave-top height and flew to the east, beginning its preprogrammed flight.

Toledo's weapons were away.

As he watched his men work, Alexander Durov felt a sharp sense of dread wash over him. No alarm Klaxon or radar track confirmed his feeling, but his instincts told him for certain that danger was imminent.

He had to leave the Command Center at once. Admiral Durov knew from long experience that he must not ignore his finely honed sixth sense.

He grabbed his fur hat and struggled into his heavy bridge coat. Zhurkov looked up. The admiral was preparing to leave? Now, when the operation was at such a critical juncture?

"Should I call your driver, Admiral?" he asked. "I'll grab my coat and go with you."

"No, Vasiliy. I'm just going out to get a breath of fresh air," Durov shot back over his shoulder. "You stay here and keep me informed." The aide would think he was a foolish old man if Durov voiced his concerns. Better to make an excuse.

The old sailor stepped through the heavy steel door and started up the stairs to the ground floor, two stories above the Command Center.

His Zil limo was sitting at the curb. Maybe a short drive would be better than a walk, he decided.

He was crossing the sidewalk, reaching for the car's door handle, when he saw a flash of silver out of the corner of his eye. The first Tomahawk plunged sharply downward, almost too quick to be seen. It drove deep into the bowels of the command building and detonated with an awful flood of fire. The shock wave from the explosion threw Durov sprawling on the frozen ground. He rose to his knees just as the second bird detonated behind him.

He stumbled again as he tried to climb into the Zil, then managed to dive in behind the wheel. The ignition key was there. The car started on the first try. He shot down the street before another rocket could fall on his head.

Flames and falling debris filled his rearview mirror and rattled on the car's roof as a third missile plunged through the same hole as the first two and exploded. Durov jammed his foot down harder on the accelerator. He had to get away, get to someplace where he could give the command to his submarines in the White Sea to begin firing.

He raced around an icy turn. The heavy car slid side-ways, clipping the corner of a building. Somehow he got it straightened. The big automobile rocketed down the street toward the waterfront.

He gritted his teeth as he drove fast toward the one spot where he felt most at home. There, at the submarine pens, the symbol of the awesome naval power he had built, in spite of the meddling of his country's weak-kneed government. It was even more perfect that his ul-timate command to commence firing the nuclear missiles toward their targets would come from the waterfront, overlooking the harbor and the fjord.

His instincts had been right again. Somehow they had found him and tried to kill him. Well, they missed. He would show them. All he needed to do was get to his barge down at the pier. Once there, he could escape this hail of rockets and call in the attack that would devastate Moscow. That would give him the victory he knew was rightfully his.

An unbelievably intense pain knifed through his head. His vision blurred and tunneled. He seemed to be look-ing through a long pipe.

Alexander Durov could not move his arms. His legs were locked, rigid, and his foot was stuck hard on the accelerator pedal. At first, he thought some debris from the explosion had hit him on the head, but the pain was so intense, the paralysis so complete, it had to be some-thing else.

A blood vessel deep inside his brain had torn loose, causing a massive stroke.

Admiral Durov was paralyzed but still crisply conscious, aware of all that was happening around him. His body refused to respond to any command that his mind tried to send it. His limbs had mutinied.

The Zil shot down the narrow street, just missing the fire engines racing back the other way, toward the blazing crater where the Command Center had once been.

The limousine, out of control, reached the end of the street and flew across the pier. With so much momentum built up, it crashed easily through the wooden barrier at the pier's edge, over one of the slips where his beloved new Akula submarines had been berthed only days before. The car plunged through the air and dropped hard through the skim ice. It sank into the black, oily water.

Inside the car, the water closed greedily around the old sailor. Admiral Alexander Durov could not protest, could not fight back. He could only wait, immobile, until this little corner of the sea he knew so well claimed him as its own.

Mark Stern leaned back in the car's rear seat and tried to relax. The big Lincoln Town Car wove as best it could through the thickening afternoon traffic. The Long Island Expressway resembled a slowly moving parking lot. The driver was using every trick he knew to get down the road more quickly. It wasn't enough for the frazzled venture capitalist.

Stern leaned forward and growled, "Can't you make this thing go any faster?"

The driver had been listening to these complaints ever since Stern flagged him down and hopped into his car in front of the Plaza Hotel. It didn't matter to the driver if the stiff wore a thousand-dollar suit and promised a fifty-buck tip if he got him to JFK in thirty minutes. No reason for the son of a bitch to behave like that.

"Listen, bud, we goin' as fast as we's can," the driver said in his thick Bronx accent. "I ain't losin' my license for youse or anybody else. Youse don't like how I'm drivin', get your ass out an' walk to da friggin' airport."

A lane opened for a few feet. The Lincoln shot toward it, only to grind to a halt again when that space closed up.

Stern sat back again and tried to relax. He didn't know why he was in such a hurry. There was still plenty of time. The flight didn't leave for a couple of hours. It looked as if he had made a clean getaway.

Stan Miller's call had caught him off guard. He reported that Andretti was in custody and singing like a bird. Telling all the world about the great caper he had set up for Mark Stern.

Stern had not expected Andretti to fold so easily. In retrospect, he wondered why he had ever been so naive. The man was nothing but a sniveling drunk. There was no reason to think the fat slob would have even an ounce of backbone. But the CTO had held the keys to the kingdom. There had been no choice.

Miller was already on the run. He called from a pay phone somewhere on the New York Thruway. He was headed for Canada. The SEC deputy director told Stern that the feds would be on his tail as well, and very soon. Andretti had made certain of that. He had better run while he had a chance. Otherwise, he was looking at some very nasty jail time.

Stern managed to find a first-class seat on a Varig

flight, nonstop to Rio. That would do for the first leg. Once he was safely hidden in Rio, he could plan what to do next. It was a big globe with lots of places to hide if one had the money to do so.

Traffic thinned a bit after they passed Atlantic Avenue. The ride through Jamaica was quick. The driver pulled up in front of the concrete-and-glass front of Terminal Four. Stern grabbed his carry-on bag, threw a couple of twenties over the seat, and hopped out. The driver didn't bother to thank him for the two-dollar tip.

An hour later, Stern was sitting in Varig's First Class Lounge, enjoying a reasonably good Scotch before boarding the flight. He relaxed. Brazil would be nice this time of year. It was late summer and the girls on the beach would be wearing very little. With the money he had stashed away in offshore accounts around the world, life on the beach could be very comfortable. The take had been nothing like what he could have made if the OptiMarx scheme had not blown up in his face, but he would still be comfortable. There was also the matter of the considerable debt he had amassed with some very bad people. He was skipping out on that. Too bad. If he covered his tracks properly, that little entanglement would eventually be forgotten as well.

The pretty young waitress brought Stern another Scotch. She smiled as she told him it was time for him to board his flight. He made his way down the ramp to the first-class boarding gate, through the passport security check. He tried to look nonchalant while his papers were checked, but he held his breath anyway. The officer smiled, wished him a nice trip, and waved him on. He eased down into the luxurious, heavily padded seat that would be his for the next eleven hours.

The stewardess offered him another glass of Scotch. He leaned back and allowed himself to breathe normally. It was over. He was on board. He had passed through screening with no trouble.

Maybe Stan Miller had exaggerated the danger. Maybe they weren't onto him yet. Still, it was prudent to leave, to go south, where he could start a new life with the fortune he had tucked away.

He sipped his drink as he watched the beautiful stewardess work her way down the aisle. One of the perks of flying the Brazilian national airlines was that they had not succumbed to the political correctness of American carriers. The stewardesses in first class were all quite lovely, very accommodating. It promised to be a comfortable flight. If he played his cards right, he might even have a beautiful dinner companion on his first evening in Rio.

The big triple-seven aircraft lumbered away from the gate and out toward the tarmac as Stern finished his latest drink. The stewardess replaced it at once without even asking. Her smile was dazzling.

He searched the flight entertainment system, looking for some restful music. As he adjusted the headphones and the pillow behind his head, he heard the pilot make some sort of announcement, something about having to return to the gate.

Must be some mechanical problem, Stern thought. Better to find it now than out over the Atlantic. He just hoped the delay wasn't too long. The dinner menu he had just surveyed included lobster. He had not had a chance to eat yet today.

Stern didn't pay much attention as the jet eased back up to the gate. He traveled enough to know this sort of thing was routine. And besides, he was watching the rather fetching shape of the stewardess and didn't see the cabin door behind him swing open. Or notice the big black man who led a group of four other men on board the aircraft.

Stern looked up when he sensed the man standing in the aisle over him. He flashed a badge in Stern's face.

"Mr. Stern, I am Special Agent Decker from the FBI. If you will, please, come with us. You are under arrest."

"That's ridiculous," Stern sputtered. "There must be some mistake." He saw the beautiful stewardess, now looking at him with wide eyes, as if he was some kind of pariah. "What are the charges? I want a lawyer."

"There is no mistake," Decker answered. "You are charged with several counts of federal investment fraud. And the New Jersey authorities have a warrant for your arrest for the attempted murder of a Mr. Alan Smythe."

Epilogue

The frumpy spinster took her seat at the back of the courtroom, sitting in the same chair she had occupied all week. No one paid her any attention. She was just another lonely soul, looking for someplace, some real drama to occupy her otherwise empty life. She sat quietly knitting, while the production played out up front. She appeared to working on a baby's sweater, maybe for some newborn niece, the daughter of a prettier sister. She sometimes smiled, sometimes frowned, but otherwise, it would have been difficult to tell that she was even paying attention to the legal give-and-take going on up at the front of the room.

Not all the seats were taken. There was the usual crowd: "legal eagles," curious onlookers, law students, a few members of the press who had been unfortunate enough to draw this duty. Dmitri Ustinov's trial did not provide the high drama that the others had done. He was such a small cog, a technical geek caught up in a complicated mess, more along for the ride than in it for the really big score. Smythe and Stern, the big-buck guys, with their billion-dollar scheme and their ties to the Russian underworld and, in turn, to the Durov plot, had captured everyone's imagination. Those were the trials that dominated the network newscasts and cable shows for weeks.

The stocky Russian's day in court was much more cut-and-dried. Yes, he was clearly guilty of the federal stock manipulation charges. He had made changes to the system to reap tremendous gains. He had been caught red-handed, too. There was no earth-shattering testimony in this case. No courtroom heroics.

The only time any of the audience took note was when the prosecutor demanded to know where Ustinov had stashed the money he managed to steal before his cover was blown by Carl Andretti. Even the old spinster knitting in the back paused her clicking needles long enough to listen closely to the exchange.

"The numbered accounts you provided us are all empty, Mr. Ustinov," the tired prosecutor reminded him. "Where did you move the money?"

But no amount of browbeating seemed enough to make Ustinov waver from his story. Those were the accounts into which he transferred all the money. Every penny. It was all there the last time he logged off, just before the FBI busted him. He could not account for where or how the money had been moved. This was the reason the government would not allow Ustinov to plead to a lesser charge. He would not tell them where the money was. That being the case, the prosecutor was going to make certain he would be in prison long enough that he would never be able to get any use from it.

This would be the final day of testimony. The prosecutor was out of questions and Ustinov's defense counsel didn't appear to have much to work with.

One of the prosecution's younger attorneys, neatly dressed in his conservative gray pin-striped suit and red power tie, rose to start the day's proceedings. Dmitri Ustinov sat on the witness stand, fidgeting nervously, his ill-fitting brown suit already rumpled and sagging.

The attorney walked slowly toward the witness stand. It appeared he was still forming his first question in his mind as he approached. Halfway there he stopped and turned back toward his table, as if he had forgotten some important fact. He picked up a yellow legal brief and turned again toward Ustinov as he read something scribbled on the page.

"Mr. Ustinov, it says here that you had an accomplice. Mr. Andretti testified that there were two of you operating the system when he overheard you talking of the plot. Who was your accomplice?"

Ustinov took a drink of water before he answered. Beads of sweat formed on his forehead and trickled down each side of his face. He looked around the courtroom quickly. The question had been asked before, at least three times, and he had answered it the same each time, in a low voice, almost a whisper, with the pronounced Russian accent he had thickened for this trial.

"I vork alone. I have no accomplice."

The prosecutor took a step backward and stared hard at Ustinov. He waited several seconds before he spoke, the disbelief heavy in his voice.

"I don't think I heard you correctly. I thought I heard you say you worked alone. Is it not true that someone was with you in the testing room when Mr. Andretti discovered you? Who was that?"

Ustinov spoke more firmly now. "As I have told you, this girl, she was only a clerk, someone Andretti hired because she is Russian and she vork cheap. And because she had nice legs. Me, I try to . . . how you say? . . . get in her pants, bragging about money I make with system. No way she could be involved. She is only talented in one area . . . filling up tight sweater."

Several people in the gallery laughed out loud. Even the spinster smiled and shook her head. It was the closest thing to juice in an otherwise dry week. The judge spluttered and tried to rein the proceedings back to their mundane norm. He ordered Dmitri Ustinov to restrict his answers to the questions.

The prosecuting attorney had lost interest. They had never believed Andretti anyway. There had been no reason to involve any of the other OptiMarx employees in the scheme, especially any of the entry-level Russian coders. Ustinov had clearly done what he did alone. The other two, Stern and Smythe, were the leeches, ready to suck out the money, until the Russian decided to skim some off the top on his own. Besides, most of the Russian programmers the company hired had turned up with immigration problems and had managed to disappear by the time anybody got around to talking with them.

The attorney wrapped up a few other loose ends, and by noon, all the testimony was completed. The judge called for a lunch break. Closing statements would start at two o'clock.

No one took notice of the spinster when she stood to leave. She casually dropped an envelope on her chair as she gathered up her knitting and made her way out the door. She disappeared into the ladies' room around the corner from the courtroom. Half an hour later, a pretty young brunette in a flattering business suit emerged from the ladies' room. She walked confidently out of the Federal Building and hailed a cab.

The young woman sat back in the seat. Her voice carried a noticeable Russian accent as she told the driver, "JFK. I have a flight I need to catch." She held a folder on her lap. It contained first-class tickets on British Air to London and on to the Seychelle Islands. The remote tropical islands, deep in the Indian Ocean, were a perfect place to continue her disappearing act.

Twenty minutes later, as he made his regular sweep of the courtroom, a bailiff noticed the envelope. Across the front, in a dainty feminine hand, was written "Dmitri Ustinov." It smelled nice, clearly held no weapon, so he decided to give it to the defendant. Even Russian computer nerds could have secret admirers, he decided.

When Ustinov opened the envelope, he found it contained only a small card with a short message in Russian.

"Thank you, Dmitri, my love. It would have been spectacular. Good-bye."

The late spring brought a smattering of cold rain to the fog-shrouded Arctic Ocean. Russian president Gregor Smitrov watched the gray swells rise and fall forlornly out ahead of the ship on which he rode. The wipers beat a slow rhythm as they cleared desultory raindrops from the bridge windows. There was no sign of any springtime rebirth in this dreary place. The cold, damp weather was causing his shoulder to ache dully. His wounds were still slowly healing. It was all too perfect for a funeral.

The bridge of the cruiser was crowded with dignitaries, civilians, and ranking officers from the Russian military. Their idle chatter almost overpowered the somber day. Here and there in the crowd men stood wearing the uniforms of lower-ranking naval officers. Even the most self-important dignitaries seemed to treat these men with deference.

As well they should. Those men were the survivors of the K-475, *Gepard*, and one of the reasons everyone was out here on this desolate stretch of sea. They were about to hold a memorial service, say their final good-byes over the site where *Gepard* and her dead now rested.

Smitrov noticed that Sergei Andropoyov, former commander of the *Gepard* and a true hero of the Russian Republic, stood apart from the others, his elbows resting on the sill as he stared out at the churning ocean. No one approached the silent captain. Something about his demeanor warned everyone away, told them that it was best to leave him to his solitude. After all, three hundred meters below them lay the wreckage of his submarine, the watery grave of twenty-one shipmates, the hulk in which he and the rest of his crew might well have perished.

When the captain finally turned from the window, Smitrov stepped over to the lone sailor. Andropoyov snapped to dutiful attention and saluted. The president waved it away.

"Sergeiovich, stand easy. We have been through much, you and I. You are remembering your lost comrades. I am mourning the many brave sons of the *Rodina* so needlessly sacrificed."

"Not just sons of the *Rodina*, President Smitrov. Many brave men from two nations died needlessly before that madman was stopped."

Andropoyov nodded toward the two ships that were steaming a few hundred meters to port of the cruiser. It was the *Anzio* and the *Toledo*, the American cruiser plowing high in the water, the submarine running low into the swells. The signal bridge on the American cruiser was crowded with civilians as well, mostly the families of the lost crew of *Miami*.

"Yes, he was quite mad," Smitrov acknowledged. "And he came within a breath of succeeding. If he had been able to give the command for those other boats to fire their missiles, we would have faced a holocaust. We can be grateful that Durov was such a control freak, that he demanded that he personally give the key orders for every step. Otherwise, I fear . . ."

The president did not have to tell Andropoyov more. Both men breathed deeply as they relived yet again how close they had come. The search for the four missing Akulas, hiding in the White Sea, had taken over a week. They all eventually surfaced and surrendered once they were convinced that their leader was gone and the coup aborted. Those new boats were now tied up in Polyarnyy again, the officers imprisoned in the Lubyanka. There was confidence that all involved in the plot were either dead or imprisoned, but there could never be total assurance that the cancer had been eradicated.

The small flotilla of ships glided to a stop as the pair

talked. Sailors were preparing the wreaths at the ship's rail so the ceremony could be quickly conducted and they could get back to warmth. Everyone was buttoning his coat tighter, getting ready for the icy bite of the brisk wind off the water.

Smitrov clapped Andropoyov on the shoulder. "Come, Sergeiovich. The others are waiting. It is time to say good-bye."

The submarine captain seemed reluctant to go. He walked slowly toward the doorway but stopped before following the rest out onto the deck.

"It is a captain's most difficult chore, Mr. President, saying such a final good-bye." Andropoyov looked Smitrov in the eye. "Just promise me one thing, sir. Promise me those men did not die in vain. That their legacy will be a more peaceful world. That all of them . . . Russian and American alike . . . gave their lives so their sons and daughters will have no need to die in war."

Gregor Smitrov thought for a moment. He rubbed the bridge of his nose as he pondered the sailor's request. "Captain, I desperately hope that is so, but I cannot promise it. There have been too many 'wars to end all wars' for me to be confident of it. One thing I can pledge to you, though. I will give my best . . . even my life . . . to try to make it so."

The submariner smiled. "Mr. President, when the waves mount and the winds blow, that is what any true sailor would gladly do," Andropoyov said quietly.

With that, the two men embraced, then stepped outside to the rail, to scatter the colorful, fragrant spring flowers on the cold, disdainful waves of the Barents Sea.

Available Now

INTREPID AVIATORS

The True Story of U.S.S. Intrepid's *Torpedo Squadron 18 and Its Epic Clash with the Superbattleship* Musashi

Gregory G. Fletcher

Intrepid Aviators is the thrilling true story of the aircraft carrier USS *Intrepid*'s brave torpedo bomber pilots, their daring duel with the Japanese superbattleship *Musashi*, and Will Fletcher's struggle to survive as a guerrilla soldier in the jungles of the Philippines after getting shot out of the sky. The sinking of *Musashi* inflicted a crucial blow in the Battle of Leyte Gulf, and would mark the first time that aviators had sunk a Japanese battleship in what would become the war's greatest—and last— epic naval battle.

Available wherever books are sold or at
penguin.com

"Like" us at facebook.com/CaliberUSA

INTO DUST AND FIRE

Five Young Americans Who Went First to Fight the Nazi Army

Rachel S. Cox

In the spring of 1941, with Europe consumed by war and occupation, Britain stood alone against the Nazi menace. The United States remained wary of entering the fray. But for five extraordinary young Americans, the global threat of fascism was too great to ignore. *Into Dust and Fire* is a fitting tribute to five men who put their lives on the line to honor a commitment to freedom which transcended national boundaries. It is an inspiring true tale of idealism, courage, camaraderie, sacrifice, and heroism.

"An inspired saga." —Douglas Brinkley, author of *The Boys of Pointe du Hoc*